The Afflicted Saga
Despair
Tale of the Fallen: Book V

Katika Schneider

ISBN: 978-1-952673-00-9

ABOUT THE AUTHOR

Patrick Lindsay came to Texas by way of Missouri, Canada, and California and has been proud to call the Lone Star State his home for more than forty years now. He retired in 2017 from "another life" as a CPA, whereafter he turned his hand to writing.

He has read just about everything by Louis L'Amour and first decided to give Western writing a try on his initial day of retirement. He has been writing ever since and loves the idea that so many people get enjoyment from his work.

Patrick and his wife Michelle live on a cattle ranch near Fort Worth along with cows, horses, chickens, and a very spoiled Great Pyrenees dog. He is an avid fan of the St. Louis Cardinals in baseball and the Kansas City Chiefs in football.

For Ms. Miller,
You opened my eyes to
the real magic of crafting stories.
Thank you for telling a fourth grader
that she was creative enough to pursue this path.

ACKNOWLEDGMENTS

To be shamelessly redundant to my previous books, my first load of gratitude goes to my beta readers. Despair reached them when a whole lot of the world *was* despairing, and they helped me make something beautiful to set free in the wilds.

My continued thanks to Sarah of Sarah Miller Creations for my first visual peek at Zeal and for truly being one of the best friends I could ask for. Keep creating, beautiful!

My utmost appreciation goes to my mentor, David Farland, and the support and encouragement of his Apex Writers Group, as well as to the Superstars Writing Seminar Tribe for much of the same.

Finally, as always, all of my love and gratitude to the wonderful readers I've met at conventions, signings, and through social media. You're all the best and I couldn't be doing this without you.

ONE

Edmund Swift sat back in his bejeweled chair, mouth gaping open and eyes wide in silent shock. Every five days, for as long as the middle-aged human could recollect, he'd spend the evening in the Swift manor's temple. He'd drink a shot from one of the casks of bitter elixir which lined the east and west walls of the room and sit in his tiny throne worth more than the cumulative fortunes of all those in the county to await whatever visions his god might send his way. As his father and his father's father before, Edmund was one of the few surviving priests of Ceredulus who hadn't been trapped behind the Veil at the conclusion of the Age of the Undead.

He'd grown up learning only two rules. First, no mortal outside the direct lineage of the Swift family was to ever be given reason to suspect Ceredulus's influence remained a quiet force on Abaeloth. Second, he was to devote the entirety of his heart and soul to his god. Given the luxurious life which his family had enjoyed thanks to that god's favor, Edmund had fully respected the first and, at least every fifth day, made a committed effort at the second. His rewards were an easy life and the delightful hallucinations of power and glory which danced through his mind when the sacred elixir warmed his blood.

But this evening was the first time these visions had ever presented Edmund a direct audience with his god.

1

Though the righteous dolts of the Order of the White Circle had done a thorough job destroying the written records of Ceredulus and his ways, Edmund recognized the dark elegance instantly. Ceredulus swept into his psyche like a brutal gale, freezing his mind and any disbelief he might have struggled with after a lifetime spent wondering how much of his dutiful worship had been due to tradition and how much of it was real. The force of the god's arrival tossed Edmund's doubts and fears about, landing him at the point of only one conclusion.

It was time for the god of the undead to reclaim his influence over the mortals of Abaeloth, and Edmund Swift was the priest who would usher in his glorious return.

Then snap out of your stupor and get to work!

The command thawed Edmund's frozen thoughts and an overwhelming compulsion shot him to his feet and spun him around. The sacred chair toppled to the floor as the portly human hastened past it for the door, its thud ignored as he concentrated solely on the unexplained impulse to reach the cellar. He neglected to pause and lock the temple door, risking the chance of one of his housekeepers peeking inside the secret chamber and thus breaking the first rule he'd been taught, but a gentle reassurance cooed in the back of his mind that it wouldn't be long before Ceredulus's priests no longer had to hide their devotion.

Grinning wildly, overcome with his objective, Edmund raced through the halls of the manor until he reached the narrow staircase which led down into the cellar. He didn't stop to locate a lantern to light his way, trusting his knowledge of the home generations of his family had lived in and the persistent guidance of his god.

The air grew chilled and damp against Edmund's flushed skin as he descended the stairs, shivers of discomfort adding to the trembling of his excitement. Less than a minute after he began this mad dash to answer his god's bidding, Edmund had reached the bottom of the cellar stairs. A pale beam of moonlight stretched down the stairwell from a window on the floor above, allowing the shelves of root vegetables and barrels of mead and wine to cast long shadows across the wooden floor. Standing now in the dank, dim cellar, Edmund was acutely aware of the pounding of his heart and the rasping of his rapid breathing. The excitement tapered into confusion and a deep gulp preceded his anxious question.

"Now what?"

Ceredulus, unlike even the best of his peers, was a patient god, and he'd been smart enough to predict the Order's ultimate response to his hordes of the undead all those centuries ago. Zeal had painted his vampires as disgusting beasts, but all they'd wanted was a way to surpass death—and armies to protect them from those who sought to stop them from achieving that goal. Always the schemer and ever the opportunist, Ceredulus had initiated one last cunning plan before the blasted Sagewind siblings and the meddlesome Azerick and Drao locked him within the Veil. Now that his dear friend Mathias was all worked up over the demons stealing souls, Ceredulus had a reason to play this devious hand. And after hearing the pathetic whimpering of that little whore who the paladin had whisked away to Zeal's arrogant splendor, Ceredulus the means in which he'd do so.

Now, came the smooth reply in Edmund's mind, *you dig.*

"...Dig?" The cluttered dimness of the cellar absorbed most of Edmund's squeaking whisper and though the command made no sense to him, neither had the compulsion to race down here in the first place.

Somewhere in the back of the human's mind, where part of his senses were still sober, he felt foolish, but Ceredulus had already secured his grip on him. Edmund fell to his hands and knees and frantically ran his fingers along the wooden planks of the floor, instinctively hunting for the subtle crease where the boards didn't quite sit flush together. Sensitive fingertips which had never worked a day of physical labor brushed across the gentle rise and though confusion had stolen the zealous grin from Edmund, his heart skipped a beat in knowing that he was serving his long-silent god.

Clawing his manicured nails into the edge of the plank, Edmund threw his weight backwards. With a groan of protest from the snuggly-fitting boards around it and a sharp jolt of pain which came from his fingernails bending backwards from the pressure,

Edmund dislodged the board and tossed it aside. Taking just a moment to mop the beading sweat from his forehead, the priest of Ceredulus fit a dutiful grimace on his face and continued to rake his fingers into the dirt, his hasty digging jostling a vital mechanism below.

* * * * *

Tristan Swift last remembered vowing his service to Ceredulus before darkness settled over him like a peaceful winter's snow. Those promises crept back to him now, tapping at the doors which had been closed in his mind as each drop of rancid, cold blood struck his tongue and rolled down his throat. He didn't yet have the energy to close his lips and escape the vile taste, but he did have the energy to listen to his god's cool, calm voice.

I promised I'd come for you. Now is the time.

A frantic scratching welcomed the youthful vampire lord through this surreal haze and back into consciousness, and when he opened his hazel eyes, it was to darkness. Comforted by his god's nearness, the inability to observe his surroundings didn't bother Tristan, but something else did.

"Where am I?"

You were entombed beneath your uncle's estate, came Ceredulus's reply. *Volunteered to do so. Or have you forgotten?*

The god's voice was just as smooth as Tristan remembered, drawing out his slumbering memories of the frustrating events which had driven his kind into a corner. Freshly woken, Tristan didn't have the strength to engage one of Mathias Sagewind's power, but the very fact that he had been woken meant that time must be near. There was no greater thrill than being rallied by his generous god to execute his will, and Tristan closed his eyes, a smile playing at his blood-spattered lips.

"Of course I remember, my lord. Is it time for my brothers and sisters to march again?"

A brief moment of silence passed, just long enough to stoke a flicker of concern in Tristan, before Ceredulus replied. *You will be marching alone, and you will be marching on Zeal.*

4

That concern ignited and Tristan's eyes flew wide, body rapidly expending the limited energy which the vial of blood had lent him. He groped at his waist to retrieve the steel flask on his hip. Ripping it from his belt, he opened the container and guzzled half its contents, rolling to his side in the snug confines of his tomb to avoid choking. This blood was no more appealing than the first, and Tristan swallowed rapidly in an effort to drive the bitterness from his tongue.

"Far be it from me to question you, my lord," he said, words straining against his urge to gag on the stagnant blood's aftertaste. "But where are the others? Why Zeal?"

Nine-hundred and seventy-six years have passed since you last walked Abaeloth, Tristan. Ceredulus didn't wait for that announcement to sink in, as time was only a relative concept to the ever-living. *Mathias Sagewind and his sister succeeded in containing me within a single region of Gelthin, and so my influence has spread no farther than what you knew.*

Tristan grimaced and finished off the contents of his flask, lowering the empty vessel slowly. He appreciated his god's ominous answer even less than he appreciated the reflexive surge from his stomach. "Am I to confront the siblings about their actions?"

No, no... The suggestion of humor had worked its way into Ceredulus's voice. *They've only grown in power since you last saw them and I'll not risk my most loyal and trusted servant to the potential of their tantrums. I've got a much more delicious plan for those two brats than some crude revenge. And I need you to execute it for me.*

The fact that Ceredulus wasn't after a fight—at least not a direct one—with either Mathias or his terrifying sister bolstered Tristan's confidence. "Give me your orders, my lord, and you will have my obedience."

That was precisely what Ceredulus had hoped to hear. *I need you to be my eyes and ears within Zeal, and to share with me what you discover about the demons and their dastardly practices.*

"The demons have become a concern of yours?"

They have begun raising the dead through means other than my grace and they must be made to pay for their crimes.

What vile beasts demons were! "Of course, my lord. My life

and death are yours to command. Just give me the word."

Very good, Tristan. Your distant cousin, Edmund, is nearly through exhuming you. Once he does, your first priority is to replenish your strength. Find some modern, clean clothes while you're at it. Make yourself approachable. Your mission begins with charming a young woman.

Tristan smiled as the scratching above him turned into the rapid drumming of fingers against wood. There hadn't been a mortal born who he couldn't charm. "I will obey, my lord. In your name and for your honor."

Then rise, Tristan Swift, Ceredulus commanded. *And feed.*

* * * * *

The nails still attached to Edmund's bleeding fingertips were jagged by the time he reached the next layer of wood. Confused, but still compelled, he ran his aching hands against the smooth surface in search of the key to satisfying his god's desires. He didn't have to look for long.

A powerful thump came from the opposite side of this barrier. Startled, Edmund froze and rocked back onto his haunches, pulling his hands closer to his chest. Had he been fully sober or less motivated by his god, the unexpected strike would have chased him out of the cellar, but comfort cooed to him through his confusion, reassuring him that this was the objective he'd been hunting for. As his eager hands reached forward again, a second strike succeeded in breaking the plank, a velvet-enclosed elbow jutting out through the splintered board. Not questioning anything else about this strange encounter, Edmund grabbed the plank closest to him, its broken edges digging deep into the meat of his palms as he heaved it free from the ground.

The elbow withdrew back into the darkness of the tomb as Edmund continued to tear the hole larger, driven by a blind frenzy as he pulled up each chunk of wood. After the third board was tossed aside, Edmund paused again. Part of the man was well aware that someone had been buried here in the cellar—that fact had been made obvious when the elbow had bashed an opening from within the tomb. Looking through that opening now, down into a

6

pair of calm, hazel eyes was just the shock he needed to forget those wild impulses which Ceredulus had assigned in him. When the body harboring those eyes sat up, Edmund scurried away.

"Well met, cousin. I am Tristan, Lord of Fallsmouth, and I am most grateful for your assistance and loyalty to our lord Ceredulus." Tristan swept a disgusted glance across his descendant's unfit frame and thinning hair before shaking the dirt from his blond curls and fitting a manipulative smile on his lips.

Edmund tried futilely to find his tongue, his jaw flapping in an attempt to reply with anything appropriate while he patted the debris-strewn floor around him. Locating one of the lengths of torn floorboard, he curled his weak fingers around it.

"Oh, please," Tristan scoffed, grasping the edges of his tomb to push his lean frame out of the hole. The effort taxed him after centuries without proper nourishment and he settled on his knees, tossing another appraising glance at Edmund. "Put that board down and help me stand. Lord Ceredulus is in need of us both; your task tonight is not yet through."

Edmund flexed his fingers tighter around the board for a second longer before sensibility returned to him. He'd spent his entire life more than a little skeptical of his god's interest in the Swift family and in the span of ten minutes, all of those doubts had been shoved aside. There were no records left depicting what Ceredulus did to those who disobeyed him, but the fact that he was the god of the undead suggested more than a few unpleasant options. Edmund released his grip on his makeshift club and rolled to his hands and knees to push himself up onto numb legs.

"You are Tristan?" Edmund asked, inching closer to the elegant man kneeling in the hole he'd just dug. "L-lord Tristan Swift?"

Tristan allowed himself a modest chuckle for this buffoon's benefit. "One and the same."

"B-but you... you died—"

"Vampires do not die, Edmund." The correction stopped the mortal man's cautious progress toward the hole, and Tristan blew out a sigh of frustration. "But you are right. I was entombed here generations ago."

7

Edmund nodded briefly, his sagging jowls flopping about, and he inched forward once again. "And you said Ceredulus, our most gracious god of the undead, master of the ever-living, has need of us?"

Tristan smirked at the embellishments the nervous human added to the god's name, catching as much guilt as fear in his voice. Not one to care about the mistakes of mortals, Tristan made no mention of this observation and held out a delicate hand bedecked in a year's taxes worth of rings to Edmund.

"He does," Tristan replied, "and by no result of chance."

The fear flashed out of Edmund's eyes after a brief moment of consideration, and he scuttled forward, grasping the pasty hand extended toward him. Copious layers of fine lace hung at the wrist of Tristan's velvet sleeve, brushing against Edmund's forearm as he awkwardly hauled the vampire to his feet. Eyes wide and hungry for the praises and riches which must be soon to follow for his assistance, Edmund squared his stance to offer his rendition of support as Tristan carefully climbed out of his tomb.

"So… what great plans does our most gracious of gods have for us?"

Tristan didn't lift his gaze to his bumbling companion, sneering instead at the wrinkles which had gathered in the once fine velvet of his overcoat and the thinned patches time had deteriorated into his cotton leggings. "Are your housekeepers about?"

Edmund frowned at the irrelevant question. "This late in the evening, I suspect but one of them will be awake."

"One of how many?"

Edmund cocked his head. "Four. But what does that—"

Tristan finished dusting off the front of his clothes and looked up at Edmund at last, flashing him a broad, inviting smile. "It has been nine-hundred and seventy-six years, Edmund. I am absolutely famished."

"Oh!" A relieved chuckle left the large man as understanding dawned on him at last. "Of course." He turned to begin his ascent of the stairs. "I'll have Miriam fire up the stove."

"Edmund." Tristan's call drew the mortal's attention just long

8

enough to enact his true objective. "Stop."

Perhaps if Edmund had been more diligent in dedicating his life to the god he'd only tonight begun professing the greatness of, he'd have understood his place in serving Ceredulus. Perhaps if he'd bothered to research the different classes of the undead, he'd have recognized that the sudden locking of his knees had been the result of the compulsion of this vampire's command. Perhaps if he'd been of average intelligence, he'd have sooner recalled exactly what a famished vampire would want to feast on. As those answers caught up to him, Edmund's cheeks paled and his eyes widened.

Tristan smiled, those hazel eyes narrowing in delight. "Silence."

That second command stole away Edmund's screams as the vampire lord rushed toward him.

TWO

Etha, ever conscious of the flow of Abaeloth's divine energy, was well aware that while Mathias had been the first Afflicted, he was not the only one. These mortals, bound to shards of the legendary god spear, could not be considered abominations in the manner which demons and the undead were. Etha had crafted Affliction herself and made the conscious decision to cast its shattered remains across the surface of Abaeloth at the end of the Divine Battle. Those shards now served as powerful resources to those who understood their value, capable of enhancing any number of natural abilities, but they still existed within the laws of creation. And so, Etha wasn't bothered by the average Afflicted mortal as long as they didn't cause any trouble.

That was, of course, until she'd met Talier Dalton.

Every other Afflicted man or woman Etha had come across was ambitious; one had to be to risk the chance of death simply to enhance their attributes. To Talier's credit, he'd timidly remained on the sidelines as Nessix and Mathias battled the inoga while so many others screamed and fled. He'd trembled with regret that he couldn't join the fight, and had gone as far as to throw a weak retaliation against Mathias when he'd thought Nessix was destined to die. Both of those observations spoke of a great degree of loyalty to Nessix, but neither reflected the confidence which accompanied every other Afflicted Etha had encountered.

Yes, Talier was quite the intriguing anomaly, one which played an important role in recovering Nessix, and so Etha whisked his unconscious body away to Zeal after Mathias had safely loaded himself and Nessix aboard Ceraphlaks, so she could investigate the magnitude of the role this young human filled.

As she situated her patient on a vacant cot in a quiet room in the Citadel's infirmary, compassion urged Etha to let Talier continue sleeping off the trauma of his recent ordeal, but curiosity and her self-ordained right to know the goings on of the world she'd created trumped that notion. Besides, if she satisfied Talier's questions—and she knew he'd have many of them—it would save Mathias from needing to do so; between Nes's recovery and the Council's inevitable demands, all of her champion's time and patience would be spent. Etha, in her guise of a friendly young woman, would be much gentler on the terrified man's eyes than her battle-damaged paladin was, anyway.

Stooping over Talier's face and tilting her head back and forth, Etha contemplated once more how he'd managed to become Afflicted. Perhaps his binding had been an accident and he was unaware of his status. Etha had certainly witnessed enough strange occurrences over the past year to not dismiss the idea quite yet. Shrugging off her little musings, she straightened to tuck her hands behind her back and allowed Talier to wake.

He did so with a heartfelt cry, grasping fistfuls of the blanket as he sat bolt upright. "Nessix!"

Etha approved of the honesty of his concern and laid a gentle hand on his chest to impart some calm into him and keep him from throwing himself from the bed in his sudden burst of dismay. "Your friend is well. She sustained grave injuries, but is in the care of one of Etha's paladins. You need not worry about her. What can you tell me of what happened?"

An identical question flew to Talier's mind as he cast his frantic eyes around the airy room, searching for some answer to where he was and how he got there. It was a clean chamber, furnished only with the cot he laid on, the fresh quilt draped over him, and a plain wooden table and chair sitting beside his bed. An open window framed by heavy linen curtains revealed that it was daytime, and the warmth of the sun carried with it the ruckus of a busy city on the streets below. He didn't hear any of the panicked screams from Fairmont, and couldn't fathom how he'd been unconscious long enough for such terrors to have left the remaining population. He clutched the blanket tighter, curling his fists up toward his chest.

"I don't think I can, ma'am," he murmured.

Etha smiled at the polite address. No off-handed remarks about her chest from this young man! She brushed the flop of chestnut bangs from his forehead. "I'm sure you can tell me *something* that happened back there to help me understand why you're so worried about your friend?"

Talier slowly uncurled one of his hands from the covers so he could rub his fingers against the spot where Etha's caress had warmed his skin. "I'm sorry, but I... we just..." He grimaced, tears surfacing as he debated what to do. Nessix had made it clear to him that she wanted to hide her affiliation with the assassins from the rest of the world, and Talier had wholeheartedly agreed that was for the best. Kol had demanded Talier hide his affiliation with the demons from the world, and he'd agreed with that, as well. Talier didn't even know where he was or who he was talking to, and all he wanted to do was get back to his brother! But in order to do that...

He broke down into a mess of ugly sobs, not acknowledging when Etha slid her arm around his shoulders and grasped the hand still blanched pale from its grip on the blanket. She pressed her peace toward him, ebbing the intensity of his memories of the attack, but the tears continued to fall, signifying something far greater than the simple exhaustion Etha had assumed he struggled with. It was well within her capabilities to dip into this young man's mind to pick out the information she was after, but she respected his free will and trusted he'd express himself better on his own than she'd be able to do for him by sneaking into places that were meant to be private.

"You're safe from whatever you're frightened of now, dear."

Talier highly doubted that. He'd never be safe from what he was frightened of until Marcoux was laid up in a bed next to him, being tended to by one of Etha's paladins, as well. Wait. Etha's paladins.

Talier gasped, tears stopping in an instant as he spun his bleary and bloodshot gaze to meet Etha's clear amber eyes. "Where am I?"

Etha smiled. "You're in the infirmary at the Citadel—"

"No, no, no!" Panic struck Talier before logic was able to debate how far he and Nessix had been from Zeal. Kol had expressly told him to keep her far from the holy city, and now they were cozied up in the core of its operations, of all places! Talier kicked as he tried to slide over to stand up, his legs tangling in the covers as he toppled toward the floor. Etha barely caught him, and she furrowed her brow as he failed to coordinate himself through a second attempt at what appeared to be running. "I need to be not here." His stomach lurched and then dropped to his feet. "Is this where Nessix is? Is she with one of Etha's paladins *here*?"

Cramming the heels of his palms into his eyes, Talier moaned in anguish. *Etha herself help me…*

Etha cocked her head, ripples of confusion forming between her brows. She approached the topic more carefully this time around. "Your friend is not yet here. Her wounds were severe and she needed a more… stable mode of transportation than that which brought you here."

Talier blew out his relief so rapidly it forced him to sink back down onto the cot, and he resumed rubbing his head as a wave of dizziness tickled his scalp. "So she's not here yet?"

Etha shook her head.

"Can you tell me what road she's taking? I need to meet up with her. Fast." He flushed with guilt and fear of what must have sounded like a ridiculous request. "I need to… I need to make sure she's safe."

Etha smiled at the man's desperation and desire to continue watching over the one woman she suspected would never need a mortal guardian. "She's safer than she could be anywhere else. And *you* need to get rest, young man. Do you not remember anything that happened?"

Of course Talier remembered what happened! How could he have forgotten? Nessix had recruited him to stand guard while she killed a man which had almost resulted in his own death, been part of another four murders, then gone on the run. After swearing off the vile career path—or so she'd led Talier to believe—she'd taken on another assassination request and then they were attacked by giant, monstrous demons who she demanded on fighting. The details got hazy and frantic after that, but Talier did remember Nessix's screams. He remembered seeing her mangled body and thinking about what her death would mean for Marcoux's safety. He remembered a man who looked chillingly like the one Nessix had been hired to kill handling the situation with a dutiful calm which defied the terrifying chaos around them, and then he woke up here. Talier remembered what happened, he just couldn't figure out the how or why behind any of it.

"I only remember a lot of death," he said. It seemed the safest way to answer the question without spoiling any of the secrets he was supposed to be keeping.

Etha frowned again and prodded around at the reaches her laws permitted her to access for signs of Talier's uncertainty or doubt. Unfortunately for Etha's gentle approach, those signs were everywhere within this young man. And unfortunately for her hopes of bringing comfort to his racing fears, the unmistakable pull of Mathias's dismay as he entered Zeal's boundaries tugged her curiosity closer to concern. Etha eyed Talier carefully. The droop of his shoulders and vacant wandering of his troubled eyes suggested he had neither the strength nor inclination to disobey at this time, despite how desperate he seemed to be to reunite with Nessix. No matter how badly Etha wanted to stay here and study Talier, Mathias was in greater need of her right now, and she was even more interested in investigating what the demons had done to Nessix. Giving Talier's hand one more tender pat, Etha stood.

"There are other patients I have to visit, so I must leave you now. Stay here in your room, rest, and don't go wandering, lest you get lost." When Talier opened his mouth to protest, Etha added, "There's a constant patrol of guards in the Citadel, and the priestesses frequently make rounds here in the infirmary." Hopefully, her reassurance would serve both to keep the flighty man where he could easily be found and help alleviate some of those fears which tainted his eyes.

"Guards?" Talier reactively hopped to his feet, pressing a hand to his throbbing temple. He had to get out of here… how could he do that amid Zeal's soldiers? Scratching at ways to hide his rampaging guilt and terror, he stammered over a hasty excuse for his outburst. "I thought you said I was safe here?"

Etha grasped the Afflicted man's elbows and, with a firm shove, deposited him onto the cot a third time. "Physically, you are, but you witnessed some terrible events few have ever survived. Besides, you are harbored in the Citadel, amid masses of politicians and dignitaries who would offer you no end of headaches and hassles if you were found lost in the mazes of its halls. The best place for you right now is here."

Talier whimpered at Etha's sound reasoning. What would all of this mean to Kol and Annin? What would it mean for Marcoux? He'd never in his life commanded the slightest bit of authority, always following instructions and seldom pitching fits about them, but he was trapped between so many different orders that his simple mind couldn't process which was the right one anymore. Sick to his stomach, he lifted his troubled eyes to Etha's.

"When can I see Nessix again?"

Nothing about Mathias's energy gave Etha reason to suspect Nessix had delivered on her broken promise of being able to come back from the dead, and Etha frowned. "Her wounds were extensive. The best medics in all of Abaeloth will tend to her, but I cannot answer when she'll be able to visit with you next."

Talier's eyes rimmed with tears once more. He could already hear Marcoux's screams as the demons carried out their torturous plans for him, venting their anger over Talier's failures on his helpless brother. He could already feel the burning in his lungs and legs as he futilely tried to outrun Kol and Annin when they came for him next. How had he, a simple messenger, ended up in this position? His entire body jerked and he gave a reactive yelp as a hand touched his knee.

"Have heart," Etha said softly. "Your troubles will soon be behind you."

Terror and regret kept Talier's frown from warping into a

scowl at Etha's assumption, and adequately hushed any argument he'd have tried to make before it was more than a pathetic squeak in his throat.

"I'll send for someone to bring you food and drink," Etha continued. "In the meantime, get your rest. You have my word. You've nothing more to fear for yourself, and I'll ensure you are notified when Nessix's status improves."

Neither the offer nor the reassurance soothed any of Talier's troubles the way Etha had intended them to, but his ruse of confidence had burned out back in Fulton when he'd watched Nessix kill all those assassins. Dread choking him into silence, Talier accepted Etha's tight smile with bereft eyes, and watched helplessly as she slipped out of the room.

THREE

Nessix lay on the bloodied ground she'd come to know so well, the same bloodied ground which had always caused her so much fear and sorrow. It wasn't a grief she owned, but one she'd had forced on her after Kol had taken her captive.

Screams of terrified and tortured men petitioned to the heavens for mercy. A deep, rolling rumble rushed beneath the singed earth, as though laughing at the frantic efforts of the mortals who struggled to accept their impending doom. Bolts of wicked lightning crackled and hissed through a sky so saturated with smoke that only those broken on the ground stood a chance at breathing, and even down there, it was contaminated with the vile stench of blood and waste of the dead and dying. No stranger to battle and intimately familiar with this precise one, Nessix allowed the foul air to flow in and out of her lungs with each of her wracked breaths, welcoming the sensation as she closed her eyes and smiled.

This time, Kol could keep this terror for himself. This time, she was safe.

Gone was her urge to sift through Kol's memories for wisps of information which might help her overcome her position beneath the demons' rule. The instinct to push through agony in her desperate race to figure out who or where she was no longer launched her to her feet. Not even her persistent longing to

17

uncover the mysterious Berann's identity and worth motivated her to move. Horror rained down on the age of Abaeloth's innocence and crashed all around her, and Nessix relaxed into the blood-soaked mud of the battlefield and into the peace of lingering death. This would never be her nightmare again.

The mortal version of Grell screamed for her—for Kol—through the heartrending din of the dying. In her past traipses through this dream, his hoarse cries had stirred in Nessix the unstoppable need to answer his call, to let him drag her toward their ultimate demise in the hope that safety might be found. Never before had she even thought of attempting to ignore his efforts, but she did today. Her smile broadened at this subtle jab of defiance against the man who would soon become an inoga.

Get up… You must get up!

The whim crept into Nes's mind, trembling to her past the raging chaos of the battlefield, and her brows wrinkled as she contemplated how thoroughly it contradicted her decision to stay put.

Get to Grell. You must find safety.

Moments after addressing her delight in avoiding just that, her eyes flashed open.

I am safer here and now than I've ever been, she calmly told the rogue thought to stave off the manner which it tried to seep into the peace she'd found. *If I get up, that's when the end begins.*

When the… The words clipped short and the snap of a sharp gasp came from the back of Nes's mind. *The end has already begun, little one. Where are you?*

Nessix gasped, chilled to the bone, as she recognized the tone of those thoughts, and she actively had to fight the reaction to leap to her feet and push past a broken hip to drag herself, screaming, toward the friendlier, mortal version of Grell. The sooner she was with him, the sooner the dream would end. And the sooner this nightmare ended, the sooner she could once again escape Kol. The notion that the alar had breached her defenses to slip into her mind—though perhaps it was more accurate to say she was in his—frightened Nessix worse than any threat of lightning bolts or the agony of being twisted and torn into a demon. And if Kol had

18

found a passage into her mind…

Scrubbing her thoughts clean of her recent memories of Mathias's rescue, Nessix engaged her demon as boldly as she could. *I am where I need to be. Far from the hells. Far from you.*

You are assuming you know where I am. Despite the playfulness of Kol's choice of words, his tone was grave and terse.

I know you haven't caught me, Nessix countered, gaining courage. *So you can't be that close, can you?*

Wherever you are, little one, you are not safe. Quit with this nonsense and come back to me. I can protect you. There are—

Inoga after me? she finished for him. *You've told me that and I've seen it for myself. And I will tell you now that I'm not worried about them.*

Not worried *about them?* Confusion ran as thick as the carnage of the battlefield in Kol's words, garnished with faint hints of outrage. Everyone was afraid of inoga. Kol suspected even Annin, despite the boldness which he used when addressing them, was afraid of inoga. Nessix had tried to fight Grell once before and failed miserably, and she'd been killed by Inek on her first day as an akhuerai. *What has happened to you that you no longer fear inoga?* It would be a nice trait to develop for himself.

Nessix hesitated, conflicted as to how much she could risk disclosing to the demon who had appointed himself as her master. She knew this was a dream and that several miles must be between her and Kol. She knew that if she could trust Mathias—and she liked to think she could—she would remain well out of the demons' grasp. But she'd also learned long ago to not underestimate Kol's tenacity or intelligence. He'd be quick to spout any insight he gathered on her whereabouts to Annin. The damned oraku would find a way to fill in any missing information, and Kol would keep on his hunt.

Nessix might be safe in the conventional sense, but her problems were far from over.

Inoga don't frighten me anymore. She stuck with the claim, despite how ridiculous it sounded. The ground rumbled against her back and a fresh wave of screams covered the sound of Grell's desperate calls.

They don't frighten you anymore. Kol could have repeated this statement ten thousand times and it couldn't have sounded more ludicrous. *Tell me where you are, little one. I can get you out of whatever trouble you've found, but only if you quit this silly rebellion.*

Nessix smirked, wondering if the intentions of her expressions were conveyed to Kol as clearly as her messages to him were. She suspected the alar did have the desire to protect her, but she also knew that he wasn't looking out for her half as much as he was looking out for himself. Grell must have been livid that she'd escaped Kol, and demon hierarchy would place the blame for her disobedience heavily on the alar's shoulders. In all honesty, Nessix was surprised Kol was still alive. A niggling fear squirmed about in her belly at the thought of the punishment her actions would ultimately earn him, and she pressed the conversation forward to escape the emotions that thought tried to rouse in her.

I got myself into the trouble I'm in, and I can get myself out of any more I find, she said, savoring how it felt to finally talk back to Kol without the risk of repercussion.

I don't think you understand the trouble you've found.

I've got a good enough idea of it.

Kol snorted in the back of her mind. *You think you're that clever? That just because you slipped between my fingers you've escaped your troubles? I know you're on Gelthin, but I suspect you've put that much together.* Another bolt of lightning streaked across the sky and this time, both Nessix and Kol recognized the timbre of Grell's agonized scream. With time running out, Kol hastened his words. *I know you've gone seeking Mathias Sagewind.*

So what if I have? Though Kol had hurried his words, Nessix remained calm. In just a few more moments, she'd be awake, Kol gone from her mind so she could tell Mathias everything he needed to hear. *As kind as you've been to me, that shouldn't frighten you so much.*

Nessix, you need me.

Are you sure it's not you who needs me, Kol?

Wherever you are, whatever you're doing, turn around—

Through Kol's frantic delivery, Nessix heard the tinge of desperation. It wasn't the same arrogant demand he'd used at the start of this conversation, but it bled with a very mortal longing, dredging up feelings Nessix had tried to fight for months now. So long without dream stop, even languishing in this nightmare, Nessix easily recounted her defiant stand against Grell in Kol's defense. She equated her own longing for Mathias to Kol's pleading to her now, and that connection to him which she'd never asked for begged her to take pity on him. There was a strong chance he'd die because of her actions—if Mathias didn't kill Kol when his hunt for her led him to Zeal, Grell would once he crawled back into the hells. Even Annin stood the chance of being Kol's demise, if the oraku finally lost his patience with him.

Before Nessix had the chance to react to this deluge of fear, the bolt destined to strike Kol diverted its natural path to slam into her where she lay on the ground. The surge of the strike coursed through her body, burning its corrupt power through her veins and snapping parts of her she didn't know how to describe. Kol had silenced his objections, his fear for her fate and his hunger to see her again echoing in the silence of her agony as divine might reforged the vessel she wore into what would become a demon.

The sensation raked through Nessix and, with a brilliant flash cast against the back of her eyelids, this nightmare and all of its horror ended.

* * * * *

Kol woke with a humiliating start, gasping on his shock and fear and, if he'd been able to calm his mind enough to realize it, his anger. Nearly choking, he flailed his arms around himself, grabbing for purchase on anything that might be able to pull him out of harm's way. From his watch point perched on a branch overhead, Annin gave him a fleeting glance and frowned.

The alar was worse than most at hiding when he suffered nightmares of the past, and neither was he particularly skilled at masking his emotions, least of all to Annin. And after pushing every ounce of restraint and resilience centuries of being a demon had conditioned into him close to depletion in his search for Nessix, it was no wonder Kol had such an embarrassing return to the waking world. It had only been two hours, and Kol genuinely needed sleep. Grumbling his dissatisfaction as the alar continued to hyperventilate, Annin stretched out his wings and glided down to the ground.

Kol smashed an open hand against his face and rubbed at the sleep in his eyes, hating the headache which crept up on him more than ever. "Where was she…?" he groaned, pushing himself to his knees with his free hand.

Annin sneered. "That was quite a dramatic display for having been dreaming about your pet."

Kol shuddered at Annin's cruelty but didn't call him on it. "I was dreaming about more than just her, and you know that damn well."

Annin shrugged. He could have guessed as much, but the route which he led the conversation was more likely to keep Kol's mind tracking the realities of their task at hand rather than getting hung up on his fantasies. "Okay, then. Where was she?"

Kol shook his head and dropped his hand to his chest to press the pendant which contained half of Nessix's soul against his flesh. At first, he let the tension which had launched him out of sleep blow out of him as the warmth of the vessel wrapped him in the embrace he'd never been able to enjoy from Nessix herself, but that relief didn't last long.

Nessix had been on the run from him for over a month now and through it all, Kol had felt faint pulses of her nerves or nothing at all. Her soul had been nearly silent to him this entire time, and now it throbbed with a deep contentment he hadn't felt since she'd been thriving under his guidance and protection down in the hells. Brows furrowing, Kol held his breath and stuck his hand down the neck of his shirt to fish out the crystalline pendant.

It glowed with an ethereal brightness, a milky haze tinged with the pale blue of bliss. Tiny sparks formed and burst throughout the vessel, celebrating the victory she assumed she'd found. There had been a brief flicker of a similar response when she'd stumbled upon Talier, but that had generated only a pathetic fraction of what she now expressed.

This glow was persistent, tumbling about in a contented manner which gave no signs of fading. That could only mean one thing. Nessix hadn't lied to him when he'd encountered her in his dream. She truly had no reason to be afraid, or at least that was what she believed.

Annin studied Kol and his trinket with the same appraising eyes which he judged all of their interactions. "Does that mean what I think it means?"

Kol gulped down the excuse which raced to his tongue and attempted a shrug of indifference which fooled neither him nor his companion. "She's… she's got reason to believe she's happy."

"Happier than she'd ever been with Talier, I presume?"

Kol nodded. "And she doesn't think she has any reason to be afraid anymore."

Annin cocked his head, brows furrowing. "You can tell that just by watching the swirls in her soul vessel?"

Kol hesitated once again. Speaking of the nightmares of the Divine Battle was frowned upon by the demons of the first wave. After establishing that they all experienced personal renditions of their final moments of mortality, they'd unanimously agreed the dreams were nothing but signs of weakness which needed to be hidden and suppressed. Of course, Annin knew of Kol's nightmare, as they shared several aspects of the same one, and they'd discussed it in full after Nessix had disclosed how she'd unwittingly found a way to invade it.

"I don't need her vessel to tell me," Kol muttered, looking away from his lifelong friend. "She told me, herself."

"How?"

Kol hunched his shoulders up around his ears and refused to turn his face back to Annin. "Haven't you pressed about this enough?"

"I thought I had. I'd hoped I had. But it sounds like I haven't. What have you held back from me, Kol? Or need I remind you that my fate is tied up in this mess, too?"

That excuse to force his compliance had grown old and if Kol wouldn't have had to rely on Annin as severely as he did, he'd have addressed that fact several times over by now. As it was, Annin was of a far more rational mind than Kol, even on his bad days, and he needed the oraku content and well informed, more so now that he suspected the reasons why Nessix had so suddenly found her happiness.

"I spoke to her in my sleep."

Annin's eyes narrowed as he contemplated what that meant. He'd bound Kol's soul to Nessix's once before to allow them to converse via dreams, but as far as he could tell—and evident by how the woman's soul swirled so peacefully in the pendant in Kol's hand—there had been no direct connection between their souls now. Either Kol had grown madder than either of them had allowed themselves to think, or something quite amiss truly was underway. Annin hadn't credited Nessix for any strengths outside of her ability to control an army, but perhaps he'd misjudged her ability to access and manipulate the spiritual realm.

"Would you mind telling me how that happened?"

Kol had always hated it when Annin asked him if he'd mind doing anything for his benefit. Would he mind telling him how he spoke to Nessix? Would he mind explaining why he thought he could trust her out in the wild? Would he mind sharing why he thought it was a good idea to bind himself to her in the first place? Of course, Kol always minded telling Annin those things, but every single time, he was compelled to answer as honestly as he could. Perhaps it boiled down to the past they'd shared as mortals and demons, but in his moments of weakness, when he knew he was going to cave to the demand, Kol liked to tell himself it was because of some sort of magical influence Annin held over him.

"You heard her talk about dreaming of the Divine Battle."

Annin sneered again and shook his head in disgust. "I have. And I've heard you confirm quite a few suspicious aspects about those dreams, as well."

Kol was through being chastised, but was too wound up over tonight's experience to put up a fight about it. "She experiences these dreams through my eyes, by inhabiting my body."

"That's a given, considering how you bound yourself to her. What's this got to do with anything?"

Kol stayed silent for a long moment before breathing out his question in a hushed voice. "Are your dreams of the Divine Battle ever lucid?" When Annin pointedly looked away, frown pinching deeper and arms twitching as though he was about to cross them,

Kol continued. "Mine are, too. I've tried countless times to change it. I don't know, maybe it's out of some strange hope that I can break the cycle and escape the fate which landed me where I am now."

Annin's eyes flashed back to Kol and he went ahead and crossed his arms. Not so much to hide any weaknesses that might be lurking in him, but to keep from rushing forward and dragging his friend to his feet. "Trying to break the cycle? Careful, Kol. You're beginning to sound like *him*."

Kol hung his head even lower, having realized that for decades now. He was proud of what he'd become, proud of the strength he commanded. He reveled in the influence he had over the weaker races of Abaeloth. But there was a part of him, as he suspected there was even in the fiercest, most conceited of the inoga, that would have done anything to have simply died on the battlefield on the day of their creation.

"It doesn't matter," he said. "We both know there's no escaping the fate we found besides death."

Annin glared down at Kol a moment longer, huffed a sigh, then cast his gaze back out toward the horizon. "Alright, go on."

"I suspect it's my eagerness to push the limits in my dreams which allowed Nessix to gather as much of the past as she has, and I suspect it was her comfort and confidence in knowing how to control the actions of my memory which allowed her to ignore the fact that she was on the battlefield tonight. She refused to move, and when I tried to motivate her to do so, she argued. Once I worked past the… the memories, I was able to communicate with her."

Annin's arms dropped to his sides, his suspicion and anger shifting to curiosity. Gaining access to new information often worked that way with the oraku, sparing Kol the other sorts of judgement which Annin was forming against him. "That sounds unusual… it's a shame we bled all of the aranau donors dry when we raised the other akhuerai. It would be interesting to cross reference such a phenomenon."

Kol smugly kept to himself his doubts that any other akhuerai would be able to produce the same results; he'd selected Nessix carefully and after studying hundreds of other candidates. She was smart. She was devoted. She was the sort of woman who figured things out for herself and wasn't afraid to take the hazardous route to get there. It was highly unlikely any of the other akhuerai had even figured out what their dreams were about.

"Phenomenon or otherwise, I spoke with her. She told me she was no longer afraid of the inoga, and when I woke, this"—he dangled the crystal around his neck for Annin to get a better look at it—"is what I discovered."

Annin stared at the pendant a bit longer before shaking his head and picking up their packs. "Then let's get moving and figure out why she's so happy. The last report we received was that she and Talier were sighted entering Fulton. We'll start our search there and flush out whatever it is that made her so brave."

There had been a time when Kol had been the leader of an army. There had been a time when he'd demanded—or had at least borrowed—Annin's respect. The longer he deluded himself into thinking Nessix cared about him, that there was a chance she would have ever chosen to stand with him, the less he believed he was any sort of leader at all. Kol had surrendered so many aspects of himself over the past several centuries, but this one was the hardest to let go of. He'd been born into his position, just as Nessix had. He'd had his title and rank forcibly removed from him, just as Nessix had. But now, as he was losing the last bit of respect and influence he had, the bliss radiating from Nessix's soul vessel bragged about how she was beginning to find hers all over again.

His desperation to reach Nessix was past the dreamy lust he'd had for her soul when she'd been a mortal, past the attachment he'd forged for her during the months he'd carried her soul around in a jar. It had little to do with the fact that he looked at her with a fondness he'd never had a reason to assign to any other living being in his entire existence. Kol was desperate to reach Nessix now because she had so many things he wanted, and he had to take them from her.

Kol waited until he was reasonably certain his legs would obediently carry him before he pushed himself to his feet. He closed the distance between himself and Annin and accepted his pack, securing it at his waist to give freedom to his wings.

"Well?" he asked. "If she was last seen in Fulton, what are we waiting for?"

Annin studied his friend silently, trying to decide if that had been a rhetorical question. There were many things which Annin was waiting for in regards to Kol, least of which was his permission to go flying off to where their quarry was last seen. No matter who Kol was trying to delude, whether it was Annin, or Nessix, or himself, the alar wasn't doing nearly as good of a job of it as he seemed to think he was.

None of this would bode well for Kol once they returned to the hells, but Annin supposed that, at least, wasn't his problem. For as many problems as Kol had landed him in through the time they'd known each other, Annin should have no longer been surprised that Kol found him trouble, though sensibility did question why he continued to let him do so. Kol, the steady, stoic alar, was losing himself through his loss of Nessix, and that made him weak. Annin would carry him as far as he could, but when it was time to drop him into the river… Annin sighed and braced himself for the day in which he would let Kol drown.

"I'm waiting for your lead, my lord."

With nothing but a firm nod that didn't convey half the confidence Kol had hoped it would, the alar launched himself into the air, followed shortly by the last reliable friend he had.

FOUR

Etha found Mathias exactly where she'd expected to—stooped over his bed as he tried to position his outwardly dead lover's body in a comfortable manner—and in just the condition she'd expected to find him in. Still exhausted from the exertion he'd expended during his stand against the inoga, the slow flight from Fairmont to Zeal had allowed the mote of relief he'd found amid the imminent crisis and needing to ease Nessix into death's arms to fizzle out. His posture was slouched, shoulders hanging heavy and arms dragging as he adjusted the pillows and blankets instead of moving with the strength of a man who had survived an inoga attack. Lines of worry and age and sorrow creased his forehead and tugged at bloodshot eyes which had lost more than one battle against his tears.

Through all of the long months spent looking for Nessix, Mathias had always thought he'd find peace when they were finally reunited, but now that he had her unresponsive body in his bed, he was more distraught than ever before. The anticipated muscle aches took gleeful advantage of his mental fatigue, and his head pounded at the thought of how to form his report to the Council. What broke him more than those pains, however, was the acute ache in his heart. All of the hopes he'd had for Nessix and the future they could have shared had been dashed upon discovering the roads—both forced upon her and willingly chosen—she had travelled since

28

he'd last spoken to her.

He was a knight of the Order of the White Circle! Their very own White Paladin! How could he possibly stand in defense of the evil intentions that inevitably lurked in Nessix? How could he continue to claim to uphold Etha's word and will when taking pity on, even *loving*, a demon-perverted assassin? He gazed at her bruised and lifeless face, at the scar on her neck and the nearly-mended puncture he'd sank beneath her collar bone. He gripped her cold hand, slipping his fingers to her wrist as he hopelessly waited for a pulse he knew he wouldn't feel, and fretted.

"I can still feel her," he said to Etha as she stood silent vigil at the foot of his bed, his voice rickety and worn. "Somewhere. Not much, but something. She *will* come back to me, won't she"—his voice cracked and he flicked a brief, torturously longing gaze at his goddess—"Etha?"

In all of her infinite wisdom and deep compassion for Mathias, Etha didn't know what to say to him, no less confused over what to make of the wretched answers they'd discovered than he was. She walked around Nes's dented breastplate where Mathias had discarded it on the floor and to his side as he smoothed Nes's hair and forced himself to let go of her wrist.

"I can only guess she will." Etha quietly went to work unbuckling the straps of Mathias's armor so he could shed its physical strain. "She knows what the demons did to her much better than we do, so all we can do is trust what she told us." Try as she might, Etha hadn't yet found any excuses or ways to make sense of what the demons had done to Nessix, which made her next words that much harder to deliver to her distraught son. "Julianna will be here shortly, and she's going to demand answers."

"I don't *have* answers," Mathias pled, unconsciously shrugging off loosened pieces of armor.

Etha frowned and caught the plates of metal before they crashed to the floor. "That's not going to stop her from expecting them." Mathias invested the bulk of his remaining strength into an indignant snort, but Etha continued before he had the chance to interject. "Whether you have answers or not, I suggest you let her in. Fighting her will do nothing to help your cause or prove Nessix as a nonhostile force."

Mathias still hadn't lifted his forlorn gaze from Nessix save that one fleeting glance to petition for Etha to miraculously fix this problem, his hopes for her lashes to flutter or her nostrils to flare with breath as strong now as they had been when he'd first lost her on Elidae. He didn't want Julianna anywhere near Nessix. His sister had made it no secret that she hated the very idea of his lover, and he didn't have any answers—satisfactory or otherwise—to use to offset her prying. Whatever Mathias couldn't prove or provide, the High Priestess would simply concoct for herself. What Mathias needed, what he knew he stood no chance obtaining, was to be alone while he sorted out what to do with his emotions—his excitement and relief, his sorrow and rapidly compounding fears—while he came to terms with and determined the most logical, least obvious way to privately interrogate the woman he loved once she came back to life.

As with every other aspect of this quest, however, what Mathias wanted and what fate threw at him were not remotely the same. A rapid knock sounded at his door, followed promptly by Julianna's demand to be let in. Mathias allowed himself a glance at Etha as she ceased her actions of removing his armor and frowned at the stoic intensity with which she focused on Nes's still form, scouring for clues as to what had happened to her. If he didn't let Julianna in, Etha would, but with disappointment in his behavior and frustration for the distraction. At least she'd been able to give him a few moments' warning that this disruption was coming. Still wearing half his armor, Mathias pulled his desk chair over to the bedside, sank into it, and waved a hand at his door to scatter away its wardings as he brought his fingers to cover his mouth.

Julianna blustered into the sacred chamber in an entitled flurry of her powder blue gown, but when she met the somber pair of her brother and her goddess, she dropped her assumed authority. When she turned her gaze to the subject of their attention, she froze in place. The door thumped shut behind her.

The High Priestess didn't need to voice her question for it to be heard, and Etha answered it to give Mathias another precious few moments to try pulling himself together.

"This is Nessix," the goddess confirmed softly, as though her voice would disrupt Nes's repose.

Julianna took another few steps closer to the bed, drawing a hand of curled fingers closer to her gaping lips as her eyes widened. "What happened to her?"

Mathias visibly winced at his sister's horrified question, his respiration rate ticking faster as memories of how the inoga had nearly succeeded in seizing Nessix returned to him, compounded by the act of obliging her request for his mercy. After how hard he'd worked to convince Julianna that he genuinely had feelings for Nes, how was he supposed to explain why she was dead on his bed? How would he justify the darkness lurking inside her once she woke from this death? *If* she woke from this death…

Etha, please *let her wake from this death…*.

Etha bowed her head at her son's fear and persistent pain, then looked up at Julianna. "He found her just as she found the inoga we'd been tracking. This ended up being less of a reunion and more of a rescue mission."

Julianna had served as Etha's High Priestess for centuries and in that time, she'd seen enough dead people to realize that Nessix had not been effectively rescued in the traditional sense of the word. Under normal circumstances, ones which Mathias had fewer emotional ties to, Julianna might have been willing to watch her brother wilt a bit further by pointing that out, but she suspected, if he was able to pull himself together even just a little bit, he'd have more than fiery retorts for such a blunt observation. Because Nessix, though all outward and most inward signs proved was dead, sported one terrifying anomaly Julianna had never seen before. Not from mortals, not from demons, not from the undead. Not even from Mathias.

This woman's soul—or at least the battered and scarred remnant of it—was pulling at the frayed ends of her threads like a diligent seamstress… and then coiling and twisting them into ugly knots like an undisciplined child. A mortal created in the manner which Etha had intended had smooth, snag-free threads which kept souls tied in place and the body functioning. Here was a soul pulling threads together on its own accord and tangling them up in the way the first god children's tantrums had snarled the threads in the mortals who had become demons. Mathias, blessed by Etha though he was, had only learned how to feel souls and the threads of the living, never able to see them, and so he had no way of knowing the chaos which he silently mourned over from his bedside.

And he will not learn of it. At least not yet.

Julianna snapped her attention from the abomination stitching itself back to life before her and up to Etha. The goddess's brows were set grimly, no doubt as troubled over this phenomenon as Julianna was, but she was calm over the entire matter. If only to save Mathias's sanity, Julianna would not argue Etha's instructions. As she silently accepted that, Etha's narrow shoulders relaxed.

Our limited intelligence and firsthand experience suggest Nessix is not quite the abomination you're thinking she is. All we can do is wait for her to wake and see what she has to say for herself.

Julianna looked at her brother again and frowned. He hadn't even acknowledged her arrival besides letting her in, never taking his forlorn gaze from Nessix as he rhythmically studied her face and still chest, eyes snagging on the ring under which the woman's remaining bit of soul dwelled along the way. He was worried, undoubtedly, though Julianna couldn't completely settle on what exactly he was worried about, but the way which he leaned forward and the desperation which streamed from his eyes confirmed that he'd put up a tenacious fight if anyone—no matter how sensible—questioned this dead woman's intentions.

Hefting a sigh, unwilling to fight Etha—or her fragile brother—on the matter, Julianna walked up to the opposite side of the bed at last. "Has word been sent to the Council?"

Mathias's frown pinched toward something akin to disgust. "I only just got back with her. What sort of paladin would walk away from his charge without first ensuring her well-being?"

Julianna crossed her arms and raised her chin at Mathias's defensive tone. "Do you plan on leaving her side once you *can* be sure of her status?" She chose to leave out the fact that there was no place more secure, either as sanctuary or prison, in all of Abaeloth than Mathias's chamber. Somehow, she didn't think that would mean much to him in this debate.

The paladin knew both Julianna's implications and the answer she expected him to give her—that he had no intention of ever leaving Nes's side again in this lifetime or any other—but having such knowledge wasn't enough to make him speak of it. "If you're so worried about those dolts, you are welcome to go tell them that I have found the key to stopping the demons."

Julianna scoffed and rolled her eyes, missing Etha's sharp glance meant to silence her haughty retort. "If she's even acting against them…" She might not have caught Etha's scolding glare, but she did note the obvious clench of Mathias's jaw and the darkening of his eyes. "You, my dear brother, are the one who said you'd deliver reports—"

"No." Mathias drew the correction out with a combative edge which prompted Etha to raise a warning hand to her priestess. He teetered on the unstable cusp between an emotional meltdown and a fit of unfulfilled rage, and not even the Mother Goddess was prepared to deal with the results of either way he might fall if shoved. "Eldon Blaxton said I'd report to them. I said you'd tend to the details. Besides, I must speak to Nes before we throw her to the Council's nonsense, make sure she's alright and has her bearings."

"You mean make sure she's not some tool the demons sent here—"

Mathias's eyes snapped up to his sister's, fiercely spearing her blunt remark and shoving it back into her throat. He'd do nearly anything for his sister, but he would not allow her to baselessly judge Nessix, not after the sacrifices he'd seen her make or the harrowing encounter he'd so recently rescued her from. He tilted his head, brows tipping at an argumentative angle, but before he could open his mouth to engage in this battle Julianna seemed so eager to wage, Nes's eyes flew open. She gasped Mathias's name, legs coiling toward her body and hands clutching at the blankets around her. As Etha flit back to the divine realm to let her children sort out Nessix's fate between themselves, Mathias pulled Nessix into a tight embrace.

"I'm here," Mathias breathed, holding her trembling body close. He bowed his head so her hair soaked up his tears. "I'm right here."

Fresh from Kol's most recent intrusion and with a vivid recollection of the inoga crushing her armor around her, Nessix's instinct was to fight the restraint holding her still, but the cushion of the mattress, the lack of pain in her torso, and the comforting strength of Mathias's arms lulled those lingering fears away.

She'd found her safety.

It wasn't quite the peace or salvation she'd dreamed of while trapped in the hells—at least not yet—but it was a start. The promise she'd made to her akhuerai soldiers, that she'd find a way to right the wrongs the demons had done to them, was closer to being achieved. She didn't know where she was or how much time had passed, but she didn't have to. Worries abated for this brief moment, Nessix sighed and melted into Mathias's arms.

Her moment of reprieve, this tantalizing glimpse of bliss which the inoga had stolen from her reunion with Mathias was snatched away by the rude clearing of a throat. Nessix tensed, instinct berating her over her vulnerable position, but Mathias didn't react to the sound, the warmth of his embrace gently promising her that nothing around them intended to do her harm. She would have believed his unspoken statement without hesitation, had it not been followed with the snip of an entitled, feminine voice.

"You have some explaining to do, General Nessix Teradhel of Elidae."

Nessix didn't have a chance to savor the thrill of being addressed by her formal title as Mathias sharply sniffed back his tears and slowly pushed himself away from her, leveling a frigid glare over her shoulder.

"Now is not the time for this."

The tension in the room intensified, further sapping that sense of security from Nessix. Grasping Mathias's arm for support, she turned to assess the woman who he'd addressed as a challenger.

"This is the perfect time." The woman had her arms crossed, faint creases around her petite nose suggesting her efforts to conceal a sneer as she judged Nessix.

No stranger to scrutiny, having been enslaved by demons and

indentured to the assassins guild, Nessix pulled her shoulders back and raised her chin. She had finally fought her way free of both those evils, and she was through being pushed around. "I owe answers only to Mathias," she told this woman. "You have your leave."

A strangled choke left Mathias as the woman's eyes widened, arms dropping to her sides in her shock, and Nessix got the distinct impression that she'd said something wrong.

"Nes," Mathias said, his voice low and treading carefully between the growing ire of both women. "This is my sister, Zeal's most esteemed High Priestess Julianna Sagewind."

Nessix had heard the clear warning in Mathias's words and recognized the same in the arrogant arch of Julianna's brows, but she'd already sank her teeth into the High Priestess's initial greeting. No matter how long ago it was, no matter how far removed from it she might be, Nessix was a general, and here on the mortal realm, backed by a man who proclaimed to uphold justice, she was ready to resume acting like one.

"Begging your pardon, then, High Priestess," Nessix said. "But the officers need to discuss battle tactics. You may leave us."

That air of conditioned control flashed from Julianna's eyes. "Do you have any idea who you are speaking to, hellspawn?"

Nessix bristled at the address and slapped away the hand which Mathias reached forward in an attempt to calm her. "Yes, fool," she snapped, ignoring, too, the pleading way Mathias groaned her name. "Mathias just told me, though I must say I'd expected someone much more insightful to hold such a prestigious title."

Nessix had been raised within an army and had grown accustomed to goading. She'd been belittled by demons and endlessly judged by mortals lacking all sense of moral fiber. She could give ten times as much as she'd ever receive. But Julianna hadn't been spoken down to since she'd been a little girl wrestling with her siblings, when Etha was little more than a name she'd heard a couple times. Her pretty face screwed up in resentment, delivering just enough satisfaction to Nessix to calm the knot of chaos tumbling about inside of her.

"Call yourself whatever you want," Julianna said tersely, "but you are in Zeal now, and any rank which you might have held on Elidae or among your demon peers does not apply."

Nes's fingers dug into Mathias's arm and he stood at last, grasping Nes's upper arm before she had the chance to shove him away. He knew both of these women well, and neither was inclined to back down from a confrontation in which they felt they were in the right. He didn't know if he had to interject to protect Nessix from Julianna's proven might or to spare his sister from whatever newly discovered power Nessix had tapped into, but he was certain that if he didn't step in, he'd lose his ability to reason with either of them. Desperate to pour water on these coals, Mathias blurted the first thought that came to mind.

"Jules, the Council will have their report from me." His words broke through the High Priestess's bubbling ire and untwisted the scowl on her face. "Let me assess Nes's physical soundness, and I will meet with the full assembly at a time of their choosing."

Julianna narrowed her eyes. Her brother was taking a sly approach to this; a full assembly wouldn't be able to be arranged until the following morning at the absolute earliest. She'd been through this dance enough times before to realize Mathias was planning something, but his willingness to keep compliance on the table would diminish the longer she took to counter his offer. "Fine," she seethed. "But that"—she jabbed a finger at the fuming woman half-risen on the bed—"does not leave your chamber."

Nessix drew in the breath to debate, but Mathias beat her to speaking and gently squeezed her arm. "Deal," he said.

Julianna scoured Nessix over once more, shot a bemused glance at her brother, then gave an exaggerated scoff. With a disgusted flinging of her arms, she spun from the pair and saw herself out of Mathias's chamber, slamming the door closed behind her. Mathias was quick to leave Nessix to reassemble the wardings on the door, hesitating for a moment before adding those which would keep Nessix contained inside, as well.

"You never told me your sister was so pleasant."

Mathias closed his eyes and leaned his forehead against the door. "I'd have better prepared you for what to expect of her if I'd had the chance to."

"I'd imagined the woman assigned to serving as Etha's voice to the masses would show a bit more… warmth." Nessix waited for a response that didn't come before digging a bit further. "Have I done something to offend her?"

Mathias was grateful he hadn't yet turned to face Nessix. If not for the past they'd shared, he would have been just as wary of her as his sister was, though he liked to think he'd express himself better. He had little more than his memories and what was left of his hope believing that Nessix was the same woman he'd fallen for on Elidae. The demons had changed her in ways he'd already observed and others he was sure he'd uncover, and she'd somehow fallen into the ranks of assassins. Even those civilians she passed without intending to kill, she'd endangered by leaving a trail for the demon forces chasing her. Maybe Julianna and Sazrah had been right. Maybe Nessix wasn't who he thought she was. Mathias didn't know how to handle such a revelation, but honor and loyalty demanded he fight for her in any manner necessary. He sighed, found a smile sleeping inside of him, and turned back to Nessix.

"Julianna is the head of the Order," he explained, loosening the straps of the remaining pieces of his armor. "And she takes her duties rather seriously."

Nessix flexed her calves to test their reliability and slid out of the bed, glancing about the plainly furnished chamber. This was the first time she'd woken from death without Kol shoving dream stop down her throat, and she had to wonder if that would make a difference in her recovery. "I'm hurt, Sagewind," she said, trying to make light of what she recognized as an uncertain situation. "You hadn't told her about me?"

He tried a chuckle that didn't come out past a puff of disappointment. "I told her a lot about you, more than she wanted to hear. And it was telling her about what happened to you and discussing the report which Sazrah sent me and the events surrounding it that dimmed her opinion of you."

Nes's features fell. Able to concentrate on matters not immediately imperative to survival for the first time in weeks, she finally had to face the consequences of her actions. The inoga had taken a mighty gash out of Fairmont before she'd stopped them, and she was certain they'd been no gentler in the other cities they'd passed through before finding her. Kol's tracking parties, smaller, smarter, and far more agile than those brutes, had to have done as much, possibly more, damage than that.

And, oh, how she must have hurt her damned alar…

Nessix shuddered and shook her head, crossing her arms tightly as the sudden sting of tears rushed to her eyes. Mathias frowned, Nes's apparent helplessness pushing past the assumptions Julianna had tried to plant in his mind. He kicked off his boots and returned to the bed to take Nessix in his arms again. She nestled against his chest, drawing on his comfort in place of dream stop, until his question interrupted their silence.

"What happened to you, Nes?"

She swallowed hard and her heart rate ticked up. "That would take a long time to explain."

"We've got all night, if Julianna does her job right." Unlocking his embrace, Mathias ran his hands down Nes's arms to push her back a step so he could look her over. "I want to help you, more than anything. And I very well may be the only person in Zeal willing to do so. Tell me what happened to you so I can stand beside you when their accusations come."

"Accusations?"

Mathias glanced away. "You must know that the Council has been holding you accountable for the current demon resurgence."

Nessix glowered at Mathias. "I know I've been blaming myself for it, and it seems you have, too." Guilt flashed across Mathias's face, and he creased his lips as he focused more intently at the floor. "But what have you told your officials that would lead them to believe it?"

Mathias didn't answer immediately, keeping to himself how he hadn't shared evidence of her most recent form of employment with anyone, nor how he'd witnessed the devastating results of both legs of the demons' search for her firsthand. "I told them all I knew. I had to. The priestesses have been studying tirelessly to find answers as to what's happened to those like you. All we've been able to uncover are breadcrumbs, names for that alar who killed you and the oraku who trapped your soul—" It was Nessix who had to look away now, and she even gave a tug against Mathias's firm hold. He'd hit a nerve he hadn't expected to locate so easily. "Is there more to it than that?"

Nessix struggled against Mathias's grasp once more, and he released her so she could sit on the edge of his bed. "There's a whole lot more," she murmured, picking at the cuticle of her thumb. "Kol is—was…"

Did she have it in her to divulge Kol's sins to the one man capable of righting them? This had been the reason Nessix had set out to reach Mathias, but she couldn't shake the fact that part of her was—and likely always would be—loyal to the demon who had risked his life so many times to keep her in it. Her shoulders slumped and she folded forward at her waist to rest her elbows on her knees. "He's who discovered how to create the akhuerai."

"The akhuerai… is that what they demons are calling the souls they've stolen?"

She nodded silently, feeling her grasp on her calm slipping as she stood poised to throw Kol to Mathias's wrath.

"I was told thousands of souls have gone missing over the past century," he said. "Have they all been taken by Kol?"

Nessix winced at the malice in Mathias's question, as well as her reflection on how many disrupted lives she'd been made responsible for. The nauseous lump climbed out of her stomach and pressed into her throat. There was no way to protect Kol's reputation in any of this. "My army consisted of just over one thousand men and women from all reaches of Abaeloth, but I'd been told that there were earlier, failed trials."

Mathias nodded slowly, the pieces of recent events falling into place even as new ones cropped up. Nessix was avoiding his questions. "And Kol managed all of this?"

Nessix perked up as means to possibly lighten Kol's sentence—or hasten his death—showed up at last. "Kol is the scholar, the one who came up with the theory, but he works closely with a winged oraku, Annin. He's the one who executes the process."

Dismissing Nes's hope for leniency for Kol, Mathias brushed

right past Annin's involvement in Abaeloth's brewing crisis. "What theory did Kol base these crimes off of?"

The entire reason Nessix had risked fleeing the hells was to give Mathias this information so he and his great Order could put a stop to the demons'—to Kol's—plans and possibly find a way to fix what had been broken. But now that she had the opportunity to do just that, Kol's desperate pleas for her to return to him, the threads of fear which stitched together his fabricated confidence, came back to her. Tears of frustration and regret rimmed her eyes, blurring her vision of Mathias's expression falling into helplessness. His calloused hands, so gentle and strong, grasped hers. Right now, in this moment, both of them wanted few things more than to simply hold each other and remember what was and what should have been, but that was a luxury they didn't have.

"Nes, this is important." Mathias's voice had softened, losing its strict edge.

"I know." Nes's reply came out on little more than a whisper as she continued to fight with her demon's influence over her. "This is why I came to find you, why I…" She shuddered and gripped Mathias's fingers tighter as she mustered the courage to lift her bleary eyes to meet his. "I've been the cause of some terrible, unforgiveable sins to ensure I could find you, but I… Now that I have to face what…"

Try as she might, Nessix couldn't force out the words that would ultimately betray Kol. She'd been able to admit, or at least hint at, how she'd funded her journey, but she couldn't simply hand over the demon who had caused so much suffering, who she had such a deeply ingrained instinct to protect.

Mathias had never been comfortable seeing Nessix cry, and he'd witnessed her tears only a few times in the past. These ones were no different than before. The mortal version of Nessix had masqueraded as a strong woman, as her title had demanded of her, and after her defiant stand against five inoga, a valiant act not even Mathias would have volunteered himself for, he knew that the hells had tempered her strength well beyond her mortal limits. Yet here she was, so broken and alone in her plight, and she was crying.

Mathias had been a prisoner of the demons' in the past. He'd been cut open and broken by them, forced to watch them operate upon and defile those he'd loved. He knew well the sorts of tortures they employed and had seen them break those just as strong as Nessix. He was acutely aware of the risks which ran with being a notable prisoner to the demons, and suspected it meant nothing good that Nessix seemed so familiar with those as high ranking as Annin and Kol. He had no doubt that they'd made a pet—and an example—of Nessix in the time they'd held her captive and he felt his own bite of tears as he had to accept that his dear, beautiful Nessix, even as broken as she was, had been their plaything for so long.

"I'm sorry," he murmured, sinking down beside her to hold her once again. "I don't mean to pry. I want to be able to give you time to recover, but the Council needs its report. We need to find a way to stop the demons' progress."

Nes leaned into Mathias's embrace, letting her tears fall, hating herself for Mathias's assumptions and all the more for the fact that she didn't fully understand why this was so hard for her. She'd been so determined to do whatever was necessary to find justice for her people, to be the good general who would throw herself at death in defense of those who needed her, that she had suppressed any contemplations over what she'd do when Kol was the one needing her protection. Safe in Mathias's arms, Nessix knew there would be no saving both the innocents and her guilty demon lord, unless…

"I was dead when they did all of this to me." Nessix pushed away from Mathias. "And I never witnessed the procedure performed on anyone else. All I know is that it involves blood and these metal rings"—her fingers pressed against the one protruding from her sternum—"we're not supposed to mess with."

"Blood magic." Mathias's eyes darkened, the warmth draining from his expression as he regarded the ring Nessix referred to.

She hesitated at the rigid clench of Mathias's jaw. Kol had done a marvelous job evading her questions about her creation, but could Mathias know something about how she'd been pieced together? She deserved the answer to that more than anyone else on the surface of Abaeloth, but wouldn't risk losing her chance to try teasing Mathias's attention away from Kol.

41

"You managed to uncover specific demon names," she said, purposefully avoiding mentioning any of them herself.

Mathias nodded, lips twitching with his desire to rediscover a friendly demeanor. "I had a connection overhear who was responsible for this blasphemy, and the priestesses went to work researching their relevance, but the furthest they've been able to dig so far is that Annin and Kol are ancients."

A relieved laugh left Nessix, chasing away the last of Mathias's anger to be replaced with confusion and the slightest glimmer of hope. "In their research, did your priestesses learn anything about a demon named Berann?"

Just as quickly as that hope lit in Mathias's eyes, it was blown cold once more. "What do you know of him?"

Nessix caught her breath, eyes flying wide at Mathias's reaction. That hadn't been an idle question; it had been recognition. "Only that he exists, that Kol and Annin know him, and that I'm supposed to forget I've ever heard his name. Who is he?"

"He was a winged oraku, like that Annin, but he was slain before the first demon war began."

Nessix lowered her eyes and gnawed on the inside of her cheek. Berann had survived the Divine Battle but had gone on to be slain—most likely by Mathias's precious Order? Not even in the furthest stretch of Nes's imagination would Kol have gotten violently defensive over another demon's fate out of mourning. There had to be more to this. "Under what circumstances was he slain?"

Mathias leaned back, gaze turning in on itself as he thought back to his youth. "He could be credited as the demon who catalyzed the outbreak of the demon war. He and three alar flew on Zeal just as news of a resurgence began to circulate. He demanded entry and to speak to the Council. Our records say he was diplomatically turned away, and that he attempted to force his way into an audience at which point he and his escorts were slain. The war broke out in full within a week of that incident."

Nessix cocked her head, tactical mind hard at work dissecting the report. "Do your tales of him state what he wanted to speak to the Council about?"

Mathias grimaced and he looked down at his hands. "The spoken tales all say he'd been sent to demand Zeal's surrender of its watch over Gelthin, but the historical recounts state nothing about his intentions." He could clearly see the wheels turning in Nes's head as she desperately tried to tie this long-ago incident to the current crisis, and he shook his head. "Zenos's research suggested that the demons' practice of stealing souls began quietly over the past century. Berann could not possibly be involved."

Nessix shook her head firmly. "Kol wouldn't—" She stopped her excuse of how the alar wouldn't have beaten her needlessly before it came out, dreading how she'd explain her reasoning to Mathias. "He wouldn't tell me anything at all about Berann, which means I was being kept ignorant for a reason. An important one I was never meant to uncover."

Mathias scoffed and stood so he could pace off some of his growing agitation. "Kol is a *demon*, Nes. The one who killed you. What makes you think he'd give you anything you asked for?"

"I was the general of the army he built." Her stubbornness, feeding off the chaos churning inside her, flared to life as she remembered with righteous fondness the long afternoons she'd spent studying demon warfare by Kol's side. "He told me more than you'd think."

A bitter chuckle left Mathias and he shook his head. He'd thought Nessix was smarter than this… "Demons use people, Nes. It's how they get ahead."

"I know that, better than you'd believe."

"Yet you're still shocked that Kol found pleasure in withholding from you the information you were after?"

Mathias's cold, harsh tone wore on Nessix, rapidly devouring what little calm she had without her dream stop. The quick beating she'd received for asking about Berann had stuck with her, just as Kol had hoped it would, but so did his embrace and affirmation of not wanting to hurt her which had come immediately afterwards. She sprang to her feet, muscles primed for a confrontation. "He derived no pleasure from withholding that information from me."

Mathias grabbed Nessix by the forearms and shook her, his voice cracking with fear and disbelief. "He is a *demon*, Nes!"

She struggled against his hold, ready to face Mathias's unbeatable might in Kol's defense just as she'd stood against Grell for the same reason, but his grip bit down too tightly, crushing the tendons which she needed to strike at him.

"You know nothing about him!" she yelled back, only realizing what she'd said after Mathias gasped, discipline draining from his face as he gaped at her like she'd just run him through.

Nessix knew instantly that she'd said the wrong thing, that her single statement was more than enough to incriminate her in anyone's eyes. The strength filtered out of her limbs as her bout of defiance abandoned her, and she almost wished she'd been facing Grell again instead of Mathias. At least then she'd be likely to find a reprieve from her shock in death. Instead, the paladin supported her as she sank back on the edge of his bed, his eyes still wide and cheeks pale.

"I think I need some time to sort out my thoughts before I meet with this Council of yours," Nes murmured.

"That sounds like a great idea."

Nessix flinched at Mathias's curt reply and was too afraid to sneak a look at the severe disapproval he regarded her with. As Nessix slumped there in the safety of Mathias's enchanted chamber in the Citadel, staring at her blood-stained hands, she heard Mathias stalk from the room, door slamming behind him. Helpless and terrified, Nessix cursed Kol all over again for what he had done to her, and did something she'd never done before.

She prayed to Etha.

FIVE

It had taken Khin a few days wasted on bitter fretting to come to terms with Julianna's words, that she was a survivor and not a warrior, but a grudging acceptance did eventually reach her. She'd approached the High Priestess then, extending her regrets for her selfish behavior and requesting a way for one of her limited skills to assist in this erupting crisis she still knew so little about. Julianna, relieved by the girl's maturity, had appointed her the simple but vital tasks of relaying reports between the Citadel's temple and Zeal's perimeter guard posts and circulating research material to and from the library. It wasn't an exciting mission, and Khin had to stretch her imagination as far as she could to find ways it would play into her desire for vengeance against the demons who had slain her family, but it kept her busy and feeling useful.

That morning, Khin returned from the eastern post with a satchel full of reports to find the studious atmosphere of the temple degraded into disorder. The younger priestesses struggled to focus on their research, fidgeting uncomfortably in their seats and losing their places in the text when they'd cast anxious glances at their seniors, who raced about the temple, delivering hushed words between one another. Heart leaping to her throat and skin chilling with a fine misting of sweat, Khin clutched her satchel's strap as she crept into the candle-lit dimness of the temple. She'd never before seen this disciplined group of women express such a lack of composure, and witnessing it now brought back so many terrible memories of other people darting around in confusion. Had some answer been found? Were they under attack? Desire and sensibility argued as to whether or not that notion excited or frightened Khin, but she so badly needed to get answers. Steeling herself with a deep breath and a firm press of her lips, she approached Abbess Diana, the priestess who'd been assigned to accept her deliveries, and slid the satchel from her arm.

"Abbess," Khin started, realizing in that moment that most of her confidence had fled her. "Has something happened?"

"Oh…" Diana drew her concern out like a fretting hen as she accepted the reports. "Sir Sagewind has returned." She turned to bustle off with the delivery.

Mathias had returned? And he hadn't sent word to Khin? The girl cast a quick look around the sanctuary, hunting for some messenger who might have been there for that purpose. Finding none, she soaked in more of that frantic and distracted buzz and gasped. What if he'd returned unwell? Gritting her teeth to fend off her tears, Khin grabbed the sleeve of the woman's robe before she could leave. "Is he alright?"

Diana sent a pleading gaze toward Julianna's office. "He's physically sound as far as I heard, but…" Her weathered lips puckered in a tight frown and she tilted her brows in what was meant to be an apology before firmly prying Khin's fingers off her sleeve to resume rushing toward the office.

Khin's faith in the world had been shaken several times in the past, and though she longed to learn to trust again in the safety of Zeal, she hadn't spent quite enough time here to not press for more answers. Clearly, the abbess was hiding something. Khin pursued her promptly.

"But what?" she asked, sticking close to the older woman's side.

Diana refused to look at her, struggling between commitment to her duty and desire to be kind to the undisciplined young woman assigned to her. "But he is busy," the woman snapped. "Much as the rest of us are. It is best you occupy yourself with unrelated matters."

Khin had never been spoken to so sharply by the gentle woman, and those words did succeed in stopping her from following as the abbess integrated into the flow of other clergywomen rushing about the temple. Painfully undereducated in political matters, Khin had no idea what conclusions she should be making right now, but she had seen enough of the world and the behavior of others to realize that something terrible was underway. Though she'd been told to find something else to occupy her time not even ten seconds prior, Khin had always had a terrible track record for following instructions.

She moved from priestess to priestess, eavesdropping where she was able until she deduced that Mathias had found the woman he'd been looking for and had brought her back here to Zeal. By these hushed reports and rumors, Khin gathered enough to know that there was something suspicious, possibly dangerous about this woman, which only complicated those jealous inklings Khin had devised against this rival for Mathias's attention. Wasn't this woman supposed to be able to help stop the demons? When it seemed as though Khin had observed all of the information she'd be able to gather through passive means, she balled up her courage once more and approached Julianna's office.

It was ridiculous to think that the High Priestess would make time for her with so much tension running rampant through the temple, but Khin deserved to know what was going on. No matter how busy Julianna was, she'd be able to spare time for one question from the girl she'd personally offered to guide. The tension tumbling about the temple reinforced Khin's caution as she approached the door, and she nearly choked on her nerves by the time she peeked inside.

Amid all of the turmoil churning about, High Priestess Julianna was gone.

Khin froze, not knowing what to make of this unusual occurrence. Julianna was almost always in her office, if she wasn't actively flitting about tending to the young priestesses' questions or grumbling her way to an appointment with the Council. In this outward and apparent crisis, she absolutely should have been here to help her students find order and Khin find answers. Ignorant to the greater workings of the Order, that lump of caution began to turn into something closer to the same panic which devoured the younger members of the priesteshood as Khin grasped at where else Julianna could possibly be.

Gripping the doorframe for support, breathing so rapidly she was becoming dizzy, Khin was faced with the fact that none of this was as simple or straightforward as she'd let herself believe. Abaeloth was facing a crisis far larger than a few murdered whores and villagers; these matters which she'd fussed over and tried to excuse away were snowballing into something more dire and serious than she'd ever been able to imagine. Survivor or not, she'd been foolish to demand to be involved with any of this!

A gentle hand brushed Khin's shoulder and she would have missed it from the tingling numbness in her skin had soft words not come with it. "There is need for you in the infirmary if—"

"The infirmary?" Khin breathed, disbelieving the tales her panic had already woven about the lies in Abbess Diana's claim of Mathias's well-being. The bottom dropped out of her stomach, her thoughts unable to keep up with logic as she spun around to face an amber-eyed priestess about her age wearing a gentle smile amid this constant flow of anxiety.

"Yes," the priestess replied patiently, the only sense of calm anywhere in the massive chamber. "The travelling companion of the woman Mathias recovered is waiting there, confused and distressed. He seemed unsure if he could trust me in terms of the Citadel's desire to assist him, but perhaps he'd be inclined to listen to you, a fellow survivor."

Arguments flocked through Khin's racing mind as to why she was woefully underqualified to offer anyone assistance right now—especially if one of Etha's own priestesses had failed to do so—but that survivor's instinct hooked onto them and dragged them back to present her another option. She may have been unable to find answers about Mathias's quest from anyone affiliated with the Order, but the travelling companion of the woman both Mathias and Julianna believed was the key to stopping the demons had to know *something* worthwhile. Ignorant and unskilled or not, even half-paralyzed and choked with this infectious fear, this was a job Khin had to accept.

"Of course, priestess," Khin said. "I'll help him settle in however I can."

Etha smiled, pleased to have found a compromise to the fretting of both Khin and Talier. "His room is on the fourth floor."

Khin nodded, through with the idle talk. "If this will help Mathias's cause."

A ripple of a pout tugged at Etha's lips, but she hid it well. "It will help the cause." With one more pat to Khin's shoulder, she slipped into the flow of busy priestesses.

Grounding herself from the frantic thoughts which were so close to dragging her into despair, Khin strode for the temple's exit to head to the infirmary.

* * * * *

Talier had never been a particularly courageous man, but the longer he'd been under the demons' heels, the less peace he was able to find in any situation or from any amount of reassurance. It was simple to attribute the degradation of whatever backbone he'd had on the leverage the demons held over him and his ingrained objections to confinement on the wolf they'd bound him to, but Talier would have given anything but his brother's life—assuming Marcoux still lived—to be able to stop pacing through the pristine security of this room within the Citadel.

The woman who he'd woken to hadn't answered any of his questions to his satisfaction. He still had no idea how he or Nessix had escaped that surreal massacre in Fairmont, nor how he'd made it as far as Zeal. He didn't even know if Nessix was truly safe as the woman had gently claimed. It was his fear of these unknowns, of whatever influence or hidden powers this woman had which motivated Talier to stay in his chamber, more so than the guards he'd been told were patrolling outside his open door, and it was that fear which kept him pacing a worn path across the room's pretty rug, because he simply *had* to find a way out of this room.

He had to find Nessix—if she still remained to be found—

and get her out of Zeal before Kol figured out she'd made it here.

Talier plunged his hand into his pocket to retrieve the pendant which housed Marcoux's proof of life and flicked the face of it open. It was difficult to decide if Marcoux was still breathing or if his subtle movements were an illusion from how the steady bumbling of Talier's pacing jostled his hand, but he didn't have much time to think it over. A timid throat cleared at the doorway and Talier yelped in surprise, closing his fingers over the locket and retreating a yard from the perceived threat.

In the doorway stood a petite young woman dressed in a simple linen dress matching the ones he'd glimpsed on the other women who occasionally passed by in the hallway. Her dark curls were pulled back in a manner which kept them from straying onto the tray of steaming soup and perfectly golden bread she carried, but her big brown eyes only flicked toward his before lowering to a point on the floor.

"I was told you could use some company." She hesitated a moment longer, as if doubting her authority, and after taking a deep breath, she rushed inside to deposit the food on the small bedside table.

Despite her timid approach, she seemed no more confident in her position than Talier felt he was, and that both elated and frightened him even more. As uncertain as she was, she moved in a relaxed manner, as though she was confident, at least, of their safety. It was that relaxation which Talier clung to in order to find the nerve to speak.

"This may sound strange, but do you know what happened?"

Whether it was Talier's unusual question or the flimsy manner in which he'd delivered it, the girl straightened promptly after situating the food and clutched the emptied tray to her chest as she turned to face him. "You don't know?" She'd been counting on him being able to provide the answers the priestesses had refused to share.

Sick to his stomach, Talier couldn't even bring himself to glance at the food. "The woman who was here when I woke up made things even more confusing… All I know is that Nessix and I were in Fairmont and these giant, monstrous demons attacked."

Nessix. Was that the woman who Mathias had left Khin behind for? She squirreled away that information before pursuing a more sobering thought. "Giant demons," Khin murmured. The nightmares of her own brush with inoga still plagued her sleep, even in Zeal's blessed walls.

"Yeah." Talier had relaxed enough to cram Marcoux's locket back in its hiding place, keeping his balled fist wrapped around its warmth. "They were tearing down homes and terrorizing the people. Nessix said something I couldn't understand and charged in to stop them. Then this knight showed up and the woman—ah, *a* woman we'd met on the road was there."

Having found someone willing to divulge answers at last, Khin scooted another couple steps closer to Talier. "And that knight... is he okay?"

Talier's eyes burned and ached as though someone had shoved wads of cotton beneath their lids, and he shook his head with a helpless shrug, holding his open hand out before himself. "I don't know. There was so much screaming and I couldn't understand what was happening. The next thing I knew, Nessix was dying and the knight was trying to tend to her wounds then suddenly, I was here." He turned his pleading eyes to Khin's. "The woman who was here when I woke told me Nessix is alive and in the care of a paladin. You have access to the infirmary. How is she? Is she really alright?"

Khin's willingness to use Talier as a source of information shriveled up as her personal concerns were once again shoved aside for those tied to this woman Mathias had abandoned her for. Gripping the tray more tightly, a bitter snarl flawed her face. "I haven't heard word about this Nessix or the paladin who is supposed to be watching over her."

Talier drew a reluctant step back at the bite of Khin's tone. "I-I'm sorry. It's just that all I want is to see Nessix better, so she can deliver whatever message she thought was so important, and we can get out of Zeal."

Khin perked up, her anger dissipating like a little puff of smoke. "You want her *out* of Zeal?"

The question sounded more eager than suspicious, and so

Talier nodded. "She's, um, got other tasks to tend to. Important ones. And I'm, ah, worried that if she's kept here too long, she won't see them done. So, please. If you know anything about how she fares or where I can find her, you'd be saving a life if you told me."

With Talier wanting Nessix out of Zeal and Khin increasingly eager for the same, she saw no reason to not try to help him. After all, helping him was what she'd been asked to do. "I haven't heard anything about your friend, but I'll ask around and see what I can find out."

Talier's entire posture sagged with the first genuine relief he'd found in weeks. Maybe, just maybe, he could fix this before it became a problem. "You would do that for me?"

Khin smiled that same welcoming smile she'd used when she thought she'd been hunting for an eligible bachelor. "Of course. Zeal exists to help us all, doesn't it?"

Talier blew out a great sigh and eyed the table of food at last. "Thank you," he said, giving a small bow of gratitude. "You have no idea how much this means to me."

Khin returned the gesture with an awkward curtsey. "I think I've got an idea."

Feeling as though she could do something for herself for the first time in her life, Khin left the agitated man's room, both of them more at ease from the exchange.

SIX

Mathias made it no farther than ten stairs down the Citadel's spire before stopping to sit on the polished marble stairs to think. Crushed beneath confusion and this barrage of emotions, he looked forward to speaking with anyone who claimed official status in the Order even less than usual, which was why he'd taken the long, physical route out of his wing of the Citadel. When he'd first found Nessix, he'd planned on staying in his chamber to catch up with her and help her sort through the horrors which had chased her out of the hells. He'd never expected her to have carried fond memories with her, least of all about the same demon who'd slain her.

Groaning, Mathias braced his elbows on his knees and dropped his face into his hands. Nessix had shown so many indications that she was still the justice-seeking general he'd fallen for, but how could he look past that last desperate plea she'd made in Kol's defense? Had her inability to answer his questions been her unwillingness to further incriminate the enemy? Perhaps Kol had seduced her, conditioned her into respecting and serving him. Mathias sucked his teeth and shook his head at the repulsive notion; if that had been the case, she wouldn't have put innocents in danger by parting ways with him, and she certainly wouldn't have engaged a group of inoga eager to drag her back into the hells.

Mathias was grateful Julianna had left when she had, as he was having trouble justifying Nes's words even to himself.

Mathias had dealt with more than his share of pain and doubt in the lifetimes he'd served Etha, but this horrible situation which was quickly becoming his reality was the greatest trial he'd ever faced.

"Oh, Etha, I just want to fix her…"

A tiny shoulder and head thumped against his arm and delicate fingers worked between his own. "But, Mathias, you have," she murmured to her grieving son. "You've finally found a way to get her to pray to me."

Mathias drew in a sharp breath and looked to his little goddess, though she kept her thoughtful gaze directed toward some distant spot down the stairs. "I thought you said you couldn't find her in the divine realm?"

Etha quirked her lips and briefly hummed her discontent. "I couldn't, but I can certainly hear her when she shouts her grievances in your room right outside my door."

Mathias carefully pried Etha from his side and leaned forward to study her more thoroughly. "What is she saying?"

Etha slid a glance at him, one brow lifting. "She only just now decided to give her confidence to me, and you want me to betray that?"

A guilty flush warmed Mathias's cheeks. That was precisely what he wanted Etha to do, but he didn't miss the obvious answer in her question. "It's just that…" He ran his palms up his face and back through his hair, grasping at his blond locks in frustration. "What am I supposed to do?"

Etha turned to regard her son at last. "I don't know." She gave a shrug. "You'd spent so long and worked so hard to find her, I hadn't bothered to consider what would happen if it turned out you didn't want to keep her once you did."

Mathias hastily pushed himself away from Etha, pressing his shoulder against the cool marble of the wall. "It's not that!" he insisted, losing a great deal of his bluster at the challenging tilt of Etha's head. "And you know it…"

"Then act like it."

Mathias turned his face from Etha's blunt practicality. He had been in denial that Nessix would have changed, despite Julianna's speculations and Etha's gentle insight and even Sazrah's firsthand account of how her soul had been twisted. He knew better than most how the demons warped the minds of those they kept as prisoners, how they'd even affected his own manner of thinking in the past. Part of him, one which he'd denied daily up until the sheriff in Midland told him Nessix had been working as an assassin, had known all along that she wouldn't be the same as she was before.

"Please, Etha," he whispered. "You don't have to betray her confidence, but I need to know if she can be saved. I need to know if her heart still beats for the justice we'd once shared."

Etha sighed heavily as she weighed Mathias's request against her laws. If Nessix had been ready to discuss any of her current troubles with Mathias, she wouldn't have asked for him to leave, and if Mathias had been ready to face them, he wouldn't have done so. Besides, there wasn't much Nessix was sharing with Etha besides her frustrations and disappointment tied together by one dominant emotion which the goddess had never liked to think lurked inside the feisty woman.

"She is afraid, Mathias," Etha said at last, reaching up to pull one of his hands from his hair. "She is afraid of what happened to her, of what roads she had to travel. She is afraid of the future—not just for herself, but for many, many others."

Mathias frowned, his glare darkening. "Is she afraid for that alar?"

"Afraid for and of him, dear."

Mathias sneered and flung his free hand to his side. "I never thought I'd see the day where Nes would fear for a demon…"

Etha hummed in consideration and tilted her head from side to side. "Much as nobody within the Order ever thought Sir Mathias Sagewind would defy his own goddess and establish an entire city for the abominations?"

Mathias jerked his hand from Etha and turned sharply to face her. "That's different!"

She met his eyes unflinchingly. "How so?"

55

Mathias pursed his lips to keep from fumbling over hasty excuses while he sorted through his thoughts. Flustered, but determined to stick to his biased point that Kol was the greatest evil he'd encountered to date, he grasped the first solid answer that came to him. "Every demon who calls Heiligate home has proven to have some amount of decency and sworn loyalty to me, if not to Zeal itself."

"And it's completely impossible that Nessix could have uncovered similar traits in the months she got to know this alar?"

Fury ignited Mathias's eyes. He couldn't believe what Etha was saying, much less the thought that she might be on to something. "That alar is an ancient, Etha!"

"And one of the few remaining demons to have ever known another way of life."

Mathias trembled in outrage he couldn't possibly vent toward Etha. "Are you *defending* him?"

Etha spun to face him, drawing up on her knees and leaning forward, expression growing strict. "I'm defending Nessix."

"Defending her?" Mathias fidgeted an inch farther back from Etha, his agitation of where she'd chosen to invest her concerns conveyed freely. "Kol hunted and killed her like she was some trophy beast! He's been stealing souls from you, Mother!"

A grim tsk left Etha and she frowned, brows drooping as though that fact was a minor inconvenience she only now realized. "Yes, there is that…"

Relieved to have some degree of his goddess's backing at last, Mathias sighed and fell back against the wall. "If Nes did form some sort of… relationship"—he nearly gagged on the word— "with this demon, what does that mean?"

Etha settled back on her haunches and looked inward, concentrating on Nes's frustrations a bit longer before raising her eyes to Mathias. "It would mean that there's one more aspect to this puzzle than we'd counted on." She stared hard at the flare of Mathias's nostrils and his tight frown. "Do you still trust Nessix?"

Mathias opened his mouth to throw out a defensive response before catching himself. Did he trust Nes? She obviously carried some significant secrets, but he had no way to determine her reasons for doing so. Khin had kept secrets from him, Julianna blatantly misled him on a regular basis, and even Etha hid from him truths they'd all be better off knowing right now. And he'd yet to hold that against any of them. Nessix had fought the inoga, stepping into danger alone and of her own volition, to spare as many civilian lives as she could. She'd worked with him in flawless synchrony to battle the fiends and had faith enough in him to end her suffering and protect her while she recovered. His name had been the first word from her lips upon her coming back to life.

"Yes," he said at last, the confirmation flooding his heart with a relief he couldn't welcome readily enough. "I trust Nessix."

Etha smiled, her amber eyes softening. "Then do all of us a favor and don't be so quick to judge her for what she's been through. Remember what it takes to survive in the hells, and then imagine what it must be like to lose part of your soul to them in the process."

Mathias's mouth gaped in refined horror as Etha's words sank in. How could he have been so selfish? "I need to go talk to her again, tell her—"

Etha calmly reached over to grab Mathias's forearm as he moved to stand and pulled him back down to the step. "Give her time to come to terms with what she's been through."

"But I made such an ass of myself."

Etha nodded sagely, refocusing her gaze down the stairs. "Yes, you did. But she's a strong woman, isn't she? Strong enough to be a general, strong enough to survive the demons, and certainly strong enough to see through one of your little fits." A smile tugged at the corners of Etha's lips and she slid her hand over Mathias's and gave it a tender pat. "She's afraid of disappointing you, Mathias. Give her some time to calm down, then try that conversation again without rushing to conclusions. She's always been a fighter. Best not to tempt her with the offer of one."

Even as lighthearted as Etha's reassurance was, Mathias suspected none of this would be that easy.

And often, the most important things aren't.

Mathias found himself breathing a brisk chuckle through his nose as Etha squeezed his hand once more. Trusting him to make reasonable decisions for the foreseeable future, she slipped away to tend to other prying matters.

Sitting by himself ten steps away from his chamber door, Mathias leaned back to contemplate Etha's encouragement. There might still be many important matters Nessix had to disclose, but he'd never get to hear them if he continued down a combative route. What she needed now was his advocacy and support as she prepared to face the Council. Whether or not the demons or her life on the road or any other outside factor had influenced her, she needed morale, not judgement, and Mathias, Zeal's own White Paladin, knew how to provide that.

With a productive heading, if not hope, Mathias pushed himself to his feet and snuck through the divine pathways to escape the Citadel unseen.

SEVEN

Driven by the message which Nessix had conveyed in his dream, Kol wasted no time in tracking the route which Talier had taken her down. Toward the end of the day, he and Annin located one of Lorrin's planted scouts to receive word that the group of inoga Grell had recruited to hunt for the renegade akhuerai had abruptly stopped their rampage in Fairmont, entering the town, but never seen leaving it. The scout had been unclear as to whether the inoga had successfully caught Nessix, if they'd grown bored with the hunt, or if they'd fallen victim to some unlikely defeat, and the anxious pair grimly set their course to Fairmont to investigate how long they had left to live.

As the two demons neared the city, they were greeted by evidence of an answer they hadn't been remotely prepared to accept. A wide fissure, twenty yards long, cleaved the ground just inside the southern wall and tell-tale signs of a demon raid scarred the nearby homes. Dead bodies—mortal and demon alike—littered the ground, among them two inoga. Annin cast an ominous glare over his shoulder which Kol met with a tight frown as he fought what common sense said must have happened here. For now, he'd credit this massacre to Nessix. He wasn't quite clear on how he'd do that, but she'd routinely surprised him, and he was eager to attribute these unsettling findings to some hidden power she'd uncovered during her rebellious quest.

Despite his best attempts at optimism, a persistent whisper of doubt quietly assured Kol that she had found the power through the help of a third party.

The city was sparse of population, the citizens having either fled or hidden in the chaos which followed inoga wherever they trod. Kol and Annin met no opposition as they landed and were not of the mind to go hunting for trouble. They had a single mission, one which seemed increasingly impossible the longer they surveyed the grisly setting. The remaining three inoga roared at one another over whose fault this was from the bottom of the pit, and the alar and oraku silently walked up to the lip of the rift to look down at the bloody mass of demon flesh wrestling two dozen feet below.

Remains of twenty or so demons were strewn around the entangled inoga, unfortunate collateral to their rage. The walls of the hole were smooth and glassy, tempered by extreme temperature and pressure to prevent the great brutes from climbing free from their prison. By the time their wrestling match ended, only one would survive, and he'd remain alive only as long as he could sustain himself on the bodies of his kin and whatever nutrition fell into the hole from above. Overall, it was a fitting fate for these beasts, one Kol would have found great amusement in, had the mystery of how they'd ended up in this predicament not been so unsettling.

Annin was in no hurry to engage with these half-wits, and so Kol accepted the responsibility of obtaining the answers neither of them wanted to hear. "I thought you were supposed to be Grell's elite force."

His disdainful voice silenced the inoga's bickering immediately, and all three turned their smashed and swollen faces up to glare at the alar.

"We don't serve that piece of shit!" the least bloodied of them spat.

Kol crossed his arms and sneered at them. It felt good to be able to express his disgust for these overlords without fear of them being able to correct him for his honesty. "Of course you do.

Otherwise you wouldn't have been trying so hard to help him."

"Help him?" a second, whose right eye had swollen shut, snorted. "We were helping ourselves!"

"I see. And this is where helping yourselves landed you?"

The first inoga jabbed a finger at Kol, face contorting in a vicious snarl that would have given the alar pause if they'd been standing on equal footing. "It's in your best interest to get us out of here, alar!"

"Oh?" Kol asked, not bothering to mask the humor in his voice. "And how do you expect me to manage that?"

The inoga spat. "Get your damned oraku to—" His beady eyes widened and he took a step forward to get a better look at his rude visitors. An orange-eyed alar and his winged oraku companion… "You son of a bitch!" he roared. "Kol! This *is* your fault!"

Kol's levity filtered away at the blunt reminder of the failure he'd yet to escape. He'd beaten himself up over their circumstances enough all on his own and didn't need an inoga, even a caged one, to draw any more attention to it.

Realizing his companion was close to losing what little composure he'd scraped up and bandaged together, Annin stepped in at last. "I'd venture to guess it's more your faults, my lords. If you'd not gotten our target running scared, she'd have been caught by now."

"Oh, that little trollop got caught, alright," the inoga sneered. "And if you won't magic us out of this hole, it'll be your responsibility to recover her, you know."

Kol's self-doubt didn't need that reminder. His breath caught in his throat, his arms dropped to his sides, and he didn't have the presence of mind to care whether or not the inoga witnessed this loss of confidence. "What do you mean, she was caught?"

"That Sagewind bastard's got her."

Annin drew in a gasp so sharp Kol felt it rattle in his own chest, but the alar couldn't find his breath at all. "One of *our* Sagewind bastards?" Kol asked, voice pathetic and small with what little nerve remained alive in him.

"No," the inoga said as if lecturing a dense child. "*The*

Sagewind bastard. How else would we have ended up in this damned hole? Now you gonna help us out of here so we can fix this, or do you plan to go back to Grell and tell him how you fucked up?"

Annin's dreadful shock worked out of his system as rapidly as usual, as he'd already moved on to seeking solutions to this dilemma. It was fortunate that Annin had trained such discipline into himself because within moments of Kol's breath returning in the form of hyperventilation, the alar screamed his rage, flung himself at the nearest house, and proceeded to vent his helplessness by manually deconstructing it. Annin sighed, letting go of how pleased he'd been with Kol's behavior, and cast his haughty glare down into the hole.

"Your pathetic circumstances aside, how do you know it was Mathias who caught her?"

"Because he was *here*!" the second inoga roared.

"You had your eyes on him?" Annin asked.

"We didn't make this hole ourselves!"

Annin nodded briefly. There still wasn't much hope for a positive outcome, but these inoga's belligerence had given him a little bit. "Then we will return to Grell." From the sound of Kol's continued curses and the splintering of wood, Annin safely guessed he hadn't heard the decision. "And report to him how you drove our objective to the same city as Mathias Sagewind and that *five* of you could not neutralize one man and capture a scrawny woman."

The threat wouldn't have held water if the inoga hadn't been trapped. "You think passing the blame will buy you his leniency?" the first tried, desperate to shake Annin's resolve and gain his compliance. It was a pity, for his sake, that he had no idea how Annin worked.

"It wouldn't be passing the blame," Annin countered smoothly. "The blame hadn't been mine to begin with."

"Grell won't care! You know that!"

It was true that Grell would go looking for the most convenient party to punish for this catastrophe, and Annin felt a momentary tug of regret that Kol stood as the most logical outlet for that. There was a small chance that their lord's long-standing fondness for them and his grudging respect for Annin's honesty could buy them a bit of time, and right now Annin was content to bank on that. Besides, with this grievous turn of events, he doubted the akhuerai project would be permitted to continue, which gave him one last place to find leverage in the ploy to get Nessix away from the Order.

"Maybe he won't," Annin granted. "But I've got my ways to reason with him. The three of you would be wise to grant each other death quickly. I'm sure Grell—or the Order, if they come for you first—will drag out your executions much longer."

The oraku turned away to face Kol, his dismissive action launching his inoga audience into a vicious tirade of threats they had no way of carrying out. Kol stood on splayed legs, wings slouching, eyes in a frenzy and fingers bleeding from beneath his nails, and he didn't react when Annin came up to him and clasped a firm hand on his shoulder.

"Come on. We need to stock up on provisions."

Kol didn't move, staring sightlessly at the scraps of house he'd flung to the ground around him. "What for?"

"For our journey. I told you we would get Nessix back. I told you we would do so before she had the chance to do any irreparable damage. I still plan to do that. Now wrap up your tantrum and let's get moving. If the Order has her, our time is too short to be distracted by..." Annin cocked his head, lip curled as he looked over Kol. "...whatever it is you're going through."

Kol tried hard to react to Annin's instructions, but his mind remained caught in a stubborn loop of disbelief over how any of this had happened. Nessix was bound to him! She'd been his first taste of trust in several hundred years. He'd tried to justify her initial escape on the flemans abducting her. He'd tried to convince himself that Elidae's branch of the Order had forced her to Gelthin to reach Zeal. Even after he'd confirmed she carried a ward from Zenos, he'd desperately told himself that she only ran from these inoga who were currently roaring themselves to aneurisms. All of these notions were delusions, and for the most part, Kol knew that well. Unfortunately, he'd latched onto his fondness for Nessix like a starving lamb to the teat, and that had blinded all of his common sense.

"If the Order gets her talking, Kol, it's all over. You know that better than anyone. You're the one who gave her memories of... of *him*. Put yourself together and come with me so we can stop her before she starts running her mouth."

It took a lot to draw fear out of a demon, but there was one fear permanently ingrained in all of those of the first wave. It was a fear weeded out through strict regulations, merciless cullings, and sanitizing of histories, but it was one which none of the ancients would ever truly escape, and one which Annin's blunt reminder found even through Kol's pounding head.

Berann.

In the back of Kol's mind, his old friend whispered of passionate betrayals which would see the end of demonkind. And from somewhere else in his mind, Nessix called back to this lost demon, asking him what he knew.

A jolt of fear severed Kol's wandering thoughts, tethering his motives to Annin's. He didn't know what plan the oraku had concocted, but he didn't care. Nessix would be his before she had a chance to tap into anything that traitor knew, and he would ensure it by letting go of this fantasy that the little wench had ever cared about him.

A deep breath and tight frown later, Kol gave Annin and his unspoken plan a firm nod. "Then let's get our provisions."

Kol pivoted in a snap and marched toward the town's market to loot what he wanted, and Annin lagged behind a moment longer, wondering if his old friend would be able to be saved after all of this settled. *Assuming* any *of us will be saved...* Hating himself for his sentimental musings nearly as much as he did for the terrible plan that was his last option, Annin followed Kol to the market.

EIGHT

Despite Etha's encouraging words, Mathias had to muster his courage to face Nessix again. He didn't fear her in the physical sense—though that might have been a wise thing to do, given the new skills she'd clearly gained—but he was terrified of what she might confess to him, of making her face this past which frightened them both so much, of how her words might hurt him, and how his reaction to that pain might push her further away. There was no easy way through this, and so Mathias gripped the bundle of clothing he'd purchased in town, sucked in a deep breath, and entered his chamber.

His desk had been cleared off, his inkwell spilled on the worn rug and the papers he'd had neatly stacked on it scattered about the floor. One pillow rested in the far corner and an empty wine bottle lay on its side halfway between the door and where Nessix sat in the middle of the floor, back to him as she faced the window overlooking the city. She'd removed the final restrictions of her armor in the safety of the chamber, bracers and greaves discarded like fallen petals across the room. Her legs, bent at the knees, were out to her sides, providing a sturdy support base for her slumped shoulders. Nessix was a petite woman, more substantially built than Etha's preferred, child-like form only because of her trained and toned body, but Mathias couldn't recall ever seeing her so small.

65

She didn't react to his entry, either assuming it was him or not caring if he was a potential antagonist, and he tucked his lips in a little frown before reaching behind himself to push the door closed.

"I brought you a change of clothes," he said, his voice rudely invading the stillness Nessix had found.

She leaned back slightly, just enough to prove to Mathias that she still remembered what pride was, but she didn't answer him.

Heart fluttering, Mathias grabbed at his next option. "And I've spoken to my most trusted armor smith about tending to your breastplate."

Nessix bowed her head and took a deep breath. "Thank you."

Mathias felt the warmth of a smile brewing inside of himself, but was reluctant to let it out quite yet. He'd have much preferred Nes to express gratitude for basic luxuries over the necessities of war. Either way, he accepted what she offered. She'd displayed no obvious signs of anger, and the empty wine bottle suggested she might be more inclined to friendliness this time around. Mathias cautiously approached her.

"I was thinking about—"

"Don't talk, Sagewind." Her interruption had been a curt order, but hadn't been malicious. "Right now, you're not the one with answers. Right now, if you value justice, if you value me, you will stay silent and you will listen."

She still hadn't looked up at him, and all of a sudden, that certainty and confidence Mathias had found faltered. Swallowing the sour lump which rose in his throat, he walked the rest of the way around Nessix and sat down before her. Her torn shirt still hung open to reveal that silver ring buried in her chest and her hair was still a frayed mess, dirt and dried blood flaking from her cheeks. Mathias gripped the bundle of clean clothes to keep from reaching forward to remedy her disheveled appearance. Listening— when he had so much to say—had never been a strength of his, but he had to try.

"Then talk," he said quietly.

Nessix blinked and bowed her head a little lower, scraping at the courage she had uncovered over the past few hours of venting and casual drinking. She had burned through much of the frantic stage of her chaos, to the point of welcoming the tingling numbness of exhaustion, but had no way to determine when to expect the more treasonous of her emotions to influence her words and actions. She had to take the risk of facing them; it was the entire reason she'd run from Kol, the only reason she'd succeeded in finding Mathias. Tapping into the pride which had allowed her to carry her station through life and death, Nessix met Mathias's eyes.

"Before anything else, you must know that I never asked for any of this."

Impulsively, desperate to correct every wrong that had befallen Nessix, Mathias reached forward and grasped her hand. "I—"

Nessix snatched her hand away and firmly shook her head. "You will let me speak." She waited as Mathias grimaced at his lack of self-control and drew his hand back to the bundle of clothes before she continued. "I don't know much about how the akhuerai are created, besides that a demon's blood is used to bring us back, but I do know that Kol was the demon whose blood brought me back to life."

She spoke that last part softly, as though afraid of it, and the burn of expired tears returned to Mathias's eyes. This revelation was worse than he'd imagined. Much as he'd been irrevocably bound to Etha when she'd bled her essence into him to resurrect him, the same had been done between Nessix and Kol. That was why she'd been so defensive of him. She had no way to break this bond, not permanently, and his fate, his desires, his will, beat within her own veins. Having vowed to Nessix that he'd let her speak, needing to honor her request, Mathias gripped tightly to the fabric of the blouse folded in his lap.

"Physically, I've escaped him." Nessix explored her confession with care, just as afraid of where it would take her as Mathias was. She had to tell him all she could if she hoped for him to help her, but she wasn't convinced that she was—or ever would be—ready to express any of it out loud. "But emotionally, I may never be able to. I want to hate him, to stand by and watch him suffer, but I…"

Now would have been an opportune moment for Mathias to try interrupting again to give her an excuse to alter this course she'd taken, but he remained silent as she'd demanded. Nessix bowed her head and cleared the reluctance from her throat.

"For whatever reason, be it my value to the demons' cause or something greater and unspoken, Kol took an unusual liking to me. He doted over me, protected me from his peers and superiors, personally overseeing my development. No other akhuerai had a dedicated keeper like this and I saw, if I could play into this fondness he had for me, that I might be able to gain the upper hand."

Silence fell over the room once again as Nessix faced that confession for what she hoped would be the last time. When she snuck a look at Mathias to gauge his thoughts, she flinched at the firm clench of his jaw and the flare of his nostrils. As she'd fully expected while on the run, he was disappointed in the road she'd taken, but it was too late to change that now. She turned her face from his quietly brewing reaction and didn't attempt to stop his question.

"And did it work?"

Nessix bowed her head, her wince of shame deepening with frustration at her reluctance to answer him. She'd played Kol and she'd played him hard. It had been means for her survival to start with, but now... Now she didn't know what it was. After hearing his desperate pleas for her to go back to him, after the reminder of how angry Grell was over her actions... Nessix toiled over Mathias's question longer than any demon truly deserved, and sighed.

"It did. He let me in, granting me glimpses into his heart and soul. Into his memories."

Mathias bristled at how intimate the connection Nes shared with this demon had apparently developed, but wisely held back his opinion on it. Confident after she'd allowed him one question, he tried another.

"His memories? Is that how you learned of Berann?"

Breathing out a slow sigh, Nessix nodded, eyes growing distant in thought. "I know they'd been comrades at the time of the Divine Battle, and you confirmed he'd survived that to more modern times. I also know that Kol had thought he'd buried

Berann in his past. He'd wanted me to learn about the demons' history, clear back to the dawn of the Divine Battle. He'd answered all of my questions patiently and generously, too freely and reliably for his assistance to have been an act. He told me everything I wanted to know except when I'd asked about Berann. He'd made it quite clear that I was to forget I'd ever so much as thought about that demon, which is why I must learn more about him."

Her gaze shifted from confused and reluctant into something far more hopeful and pleading as she looked up at Mathias, and he found himself shaking his head, at a loss.

"I told you everything I know of the ancient demon by that name," he told her. "I may not... understand what all you went through in the hells and I might have trouble accepting that you found a way to coexist with the beast who killed you, but if I knew anything else about Berann, anything at all, I wouldn't hide it from you."

The answer didn't please Nessix, as she'd much preferred her lofty dream of showing up in Zeal and having Mathias spout off all the answers in the way he'd so often annoyed her when she'd been a mortal, but she'd come to terms with the fact that too much had changed since those innocent times. Her problems spanned far wider than herself, wider than Elidae. She no longer had the luxury of fighting for her pride or even her people; she now fought for the fate of the entire world.

And demons were no longer stupid beasts meant to be looked down upon and slaughtered, but cunning opponents capable of out-thinking the sharpest minds she'd known.

Nessix delved deeply into Mathias's eyes, soaking in his pain and the swells of regret that he couldn't simply erase her troubles with a few cocky words and a bold charge ahead of her troops. In her fit of chaos, amid the haunting echoes of Kol's laughter, all she could remember was Julianna's scathing tone and Mathias's disgust at her connection with Kol, but she saw now the paladin's fears, just as valid and real as her own. And she realized that she still trusted him more than she trusted herself.

That realization struck Nes with a great flood of relief and the remnants of her chaos drifted away like a receding tide. She'd fought for so long. She'd despaired for so long. There were so many matters yet to be discussed, so many problems to solve, but she'd reached her first objective, the most important one, the one she'd begun to fear was impossible. She'd found her hope once again, and more than anything else, she needed to take this moment to embrace this impossible victory she'd found. After all, Mathias was the White Paladin. There were no wounds which he couldn't heal. Nes's shoulders slumped as the last of her tension drifted away, and she reached forward to slip her hand into his.

"The demons have taken damn near everything from me," she murmured, lowering her eyes. "If we manage to reclaim nothing else from them, can we have this moment just for us? Can we put aside duty and worry for just a little bit?"

Her fingers trembled in Mathias's grasp, silently conveying how long she'd been waiting and longing for comfort and peace. Nessix had never known a time without duty, and Mathias had been so caught up in the pain he'd internalized since he'd lost her to fully appreciate how taxing her own façade of strength must be. Softening his approach, relieved by the warmth and honesty which he believed to be Nes's true nature, he opened the arm of his free hand and beckoned her closer.

"We won't let them take one more thing from us," he answered as she fell into his embrace, melting into the warmth of his chest. "I suspect it won't be an easy fight, but it is one we will win."

Nessix closed her eyes, thriving off his comfort and the certainty of his words as she had when he'd first motivated her to take up arms against the demons. "I wouldn't have risked trying to find you if I'd thought otherwise."

Mathias dropped his chin into Nes's crown, tipping his lips to press them into her hair. There were still many questions left to be answered and even more obstacles he'd have to find a way to overcome, but Nes's request hadn't been an unfair one. The demons had taken them from each other. They had taken their peace. They'd taken the joy from their reunion. He and Nessix deserved at least a moment to revel in their victory.

Etha smiled down on her most beloved son and the tortured

soul he'd fallen in love with and blanketed them in that longed-for peace, allowing them to pass the rest of the evening with small talk and daydreams. They needed this reprieve to reinforce their faith in one another, for their trials were far from over, and they would begin very soon.

* * * * *

A rapid knocking at his chamber door chased Mathias back into the waking world. He stifled his groan, hoping to avoid rousing Nessix as she nestled in the crook of his left arm, and carefully pushed his bedding off of himself. As much as he wanted to ignore the summons, he had few choices in the matter; he could answer now and give Nessix the last few minutes of her sleep, or he could let Julianna get more irritated and more persistent. After carefully dislodging himself from beneath Nes's head, he stood, rubbed the drowsiness from his eyes and staggered to his door before the next round of knocking began.

As he'd predicted, Julianna stood on the other side, eyes bloodshot and puffy from what must have been a sleepless night for her. Mathias kept his smirk to himself, not keen on starting a fight when Julianna was short tempered and they both had more important matters to address. He propped his arm on the doorframe to signal to his prying sister that while he was willing to talk, she was not welcome to enter.

Julianna tilted her chin and one brow twitched in suspicion, but, just like her brother, she wouldn't waste time on matters that were not immediately relevant. "The Council is gathered and ready to receive your report."

Despite having known this was the reason Julianna had come to find him, Mathias was no more pleased to hear it. Behind him, the subtle groans and whispers of Nessix shifting in bed signaled that she'd woken, and Mathias kept his voice hushed. "They'll have it shortly."

Julianna crossed her arms and looked over her brother's messy appearance. "And they'll be receiving it from you?"

Mathias rolled his eyes and craned his head as though

stretching his neck so he could catch a quick glimpse of Nessix as she pushed herself to a seated position and rubbed her eyes. "They'll receive it from me," he said quickly, withdrawing the arm he'd had blocking Julianna from entering as he moved to close the door.

Weary or not, Julianna's arm was quick to snap forward and stop her brother's efforts. She fixed him with a stern glare. "If you're thinking to find a way to sneak out of this—"

Mathias scoffed and shoved her hand away. "It hadn't even crossed my mind," he said dryly, an excuse he didn't even try to make sound believable. "But you'll at least let me dress out of slept-in street clothes to meet their dignified expectations."

Julianna's lips sank into a firm frown. "This is serious, Mathias."

"I'll be down there, Jules," he caved with a weary tone. "After yesterday, I've run out of excuses to avoid them." He flicked a hand toward the hallway. "Go tell them I'm on my way."

Julianna was used to Mathias making excuses to get out of official business. She was used to him deciding for himself those things that were or were not important enough to merit his attention. But she also knew him better than anyone else besides Etha herself, and she heard the clear defeat, his willingness to throw in the towel in this issue, at last. Dropping her air of strictness, exhaustion quickly rushing in behind it, Julianna shook her head and sighed.

"Fine," she said. "But don't keep them waiting long. They're quite agitated and I have nothing left to occupy them with. The sooner you get down there, the less time they'll have to fabricate their stories and come to their own conclusions."

That was Julianna's last card to vie for Mathias's honest compliance, one which, provided Etha's testament and her own observations from the previous day were accurate, would force her brother's hand. With nothing else, the priestess turned and began to descend the spire stairs.

Mathias didn't wait for Julianna to disappear from view before closing the door. Better to see to this conversation's end before she changed her mind on their terms. Breathing in deep and letting it out as a strained groan, Mathias tuned around to see Nessix shimmying her way into the clean blouse he'd brought her.

She was so beautiful, the worries of the past settled in her heart, and thinking back, Mathias couldn't remember ever seeing her so content. He'd seen her confidence and ingrained authority, but never such casual ease, never the relaxation which came from knowing those she was responsible for would be alright. Mathias worked the sour taste building in his mouth across his tongue, not prepared to ruin this moment with what he was about to say. Silently, he moved to the pile of armor he and Etha had left on the floor and began to piece it onto himself. If the Council wanted a battle, he'd show up prepared.

"You're not coming with me today." He blurted the words firmly but kept his eyes averted as Nessix snapped her attention up from her task of lacing a boot.

She stayed quiet for a long moment then voiced a chuckle which didn't balk at the idea of engaging Mathias's authority. "Of course I am." She dictated her words carefully, the way she'd always staked her claims against his. "The entire reason I set out for Zeal was to get the Order's help to free my people. Nobody is better equipped or more motivated to answer questions about what the demons are up to than I am."

Mathias winced as he tugged the strap of a greave tight and snuck a timid glance at her confident eyes. "Nes… the Council is full of jackals. Trained ones, mind you, but no more decent."

Nessix snorted and resumed her work of cinching up her boot. "Oh, please, Sagewind. Has one quiet night made you forget where my life has led me?" She tossed him a sly smirk and reached for the next boot. "A roomful of snooty nobles doesn't intimidate me."

Mathias winced, realizing this was about to turn into a fight. "You've faced graver dangers than anyone should ever have to, yes, but I've seen the way you handle your frustration… and I can assure you that the Council will do everything they can to stoke that frustration so they can use your actions against you. Before anything else, I need to hear what they plan to do with you—"

A dry laugh puffed from Nessix. "They do not control me."

He heaved a sigh and cast his gaze to the heavens before bending down to retrieve his breastplate. "No," he granted, "they don't. But they do control Zeal and all aspects tied to her."

Nessix shook her head. Had Mathias so easily forgotten so much about her? "I dealt with Veed and the demons just fine—"

"Did you?"

Nessix straightened, her cockiness sharpened with a fierce air of resentment "A handful of politicians from your fair city doesn't intimidate me. Besides, I didn't come all the way from the hells to be locked in your room. And what about Talier? He must be worried sick about me."

Despite the past day's disconcerting revelations, the past months spent missing Nessix had pushed Mathias's fondest memories of her to the forefront, allowing him to reflect most on her more charming attributes and overlook the parts of her which had always caused him such headaches. Her insistence on learning her lessons the hard way—a trait which must have caused her no end of pain in the hells, no matter how well she thought she'd played Kol—was one such thing Mathias had contently let himself forget. Until now. Having spent so long needing to force himself into patience, the finesse he needed to navigate Nes's temper had deteriorated. He had no choice but to jump into this head first.

"You will not leave this room until I permit it," he ordered.

Nessix jerked abruptly and shook her head in disbelief before flinging her irritated glare at him. "*Excuse* me?" He met her offended glower with a clenched jaw and unwavering eyes. "I don't need your permission to—"

"In here, you do." Interrupting Nessix and receiving her angry snarl for doing so beat letting her argument gain steam. "Nobody enters or exits my chamber unless I will them to do so."

An indignant fury worked across Nes's face as she straightened, squaring her shoulders. "Am I your prisoner now, Sagewind? Is that where we've ended up?"

Mathias opened his mouth to engage her, but at the last moment before his first words made it to his tongue, he saw the faint ripples of terror which lapped at the foundation of Nes's ire. She knew that he knew about the evils she'd taken part in over these past few weeks, and she was terrified, absolutely convinced, that he was punishing her for them. He'd been her only hope, her final link to the mortal world, and he stood poised to either bring her salvation or her destruction. His behavior over the past day had given her nothing but mixed signals and right now, she was facing the very real chance that he meant to side with the cold logic of the Order over her pleas.

He sighed, softening his approach as he reached out and took her hands. "Nes… please don't make this more complicated," he bid softly. "The Council is excitable and eager to point fingers, and you'll be the one they target. Give me today to soften them up and I'll let you have at them tomorrow."

She didn't fight his touch, actually relaxing her stance at the security his hands conveyed, but she did narrow her eyes as she met his. "Do you swear it to your Etha?"

Mathias did well to hold back his grimace. This was a promise he knew Nessix would not permit him to back out of, but it was also one he had no feasible way to guarantee. Cornered and desperate to hurry this along to decrease the odds of Julianna coming back and making all of it even worse, Mathias breathed a brisk sigh out his nose. He'd find a way to keep from letting Nessix down. "Tomorrow. I promise."

Nessix scrutinized his sincerity, waiting for him to buckle under her silent skepticism, but he held firm in his stance. Finally allowing both herself and Mathias to relax, she withdrew her hands. "What do you expect me to do while you're away? This chamber of yours is quite boring."

"You've already found my collection of literature." He swept his hand toward where his bookshelf stood, one of the shelves having been broken in Nes's previous bout of chaos and spilling the volumes across the floor. "If reading doesn't interest you, I suppose you could tidy up your handiwork from yesterday."

She leveled a glare at him and grit her teeth at his blunt attempt at humor, the only indication she gave that he'd struck a nerve.

At least he'd distracted her from what she actually wanted to do. "I'll do everything I can to hurry the meeting along," Mathias promised. "And when I get back, provided all goes smoothly, I'll take you out to see the city and let you stretch your legs. Until then, please trust me. Now, unless you want Julianna to fuss at us again…"

Nessix accepted this final deflection in good nature and slumped down on the side of Mathias's bed. "Go and talk to your nobles. And tell them that I look forward to my meeting with them."

That last statement took a bit of the optimism from Mathias, but he did well at hiding it. Dismissing himself from Nessix, he left the room and headed toward the frustrating task he'd been dreading, thankful, at least, that he'd bought them all more time before Nes would have to face them.

NINE

When Annin had told Kol that he had a plan to recover Nessix, the alar, adrenaline and foolishness running as hot as ever, had anxiously anticipated the pair of them storming Zeal and somehow coming out victorious. Enough intelligence still functioned in Kol for him to realize what a terrible idea that would be, but that wasn't enough to dislodge the fantasy from his mind. Battling logic and desire, aware that he was ill equipped to make such decisions, Kol followed Annin's flight south for a full day before deciding it was time to get some answers.

The pair stopped for a late lunch in the field somewhere south of Covington. Even with the provisions they'd taken from Fairmont, their journey had worn on their bodies, and both were thankful for the chance to rest their wings. Annin plopped down to the ground and dug through his pouch. When Kol chose to remain standing, the oraku looked up and froze in his actions at the unstable alar's crossed arms and fierce focus on the north.

Annin had been relieved when Kol had eased up on his pathetic whining about missing Nessix and his insistent claims that she'd never betray him. Seeing his friend filled more with anger suited to their circumstances than denial had elated Annin until Kol's steely appraisal reminded him that it had been months since he'd considered Kol of sound mind. Not moving, Annin silently traced Kol's threads, touching the tips of his fingers together where they were hidden in his bag in case he needed to drop his friend in a hurry.

"Is there a problem?" Annin asked evenly.

"You said we were going to get Nessix out of Zeal." Kol didn't so much as glance Annin's direction. "Last I checked, Zeal was half a continent to the north."

Annin relaxed enough to abandon his offensive preparations and resumed his search for the bowl which would allow him to scry Lorrin.

"Zeal is to the north, yes." Annin patted a flat spot in the grass in front of him and placed the bowl down as he drew his pick from its case at his hip.

"Then why are we heading south?" Kol snapped his glare toward Annin and his nonchalant actions. "You said we didn't have time for delays." *And,* the wicked voice in Kol's mind teased, *every wasted moment gives Nessix more time to ask around about Berann ...* Kol shuddered and flung his arms to his side. The Order had taken shape during the Divine Battle, offering sanctuary to those mortals who fled in terror of the children gods' rampage as opposed to foolishly fighting on their cursed behalf. It would be ancient by now, but there was still the chance that somewhere buried in Zeal's library were hints to Berann's identity. Thinking of that, of Nessix's persistent curiosity successfully drawing the Order's interest to that demon, was nearly enough to throw Kol into another fit, and his weary legs launched him into a bout of agitated pacing to distract him from more draining methods of venting his fear.

Annin pricked his thumb and squeezed his blood into the bowl, not looking up at his flustered companion. "I appreciate your faith that the two of us could conquer the holy city on our own, but I've also come to realize you don't always invest your faith in the soundest causes." He glanced up and smirked at Kol's perturbed glower. "When we reach Zeal, we'll need more than my magic and your might to get what we want."

"So where are we heading?"

Annin held up a finger as the blood in the bowl rippled to reveal Lorrin's grinning face.

"Annin! Have you found your prey?"

Kol stopped his pacing and moved closer to better hear both sides of the coming conversation.

"She's been located," Annin confirmed.

"That's fantastic!"

"By Mathias Sagewind."

The smile flashed from Lorrin's face. He'd never been told why finding Nessix was so important, only that doing so would humiliate Grell, but any mention of the White Paladin crossing into a demon's plans never implied anything good. "So that wolf boy of yours failed?" It was a pity; that had been a clever experiment.

"Maybe not. We were unable to recover him, which means he might still be with her."

Lorrin gave a great grumble but submitted to Annin's authority just as seamlessly as he had when they'd been mortals. "Is it safe for me to ask where you're heading?"

Annin cast a quick glance at Kol and flushed as the alar's impatient gaze locked on him, demanding the answer to the same question. Neither Kol nor Lorrin would be particularly pleased with the tactic he was about to propose, but at least he'd only have to deal with one of them. Unfortunately for Annin, it was the one he least preferred to engage in combat and the one he most doubted he'd be able to reason with without trouble.

"We're going to barter with Grell."

"*What?*"

The demand echoed from either side of Annin, conveying all of the shock and outrage and, in Kol's case, terror he'd expected. Oh well. He couldn't have kept it a secret forever.

"You have taken your liberties too far," Kol said.

"I agree," Lorrin added from his safety miles away.

"His inoga friends have failed in the most humiliating way," Annin countered, "condemned to death at the bottom of a pit carved by Mathias's treachery and his vile goddess. They were the ones who let this happen, not us. And I know just the leverage we need to convince Mathias to hand over our property without contest."

Kol silenced his objections, even the ones he'd kept to

himself, as Annin had predicted he would. No matter how strained their relationship had become of late, once Annin could prove he'd actually thought matters through, Kol was always willing to listen. Lorrin, on the other hand, hadn't learned to trust his fellow oraku's reasoning, and wasn't keen on the idea of anyone asking Grell for anything.

"What leverage is that?"

Just as Lorrin didn't wholly trust Annin, Annin didn't wholly trust Lorrin. The surface-bound demon and his men had proven reliable so far, but they weren't without their own motives that could, if relations grew tense, serve against Annin. It was imperative to keep Lorrin both content with his role in this operation and ignorant enough in its details to prevent him from posing as a future threat. Fortunately, current events had provided Annin with a brilliant solution to this problem.

"Mathias is now aware of what we've been up to," Annin said. "And you can bet that peace you've found up on your mountain that he'll get the Order sniffing around where they don't belong as soon as he figures out you've settled there. It is safest for all of us if you can plead ignorance. Let me and Kol bear this burden. You keep your men out of the Order's sights."

Lorrin thought this over, balancing out his desire to humiliate Grell with those to humble the Order and maintain the sanctuary he'd created, finally siding with the latter. He and his men were free; free of inoga overlords, free of the Order's attention, free to do as they wished in the land that had first been their home. Annin was the most clever man he'd ever known; if he said it was in Lorrin's best interest to let this drop, he'd do so.

"What should I do with my forces you've scattered about?"

"That is not my decision to make," Annin said. "Recall them if you wish to offer them safety or leave them at their stations if you want reports of movement out of Zeal. I appreciate the assistance their expertise has lent us, but I've no more use for them in the field for this assignment."

Lorrin grunted his acceptance of Annin's gratitude, too timid to make a greater show of it. "Am I to keep that human hostage alive?"

"That would be ideal," Annin said. "We may still have use for Talier."

Lorrin grunted a second time, this one sounding less accepting but conveying obedience, nonetheless. "Then I guess I'll be hearing from you again. Assuming Grell doesn't kill you."

Annin narrowed his eyes at Lorrin's offhanded remark as Kol made a quick hiss beside him. "Kol and I are operating on a short time frame. You'll hear word from us soon."

Not waiting for any other attempt Lorrin might make at humor or poorly constructed warnings, determined to keep Kol's confidence stitched together, Annin flung the blood from his bowl, stood, and turned to tend to the debate waiting for him.

"I cannot go back to the hells without Nessix in my hands," came Kol's growl before Annin had fully faced him. "You know that. Grell will not let me leave a second time."

"And I cannot go back into the hells without you with me. I gave Grell my word that I'd keep track of you until this was over, and I will not risk myself more than I already have because you are too frightened to lie to that simpleton."

Kol shook his head, lips pressed tight as he tried to sort through how and why Annin was so bent on tormenting him. "He'd be more likely to forgive you than he'd ever be to forgive me. He likes you. He doesn't see the threat you've always been to him. Let me stay here. I can keep an eye on Zeal and make sure Nessix doesn't leave."

Annin cocked his head. "You think she plans to willingly walk out of that blasted city's safety without an army at her back?"

Kol didn't look at his friend. He already knew the answer.

"You need to come with me," Annin persisted, "and we need to move quickly. We have no idea what she's already told Mathias. We have no idea what she's been able to convince him to believe. We have no idea if anyone else in that damned Order has taken what she knows to heart. We're running off very borrowed time, Kol, and the longer you protest the only solution we have, the shorter that time runs."

"There are other solutions," Kol demanded stubbornly.

"Like what? You want the two of us on our own to storm

Zeal? Even if we were to make it past their guards or all of the Order, we would be helpless in the Citadel. Don't be stupid. We need leverage, and we can find that in the hells."

The sensible part of Kol acknowledged how desperation had blinded and led him to make some terrible mistakes. But he couldn't help but fret over how returning to the hells, where Grell still ruled, was a monumental one. Even if he'd succeeded in catching Nessix before she'd been herded into Mathias's waiting hands, there was a very real possibility that Grell would just as easily decide to claim Nessix as his own and do away with Kol simply for the errors he'd made. That in itself was enough to discourage Kol from ever wanting to go back. Who knew. Maybe he'd be able to carve out a life for himself in Vesper or Heiligate…

Annin's steady, waiting gaze never faltered, and Kol had to cave into the fact that the oraku would ensure he fell in line, regardless of his desires. After all, one of them had to be the smart one.

"Fine," Kol spat. "Tell me this great plan of yours."

Annin gave a short nod. "Mathias can want Nessix however badly he wants to, and the Order is unlikely to be able to do anything about that. But you and I have something the Order would want even more than they want to keep Mathias happy."

Kol pondered this thought for some time, wondering if Annin was alluding to the very same secrets which he was so terrified Nessix would uncover. The demons didn't have much else of value to the Order or even Mathias, not anything that the paladin hadn't already discovered for himself, anyway. Dissecting Annin's words even further, Kol made the connection at last. Annin had said "you and I," not "demons" in the broad sense. Certainly, the Order would be curious to know what had been recorded in the ancient tomes which the two of them had collected, but the libraries in Zeal had to have most of that information, save the personal accounts. The only other thing they had of value was…

"The priestesses?"

Annin smirked and nodded. "The priestesses."

Kol cocked his head with an argumentative frown. "We can't get rid of them. Their extruded blessings are needed to raise the akhuerai."

Annin sucked his teeth and gave Kol a disappointed glare. "Do you honestly think there's anything left of this project when we return? Even with Nessix in tow, do you truly believe we will be permitted to continue to grow that army?"

Annin was taking the idea of seeing the past century of labor and headaches unravelling much more gracefully than Kol had expected he would, but the alar wasn't truly prepared to abandon this experiment quite yet. They still needed the akhuerai in order to overthrow the inoga.

When Kol didn't answer, Annin continued, determined to convey the truth of what they'd landed themselves in. "Grell may have taken a fancy to that fleman-based akhuerai, but it won't be long before his peers grow suspicious of Nessix's intentions. Odds are good we'll get to keep the army we have right now, but only after we've thoroughly beaten Nessix and her troops into submission. The notion of bringing fresh blood in is unlikely. Zeal will give us Nessix if we're willing to give them their priestesses. And no amount of Mathias's petitioning will do anything to stop that. Let go of the akhuerai if you want to get a hold of Nessix. It's the only way."

Annin spoke sense, as he always did, and Kol hated him for that. He hated him for that more than he hated himself for letting Nessix slip away from him in the first place. Unable to fight what truly was the last-ditch effort for Kol to get his hands on Nessix once more, the alar bowed his head to Annin's sense.

"I suspect that it is," he admitted at last. "But how do you think we'll be able to gather up the priestesses and get out of the hells without Grell changing his mind?"

"I've got enough ideas. I'll make something work."

Kol shook his head and rooted his feet firmly in place. "I don't need you to have ideas. I need you to have a plan. You're asking me to risk my life—"

Annin spun on Kol so fast it made the alar stagger backwards, his pale eyes flashing with repressed rage. "And you have asked me to risk mine! Repeatedly! I have followed you through madness, Kol, but I will not take one step farther down this path to destruction that you've gaily traipsed down. Be my lord all you want, but you will obey me now."

Kol had been waiting for Annin to declare him inferior since he'd first witnessed the mortal version of the same man fearlessly confront the frost beast the day they'd met. He'd been waiting for it since Annin had demonstrated how he could cripple a man from fifty yards away with nothing but a snap of his fingers. Annin had been a danger to those around him since the day he'd discovered he had hands, and that was why his village had tried to kill him. But Kol had been enamored by his skills and his spirit from the moment he'd first laid eyes on him, starved and half frozen in the mountains. Annin had pledged his loyalty to Kol for having saved him on that day, remaining faithful to him all these years, through terrors no one should ever have to face. It was this loyalty to Kol which had kept Annin in check against the likes of the inoga, the reason Annin had always stayed so calm when facing them instead of snapping them in half with his magic when Kol told him to wait. To bide his time. That time had come, and while Kol suspected Annin would still remain obedient to him once this threat passed, his demands now were spoken clearly enough for Kol to doubt his standing for the first time in his life.

Kol couldn't see himself ever renouncing his dominance to Annin, but he bowed his head in surrender now. "You swear I will make it back out of the hells alive?"

"You stand a better chance of it now, with me, than you would under any other circumstances."

It would have been so much easier to let himself hate Nessix for the trouble she'd gotten him into, but that part of Kol which liked to make excuses for her forbid him from doing so. This had all been his fault, from the very start, and he had nobody else to blame.

"And you're certain this will work?"

Annin flexed his jaw back and forth, running through the probabilities in his mind. In truth, he wasn't certain it would work; he didn't even know if the priestesses were still alive. An even greater wild card was whether or not Grell could truly be convinced to accept the trade. The inoga loved playing with mortals, and it was quite possible that he would be unwilling to release these girls who many of the higher ranking demons had chosen as playthings in the past. But perhaps having discovered alternative uses for the akhuerai, Grell's mind could be swayed. No, the hardest part would be convincing Grell that his inoga connections had failed him and that it was Annin and Kol who needed to clean up the mess they'd caused. For that, Annin suspected only a forty percent success rate, and a narrow twenty percent chance he'd actually be able to pull Kol out with him. But one of the things Annin had learned early in life was that a slim chance was still a chance, and if anyone could find a way to warp the odds in his favor, it was him.

"As certain as I've been about anything."

It was an honest answer, one which he let Kol assume meant was as true as it sounded. The alar didn't have to know Annin routinely doubted himself and had just grown adept at hiding it.

Faith in his friend or not, nodding in acceptance of what he saw as a death sentence was one of the harder tasks Kol had faced in recent recollection. But nod, he did, and Annin didn't wait for him to have second thoughts before leaping into the air, confident Kol would follow him.

TEN

Word had spread well through the temple of Julianna's efforts to gather the Council, and Khin had meticulously planned her morning according to Mathias's expected arrival so she could intercept him in the hall. The reports she'd heard of him successfully finding the woman he'd been looking for and the conclusions her hopeful reasoning had reached assured her that he'd have time for her as he'd promised before he left, and she found the bounce returning to her step.

Everyone who spent any amount of time in the Citadel knew where the southern spire's staircase emptied into the main hall, and Khin slipped her way through the usual crowd of visiting dignitaries and attendants to wait for Mathias to descend the stairs so she could reach him before anyone else had a chance to demand his attention. Once there, she tucked herself against a wall, out of the way of the hustle and bustle of those with official business, and waited for a dreadfully long time until the rapid steps of someone rushing down the stairs reached her ears. Smiling, she pushed herself away from the wall.

Khin had seen Mathias set for business enough times in the past to recognize the mission in his stride and the focus etched into his face. He wore his armor, flecks of dried blood spattered across the glistening breastplate and his sword unbuckled in its sheath. His hair was disheveled more than usual, his eyes cold and jaw clenched. All of the reports Khin had overheard had suggested he'd been successful in his quest, leaving her to wonder what had put him in such a stony mood and prepared for combat, but the hope he'd vowed to her still existed in her broken life whispered that maybe the results of that success had left him still wanting, perhaps with a void an cager apprentice could fill. Offering a warm smile and eyes alight, Khin hurried down the hall.

Mathias didn't even glance her direction, continuing forward with his purposeful stride, the tendons in his neck twitching as his patience floundered when he was forced to wait on the self-important nobles to move out of his way.

Khin redoubled her efforts of squeezing through the crowd, knowing in her heart that she'd be able to help Mathias reclaim his peace and alleviate whatever tension he'd brought home with him. Few people paid Khin much mind, assuming she was simply a young acolyte trying to relay messages between the wings of the Citadel, but neither did they do anything to expedite her efforts to reach Mathias. Though he didn't order anyone out of his way—a feat which surprised Khin based on the continued darkening of his glare—most were quick to recognize him and shift aside to let him pass or were too appalled by his current physical state and cleared the way to avoid fouling their own fine grooming by risking him brushing against them. His passage through the hall moved much brisker than Khin's own, his longer legs and stalwart duty carrying him faster than she'd have been able to manage, even if there was nobody else in the hall.

Desperate and despairing, Khin bit down on her lip and shoved past a snooty man in a blue waistcoat with a pristine rapier on his hip to try to get closer, and when she realized it was a lost cause, she resorted to calling out Mathias's name through the buzz of gossip in the hall.

And he continued walking, smoothly sliding a shoulder back to slip past a man whose back was to him.

Khin froze there in the hall, struck a strong blow by his blatant disregard. Mathias had promised he'd make time for her when he returned. He'd told her he'd never leave her scared and alone. Yet here she was, stuck in the congestion of this busy hallway of dandy men and arrogant women who wouldn't have bothered to address her by her name if they'd known it. Scared, past experience reminding her that she'd never been important and shouldn't have expected someone as influential as Mathias to remember her longer than she proved useful to him, Khin bit her lip and darted back into the crowd to return to the security of the temple. She made it three strides before her tears began to fall.

* * * * *

Mathias hadn't even heard the pitch of Khin's voice past his rampaging thoughts and Etha's gentle guidance in his mind. He knew what duty demanded of him, and had reached the point where he agreed that duty surpassed his own desires, but that didn't make him any more eager to speak with the Council. Julianna's insistence that the political sides of this matter were addressed immediately hadn't given him enough time to talk to Nessix about what all she knew; all he'd managed to do so far was uncover inconvenient details which fed the residue of his paranoia. The Council had already expressed their desire to hold Nes accountable for the demon resurgence, and that was before she'd returned as what was essentially an abomination to Etha's will. No matter how many times he played out the coming debate in his head, Mathias could find no way that it would end smoothly.

He could not escape this meeting, not with so many aware of it and waiting on his presence, but if he could placate them for now, perhaps that would buy him time to find a way to sneak Nessix out of the Citadel and away from the threats the Council posed toward her. With the only inoga he'd been tracking taken out of the picture, Mathias was confident he and Nessix could battle off any other demons who would try to complicate such movements if they had to take to the road while figuring out their next move.

Assuming Nes's attachment to Kol would allow her to fight him…

Mathias growled deep in his throat at the unwanted thought,

still longing to disbelieve the lamented confession Nessix had given him in regards to her relationship with the demon who had killed her. He'd been a prisoner to the demons before and he'd fought them long enough to understand the sorts of psychological games they played with their prisoners, but Nessix had admitted to a bond much deeper than such aggressive pressures alone could achieve. Her confusion over the matter did little to help Mathias identify just how deep that bond went, and though he yearned to uncover how strong that attachment was, he was in no hurry to discover it firsthand on the field.

You worry too much, Etha chided, hoping to drag Mathias to a better state of mind before he was further taxed by the Council.

He puffed out a dry laugh. *Or maybe I'm not worrying enough. Maybe Jules was right. I've made excuses for Nessix this entire time, only to discover she's been running across Gelthin as an assassin, tailed by a demon she's in love with—*

Etha's laughter echoed in his head, achieving the exact opposite goal as she'd set out to accomplish. *That's a bit of a strong way to put it, I think. If she was in love with him, don't you think she'd have been less relieved to see you? Do you think she'd have clung to you so tightly when she woke?*

Etha spoke sound sense, but that did little to erase the fears and assumptions Mathias's tired mind was making on its own. *Okay. So maybe she's not in love with him. But she's loyal to him. That's not much better.*

Etha hummed her consideration on the matter, but hadn't reached adequate conclusions about this unexpected development to comment on it quite yet. *And you should be grateful she'd played a stint at being an assassin.*

That was the first stimulus Mathias had found since leaving his chamber which succeeded in breaking his trance. He slowed his gait for a moment, eyes grounding back to the present as he blinked. *The Nessix I knew, the Nessix I loved, would have never engaged in such a disgusting, petty act.*

Probably not. But haven't you already decided she's no longer the Nessix you knew?

Grumbling at this terrible game Etha had decided to play with him, Mathias resumed his hasty pace. *Am I to be grateful for that?*

Of course. If she wouldn't have fallen in with assassins, she never would have killed the one who told me where to find her and I never would have been able to arrange to have the two of you meet in Fairmont. Her being an assassin might have saved her life and the lives of all the mortals her actions had spared.

Mathias had learned long ago to accept where fate could lead a person, but the idea that part of Nes's fate crossed that road was still a difficult concept to swallow. *What did you say to her to get her to go to Fairmont, anyway?*

Oh... that? I'd hired her to kill you.

Mathias's steady progress toward the conference hall snagged abruptly on Etha's words. Etha had hired a hit on him? The benevolent goddess he endlessly suffered for had contracted an assassin to kill him? He had no right to question Etha's motives in anything she did, and he truly believed she acted within the most reasonable means available to her, but there was a greater shock which pulled at his heart than the liberties his goddess had taken with his safety.

Etha had hired a hit on him, and Nessix had accepted it. Mathias had done his best to deny the truth of Nes's occupation over the past few days, telling himself that the sheriff in Midland had been mistaken, that she couldn't have fallen in with that crowd. This denial had become more difficult to believe as Mathias witnessed the deeper flaws Nes had carried back to the surface, and Etha's confirmation that it had been the vile act of murdering for hire which had landed Nessix in the city she'd guided Mathias to, that Nessix had gone there willingly, did nothing to soothe him the way Etha seemed to think it would.

Calm down, Etha sighed dramatically. *You have to have your head about you when you go talk to the Council.*

Calm down! Mathias still wasn't even sure he knew what stance he was going to take in front of the officials. *You just told me you'd hired Nessix to assassinate me. How am I not supposed to be worried about that?*

Etha didn't attempt to hide her sigh—nor the hint of amusement with which she viewed this entire situation. *I had to motivate her somehow, and we both know she wouldn't have been able to actually* do *it.* Her reassurance didn't do a thing to lighten Mathias's gloomy expression. *Besides, she didn't know it was you she was supposed to be hunting.*

Mathias could reflect on nothing else besides how effective Nessix was in combat, recalling exactly how much he'd admired her courageous stand against the demons attacking Fairmont. Win or lose, if she would have directed that ferocity at him, that would have been a painful fight.

But she didn't fight you, Mathias, Etha said gently, locating Mathias's calm at last. *The moment she realized who you were, she lost any murderous intent that wasn't focused on those inoga.*

That brief flicker of relief didn't last long as the fact remained that Nessix had been willing to kill him—or whatever man she'd believed him to be. *I'm not entirely sure that makes it any better.*

He continued stalking down the hall after his blunt snip, and Etha held back her thoughts a moment longer to let his settle before gently approaching one last time.

Mathias, she was being hunted by demons, she said softly, knowing that her paladin would understand the weight of that threat better than anyone other than Nessix herself. *She did what she had to in order to stay alive and get to where she needed to go. What other choice did she have?*

Mathias wasn't too proud to be proven wrong, especially in cases where he loathed the circumstances to start with. All this time, despite the conclusions he'd jumped to and the terrible stories Julianna and his own mind had concocted about Nessix, his heart had told him that she'd never strayed from her path toward justice and now that she'd found a reprieve from the immediate dangers chasing her, he was able to resume believing as much.

Etha's warmth seeped into his tense arms and aching legs. *Trust her, Mathias. Trust her like you did on Elidae. She's fighting the good fight. Just let yourself see it.*

There were still too many questions left needing answers to alleviate all of Mathias's concerns, but at least Etha had steered him off the destructive path he'd been barreling down. Now, all he had to do was carve out time to sit down with Nessix when tensions weren't running quite so high, and ask her to explain what she hadn't been able to face last night. Determined to see that happen, knowing he wouldn't have the opportunity for it until he satisfied the Council, Mathias grit his teeth and strode with greater purpose toward the conference chamber.

The guards outside of the great doors jumped to attention the moment they recognized Mathias heading their way. The one on the right patted flat the front of his uniform and turned to pull the door open to announce the paladin's arrival. Before the young man could complete his movement, however, Mathias met his eyes and deliberately shook his head. Had the young man been a bit older or more experienced, he would have understood that while Mathias commanded unrivaled power, he was not the authority figure in this case, but as he was lacking in both age and experience, he froze at the legendary paladin's unspoken order.

Allowing himself the briefest moment of smug satisfaction, Mathias summoned up his Etha-given air of authority and shoved the doors of the conference chamber open himself, leaving the flustered doormen behind him. He capitalized on the shock factor of entering the room of anxious Council members unannounced, enjoying the briefest surge of pleasure in the manner which they gasped and jumped and cast their frightful glances at his abrupt arrival. Even Julianna was quicker than usual to turn her eyes his way, and she'd been the one who told him when to arrive.

The doors of the conference chamber hadn't yet fallen closed and Mathias had only cleared a quarter of the distance toward the body of the Council when Head of Court Henrick Caldwell boldly addressed him.

"You came here alone?"

Mathias held his arms out to his sides and shrugged. "I was told you were waiting on me. What else was I supposed to make of that?"

Henrik flicked a disapproving glance toward Julianna but had sense enough to not accuse her of failing in her task of summoning her brother. He heaved an inconvenienced sigh and cast his eyes back to Mathias, who he'd always had an easier time showing his disappointment to. "It sounds as though you've been a busy man, Sir Sagewind."

Mathias bristled at the man's arrogant voice and slid a

perturbed look at Julianna, who stubbornly met his challenge. The tightness of her frown and steep angle of her arched brows conveyed her opinion of his untimely bout of mischief and the filthy armor he'd chosen to wear to such an important meeting. When she'd gone to gather him from his chamber, he'd been halfway undressed from casual clothing and had claimed he wanted to present himself in a manner more appropriate for the setting he'd been called to. It was a fault of Julianna's trust in her brother which had let her believe he'd meant he was going to find something truly appropriate for the task at hand, as the scratches and spatters of blood on his breastplate, the curl of leather straps that had been allowed to dry without sweat being cleaned off of them, gave anything but the noble appearance the Council expected from their audiences.

It did, however, draw out the exact reaction Mathias had hoped it would, and Julianna read as much in the steely determination in his eyes. Mathias had arrived here prepared for battle, and she'd been stupid enough to let him have the past twenty minutes to sort out his tactics. She gave him a slow shake of her head, silently scolding him for the words and actions he hadn't yet made.

Disregarding the balance of his sister's ire, Mathias returned his attention to the more contentious Council member. "Just carrying out my duties, Master Caldwell. Same as ever."

"And which duty is that?" The question snapped out disdainfully, as though Henrik was bored with, rather than infuriated by, the paladin's disrespectful presentation. "The one of reporting acts of demon aggression to the Council? Or maybe—"

Between his search, his battle with inoga, and the alarming insights which Nes had given him, Mathias's patience had been depleted. He reached his place behind the little corral meant to contain those addressing the esteemed officials and held his chin high, his eyes narrowed accusingly. "The one to impede the demons' progress while the lot of you sit in your comfort and bitch about why they're here."

Of the two-thirds of the Council members who were paying attention to the goings on, half of them blushed at Mathias's crude accusation. Henrik, having dealt with Mathias more personally than any of the others besides Julianna, recovered from his shock faster than most. He cleared his throat and leaned over his podium.

"There has been no… *bitching*"—he drew the word out slowly, as though pulling a long hair out of his food—"as to why they are here, Sir Sagewind. We already know."

"Oh?" Mathias sent another simmering glare toward Julianna and this time, she lowered her eyes. "And why is that?"

"When you ran off to go find this Miss Trelladell—"

"General Teradhel," Mathias cut in sharply.

"Whatever," Henrik dismissed, continuing as if Mathias had never interrupted him. "High Priestess Julianna did as you'd asked and gave a full report on what you knew regarding the… unusual events which accompanied your war efforts on Elidae."

Mathias grit his teeth and refrained from silently scolding his sister a third time; her shame in having hurt him radiated clearly to where he stood. He could see clearly where this meeting was now heading and it was too late to divert its path. Any loss of calm on his part would do nothing but discredit his defense of Nessix. "And so you must have understood how imperative it was for me to stay on the road."

"Imperative to what extent?" Henrik pressed.

Mathias furrowed his brows and shook his head. "What do you mean? Surely, it's evident—"

"He *means*," Thessia Hazlitt clarified, "was your mission ever truly to stop the demons or was it to simply protect your woman?"

Oh, Etha, stop me from strangling the lot of them… A slow breath did its best to calm Mathias, but it didn't smooth out his hackles. "My mission, as it's been for the past few centuries, was to stop the demons, and it was my belief that finding Nessix was the fastest, safest way to accomplish this."

"So her well-being played no part in your disregard for protocol?" Thessia asked.

"Disregard for—" That calming breath burst free of Mathias and he shook his head in shock. "It's your damned protocol which had kept me grounded here for a day and a half before I began my search. It was losing that day and a half which cost the village of

Fieldsdeep its entire population. I am quite literally the most senior officer the Order has ever seen and I will not ask your forgiveness for acting as necessity required me to do so."

A gentle hum of murmurs passed between the Council members, a few of them penning quick notes at Mathias's bold but accurate statement.

"So," Henrik said, "you claim her presence here on the surface played no part in the demon resurgence or even that very attack you have accused us for allowing to happen?"

Mathias bristled and grit his teeth, more thankful than ever that he'd convinced Nessix to stay in his room. He knew the answer to that accusation just as well as Henrik and the rest of the Council did, but he couldn't deliver it directly if he hoped to protect Nessix. "If you'd let me explain her circumstances and the reason she came to our realm to begin with, I'm sure you'd understand."

One corner of Henrik's mouth lifted in a subtle smirk Mathias wanted to swat from his face. "I'd prefer to hear them from her."

"Yeah, well, you got me instead."

From her corner position in the room, Julianna gave the tiniest shake of her head.

"Is there a reason you feel the need to hide this woman from us, Sir Sagewind?" Henrik persisted, voice dripping with his devious intentions and hunger for the Council's version of justice to be complete.

Mathias was prepared to bluster more excuses to cover for Nessix, but this wasn't his first dance with Henrik, and he was tired of following in the name of etiquette. "Yes. There is."

The cocky smirk flashed from Henrik's face and those members paying attention sat up straighter. Clearly, that hadn't been what they'd expected from Mathias.

"Then as Head of Court, I demand you share it." Henrik spoke this demand as boldly as he could, given the fact that experience suggested Mathias had begun to weave a trap for him.

"You're sure?" Mathias asked, catching that uncertainty Henrik had hoped he'd hidden.

Henrik drew a breath and held it. "It was an order."

Mathias chuckled bitterly at the nobleman's gall, shook his head, and shrugged, purposefully avoiding Julianna's seething glower from his side. He'd done what he could to avoid saying what had to be said. "Quite frankly, you're all a bunch of assholes." He ignored the offended gasps, neither surprised nor remorseful for having gained them. "I've witnessed several times how Nessix functions around people like you and, let's just say, it's not with the grace and ease which she handles a battlefield. In case you're all too dense to put this together, she only recently escaped imprisonment in the hells. I rescued her from the clutches of five inoga—" When most of the expressions remained dull and indifferent to the weight of that remark, Mathias pinched his eyes shut to sigh out his frustration. "Really big, really mean demons. She's secured and compliant, but still in too fragile a state to be getting riled up with your nonsense."

"Nonsense!" Henrik objected. "This is the fate of Gelthin you are dismissing, Sir Sagewind!"

"No, you arrogant fool," Mathias snapped. To his side, Julianna murmured a prayer and closed her eyes. "This is the fate of all of Abaeloth which *you* are dismissing. Nessix is a vital key in the war that is upon us. She is on the verge of breaking as it is, and if you and your blunt hand slap her before she can cool, if you push her to the point of deeming you incompetent, it will do nothing to save anyone. Abaeloth, Gelthin, Zeal, or even yourself."

"So you admit she's a threat?"

Mathias trembled with his anger now and suddenly, his prior concerns about where Nessix stood in the whole scheme of Abaeloth's safety left his mind. "She is less of a threat than the Council's incompetence is."

Henrik cocked his head belligerently and opened his mouth to rebuke, but Julianna held up a hand to stop him from the hasty course of engaging Mathias's ire. The Head of Court could claim to understand how Mathias functioned and know which buttons to push to frame an argument in his favor all he wanted, but none could dispute Julianna's knowledge of her brother, his motives, and his limits. The fact that she'd stepped in to defuse the situation now was all the chilly reminder Henrik needed to hold himself back.

Whether or not the Council sought to discredit Mathias for his impulsive nature, Henrik would not endanger his own safety to do so.

Reluctantly, and with great outward effort, Henrik swallowed his prepared retort and approached from what he prayed was a safer angle. "Can you tell us with certainty that she is of no danger to any of those we strive to protect?"

That's assuming the Council strives to protect anyone other than themselves... Mathias muttered to Etha, as even Julianna's careful watch on him suggested she wasn't a friendly audience in this moment.

You're going to want to answer this one sooner than later, Etha replied.

"She is trying to help the surface realm," Mathias said promptly.

"And how do you know?" Henrik asked.

Mathias shook his head. "Because that's what she told me."

"And it's impossible for her to lie?"

Truth be told, that was a question Mathias had found himself toiling over more often than he was comfortable doing so, but this unpleasant situation had helped put many of his concerns into perspective. "It may be difficult for you to fathom, Henrik"—he allowed himself a little smile at the way the Head of Court bristled at the casual address—"but some people are made of stronger moral fiber than either of us. The fate of innocents is on the line and Nessix needs the Order's help to protect them. She would not lie about her intentions."

Henrik did his admirable best to stare Mathias down, but the paladin, even as worn and fed up as he was, had spent lifetimes fighting demons and the undead. One spoiled mortal would not intimidate him. "It has been noted," Henrik snipped at last. "We will need to speak with her."

A gentle rumble of agreement filtered up from the rest of the crowd and Mathias's heart fell.

"She is not yet ready to—"

"Every day this brave, noble general remains cowering and—how did you put it?—*fragile* in your secret little cubby hole, more innocents are left in danger of whatever terrible fates the demons

97

have planned for them. Am I right?"

Each fiber of Mathias's being wanted to argue Henrik's logic, but he couldn't do so and maintain any sense of integrity. He could no longer hold back the outward signs of his trembling and all he could think about was how he'd failed Nessix yet again. Support came to him, as it often did, in the unlikely ring of Julianna's voice through the waiting silence.

"Master Caldwell, the Council's wishes have been noted." She turned her attention to her brother, holding it there until he shifted his perturbed gaze from where it bore holes in the floor to hers. "Mathias," she softened her voice, but maintained a strict undertone which spoke of the ramifications if he chose to disobey. "You will find a way to motivate Nessix to be prepared to speak with the Council in two days' time."

His eyes darkened into a simmering glower, one of the few times in life he'd ever expressed such fuming rage at his sister, and he ground his teeth together to keep from expressing exactly what he wanted to say to this entire chamber.

"For the sake of Abaeloth," Julianna added quietly.

Had she used any other tone for her gentle reminder that Mathias was the world's first and last line of defense against the demons, he would have been able to shove her words aside. But she'd spoken a truth he'd needed to hear, one which no amount of his anger would allow him to disregard. One he knew was true… and which Nessix would wholeheartedly agree with. He grimaced at the notion of her enthusiasm, fretting over how he'd be able to adequately prepare her for the petty nature of this particular body of nobles. She'd had a great deal of leverage over Veed, and had apparently found some degree of it with the demons. Zeal's Council, though, not even Mathias had found any leverage over.

All eyes were planted on him as he toiled over this most unpleasant duty which had just been strapped to him, and Mathias was ready to be through with this entire headache.

"Then I'd best be going to motivate her." He turned and began for the doors, pleased to not have to look at the arrogant faces of the officials any longer.

The two guards manning the interior of the chamber clutched

their polearms nervously, casting timid glances between Mathias and the officials who gave them their orders, uncertain who it was safest to offend.

"Sir Sagewind, you were not dismissed," Henrik called to his back.

Mathias waved a flippant hand in the air and raised his voice to avoid needing to turn around. "If getting Nessix down here is that important to you, *for the sake of Abaeloth*, you certainly did."

Stunned silence reigned through the chamber until Julianna's terse groan of Etha's name cut through the tension and she slipped from her seat to rush after her brother. At the High Priestess's approach, the guards visibly relaxed their stances and pulled the doors open for the departing Sagewinds as the Council members instantly launched into an argument over who was to blame for Mathias's behavior this time around.

Leaving that ruckus behind delighted Mathias, but he'd have been able to find more contentment if Julianna hadn't doggedly stayed at his heels. He pointedly ignored how closely she followed him, and she allowed him that luxury until he led her out of the main hallways so they could be alone for the reprimand they both knew was coming. Once they reached their privacy, Mathias didn't bother to look at her, though she'd lengthened her stride to march beside him.

"You should have kept your mouth shut from the start," he seethed. "You never should have told them what happened to Nessix. Not before we'd figured it out for ourselves."

"I did what I had to, and you know it," she replied, just as shortly.

"No, you did what you wanted to because of your bias against Nes, and now she's going to be the one who pays for it."

Julianna huffed a deep sigh and hustled to get in front of Mathias. He clipped to a stop as she grasped his forearms and flung his perturbed glare to the side in preparation for his sister's scolding. "You know how the Council runs. They would have gotten their answers eventually and the harder we tried to hide them, the worse their response would be."

Mathias brought his glower to meet Julianna's firm eyes,

weighing the sincerity of her words. She spoke a valid truth, one which Mathias agreed with, but he saw no hint of remorse for her actions. He scoffed and shoved her hands off his arms to push forward again. "They've already made their decisions about her, just as you did weeks ago. You should have let me speak to them before you shared your feelings."

Julianna twisted her lips in dissatisfaction and turned to resume stalking after her brother. "And *you* should have taken the chance to share *your* feelings any of the five hundred times it was offered to you."

Mathias clenched his teeth tighter and pulled another veil over his eyes.

Unafraid of her brother's anger, Julianna persisted. "If she is truly noble and just, if her intentions are as pure as you say, let her make her case before the Council."

Mathias coughed. "They won't—"

Julianna snapped her hand forward and grabbed Mathias's arm, pulling him to a stop with a force not even he could fight. "It is the only way, Mathias. It would be the only way even if she was still a mortal. Any knight of the Order would jump at the chance to march against demons under the White Paladin, but few would risk their titles to do so without the Council's approval. This is how it has to be."

Her words soaked into Mathias's sensibility and he had no grounds to fight them, even if he wanted to. The Council would have to speak with Nes before they allowed any of the Order to march per her request, and she'd have to find a way to convince them that doing so was in the city's best interest. Mathias would have given just about anything for an extra day to have prepared himself for dealing with the Council, suddenly regretting that he'd missed his chance to diplomatically lay the groundwork of Nes's proposal before she and her tainted position had to do it all by herself. He'd learned to not underestimate the woman when she had a goal in mind, and he'd seen her overcome ridiculous odds, but she had a trying battle ahead of her with negotiations, and Mathias's own temper had done nothing at all to help her. At least she enjoyed challenges…

"*You!*"

Both siblings, having been caught up pondering different aspects of the same scenario, shook their heads at the sudden interruption and turned to find a distraught young man staggering down the hall. Mathias didn't readily recognize Talier's physical traits, but the scrawny human's pathetic terror was easily recognized from when he'd rescued Nessix from the inoga. Despite Mathias's relaxed reception of this bumbling man, Julianna studied the aura of Affliction burning about him. Her brother was too sharp and in tune with this attribute, himself, to have not noticed it, and his neglect to tell her about this acquaintance only gave her more reasons to question his better judgement.

Though Julianna continued to stand by, watching the unusual man carefully, she didn't comment on his arrival, leaving the burden of sorting out whatever he wanted solely on Mathias. The paladin, so through with responsibility for one day, sighed and did his wanting best to put on an approachable smile.

"You are Nes's friend. Talier, right?" Mathias said.

The matter-of-fact greeting stopped Talier, pulling a great deal of the courage which had brought him this far from his sails. He gave a feeble nod. "And you... you..." Tears welled up in Talier's eyes to replace his misguided determination as he struggled with the memories tied to the inoga attack. Facing this man in the quiet security of the Citadel only dumped the terrible answers to Talier's pathetic questions into place. "I was told she was safe, that she was in the care of a paladin."

As much as Mathias would have loved pawning this man off on Julianna, he saw an opportunity in this diversion. "She is both of those things." He stepped away from his sister. "And she's asked about you a couple times. Would you like to see her?"

Talier choked between a gulp and a sigh. After clearing the disturbance from his throat, he nodded again. "If that could be arranged..."

Before Mathias could take another step forward, Julianna's grasp on the back of his arm stopped him and she pulled him back. "You failed to mention she'd taken up company with an Afflicted," she murmured for her brother's ears only.

Down the hall, Talier nervously drummed his fingers against his thighs and cast his gaze at the floor, his enhanced ears easily catching her suspicious tone.

Mathias shrugged. "I hadn't seen the need to. Look at him. He's the furthest thing from a threat we've seen all week. Worry about something worthwhile."

"Like whether or not you'll actually bring Nessix to the next Council meeting?"

Mathias quirked his lips and narrowed his eyes in forced consideration. "I was thinking more along the lines of your dinner plans or which of your gowns you planned to wear to evening prayer."

Julianna didn't bite on his attempt at humor. "Mathias, I'm serious."

He fought the urge to roll his eyes so powerfully that it rocked his head backwards. "Fine. I'll make the arrangements."

Julianna nodded silently, her expression strict and branding her expectations of Mathias's compliance into his mind. She gave Talier one last, critical look over, sighed in a manner which clearly conveyed her doubt in Mathias's decision making skills, and left to go manage damage control within the conference chamber.

As soon as he was sure Julianna had left the vicinity, Mathias felt the tension balled up between his shoulder blades soften and release, and he closed the distance between himself and Talier. The young man only managed a few timid glances his way, but they weren't as sheepish as the typical star-struck youth's regard for his status or station. Instead, Talier shifted about as Mathias neared, like he expected the paladin to snap and take the life of a loved one.

"I'm sorry for what you had to witness the other day." Mathias wasn't quite as skilled at comforting the masses as Julianna was, but that didn't keep him from trying. "Nobody deserves to carry such memories."

Talier hung his head even lower and concentrated on his feet as he followed Mathias's casual lead down the hall. Would he ever again face another man without crumbling in terror? He was struck with the urge to tell Mathias why he was afraid, about Kol and Annin and what they'd do to Marcoux once they found out Nessix was cozied up in Zeal's Citadel, but that greater fear of betraying them and of cluing Mathias in on his direct involvement with the demons silenced those thoughts. He crossed his arms and hunched his shoulders.

"There's a whole lot I don't think I should have seen..."

Mathias was surprised, though pleasantly so, to hear Talier open up to him, and shamelessly chose to use this opportunity to his advantage. "I'm sure whatever road Nes took you down wasn't the easiest."

"You don't know the half of it..."

Mathias cast a curious eye on his companion as he guided him to the hall which joined with the spire's staircase. "How long were you with her?"

"I don't know." In truth, Talier's days had all run together in one dismal period of feeling death constantly breathing down his neck. After finding Nessix, he'd listened to her recount her past and soaked in the tells of her scent until he felt as though he knew her far better than he actually did. "Maybe a week? It's hard to say."

Mathias chuckled and shook his head, always marveling at the power of Nes's charisma. "Maybe a week, and she endeared herself to you this much?"

Talier curled his fingers into the slack of his sleeves, struggling to suppress the whirlpool of emotions which muddled his instincts. "She... she fought a pair of demons off me on the road and promised to keep me safe if I got her to Zeal."

They reached the foot of the stairs and Mathias paused. "Then I owe you my gratitude for helping her find her way."

Talier gulped down the guilt of his true intentions—and the fear of having failed them—and nodded since his tongue couldn't navigate the concept of words.

Mathias looked up the stairs, back to Talier, and back up the stairs once again. "It's... a long climb to my chamber," he said. "If you'd wait here, I'll fetch Nes and we can all go get some fresh air."

Talier followed Mathias's gaze as it stretched up to where the spiraling stairs disappeared. He didn't want to let Mathias out of his sight, afraid of being stood up or forgotten about, but he'd already spent most of his fortitude gathering up the nerve to follow

Mathias's scent past the infirmary guards. Crushed by so many fears, Talier crossed his arms and nodded.

"That sounds great," he said, not knowing what other option he truly had. *Besides*, he reminded himself, *even if Mathias did try to disappear, I could just keep tracking him.*

"Thank you. We'll be down shortly."

Mathias left the twitchy man at the foot of the stairs, ascending two steps at a time until he'd reached the first full turn after which point, he simply teleported into his chamber. He was relieved to see Nessix still inside—though he couldn't figure out where he'd been afraid she'd escape to—sitting at his desk, his room predictably still in shambles. He was slightly less relieved when she turned her face to him to reveal the faint traces of dried tears on her cheeks.

"Nes…?" He began to rush over to her but stopped and winced the moment he saw what book she'd chosen to occupy her time in his absence. "You… weren't meant to read that one…"

The first book Nessix had found in all of Gelthin written in her native tongue had been Brant's journal. It had chronicled, in his own colorful words, his struggle to cope with his grief, Sulik's devotion to him, and his repeated attempts to build a relationship with Sazrah. He hadn't been cut out to be Elidae's general, not by a long shot, and all of those shortcomings of the role he'd been forced to fill had been logged on those pages… until they simply stopped.

Nessix swiped at the remnants of her tears and tried to bury her frustration with Mathias witnessing her grief behind a wrinkle of her brow. "I knew what it was as soon as I picked it up. It's my own fault for reading it." She slapped the cover closed and cleared her throat to dislodge the gruffness from her voice. "How'd your meeting go?"

Mathias watched her curiously as he gathered up the pieces of her armor, unconvinced by her display of resilience but seeing no need to make an issue out of it. "About as well as I'd expected."

She shoved the book away and stood, gripping firmly to the confident tone she'd built up. "And my audience with them?"

Mathias groaned and hesitated in his gathering. Perhaps he

should have thought over his plans a bit better. "You'll have it in two days." He held up a hand to halt her instant debate. "It was the soonest they could fit you in."

Nes's lip twitched at the idea of losing an extra day, but considered herself lucky that Mathias had followed through with arranging a meeting for her at all. "And what's this"—she gestured to his efforts of collecting her armor—"all about?"

"You wanted to see Zeal, your armor is in desperate need of repair, and you've got a stir-crazy friend who sounds like he's in need of an outing almost as bad as you are."

She perked up even more. "Talier's well?"

"As well as can be expected for the survivor of an inoga attack." With a tidy bundle of Nes's dented and gouged armor, Mathias swept his free arm toward the door.

Nessix readily accepted the offer, elated to be able to leave the confines of this room at last.

"He said you'd only known each other about a week?" Mathias asked as Nessix led the way down the stairs.

Nessix thought it over carefully. She'd spent so much of her journey running through the night, catching glimpses of sleep in the few safe moments she found, that she didn't even know how many days it had been since she'd stepped off the ship in Seaton.

"About that, I guess."

"Huh."

Nessix slowed to toss a look at Mathias over her shoulder. "Huh, what?"

Mathias shook his head to dismiss the question which came to mind, but it stubbornly stayed in place, waiting for him to ask it. "I understand how he, or anyone for that matter, would latch onto you in such short time, but even before the demons had taken you, you'd been slow to trust. How long did it take you to first address me by my given name?"

She smirked and blew out a weary breath before resuming a brisk pace down the stairs. "Respect and trust aren't quite the same thing." She slid a sly glance back at him. "Sagewind."

He chuckled at her levity, but found his humor lacking. "It's a serious question, though, Nes. What made you trust him so quickly?"

The humor dropped from her expression and she slowed her descent from an eager skipping to a more thoughtful plod. "I'd lost my map in a… um… a fight with demons." She flushed and kept her focus on the stairs. "I'd been travelling by myself and had no idea where I was going. When I found him and he told me he could navigate this country, I had few other options than to trust him. Besides," she allowed herself to glance at Mathias once more. "You don't think he'd be able to hurt me, do you?"

Again, Mathias wanted to find the jest in Nes's words, but got hung up on one important fact. "It doesn't seem likely, but he is Afflicted."

Nes's brows wrinkled. "He's what?"

Mathias sighed, wishing—not for the first time—that Nessix had ever cared about the workings of Abaeloth beyond those that immediately applied to Elidae. "In the Divine Battle, the first children—"

"Went to war with each other, right," she finished for him. "The war ended when the fire god Muerick wielded the god spear Affliction to strike down his siblings, then Etha bore Affliction down on her favored son before destroying the artifact."

Mathias stopped and grabbed Nes's arm. "How did you know that?"

She didn't know where to start explaining what she'd learned from the dream she shared with Kol, and so she settled for a shrug. "I told you. Kol made me read about the demons' past. A *lot* about it."

Oh, Mathias! Etha gasped in glee. *She* can *be taught!*

Mathias glowered at his goddess's enthusiasm. *I guess I should have tried claiming her as my property to get her to listen to me.*

At least she bothered to listen at all.

"Wait." Contemplation sat heavy across Nes's brows. "Are you implying that the Afflicted were born of the god spear? That there was another byproduct of the Divine Battle other than demons?" Her jaw sagged, eyes widening as she fought to understand how Talier could have lived longer than his apparent twenty-something years and still been so timid and naïve.

106

Well, look at that, Etha threw in. *She's willing to listen to you, no domination necessary.*

"Not… quite." Mathias took his hand from Nes's arm to press his palm against his chest, where his own chunk of Affliction was wedged. "We Afflicted—"

"*We?*" She gasped and lifted her fingers to the ring in her chest. "Are you saying I—"

Mathias sighed and closed his eyes. "No, not you, Nes. Me. You are speaking to the first man to ever have a piece of the god spear bound to him."

Nessix crossed her arms and leaned her shoulder against the wall. "And all this time, you let me think you got all of your strength from simple prayers."

Mathias worked his jaw against Nes's playful jab, enjoying the lighthearted mischief she threw at him more than he enjoyed Etha's echoing laughter in his mind. "We Afflicted," he started again, enunciating the words sharply to let himself pretend he was in control of the conversation, "are bound to other, outside forces, the divine might of our shard of Affliction stitching into us the powers of that which we're bound to."

Nessix laughed and resumed her trek down the stairs, logic not quite keeping up with her tongue. "You mean to tell me you're physically *bound* to Etha?"

It's about time she figured that out…

Mathias cleared his throat and huffed out a brisk sigh. "That is exactly what I'm telling you."

Mind now caught up with the implications of this conversation, Nessix threw her shoulders back to stop again, but Mathias gently prodded her to keep moving forward. "And I… I'm alive because of…"

"Because of the demon blood in your veins," Mathias answered bluntly as her voice tapered away from speaking that truth.

"But that means…"

Mathias had found several reasons to be disappointed in himself over the past few days, but none of them struck him quite as powerfully as the loss of direction which welled in Nes's eyes at this confirmation. If he'd still believed she was in love with Kol, that notion would have died a rapid death as she silently contemplated the thought that Mathias being half divine and her being half damned meant the future she'd dreamed about in those precious few moments when duty and survival didn't demand her all was a lie.

"It does," Mathias confirmed gruffly.

Nes's pace slowed some more. Her eyes flashed with a brief glisten of tears, but she cleared her throat and quickly blinked them away. "So what does this have to do with Talier?" she asked, trying—but failing—to bring the bliss back to her voice.

Mathias appreciated her efforts, and attempted to match them. "Somewhere in his past, he's had a piece of Affliction incorporated in him. It's not a common occurrence among mortals, as those who know how to carry out the procedure without killing their subjects are few and expensive to employ."

Nessix shook her head. "That doesn't make any sense." She cast another look at Mathias, blushing at the memory of when she'd been close enough to his bare chest to notice the scar that must have been from his own Afflicting. "It has to take courage or desperation to let someone stab you like that and trust you'll come out on the other end. Talier hasn't got an ounce of bravery in him."

"Now I don't think that's quite fair…"

"No," Nessix insisted. "He ran from every suggestion of danger we came across and I spent more time trying to convince him that the demons wouldn't catch us than I did actively watching for an ambush. You must be mistaken."

Mathias chuckled. "I'm bound to Etha, remember? I'm not just mistaken about this sort of thing."

Nessix rolled her eyes, but admitted that she'd lost this argument. "So what if he's one of these Afflicted? That in itself can't be enough for him to be kicked out of Zeal, can it? I mean, you're still allowed to be here."

Mathias blew out a slow breath, reflecting on those influential members of Zeal who would prefer a man's Afflicted status *could* get him banned from the city. "On its own, no, it's not nearly enough. It would depend on his conduct which, in Talier's case, I think is safe to say can be easily controlled, and what sort of enhancements he's got."

Nessix thought back on what she knew of Talier, and only one unusual attribute came to mind. "He's got uncanny hearing, good enough to pick apart conversations from across a crowded tavern."

"Yeah, well, if he's got superior hearing, we should probably quit talking about him soon."

Nes's expression brightened from her gloomy contemplations, and she hastened her step once more, eager to put her eyes on the poor man—even if he had hidden his status from her the way she'd hidden hers from him—she'd taken on as a troop. Mathias followed, trying to find comfort in her enthusiasm. He savored her excitement, the way innocence still played with the notion of coming to life inside of her despite the wrongs made against her. She'd grown up privileged and spoiled in her station, but it had come at the cost of having many of the simpler joys of life barred from her. She'd shouldered the yoke of duty when still a child and through the tragic perversion of fate she'd fallen victim to, beautiful, resilient Nessix, hadn't given up on the wonders of the world.

There must be some way to fix her... Mathias rounded the final corner before the landing of the stairs to reveal Nessix giving Talier a hearty pat on the shoulder, her warmth pulling a reluctant smile from the timid Afflicted. For the briefest moment, Mathias was able to forget the dark path Nes's life had taken, the torment and despair she must have faced, the hardships which had forced her to have to kill for money as he watched her restore some amount of light in the young man. But the frown returned to Talier's face as his eyes wandered to the crumbled armor Mathias held, his expression closing in on itself, and he remembered all over again that nobody on Abaeloth—Nessix chief among them—was safe right now.

Mathias pressed his lips together to keep from expressing such disheartening thoughts, inwardly cringing at how Nes's eyes confirmed that she heard what he was thinking. "Are the two of you ready to head out and behold the most basic of Zeal's wonders?"

"I've daydreamed about what Zeal looks like since the day Grandfather forced me to start learning about you," Nes said.

Mathias tried for a friendly smile which worked on neither him nor his two companions, and gestured down the hall. "Then let's go stretch our legs."

The enthusiasm Nessix had discovered upon seeing Talier alive and well shriveled up and went back into hiding in light of the endless dump of misgivings coming her way, but the idea of moving about—free from confinement, free from the assassins' eyes, and free from the constant threat of Kol's determination—was a welcome reprieve from what she'd dealt with over the past several months. Eager to resume normal activity, even if it would in part be an act, Nessix stepped forward to follow Mathias when Talier's flimsy hand grabbed her arm. She paused and looked back at him, wearing the same manufactured smile she'd always used to rally her troops, but the expression faded as she met her friend's haunted eyes.

"Are you alright?" she asked the man, hoping Mathias was taking note of Talier's behavior to better prove her point that there was nothing threatening about him.

Talier looked from Nessix to Mathias and back again, gnawing on the inside of his cheek as he scooted closer to Nessix by shifting his weight between his feet. "Nessix…" He sent another fleeting glance over her head to where Mathias had stopped to wait on them. "We need to get out of Zeal. As soon as possible."

She'd hoped Talier's display of cowardice would have been enough to sway Mathias's suspicions of him, but his whispered request contradicted everything that a man allegedly terrified of demons would want. Either way, she hadn't travelled so closely with Talier, risking her life for him and investing her faith in his good nature, to disregard his concerns so easily.

"Zeal was our goal, remember?" She resumed that heartening smile, tapping into her charisma and diplomatic skills every bit as well as she had when trying to encourage critically wounded soldier to hang on a little bit longer. "And now, here we are. We're okay. This is where we need to be."

Talier's nervous swaying hadn't stopped and he glanced again at Mathias's observant eyes, sweating under their steady pressure. "How can you be sure?" Half the words came out nearly silent, and Nes's brows furrowed. Even for Talier, who she'd dragged out of demon clutches and forced to be involved in an assassination plot which had resulted in four dead men, this was an unusually heavy display of cowardice.

"Because we've been here for two days now without complication." She tactfully left out Julianna's reception and the personal matters she contended with. "We have a roof over our heads instead of a hungry sky. We have access to bathing, clean water, and warm food instead of picking at questionable scraps. And we haven't had to dodge *any* sort of shady character to obtain it. It may not have been that long for you, but it's been *weeks* since I've been able to sleep through the night like I can now. I cannot and will not force you to stay, but I have no intention of leaving until I have what I need, at the very least until my armor's repaired."

She moved to gesture toward where Mathias studied their interaction from down the hall with her bundle of possessions, but Talier stopped her movement by grabbing her arm. His fear and inaction due to it had already allowed too much time to pass between their terrible mishap and now, and though his locket still displayed evidence of Marcoux's life, he'd witnessed firsthand how little patience his demon masters had and knew it would be even worse once they figured out where he and Nessix had ended up.

"I... I can't explain why," he sputtered, sending another fearful glance at Mathias. Even if he *did* manage to sway Nessix, how would he slip past the paladin's watchfulness? "Just that it's... it's not safe here."

Nessix gently withdrew her arm from his hold, relaxing away the tension his behavior had roused in her. "This is the safest place in all of Abaeloth," she told him firmly. "Quit worrying."

Dampness glistened in Talier's eyes, but he'd cried so many tears already that they couldn't quite accumulate the volume to fall. He wasn't supposed to let Nessix reach Zeal. He wasn't supposed to let her find Mathias Sagewind. He wasn't supposed to let her know his connection to Kol. He wasn't supposed to be alive, and he suspected an amendment to that last part was coming due in short time from everything else he'd fouled up. Kol was smart and Annin was scary, and it wouldn't take them long to figure out that Nessix had succeeded in her quest to reach Zeal.

"But what if…" Talier threw his head back and tried to work out how to alleviate his fears without creating new ones in the form of Nessix's anger or Mathias's intervention. "What if the demons find us here?"

Nessix chuckled, the last of her suspicions sifting away as Talier finally managed to express what was on his mind. "Talier," she sighed, turning to resume walking toward Mathias. "They *can't* reach us here."

He caught her hand just before it escaped his reach. "But what if they *do*?"

Nessix turned back to Talier and soaked in the terror in his eyes. She'd been the one to encourage him to come along with her. She'd been the one to put him to work on a quest she knew would infuriate some of the most tenacious demons she'd ever encountered. She couldn't be sure what all he'd witnessed of the demons' capabilities, but they'd killed his brother and had tried to kill him, and though Nessix had no way of understanding the helplessness which civilians felt toward those with martial skills, she ached for Talier's fear now. She walked back over to him, shaking his hand from hers, and when he frowned and tried to back away from her, she reached up to cup his face in her hands.

"You have to trust me, Talier," she said quietly. "As long as we stay in Zeal, the demons cannot touch us, and any who try will have to make it through me and Mathias." Her reassurance didn't appear to make a dent in Talier's fears, her reference to taking a stand against an attack splintering the fragile resolve in his eyes, leaving more cracks for tears to shine through. Nessix frowned, wishing she had more than mere words for him, and lowered her hands. "I've got to get my armor fixed. You can come with us or stay inside the Citadel. You can leave Zeal, if you truly feel you're safer on the road. But I will not leave until I have an army behind me to strike against the demons."

Talier gulped at Nessix's declaration. So *that* was what Kol had been afraid of. Nessix hadn't been a tool of his so much as a weapon which could be used against him. And Talier had effectively drawn her out of her sheath and placed her in Zeal's armored hand. His fingers pressed against his pocket and felt out the lump of Marcoux's pendant. He'd told Nessix that his brother had died to the demons, and perhaps it was time to start believing it. There was no escaping the situation he'd fallen into, not if he wanted to live, and Nessix's idea of staying inside the Citadel, under vaulted marble ceilings which would shield him from the eyes of demons flying above, seemed like his best option.

"I'll stay here," he murmured, drawing away from Nessix as he worked his hand into his pocket. "Just… be careful. Please?"

Nessix frowned. She'd truly hoped Talier would have found peace in the holy city, and none of her experience in consoling civilians or rallying troops or bringing heart to the devastated told her how to alleviate these persisting fears of his. "I'll be careful," she said. "I promise."

Talier nodded, bereft eyes reflecting her pitying face in their unfallen tears.

"Come on, Nes," Mathias bid gently from several feet away. "He's got the security of the Citadel's guards watching over him."

Nessix slapped Talier on the shoulder once more, frowning as he jumped at the gesture, then turned to join Mathias.

ELEVEN

Tristan didn't like to think of himself as a predator, but there were few other ways to classify himself as he casually stalked through Zeal's streets, careful to slip past guards and those who carried the air of off-duty knights. So much time had passed since the Order had had to deal with the undead that he was fairly certain few would know what he was—only the Sagewinds had been alive during his kind's first assault—and the city's concerns were currently invested in the immediate threat of the demons' activity, but Tristan took care to avoid undue notice as Ceredulus guided him down the trail of the young woman Mathias had been neglecting.

He hadn't been given a physical description of the girl, as Ceredulus's position trapped within the Veil limited his ability to obtain such information, but the vampire recognized her as his mark even before his god had confirmed he'd reached the troubled soul. She was small and of adequate womanly proportions, her mane of messy brown curls pulled back as though she had no desire to impress anyone. She marched down the street with rigid strides that kicked at the plain gray skirt which labeled her a servant of the temple. An artificial confidence held her chin high and she clenched her jaw firmly to keep the tears glistening in her big brown eyes from falling.

Tristan smirked. Mathias had certainly done a number on this one…

Already concocting a list of uses he and his god could extract from this confused girl, Tristan pointedly looked to his right as he stepped into Khin's path. Her pace too brisk and thoughts trapped fretting over how she'd ever gain Mathias's attention and kindness again, Khin collided with the tall vampire, her satchel of scrolls slipping down to her elbow. He gasped and spun to face her, catching her arms to help her find her balance as she flushed and lowered her eyes.

"I'm sorry, sir," she mumbled, shrugging her left arm free from Tristan's grasp so she could slide the satchel's strap back in place.

"No need to apologize, Khin."

It was Khin's turn to gasp as her name left his lips on a melodic and mesmerizing tenor which she couldn't imagine had once been raised in any form of aggression. Embarrassment draining from her rapidly in exchange for fear that he'd known her name, she snapped her eyes up to Tristan's face and gasped again.

If Mathias had commanded a rugged allure which Khin had found appealing, this man was suave and elegant, his fair features speaking of refined breeding. His smile was more charming than it was friendly, and his eyes spoke of passionate commands which enthralled Khin on levels she'd hoped to forget existed. Khin blushed furiously and her shoulders caved in toward each other under the intensity of this man's undivided attention.

"I… I'm sorry, sir," she stammered again, tongue fumbling to form words able to convey her thoughts. "Do we… do we know each other?"

Tristan cocked his head, eyes narrowing in delight at Khin's simplicity. "We don't yet, but I was hoping we could amend that little problem."

Khin froze and clutched at the strap of her satchel until her knuckles paled, wide eyes spewing panic as she glanced about the bustle of the market's streets to see if any passersby were concerned about their interaction, searching for someone she might be able to petition to for help if she'd stumbled across a threat she'd convinced herself lurked only in her past.

"I'm sure you're confusing me for someone else…" Her voice trembled with the rapid flittering of her heart.

"Are you not the same Khin who has been travelling with Mathias Sagewind?" he asked, continuing when her wide eyes snapped to his. "The same Khin who escaped two demon attacks to reach this glorious city's splendor?" He swept his left hand—embellished with a county's fortune of fine rings—toward the elegant architecture and meticulously groomed flower beds around them.

Khin gulped, too stunned by how much this handsome stranger knew about her to even nod, much less follow his indications.

Her reaction was of little consequence to Tristan, and he continued just as smoothly as he'd begun. "You see, I have business within the Citadel and was told you were a runner for the temple. I need your help to see my business through."

A nervous laugh tinkled from Khin as the heat returned to her cheeks, and she uncurled the fingers of one of her hands to scratch the back of her neck. "I…I'm not sure I have that authority, sir. There's appointments and officials and all sorts of things to arrange and I…" She chanced a look into the glittering depths of his hazel eyes at last, captured by their warmth, and her next words came out on numb lips. "I just bring messages in and out."

Smile sinking deeper onto his lips, Tristan reached forward and brushed a stray lock of hair behind Khin's ear.

"Do you consider the Citadel your home?"

Khin rolled her lips between her teeth to moisten them. "I suppose it's the only home I have left."

"Then you can arrange all I need."

Khin hummed nervously and glanced away, a rush of tears threatening to assault her at any moment. Even through her uncertainty and with past experience screaming about how this was a vile setup, she couldn't motivate herself to retreat from this man's touch. Her heart hammered aggressively in her chest. "Sir, I… I really have to go." She twitched as though preparing to turn back toward the Citadel, but never made it out of his steady gaze. "I'll…

um… if you stay here, I'll send for a proper aide—"

"You can quit calling me sir," Tristan said, unfazed by Khin's attempts to back out of this confrontation. "I have never been knighted and do not care for the sort of life they live. I prefer a bit more luxury, knowing where my meals will come from, warm beds." Khin gulped, and he chuckled. "You are welcome to call me Tristan."

Khin echoed his laugh, though too loudly, not knowing what else to do as it became increasingly evident that Tristan had no intention of letting her leave without first gaining the access he was seeking. She had no immediate way of securing as much, and the way which he left her so flustered despite her conditioned wariness of men disintegrated what should have been a routine outing for her into an unnerving—but oh, so thrilling—encounter.

"Well, Tristan, I'm due back at the temple." She took a quick step back to withdraw from him, and his hand was on her forearm before she saw it move, his grip gentle but holding her firmly in place. A great shudder worked from her feet to her head. "Overdue, really." She moved her free hand to begin prying at his hold but found all she could manage were a few halfhearted shoves which lost intensity each time her fingers slid over his. "As… as I said, I'll ask an aide—"

Tristan laid his free hand atop hers, silencing her frantic objections instantly as his delicate touch and the lace of his sleeve brushed across the back of her hand. "Miss Khin. None of the aides can get me what I want. Your prayers were heard and I seek to answer them. I came looking for you, and I ask that *you* take me to the Citadel. Not someone else."

Perhaps if Khin had been of a wealthier upbringing or if Zeal hadn't done such a thorough job sanitizing the evidence of the vampires they'd subdued all those generations ago, she might have had words to assign to the suspicions which came to life inside her. But she had neither an education nor insight to the uglier ages of Abaeloth's history, and was gullibly drawn in to the implied prophecy in Tristan's words. The color drained from her cheeks as she gaped at the beautiful man.

She'd never been a particularly spiritual person, especially after the turns her life had taken, and the concept of her prayers being heard by anyone seemed more than a little ridiculous to Khin. However, Tristan knew her name, knew she'd been silently begging for help, and he held more power over her than anyone she'd ever known in her life. If Mathias would have been there, he'd have encouraged her to be more careful, but Mathias wasn't there. He'd abandoned her for his quest to go find the woman who was more important than she was.

"W-what prayers, Tristan?"

He gentled his smile, his soft and alluring expression drawing her closer to him. "Prayers for help. Prayers for closure. Prayers for vengeance and answers." When Khin's expression remained troubled and her lips stayed creased in a firm line, Tristan sighed and closed his eyes, scanning the reaches of his abilities for the whispers of souls past. "Your mother mourns for the sacrifices you made for your family. She wishes she could have found a way to spare you the hardships you experienced. And your father—" Tristan jolted upright, eyes opening and pupils restricting quickly with shock. "Your father has some very unkind things to say about me prying into his conscience."

Khin gasped and her eyes welled with the tears she'd fought so hard to repress all day. "Father… father didn't believe in seers," she murmured. "He said they did the demons' work…" Given her recent brushes with those fiends and the connection she just made, Khin tugged more forcefully against Tristan's hold, nearly toppling backwards from her effort.

Tristan tightened his grip, though his fingers didn't dig into her with the bite of dominance. After he'd steadied Khin, he removed both of his hands, confident she wouldn't make another attempt to escape him, and smiled knowingly. "The demons' work? No, child, this is something far more divine than those foul creatures could ever hope to command." Her expression softened to match his, the pitiful longing he'd hoped to see slowly seeping into her eyes. "And this is a talent I would be happy to teach you, if you would only be so kind as to get me inside the Citadel."

The suppressed common sense which had told Khin that getting on the carriage bound for Seaton with the other girls from

Fieldsdeep had been a bad decision told her to run, but her desire for happiness and closure, for respect and confidence, thoroughly took that sensibility to task, just as her desperation had back then. "And I could talk to my family again…"

"Of course you could. You could have everything you need to mend that broken heart of yours."

She drew a hand to her chest to press against her aching heart and did her best with her poor judgement to gauge what it was Tristan was truly after. "And all I have to do is bring you into the Citadel?"

"Bring me into the Citadel and direct me to the libraries, yes."

Khin hesitated again, that same warning flag waving. No matter how badly she wanted to fix what had gone wrong with her life, no matter how wonderful it would be to talk to her family again—even if it came through some sort of demonic witchcraft—Tristan's request was rather specific. Khin was but a temporary servant of the Order; she had no authority to be making decisions of who went where or for what reasons. She frowned and lowered her eyes, struggling with this compulsion to please Tristan so he might help her find the life Mathias had decided was no longer worth his time to guide her toward.

"What do you need to find in the libraries?"

Tristan studied her a bit harder, delving into her scared little soul so full of doubts and betrayals to find how she idolized Mathias to the point of infatuation and smiled. Gaining her compliance, if just to spite the White Paladin, would be worth the effort of winning her over. "I seek to get to the bottom of what has caused the demon resurgence."

Khin shuffled and peeked up at him, fingers once again plucking at the strap of her satchel. "The priestesses are already researching what the demons could be after. There's nothing you could do to help them."

Tristan lifted a slender finger in the air and gave her a charming smile. "Ah. Nothing against the most holy work of the priestesses, but I believe I might have some insight on the subject which their order lacks. What if they aren't searching in the right places?"

Khin's eyes widened just a little bit more. This entire time, all of the priestesses' efforts had been directed at digging through the demons' past, all the way back to the Divine Battle. They'd started with the oldest tomes they could dig up and had barely made it up to the point of Mathias's death. Khin couldn't read and she didn't know much about history, but she had been directed on which wings of the library held different sets of information when tasked with returning exhausted volumes to their shelves. What if the information the priestesses had dismissed as irrelevant held the secrets they were after? If Tristan found the information that was truly needed and she was the one to help him do that, she wouldn't have to settle for being a mere survivor.

"And you know where to start looking?" she asked at last.

"I have my suspicions. The worst that happens is I won't be able to find what I hope to, and I will leave your fair city as elegantly as I arrived. Please, Miss Khin," he bowed to her, tilting his chin up to look at her through his lashes. "Won't you assist my prying mind, just a little bit? May I enter your home?"

Khin's heart fluttered at his flirtation, the attention she was getting far more innocent and much less crude than that she'd received from the more devious men who had crossed her path. This time when her shoulders scrunched up, a coy smile accompanied them, and she found even greater difficulty meeting the swimmable depth of Tristan's hazel eyes. "Of course you may." A trill of laughter danced on her voice. "How else would you access the library?"

This had been too easy... Tristan's fingers traced up Khin's arm to rest on her shoulder so he could turn her back toward the Citadel and gently prod her forward. "How else, indeed..."

TWELVE

Despite his vow of trusting Annin's lead, Kol did hesitate a few times on their flight back to Elidae, second guessing how far he could tolerate being distanced from Nessix. Her pendant, though it still glowed with enthusiasm, had begun to dull in its luminescence, drawing a different sort of frown from the alar. Neither was he pleased with the idea of getting close to Grell, but he didn't stop and he didn't offer any further arguments about the soundness of this plan. Skipping across a handful of tiny border islands for brief rests and to eat, the demons made good time back to Elidae, careful to skirt low along the ocean upon their approach to avoid the eyes of any of the Order's reinforcements which might spot them.

Though the flight had gone smoothly, even Annin executed caution when entering the cavern which led into their realm. When it had just been the pair of them out in the wilds, Kol had been as comfortable as he could be expressing his weaknesses to Annin, and he'd witnessed Annin at a physical disadvantage from how much energy he'd expended more than once. These were facts both of them accepted and knew about each other, but allowing a third party to witness them in such vulnerable states was risky, especially if they hoped to succeed at carrying out Annin's ploy.

They passed through the crowds of demons, their stoic airs

121

hushing most conversations, though a few of the more foolhardy underlings continued to share snide murmurs between each other. A handful of these underlings darted off the moment they recognized the two winged demons, undoubtedly rushing off to report to their respective lords that Kol and Annin had returned— unaccompanied by an akhuerai. This realization did nothing at all to motivate Kol, but Annin's steady stride drew him along, threatening to leave him behind and without an oraku's backing to the lesser demons' torments and the threat which resided within their greater numbers.

Annin headed straight for Grell's chamber. Whether or not the brute of a lord was home, he'd return there shortly once the reports carried by eager runners reached him. As he and Kol entered the tunnel which led to the inoga's room, shrill screams of torture greeted them, confirming that Grell was where Annin had hoped he'd be. On cue, he reached back, snagged Kol's arm to keep him from backing out of this obligation, and soldiered forward.

"Grell, we have returned," Annin called, more confidence than Kol had ever heard in his life ringing those words down the hall.

The screams promptly died out with a single snap, and though Kol gave a brief tug against Annin's hold, the oraku continued to drag him along. It would serve them well for Grell to see Kol's apprehension to prove that Annin was fulfilling his end of the bargain in making sure he didn't try to run away. At least that's what Annin hoped.

Seconds later, Grell's excited face poked out the door, waiting to behold the fact that his subordinates had found Nessix and were bringing her to him so he could give her a proper punishment. When all he saw were his two subordinates, one strict and confident, the other refusing to look in his direction, he frowned, the scar on the side of his face pulling the expression lopsided.

"The two of you are *alone*?" He wedged his bulk through the doorway and blocked the passage to his chamber, arms crossed as he tilted his head to rest one ear on his shoulder. "The two of you are alone and you came back?"

So close to Grell, instinct alone kept Kol from trying to draw away from Annin as they steadily closed the remaining distance between them. Just as a dog would chase down a frightened rabbit, Grell would pounce the second he thought there was something to chase. That instinct, however, was not enough to convince Kol that he was remotely safe.

"We came back alone," Annin replied in stride.

"That's not at all what you told me you'd do. You told me you'd beat my friends to Nessix and bring her back with you."

Annin nodded as he stopped a yard out of Grell's rushing distance, his fingers digging deeper into Kol's forearm to ensure he stayed put. "That is what we told you."

"And the fact that you've returned... does that imply you failed?"

"We failed in the sense that your inoga friends did find Nessix first, yes." Kol gave another feeble pull against Annin to try to escape as Grell's frown turned into a conceited smirk and he lowed a soft chuckle. This hadn't been how Annin said he'd handle this situation. "But they caused a much more severe complication in this race than either Kol or I have managed to do."

On days when his life wasn't on the line, Kol loved to watch the way Annin toyed with Grell's simple brain; it had been a means of entertainment dating back to when they'd all been mortals hunting for winter provisions. It hadn't ever quite lost its appeal, though Kol had taken to being more mindful about when he allowed himself to laugh over it. Today, witnessing Grell's flash of anger put Kol in a much darker spot, one that wanted him to stick a knife in Annin's side so he could try escaping the situation. But as Annin was his only feasible means to reuniting with Nessix, he couldn't do that, either.

"What sort of complication could they have caused? Bring me that magic bowl of yours and—"

"There is no use in scrying them, and I can tell you exactly what happened. Those fools got on Nessix's scent and they chased her right into the same town as Mathias Sagewind."

Grell sucked in a sharp breath, his thin brows springing up over the widening of his piggish eyes and his lips pursing into a shocked little frown.

"And there, he soundly decimated their ranks and abducted

Nessix. We believe she is now in his custody headed to or possibly already in Zeal."

Fast thinking had never been one of Grell's strong suits, past the gut reactions which he employed in combat, and this time was no exception. He churned over the details Annin had provided, desperate to come up with some debate or way to get the oraku to corner himself so he'd have a valid reason to vent his rage. That answer wasn't readily available, and so Grell did the next best thing. "How do you know this?"

"Because Mathias sank the three of them he'd left standing into the ground and they told us what happened themselves. Your inoga friends, sir, did not follow your orders. Kol and I had been careful to drive Nessix away from Zeal, mindful of where the White Paladin had positioned himself because we recognized the threat he posed to this mission, but your peers betrayed that trust you'd invested in them."

Grell hated a whole lot of things, and chief among them was how he hated being wrong. Rage boiled in him, pushing past the euphoria of how he'd played with his pet akhuerai, past the humor he found in imagining how he'd also get to play with Kol and possibly Annin when they failed him. His cheeks reddened and his muscles twitched, but he didn't move quite yet. Grell was slow to learn, he always had been, but he also knew to avoid jumping to conclusions when talking to Annin. Kol was smart, but he was prone to making mistakes which could be exploited. Annin, even as impulsive as he was, wasn't prone to making mistakes at all; when he wanted something done, he knew how to achieve it. And that meant he would not be standing here in Grell's hallway unless he had some means to fix this mess. Hating that he had to rely on someone else for matters he should have been able to muscle and intimidate his way through, Grell folded his arms.

"So they betrayed me," he grunted, fear ticking in his voice in a way that the single calm sliver of Kol's heart laughed at. "What am I supposed to do about it?"

Never one to balk when taking a chance, Annin's only tell of reluctance was a single, hearty swallowing of his nerves. "You let me and Kol go back out there and take her from Zeal."

That flush of rage deepened as Annin's words processed to Grell as an insult. "You came all the way back here to mock me? I'd expect that sort of behavior out of that little mouse you've dragged down here, but not from you, Annin!"

Annin held his ground. "I came down here to report to you the failings of those you thought you could trust and to remind you that Kol and I have been by your side from the very start. I'm not asking you to invest that same trust which you'd given to those who owe you nothing, no loyalty or honesty or even respect, but I am asking you to let us fix the problems which they have caused."

He tactfully left out the fact that Grell's reaction to recruit those alleged friends had been the sole catalyst of this current problem, knowing that would do nothing whatsoever for his purposes. Instead, Annin had expressed his facts as an open request, an offering which only he would be capable of fulfilling. It was a tactic he'd used against Grell in the past and one which continued to work for him today.

"The bitch is in Zeal," Grell sneered. "How are we supposed to get her out of there?"

Here came the gamble. "We offer an exchange of her for the priestesses."

Grell stared mutely at Annin for some time, trying to decipher whether or not that had been a joke. It was a strange reaction, considering Annin's dry sense of humor and the fact that he seldom wasted his time on anything remotely akin to jest, but Grell couldn't believe that had been the best option Annin had come up with. A brief glance at Kol's tiny sneer and rolled eyes confirmed that the alar knew this was Annin's answer to the problem, and Grell realized that he had nothing to laugh about.

"With how valuable Nessix is, with how long Mathias Sagewind spent searching for her, with her being the first answer the surface has had to figure out what we're doing down here, you really think they'll trade her for a handful of defiled priestesses? It's been years since we've had them in our possession. Nobody in Zeal probably even remembers the girls' names."

Annin would have loved for Kol to step in and take some of this burden off his shoulders, but he wouldn't hold it against him that he couldn't. "Zeal doesn't forget anything. You know that. And Mathias is but one man; the Council and the entirety of the temple will overrule any preference he might have."

"Have you forgotten how many times he's operated outside of that Council's wishes?" Grell spat.

"I have not," Annin answered. "But I also know he can't stand against his sister. He can come charging after us if he wants to, but we can outpace him if he's on his own. We bring the priestesses to Zeal, offer the trade. If they accept, we win. If they don't, we begin to kill the girls. Eventually they'll cave."

Grell grunted. "And if they don't?"

"And if they don't, then we're no worse off than where we are right now. But you know how squirmy mortals get at the thought of harm coming to one of their own, just like you know if we try to lead an army—demon, akhuerai, it doesn't matter—against Zeal, we will not succeed."

Grell cocked his head. "The akhuerai army…"

"Cannot march against Zeal." Annin delivered his correction firmly, leaving no room for Grell to wedge an argument. "Do not forget that you showed them how to end themselves, and I'm sure Mathias has already figured out what the ring in Nessix's chest is for. It's the priestesses, Grell, or nothing."

Grell glanced again from Annin to where Kol held his breath standing slightly behind him. "You've been awful quiet about all of this, Kol. Is that implying you've got doubts?"

Oh, Kol had a whole heap of doubts crushing down on him, but he owed it to Annin to hide them. He choked down his nerves, but not thoroughly enough to keep the rasp from his voice. "No doubts, sir. Just anger." At least that part was true.

"And do you think the priestesses are enough to pry Nessix away from the Order?"

Kol chanced a quick glimpse at Grell, shrinking away as the inoga stared at him like some sort of bored predatory cat. On normal days, Grell liked to see a struggle; he enjoyed people declaring their intentions to do something he expected them to fail at, as he had when Kol and Annin first claimed they would find Nessix. But Kol, even with the roar of nerves pounding through his head, had caught a tick of apprehension in Grell and suspected that he was as desperate for a solution to this problem as he and Annin were.

"If we bring what's left of Auden, we can lure Nessix out of hiding," Annin suggested when it became apparent Kol had spent the extent of his courage with his previous statement. "Between him and the priestesses, we can leverage the Order to cooperate with our demands. I believe this is the only way to recover her."

For the briefest moment, a sense of obedience passed between the three demons, a tiny nod to the fellowship they'd once shared. Grell was frightened, though he'd never admit it, and as always, Annin and Kol had come up with a solution to his fears. All he had to do was trust them. Unfortunately, he'd also spent centuries never needing to rely on others past their entertainment value, and the notion of following instructions didn't sit well with any part of who Grell had become. There had to be a way to make all of this work in a manner which would allow him to maintain his command over both of these demons.

"You are sure this is how you want to proceed?"

"I am," Annin said, without the faintest hint of reluctance.

Unable to see a way around this, Grell nodded once, shortly. "Very well. Annin, you may take what's left of the akhuerai commander and the priestesses to Zeal to arrange an exchange. Kol, you stay with me as collateral."

The blood drained from the alar's extremities. He didn't need Grell to elaborate on what that meant, and neither could he petition for Annin's support in trying to get out of it. As determined as the oraku was to get his way, this would be just the kind of trade he'd be inclined to agree to. Despite how many times Annin had sworn he'd get Kol out of the hells if he agreed to return with him, having now received Grell's ultimatum on the situation, Kol was left on the cusp of a frenzied fight. Despite Annin's magical prowess, Kol was smarter than him; he knew how to read people on an emotional level Annin often denied existed, and he had *known* beyond a doubt that matters would come to this. Had that been Annin's plan all along? Kol knew he'd been trying his friend's patience in the worst ways…

"It is imperative that Kol returns to the surface with me, sir."

Grell snarled and advanced a step on the pair. While Kol flinched, Annin stood his ground admirably, and that only stoked Grell's anger further. "Are you arguing with me, oraku?"

"I am stating that I need Kol to come with me in order for this trade to work. If he can't come, I cannot promise I will return with Nessix."

"Is that a threat?"

"To you?" Annin puffed out a dry laugh. "What sort of threat could one of my stature possibly pose one of yours? No, I am stating facts. We were fools to let Kol tote her soul around for so long before she was raised, more foolish still to let him source his blood for her. He has not just bound himself to her physically but has bonded to her soul, which he has made evident to me through his behavior several times now. I need him with me when she enters my custody in order to guarantee her compliance and obedience."

That sneer developed dangerously close to a full growl. "Like he controlled her when she ran away from him?"

"Exactly like that," Annin said. "Because he wasn't with her when she ran. He was back here in the hells, as you'd requested. You've witnessed her obedience to him when he's physically with her. You've seen her nearly kill herself to please him when he's overseeing her. He is the only one of us who can truly control her, but he has to do it within an effective range of her in order to see it done. If I cannot bring Kol with me, I cannot promise I will return with Nessix."

Kol thought back on all of the instances which Annin had referenced, the chill of his fear now compounded by that of this realization. Was Annin sputtering nonsense to get his way, or was he actually on to something? Could that be why Kol was so drawn to Nessix? A bond of the soul? That would explain all of the moments of weakness which had passed between the two of them in the privacy of his chamber. Part of him was so relieved to consider this phenomenon, to know that he wasn't simply going mad but following a normal response to the actions he'd taken, but that glimmer of relief disappeared when Grell spoke.

"If you take Kol, I'm going, too. I've watched too many mistakes be made, and I will ensure things are done right this time."

Kol already saw exactly how this would work. No matter how badly Nessix wanted to deny caring about him, he knew she did. He'd felt it as recently as the past dream they'd shared. She may want to run from him. She may long for the life she once lived. But she would do what she had to in order to protect him. If Annin's theory was correct, she may not even be able to stop herself if she saw harm come his way. And that was precisely what Grell planned to capitalize on. He'd wait for Zeal's forces to face them, and if there was any sort of reluctance, Grell would use Kol to force Nessix's compliance. Kol swallowed a grim whine before it had the chance to encourage Grell's intentions.

"It would be unwise for you to travel with us, my lord."

Neither Grell nor Kol had expected Annin to continue this debate. He'd already asked for—and received—so much; how could he possibly think to get away with more? If anyone could do it, it would be Annin, but that didn't make Kol any more comfortable with the thought that he was trying it with Grell within arm's reach and Annin already half-worn from their flight.

"Are you *forbidding* me to go to the surface?"

"I'm not forbidding you from going anywhere. But here are the facts. It takes just shy of a week to travel between Elidae and Gelthin through the Undersea Pass. It would take at least two weeks of a steady charge on foot, even with our stamina, to clear Harborswatch to Zeal, and that would be assuming the priestesses could hold up to that pace. If we were to fly from Elidae, however, two alar to tote each prisoner with enough to rotate fresh arms and wings, at the right speed and elevation, we could make the entire journey in under a week by air. Your indisputable might has rendered your body less suited for such lengthy and intense flights. I am not saying you cannot come with us, but I can tell you that if Nessix is in Zeal, every second we lose matters."

Kol held his breath, hardly able to believe that Annin had had the foresight to think through such a detail nor that he'd had the nerve to so directly contradict Grell in something he so clearly wanted. He spoke complete sense, though, sense which Grell could not debate, and Kol's heart nearly stopped beating when Grell's snarl relaxed into a contemplative frown, his eyes growing distant as he thought over Annin's words.

Grell, in an unusual bout of maturity and lenience, accepted Annin's logic, evident by the slow falling of his features and the faraway look which seeped into his eyes. He didn't have to like the answer, but the threat Nessix had the potential to pose—though he had no way of knowing the worst of it—was too great to risk on something as petty as his whims to torture Kol. Besides, if Annin was speaking the truth about Kol's influence over that cursed akhuerai, he'd be able to hurt them both in much more interesting ways if he could access them together.

"You're taking your alar, then?" Grell asked.

Kol didn't dare to start breathing, but Annin had never stopped.

"Those who want to come with us."

Grell's brows stitched closer together. "And what ever happened to that sorry lot you'd originally taken with you?"

Annin was too smart to bring up the fact that they'd partnered with Lorrin, as Grell's hatred for the surface oraku was no less severe than Lorrin's hatred of Grell. "We've assigned them to continue patrolling the far reaches of Zeal's borders," he said, "to keep an eye out for whether or not Mathias decides to try to mobilize Nessix."

Grell's features fell, as he'd been hoping for an excuse to draw out this argument a little longer. Since he had none, especially with Annin's reminder of the borrowed time they were running on, Grell voiced a spoiled harrumph, and turned to go back into his room.

"Do whatever you'd like, then, so long as it brings Nessix back to the hells. Her army needs a leader after what happened to that commander of theirs."

With Grell's back to him, a surge of bitter confidence returned to Kol in an overwhelming rush after how casually the inoga dismissed the damage he'd done to Auden. The tension ran through his muscles and into his arm, and Annin gave it a sharp wrench to keep him silent. There would be nothing gained for drawing Grell's agitation or curiosity back to them now.

"Thank you, my lord. We will be victorious."

"You'd better be."

The damp flop of a limp body being peeled off a bloody floor left the room and Annin released Kol's arm at last so he could forcibly turn the alar back down the hall and prod him to the safer reaches of the hells.

* * * * *

Grell had long ago quit keeping track of how much time had passed since he'd been a mortal. Unlike most of the demons of the first wave, he didn't look back on the events which ushered in the conclusion of the Divine Battle with fear or contempt, but with a humble—or as close to it as he could get—gratitude. If not for the Divine Battle, Grell would have lived and died an average man of average strength and average influence. He'd have dutifully served Kol as his young tribe's developing traditions had dictated, never to find glory for himself but for others.

The Divine Battle had condemned the likes of Kol and Annin and countless other demons to a life of bitterness, but it had saved Grell, giving him the power he hadn't let himself dream of as a mortal.

Hemorrhaging with might and commanding the frightened respect of those beneath him, Grell resented the notion of following any lead Kol might give him, but his longing to catch the pesky alar, the pathetic little man who had been granted position over him by a dead goddess, in the act of failure, to watch him squirm and suffer and realize he'd never stood a chance at success was simply too sweet.

Within the hour of Kol and Annin dashing off to collect their prisoners and reinforcements, Grell's akhuerai toy groaned as life crept back into him, giving the inoga a reason to smile. He lumbered over to the battered man and clapped a meaty paw over his wrist to haul him to his feet. "There's been a change of plans."

The haunted man didn't have the strength or will to weep, much less fight Grell's hold, only able to sputter a pathetic whimper at his interpretation of the inoga's words.

"Your general has been located," Grell continued, dragging the fleman across his room when his feet failed to carry him on their own. "And now she has to be caught." He pulled his toy out into the hall, leaving a bloody smear from saturated clothes as he dragged the man back toward the chasm. "Kol and Annin have set out to reclaim her, but I'm not sure they can be trusted. Are you?" He glanced at the whimpering akhuerai who kept his head bowed low beneath his shoulders, and growled, stopping abruptly to grip the man by both shoulders to shake him.

"Do you think they can be trusted?" Grell roared.

"No, sir!" The akhuerai's yelp ran together like it had been one word and he would have been trembling had Grell's crushing grip not held him immobile. He had no idea what Grell was talking about but did have sense enough to agree with him and hope that would buy him some mercy. "I don't think they can be trusted!"

Grell smirked and took one hand off the akhuerai's shoulder to roughly pat him atop the head. "Of course they can't." He continued his way down the hall. "You don't much care for them, either of them, do you, friend?"

The ragged akhuerai, having found his feet after Grell had put him down, scampered along behind the inoga like a toddler being dragged by an inattentive parent. "No, sir," he answered hastily, the confession that the fear he'd developed for Kol and Annin paled in comparison to his fear of Grell getting stuck in his dry throat.

"Good." Grell drew out his reply. "I'm going to have to leave you for a little while."

The man bit into the inside of his cheek at Grell's words, too afraid to show any sign of hope before his domineering master, too afraid to contemplate what would be involved with an inoga leaving one of his playthings behind. So much trauma had been piled on him since he'd last been back to the chasm that he hadn't recognized where they were until the hallway opened up before them. Grell continued to pull the man, more willing to move with the possibility of an escape from torture so close, to the lip of the chasm. Below, the akhuerai had resumed the uncertain milling they'd known before that traitorous woman had arrived to teach them how to disobey, sending frightened glances at the guard posts and jumping at every unexpected noise.

"Don't you worry, friend," Grell purred, squeezing down on the man's arm until he cried out and his knees buckled. "I'm going to make this right once again."

Not waiting for the akhuerai to form another one of his halfhearted replies, Grell flicked his arm forward and launched the man into the air above the chasm, enjoying one last moment of terrified screams that were silenced by an abrupt landing on the chasm floor. Grell smiled, trusting his toy would be safer among his peers than in the hands of any of the region's other inoga, and turned to head for the Undersea Pass. Annin and Kol would not escape him so easily.

THIRTEEN

Sleep only came to Nessix in fleeting glimpses the night before her scheduled conference, her thoughts racing with how she'd best present the plight of her people to the Council Mathias so dreaded, but equally excited to finally put her plans into action. She'd promised the akhuerai she'd come back to them with an army of knights of the Order, and she'd convinced Mathias to give her the chance to recruit that force. All she had to do was remember what it meant to be a politician for a couple of hours, and she'd have the biggest of her problems solved.

While Nessix anxiously watched the moon's passage toward dawn through the window in Mathias's chamber, the paladin had rested no more than she had, though he'd done well to hide it. There wasn't one part of him which believed Nes's meeting would go well for anyone involved, but he was out of excuses to give the Council and out of means to try to stall Nessix without stoking her irritation. He didn't have much to say the next morning as they dressed and dined, convinced that there was nothing to be said that could make the situation any better.

Nessix is a big girl, Etha assured Mathias as he made the final adjustments to the plain green tunic he'd donned in favor of his armor. *She'll be able to handle them just fine.*

That's just it, Mathias grumbled back, unrolling the cuffs he'd

made in his sleeves to roll them again. *I know she can handle them…
but I'm not quite sure they'll be able to handle her.*

"You look fine, Sagewind." Nessix caught his hand from
where he attempted to go through the process of straightening his
pressed collar for a third time. "All we're doing is going to have a
chat with some nobles. I've seen you charge into battle more
relaxed than this."

Mathias heaved a sigh and shook his hand free from Nes's to
smooth out the chest of his shirt once more. He'd been over his
reasons for dreading this meeting a hundred times with her, and
she still doubted his tactical assessment. "Charging into battle is
much more predictable than a meeting with the Council…" he
muttered as he finally motivated himself to step toward the exit of
his chamber.

Nessix, unarmed and dressed in the finest blouse and breeches
she'd been able to find on her day in the city, rolled her eyes at his
words and hurried after him, just in case he'd developed second
thoughts and planned to lock her inside his room again. "You
survived your meeting from the other day, and you've clearly
survived all the other ones in the past. You've got a way with
flowery words, and I've had enough diplomacy trained into me that
I'll be fine. Quit worrying."

Her casual approach to this formal situation did nothing to
ease the heavy sense of dread Mathias had been carrying with him,
and he didn't bother to hide his groan at her attempts to direct his
mood in any other direction as they descended the stairs. His
gloom didn't dampen Nes's enthusiasm, and so he thought little of
it until they reached the landing of the stairs to be greeted by a full
detail of armed guards.

The guards moved instantly, not waiting for the pair to
descend the last few steps, and the first of them grabbed Nes's arm.
Her brows furrowed in irritation and she jerked free of the grasp
which she'd clearly been meant to comply with. "What is this
nonsense?"

A second guard stepped forward and joined his comrade in
restraining the petite woman, one on each arm. This time her
attempt to pull free from their holds ended in failure.

Mathias should have seen such an underhanded tactic coming, but had allowed Nes's optimism to soothe away his better judgement. The Council had already lost their patience with him and he was willing to shoulder another dose of their ire if he could keep Nessix from tipping from her eagerness to speak with them to a righteous tirade.

"Gentlemen, there is no need—"

As Mathias stepped closer to Nessix, the balance of the guards closed in on him, pointing quivering spear tips at his throat. There wasn't one neck tendon among the group which wasn't tense, not one pair of eyes which didn't glisten with frightened regret for the action they'd been ordered to execute, not one jaw left unclenched. Mathias swallowed his initial response to swat away the spears and remind these soldiers of the valid reasons they had to be so afraid of crossing him, but had sense enough to realize that none of them were pleased to be in their positions. Instead, he slowly raised his hands from his weapons, splaying his fingers wide.

"I implore you to lower your weapons—"

"You are to remain silent, Sir Sagewind."

The command came from a voice which squeaked as though stuck midway through puberty, and Mathias shifted his glance toward the guard farthest to his right.

"By whose orders?" Mathias asked.

"Master Henrik Caldwell, Head of Court."

So this was how the petty man wanted to play... "And what did High Priestess Julianna have to say of the order?"

The soldier balked at Mathias's question and his comrades sent the paladin nervous glances, but held their ground admirably. "She was not present when the order was given, sir."

Of course she hadn't been, but that wasn't the fault of these young men. "Both Nessix and I will accompany you without objection," Mathias said calmly. "On my word as the White Paladin, neither of us pose any threat to you, the Council, or any who reside in Zeal."

The soldier gulped and gave Mathias a curt nod. "It is noted."

Mathias stared at the young man a moment longer, the pressure of his gaze squashing what was left of the soldier's confidence until he shifted his eyes away from the legendary hero's. "Might I encourage you to lower your weapons, then?"

It was clear by the firmness of Mathias's tone that his words had been more than a simple request. Though Henrik had the authority to strip the titles from them for any disobedience, Mathias had always been held in the highest regard among the Order's combatants, and wronging him frightened them all more than upsetting an entitled noble. Trusting the hero, having faith that his good nature would not permit him to cause them any trouble if they chose to comply with him, the guard who had been speaking nodded again and drew his spear back. Moments later, the five others around Mathias did the same, but Nes's two guards maintained their firm restraint on her.

A faint tremble coursed between her shoulders and she slowly tilted her face toward Mathias, pointed glare demanding to know if this was considered acceptable treatment of a visiting dignitary to Zeal, and Mathias's feeble hope for a positive outcome plummeted as a lump in his stomach. Nessix was already forming her opinion of how the Council operated, and she hadn't even faced one of the officials.

"And the lady?" Mathias prompted the leader. "I assure you she is well within my influence and means you even less ill than I do, provided you treat her with respect."

The guard didn't meet Mathias's eyes, focusing instead on the anger brewing within Nes's expression. "This *is* respect, Sir Sagewind," he said curtly. "We'd been encouraged to bring chains."

A deep breath straightened Nes's posture and the guards restraining her shifted their stances in case they'd need to use force against her, but Mathias quickly held out a hand to stave off all of his reactive company's responses. He speared Nessix with a commanding glare, reminding her that he'd told her exactly what to expect from the Council and assuring her that he could still control the situation as long as she didn't do anything to further complicate it. Acceptance worked through Nessix slowly, but faster than it had when she'd been a mortal, and though she didn't relax her posture, she did turn her face away.

"Nessix will accompany you without resistance," Mathias

addressed the entirety of the group. "And Nes—"

The lead guard stepped forward again, keeping his spear vertically aligned as he reached a hand out to silence Mathias. The paladin glanced down at how it had stopped an inch from his chest, then slowly lifted his gaze to the young man who still couldn't hold his eyes longer than a heartbeat.

"You are to remain silent, Sir Sagewind," the guard repeated, having found a pinch of his confidence through Mathias's cordial behavior. "Per Master Caldwell's orders."

Mathias raised his glare to the leader, silently scolding him for following an order he must have known was neither necessary nor right. This was a fine setup the Council had arranged, shortening the amount of time Mathias had to guide Nessix through how best to approach the finicky officials. Over the past few days, he had exhausted his capacity for trusting almost everything around him, but he had to do so now. Nessix had spent every waking moment since he'd found her reminding him of her past as a diplomat and, despite this rude handling—no worse than she'd likely received from the demons, but far from the generous welcome Mathias suspected she'd anticipated—he had to believe that she would conduct herself accordingly.

He sighed and lowered his head in compliance. "Very well. Lead us to wherever Henrik wants us."

The men standing guard over Mathias relaxed notably and positioned themselves between him and Nessix, further enforcing Henrik's desire to keep the two from communicating in these final moments before their appointment. The two guards leading Nessix gave her a firm tug to get her moving along. Mathias was relieved that she offered no further objections to their handling as they marched the pair through the halls of the Citadel.

Whispers chased the procession to a cozy antechamber located off the main conference hall and despite the circumstances, Mathias felt his calm trickle back into him. No matter how much bluster and sway the Council had in Zeal, the citizens present in the Citadel this morning were watchful and curious, observing Nes's steady nature firsthand. The Council would have a hard time persecuting her for their preexisting grudges with so many witnesses able to contradict their biases. Once inside the antechamber, the guards directed Nessix to the corner diagonally opposite the door and herded Mathias to the one straight across from it. Once it seemed evident that Mathias was content in his position, the lead guard and one of the others changed positions to watch over Nessix.

When Nessix had been a general on Elidae, she had wasted more time than she was proud to admit dreaming about what splendors Zeal held within her marble walls, of the great fields of lilies which embraced the city and gave the Order of the White Circle its name. When she'd been a prisoner and plaything of the demons', she had clung to the belief that the holy city was the one place she would find salvation for herself and the ragtag army she'd been ordered to build, in the form of ranks of disciplined knights who sought to protect innocents. And after she'd slipped away from her captors, lying and killing her way across this foreign continent to reach the blessed sanctuary before the demons caught her, Nessix had expected some amount of safety and peace to be waiting for her in the name of the justice which Mathias had allowed her to believe Zeal stood for.

She let out a slow breath and glanced at the nearest of her four tight-lipped guards. He was young and lanky, hardly filling out the arms of his pressed uniform, and his eyes glistened with self-doubt. A faint glimmer of sweat beaded along his brow as he gripped his pike in a gloved hand. The guards, while serving as an irritating inconvenience, didn't frighten Nessix, but their presence did offend her. She'd risked her life, her very soul—and quite possibly those of the army she'd left behind in the hells—to bring word of the demons' activities to the holy city that was meant to hold all of Abaeloth's answers, and their Council's response was to detain her?

Near the door of the antechamber, across the open room from Nessix, Mathias leaned against the wall, arms crossed and eyes directed away from her as he stared at the feathering in the white marble floor with an undue intensity. He didn't look up as he spoke to her. "I told you this was—"

The lead guard spun on a heel to face the paladin. "Silence—" His voice cracked and he self-consciously pulled his spear toward his chest, clutching it close like a child would hold his security blanket. "Erm... Sir Sagewind. No speaking, per Master Caldwell's—"

"Henrik's orders," Mathias grumbled, casting a challenging gaze toward the sweating young man. "Yes. You've told me."

Nessix allowed herself a smirk at last as the guard swallowed an audible gulp, and she raised her eyes to Mathias's. She had a sound enough political mind to know better than to encourage his sense of humor, well aware that she was the cause of the tension which had prompted the order for his silence, but that didn't stop her from appreciating his efforts.

As quickly as that reprieve from the dire urgency of her quest had come to her, it was chased away by the echoing clomp of a second unit of guards marching down the hall. Moments later, their reflections stretched long across the polished floors of the hallway.

The lanky guard pressed a brief grimace across his lips and reached his free hand toward Nessix's arm, pausing before he touched her, as though afraid she'd curse him if he did. "Miss Teradhel. If you'd come with me."

Nessix bumped her arm up into the young man's grasp, smirk broadening at his nervous gasp as she did so. "Lead the way." It was time to deliver the answers the world needed to hear.

The guards didn't relax into any more confidence until they were joined by the unit which had come to retrieve them for the Council. Now flanked by sixteen soldiers and followed by a growing crowd of the curious public, Nessix and Mathias passed through the Citadel's main artery, exposing Nessix—being handled with the caution allotted to dangerous prisoners—to the greatest density of nobles as possible. It was a fine plan Henrik had orchestrated to try boasting how much power he possessed, but the quick glance Mathias snuck at Nes's dignified expression between the strides of her guards told him she'd yet to be threatened by this reception. As always, duty came first for her. Mathias sighed as they were stopped before the great doors of the conference chamber.

Nessix straightened her posture with the confident authority she held even when facing most demons as the doors swung open. She was so eager to resume some sort of activity reminiscent to what she considered normal, and with a thrilled flutter in her chest, she looked forward to this meeting as the first step toward reclaiming this part of her identity. That hope froze in its tracks as a third unit of guards marched toward her from where they'd been stationed before a panel of three dozen stone-faced men and women who looked down on her with expressions ranging from caution to disgust. Their escorts pushed Nessix and Mathias forward to meet this additional unit in the center of the great room.

"Sagewind, is this normal—"

Henrik stood as Nessix began to speak, slamming a gavel on his podium. "You, Miss—"

Nes's attention snapped to the arrogant human at a speed which made Mathias groan. "General," she snapped, her voice ringing defiantly through the chamber and cowing the greenest of the soldiers.

Henrik delivered a willful cock of his head at her sharp correction and swept his amused glance at Mathias before narrowing his eyes at Nessix. "*Miss* Teradhel," he said stubbornly, "it is my understanding that you have put all of Abaeloth in peril."

Nessix bit back the rush of defenses which came to her tongue, knowing well that spouting them now would only confirm this human's implied impressions of her. "Please," she said instead, more polite than before, but no less authoritative. "I came to Zeal to petition for your aid. Though I will not criticize your wariness, I offer no threat to any innocent, and these guards are *completely* unnecessary."

"You are considered too much of a flight risk to—"

"A flight risk?" Nessix laughed at the absurdity of that suggestion. Half of the panel before her awkwardly looked away or busied themselves by needlessly shuffling papers. Even Mathias made a subtle cough. "Where in all of Abaeloth do you think I'd run to? Where do you think I *could*?"

Henrik turned his gaze back to Mathias and shook his head. "Like certainly does attract like, doesn't it, Sir Sagewind?"

"In that Nessix and I have both lived longer and experienced more of Abaeloth's hardships than your own grandparents, Henrik?" Mathias challenged.

The obstinate official pursed his lips, cheeks trembling as he clenched his teeth.

"Sir Sagewind," Eldon Blaxton, Regent of Pleibian Affairs, spoke up when it seemed apparent Henrik was too flustered to do so. "We beg you to take into consideration the current state of affairs and ask that you and Miss Teradhel"—though his eyes reflected his wariness, the human gave her a respectful nod—"understand that certain precautions must be made."

Nessix glanced at Mathias, wanting so badly for him to translate what was going on, but he hadn't shifted his firm glower from the Head of Court. "It had been my understanding, Master Blaxton, that when the Council had requested an audience with *General* Teradhel that she was to be a guest in this chamber," he said, willfully aiming to trick Henrik into exposing his less-than-honest intentions. "But now I must ask, Master Caldwell, had I been misled?"

Henrik, well accustomed to Mathias's shrewd sense of what he considered justice, stepped over the trap the paladin was laying. "She is our guest," Henrik replied coolly amid a varying collection of averted eyes and approving nods from his peers, "but as my esteemed colleague pointed out, she has come to us under the most alarming circumstances. Certainly, neither of you, being experienced officers of the battlefield, can fault us for our caution."

The excuse didn't do a thing to convince Mathias of Henrik's sincerity, but Nessix accepted it at face value and rolled her eyes. "It's fine, Sagewind." If someone didn't do something to take the edge off Mathias, she'd never get to have her words with this Council. "It's a valid point. You'd be cautious of me if you didn't know who I am."

Mathias eyed Nessix skeptically, ignoring the cocky turn of Henrik's lips as Nessix slipped into the noose he'd set. "Regardless, I'd have treated you like a person and not a vicious animal."

Henrik sent a disapproving look over his shoulder at the smattering of chuckles poorly concealed behind coughs. "You, Sir Sagewind, are equipped with powers the rest of us lowly servants of the Order have not been blessed with," he replied smoothly. "Of course you wouldn't feel the need to protect yourself from a possible threat. And speaking of threats." He turned to his left. "I believe Master Aligoth has a request to make of you?"

Willard, cheeks pink with shame, had kept his eyes on the desk before him this entire time, fiddling obsessively with the worn edge of a piece of parchment, and Mathias grimaced. The Minister of Petitions was a decent man, more so than most who served on the Council, and Mathias had no doubts that Henrik had arranged whatever request Willard would make. Slowly, the middle-aged human stood, fidgeted with the corners of the paper in front of him, and cleared his throat.

"We've a request to send you to monitor the activities in and around Heiligate." As soon as his statement was through, Willard flattened his lips in a grim frown and sat, having never raised his eyes from his desk.

Mathias shook his head and directed his confusion straight past Willard and speared it to Henrik. This was a highly inappropriate time to bring up a mission they all knew served little purpose. "Not even a month ago, they were busy licking their wounds from a grievous attack. I hardly think they'd be able to cause any trouble if they wanted to."

Henrik gave a brisk little snort and sent his haughty gaze to Willard. When the Minister of Petitions didn't acknowledge him or offer to speak, Henrik scoffed and flapped his hand impatiently until Willard handed his report to the official to his right to be passed over to Henrik. The Head of Court snatched it and smoothed it flat on his podium as he reviewed it. "The villages nearby are growing more nervous of those demons' presence than normal in light of..." he raised his gaze to Nessix once more, "recent events."

A fresh strain of agitation worked through Nessix but, surrounded by guards as she was, she held back her opinion, determined to prove to this Council that she was more stable than she truly was.

"Send Sir Roderick to go check on them," Mathias said. "Mehalco and his crew know him well enough and he's proven to be of a more understanding nature than the rest of the demon hunters."

143

"They are *your* pets, Sir Sagewind," Henrik said sharply. "You will go tend to them."

Mathias narrowed his eyes at this political opponent and ignored Nes's prying gaze at the subject of this revelation. "Now?"

"Now. Per official orders."

Mathias allowed himself a bitter laugh at Henrik's audacity, gaining the shame of more than a few of the soldiers and more reasonable officials. So this was how it was going to be… He cast Nessix a long glance. None of his efforts of preparing her for what to expect from the Council had set her up to handle Henrik's current mood, and the last thing he wanted to do was leave her alone in this man's incapable and judgmental hands. His disobedience now, however, would only serve to increase the officials' existing bias. Besides, Mehalco might be able to provide answers to some questions Mathias wouldn't be able to hunt for in Zeal.

There were so many final warnings Mathias wanted to deliver to Nessix, to tell her to be patient with these nobles, to beg her not to bite the bait they would inevitably throw her. He wanted to have a quiet moment to remind her that she was an educated and experienced politician in her own right and that her willingness to let go of the insults and accusations bound to come her way would be the only way to achieve the outcome she hoped to obtain. Unfortunately, Mathias wasn't in the position to deliver any of those thoughts or warnings, and that knot of nausea he'd been struggling with all morning squeezed tighter.

"I'm where I need to be, Sagewind," Nessix said softly. "I know what I'm doing. I'll be fine."

Mathias expelled a slow breath to keep from telling her how wrong she was and bowed his head, nodding slowly. There was no getting Nessix out of the trouble that closed in on her, and so he would have to come up with a way to manage whatever damage he returned to find. He raised his eyes once more to Julianna's. The High Priestess watched her brother steadily and with a pleasant expression of surprise that he hadn't made more of an issue over this turn of events.

You keep them in line… he threatened her silently.

Only if she stays in line, herself, came the unspoken reply.

Mathias sighed and looked once more to Nessix, admiring the confidence in her eyes, the proud lift of her head and shoulders, the acceptance of duty and honor which radiated from her. Here, surrounded by two dozen guards, unprotected by her sword or armor, and facing an opponent she had no way of judging as she prepared to give whatever was demanded of her to secure the necessary aid to protect those she'd sworn to protect, Mathias had never seen her so stunning. All the time he'd spent searching for her, through the mishaps and side quests he'd been dragged down, he'd stubbornly repeated to himself that Nessix would be fine because she was strong and clever. He'd managed to convince himself of that when he'd been so afraid of never seeing her again and now, as she stood just a few feet and several armed guards away from him, he believed it still.

"Save your people, Nes," Mathias said softly, treasuring the smile she threw his way.

"That's still the plan, Sagewind," she answered in turn.

The exchange did more than raise Nes's confidence and ease part of Mathias's mind, and the guards around them shifted uncomfortably at the implications of honor which passed between the pair. They'd been told by Henrik that this woman was an unpredictable beast, some insider of the demons' sent to crumble the Order from within. But Mathias's faith in her and her heartfelt acknowledgement of the mission they'd never been told she was on did a fair job at jumbling up what they understood for themselves. Satisfied with the discomfort he and Nes had laid on the less corrupt minds in the chamber, Mathias turned and dismissed himself from the hall.

Nes's confidence held as Mathias departed and as the doors thudded closed. All eyes stayed focused on her, waiting to see what she would do now that her handler had been drawn out of the room, and when it became clear that nobody knew how to proceed, she took the initiative for herself. "I am General Nessix Teradhel of Elidae, prisoner of war to the demons, protector of innocents, and I have come to Zeal with the utmost urgency to petition for help in freeing those who the demons have captured."

145

"Protector of innocents," Henrik repeated, sitting down behind his podium and drawing out the title Nessix had given as though he had difficulty understanding what it could possibly mean. "All innocents? Or only the ones you've decided are worth your while to care about?"

Nessix eyed this opponent carefully, realizing now what Mathias had been worried about. She'd dealt with politicians all her life, but always ones who served beneath her or held the title of guardian or overlord of some group of people they'd accepted responsibility for. These nobles had no solid grasp of war or sacrifice, they only understood how to prioritize matters for their own gain. She'd fallen into their first trap, but she'd done so with her eyes open and was undaunted by it.

"I am a general," Nessix answered firmly. "I protect those I vowed myself to first and foremost. I will help others when I am able, but it is not my responsibility to manage the safety of those under the sworn care of others."

"So you have no qualms endangering those you have not expressly sworn service to?" Henrik dipped his quill in an inkwell and looked up to await Nes's answer.

Nessix worked her jaw from side to side to push her growing ire to a more productive location in the back of her mind. "I never said that."

The pen scratched across the parchment. "But you do not consider them your responsibility."

Nessix grit her teeth and let her flare of indignation die down before answering. "I do understand that you have never led a warfront, and so I will accept that it is impossible for you to understand that one woman—or even an immortal paladin—is unable to protect every innocent life she comes across. I consider those I've vowed to protect as my responsibility and trust that there are others who will step up for those I cannot aid. That is my duty."

Henrik paused in his writing to look up at Nessix. "Sir Sagewind told us you were of stronger moral fiber than to willfully risk the lives of innocents."

"Sir Sagewind," Nessix answered tartly, "told you correctly."

The Head of Court laid down his quill and momentarily

ducked beneath his podium, reappearing with a handful of tattered sheaves of parchment. "I am declaring this meeting fit for High Council," Henrik announced. Excited chatter bubbled up immediately and a devious grin sliced across Henrik's face before a bold objection from a weathered woman in the back left corner challenged him.

"Now, Henrik, I'm not sure that's necessary."

"It's more than unnecessary, Lady Stele," agreed a dignified young man from the center of the group. "It's entirely unreasonable!"

Henrik's smile degraded into a righteous chagrin and he pressed his soft palms against the top of his podium to turn and face his peers. "Perhaps you could provide me a valid reason why we should avoid it?"

"High Council is meant to deal with one of our own," Eldon said.

"And has *our own* Sir Sagewind not already laid his claim to this..." Henrik threw a shoulder back to sneer at Nessix and wave a hand at her. "...woman?"

Nessix snarled back at him and tilted her head defiantly, but Julianna popping to her feet silenced her retaliation before it took form. "Master Caldwell," the High Priestess snapped, "you are making quite a leap there, and Master Blaxton is right. Foreigners are not meant to be subject to High Council."

Had Julianna made any effort at all to present herself as a potential ally, Nessix might have accepted her declaration as aid, but the High Priestess had shown her very little regard, and Nessix took her statement as a most unwelcome interference to getting what she wanted. "Subject me to whatever you want," she said. "I'm here for my people, and if this High Council of yours is what it takes for you to see that, then I accept it."

A smattering of gasps answered her reply, the vocal opponents of Henrik's demand shaking their heads with distinct, horrified expressions. Even Julianna's full lips had turned into a grim frown as Henrik turned back toward Nessix and settled into his seat once again.

"High Council, it is, then," the smug man said. "Now, do you,

Miss—"

"General," Nessix corrected again.

"Do you, *Miss* Teradhel, know what these are?" Henrik gripped the stack of parchment on his podium in both hands and waved them before himself.

Nessix sighed, patience abandoning her faster than she'd anticipated. She'd opted to come to this meeting sober, having hoped a clear mind would improve her odds of successful negotiations with these officials Mathias had been so concerned about, but as the chaos tickled about inside her, she began to regret that decision. "As I have not had the opportunity to review them, no. I do not."

"Well!" Henrik slapped the pages down on his podium so he could leaf through them. "You ought to. These are reports of the damages caused by demon raids over the past three weeks."

Despite her best intentions, Nessix caught a quick gasp and her cheeks drained of their warmth.

"And you may *think* Sir Sagewind has some sort of fondness for you, but he told us himself that the demons had only ventured up to the surface in pursuit of you."

Nessix's fists clenched at the goading, and she was conflicted as to whether she was grateful she'd left her weapons back in Mathias's chamber or discouraged by it. She had no doubt that Mathias, in all his blatant sensibility, had mentioned the correlation between his quest to find her and the demon resurgence, and she couldn't fault him for doing so, but she saw at last what he had meant when he'd told her this Council was full of jackals. She sent an inquisitive gaze toward Julianna, who sat primly to the side of the rest of the gathered officials, her face as set and cold as the marble walls. Nessix accepted that the High Priestess wasn't thrilled with her, but she'd have thought the woman would have shown some amount of concern for her brother's name being dragged into this.

"Mathias was right about you," Nessix sneered.

"Oh?" Henrik asked, humor lighting the accusations in his voice. "And what did our esteemed Sir Sagewind have to say about us?"

148

Nessix puffed out a short laugh and shook her head. "That is none of your business."

"No, that was an order, Miss Teradhel."

Nessix bristled at the Henrik's continued disregard for her station and title, aspects even the demons had respected and allowed her to carry—though she knew better than to mention that here and now. "And I am not one of your subjects to be ordered about."

A second round of gasps echoed about the hall and the guards immediately surrounding Nessix tightened their holds on their weapons. It seemed as though she'd succeeded in striking a nerve.

"If you reside in Zeal," Henrik said slowly, as though talking down to a peasant child, "you are our subject and will do as you are told."

Nes's eyes hardened and she flexed the fingers of her sword hand at her side. "I am a visiting dignitary."

Henrik snorted. "From *where*, Miss Teradhel? The *hells*?"

The soldiers fidgeted on their feet and with their weapons, and Nessix easily identified the discomfort of troops weighing out the validity of a shady order. If there weren't so many of them around her... "From Elidae," she snapped.

"Shall we send an inquiry to our contacts on the island to verify your claim?" Henrik asked.

Nessix sucked back her angry retort. She'd been too preoccupied with her mission of reaching Zeal and staying ahead of Kol and the assassins to dwell on what had become of her homeland, but that curt reminder was all she needed for those furious emotions to return to the front of her mind. Pride begged her to take Henrik up on the challenge he was so eagerly presenting to her, to turn the blame of what became of Elidae in the past year back on the Order and its presence in her homeland, but she suspected that was exactly the sort of situation this devious human was aiming for, and she would not indulge him in such a childish game. She may not know how to deal with corrupt nobles, but she had twenty soldiers around her, and they were precisely who she knew how to address.

Throwing her shoulders back, Nessix turned to face the tense men nearest her. "*This* is the leadership you've been forced to follow? It is utter madness!" Jaws clenched and glares stubbornly hardened, but Nessix had only just started. "There are townships actively falling to the demons, and you turn your sights on *me* as I seek to rally help against them? Civilians you and I have both sworn to protect are—"

Henrik jumped to his feet as a handful of Nes's guards snuck grudging glances his way. "Miss Terad—"

"General," came a rough cough from the back of the chamber, silencing Henrik's objection.

Nessix nodded her appreciation in the direction of her unknown defender, and continued her plea, encompassing the rest of the chamber in her address. "The souls which have been stolen by the demons do not have the time for us to waste trying to shame one another."

"You have been trying to shame the Council?" Henrik sputtered before Nes's words could sink into his growing opposition any deeper.

Nessix shifted her stance, toes curling in her boots as she fought to contain her ire. "I have been waiting for you to address Abaeloth's true concerns. I came to Zeal under the impression that this city harbored honorable, just men who would do what they must to protect civilians from the demons, and that is what I insist on doing."

Mumbled commentary bubbled up from the politicians until Henrik's noxious laughter cut them off, soon joined by the tittering of a few of his peers. Nessix bristled. As long as this body was so split in their principles, she'd gain no ground. She'd had enough, and she successfully pushed past the closest of her two guards.

"*Demons* have returned to the surface." Her words were short and scolding, yet they did nothing to wipe the arrogant humor from Henrik's face. "They've been stealing *souls* from mortals. And you *laugh*?"

Henrik turned his haughty gaze toward the offending officials, his expression giving them little more than a tap on the wrist, before he swung his attention back to Nessix. "We are not laughing at the crisis Abaeloth is facing, no. We are laughing at the notion that *you* assume you can insist on anything."

Suppressed rage boiled inside Nessix, the pressure building toward a hot whistle, and she dug her nails into the meat of her palms. "There are over two thousand souls currently counting on me to find them help," she seethed, "and countless others who could be forced to join them, not to mention all of the mortals who will be subject to the demons' whims in the process. Your great Etha cannot hear the prayers of the men and women who depend on me, and so I have appointed myself to answer them instead."

For the first time in this conversation, Julianna's expression changed, her pretty mouth dropping open in an abhorred gasp and eyes widening at Nes's nerve of mentioning the goddess in such a dismissive manner. The balance of the Council stared at Nessix as though she had just declared war on them, and Henrik shot to his feet once more, raising a shaking finger high in the air.

"You, hell dweller, dare to impose yourself above the will of our goddess?"

Nessix eyed the guard beside her, contemplating whether or not she'd be able to grab a weapon and remove herself from the middle of their confinement before getting caught. "The hells were never my home. They were my prison. And there's not a thing I wouldn't do to be able to have your goddess take care of this problem for me. If she's willing to step in and shoulder it all in my stead, she is welcome to do so."

A rumble of murmurs sprouted up through the room and Nes's guards shifted about again in anticipation of the situation turning even further south. The color had slowly returned to Julianna's cheeks, and though the outrage remained in her eyes and she'd pinched her lips together in a tight frown, her dissatisfied scowl seemed directed more internally than at Nessix.

Henrik hissed and shook his head, lip curling in disgust. "It was bad enough that you had the insolence to assume the Order would fix the problems of demon kind, but to imply that Etha herself would be of the mind to do so…?"

Julianna stood at last, seeming to be launched to her feet against her will, and her nose wrinkled through the entirety of her statement. "Master Caldwell, Etha's will *is* such that the demons' blasphemy is put to an end." She promptly clamped her mouth shut and grimaced as though swallowing a bite of rotten apple.

"I wouldn't dream of contesting that, High Priestess," Henrik replied, speaking far more graciously to Julianna than Nessix thought was either prudent or believable. "But you must consider the source…"

Nessix was through with diplomacy. She was through with forcing herself to be polite simply because she was in a foreign hall. "Do you mock my honor?"

Henrik smirked and his shoulders bobbed with a silent laugh. "Of course not. I simply refuse to acknowledge it, as I've yet to see evidence that it exists."

Struggling between the balance of asserting herself and keeping her boiling chaos at bay, Nessix shook her head in disbelief and struck a hand out at her side. "I risked my life and soul to escape the most dangerous, vindictive enemies Abaeloth has ever seen to try to keep them from harming anyone else."

Henrik waved a hand at the guards who had turned their waiting eyes toward him as Nes's agitation snapped at the cracking bars she'd caged it behind. "You've rattled on about being a general, have you not?" Henrik asked. "Shouldn't protecting Abaeloth from dangers such as demons be expected of you?" He reveled in the heaving of Nes's chest and the flare of her nostrils, drawing out a keen darkness from her glare with his smirk. "Doing the right thing doesn't make you honorable. It just makes you desperate."

Nessix's muscles twitched as she instinctively sought to lunge forward, but she caught herself before any of her guards felt the need to restrain her. "I *am* desperate!" she shouted, bending at the waist from the force of her plea. "There are *thousands* of souls at stake and Mathias and I cannot possibly manage the magnitude of this threat on our own." She held her empty hands open before herself and cast her gaze toward the men around her. "I am *begging* the Order of the White Circle for aid in this crisis."

Henrik crossed his arms. "Is begging what passes as honorable these days?"

Tears of frustration and restraint and frustration at her

restraint welled up in Nes's eyes. "If begging for help for those in need discredits my honor, then tell me how I can prove it to you."

Henrik's expression ignited with a sly enthusiasm. "Don't you barbaric combative types manage such feats through duels?"

Nessix looked over Henrik's doughy cheeks, soft arms, and rounded shoulders, and chuckled bitterly. If it would take a test of arms, whether against him or any other man or woman in this chamber, Nessix would comply. "Is that where you want to take this, *Mister* Caldwell?"

The human's face contorted in laughable rage at Nes's pointed jab, and Julianna sprang to her feet once again. "Master Caldwell!" Her voice was harsh and filled with an authority Nessix might have respected, had she not been so close to losing reason. "Consider the consequences of your words."

"Oh… I have," he replied, the challenge running even thicker in his voice.

Julianna had hoped for many things to come from this meeting with Nessix, but misleading the woman into taking incriminating actions hadn't been among them. She had few reasons to care about Nessix or her fate, but was desperate to disarm a situation that was destined to push Mathias past the point of tolerating the Council in this time of need.

"Miss—" Julianna stopped herself, hoping a show of respect would spread some salve over Nessix's wounds. "General Teradhel, I urge you to stand down."

Nessix swung her heated glare toward Julianna, appreciating the High Priestess's opinions as little now as she had upon her waking. All that mattered to her was obtaining the justice that was so long overdue, and she wasn't about to abandon that because of some woman's request. "Oh, you'd like that very much, wouldn't you? My honor was called into question and I've been told to claim it back. If that's what it takes to make you daft dandies take notice of the crisis that's in front of you, then I will do so." She brought her attention to the crowd of guards. "Someone, provide me with a sword so we can get on with it."

Every last guard, both those swayed by Nes's charismatic stance and opposed to it, swung his attention through the superiors in the room, shocked expressions pleading for definitive orders in this abrupt and unexpected change of events.

"*Nobody* provide her with a sword!" Julianna demanded.

The guards began to shift back into their positions, summoned to uncertainty once again as Henrik's offended snort countered the soundness of Julianna's order.

"You heard the woman, High Priestess," he scoffed. "She wishes to reclaim her honor."

Julianna shook her head fiercely, flinging her loose hair about her shoulders in a manner most unfitting for one of her dignified station. "You, Master Caldwell, have allowed your station to go to your head!" With Julianna's backing, those hushed murmurs of agreement about Henrik's behavior were twice as loud as before. "I do not and cannot stand for this."

Nessix rolled her eyes. Of all the times for the troublesome woman to choose to stand up for her, she chose the one which held actual meaning. And, just like the time when Kol had taken on Grell's fury to try keeping her safe, Nes's sense of reason slipped free from her grasp. "Then sit down, High Priestess."

The entire chamber, Henrik included, gasped at Nes's bold tongue. All they could see in Nessix now was the courageous, commanding woman they'd all tried so hard to deny she was. The guard to her right briefly met her heated glower and subtly shifted his arm from his hip, inviting Nessix to the rapier on his belt. A second gasp consumed the chamber as it became apparent that this trained combatant who had worked amid and somehow slipped free from demons was armed and prepared to engage Henrik—and likely any who attempted to go to his aid—in combat.

Henrik had been aiming to goad Nessix into openly declaring hostility at High Council, but as he stood among his peers, frozen in horror at the discipline etched on Nessix's face, all he could see was a fate he didn't truly want, no matter how it would discredit the foul creature in question. Trembling, having not thought through what he'd do if this woman actually accepted his taunts, Henrik belted out a humiliating cry and ducked behind his podium as Nessix dipped from view to crouch down and weave through the guards in front of her.

She made it past that first guard with little trouble and lowered her shoulder to knock the next down when a powerful force collided with her right side. With her center of gravity lowered, the blow wasn't enough to take her off her feet, but it did steal the breath from her. A second impact slammed against her back and succeeded in dropping her to the floor. By the time she realized the guards had organized themselves into two factions, a third grabbed her right wrist, twisting it and bending it backwards until she yelped and was forced to drop the sword.

"Coward!" she roared, aiming her fury at Henrik as he peeked from around the side of his podium. "This is not how—"

A blow between the shoulder blades cut off Nes's words and Henrik cautiously pushed himself to his feet. Tugging at the hems of his sleeves and straightening the front of his robes free of wrinkles, he turned to his peers and swept an arm toward where seven guards invested the better parts of their strength and skill to keep Nessix pinned to the ground.

"And you see, my fellow Council members. That is not the behavior of a sane woman. This is why we cannot trust this... this *abomination*, nor the word of Mathias Sagewind."

"It is the behavior of a *desperate* woman," came the heated retort from a feminine voice Nessix hadn't previously heard.

Nessix could only open her left eye for how her right one was smashed against the courtroom's floor, but she managed to shoot a glare at Henrik's feet as she wheezed in a breath. This was about Mathias now? "Unhand me!" she growled to the guards on top of her.

Her answer came in the form of a hand grabbing a fistful of her hair to give her head a dazing rap against the marble floor.

"Take her to the dungeon," Henrik cried victoriously, "to await a proper trial."

Nes's head swam from the mishandling and the gusts of chaos heaving inside her as the guards hauled her upright, holding tight to her limbs and waist. She flexed her muscles to try to wriggle her way free, but even so filled with rage and desperation, she couldn't throw the men off balance.

"You're making a terrible mistake," she demanded alongside

the firm verbal support she received from a few of the Council members as the procession of guards carried her toward the doors.

"The only mistake made," Henrik declared, "was Sir Sagewind's lapse of judgement in bringing you into our city. You will be tried for your crimes and dealt with accordingly, Miss Teradhel."

Nessix didn't have the presence of mind to contemplate what crimes Henrik referred to, moved by the single motivation she'd had all along. "Try me how you must," she said defiantly. "I do not matter. Only the people matter. How can you call yourselves just and continue ignoring what's going on around you?"

"You will see your justice, Miss Teradhel." Henrik had to raise his voice until it threatened to squeak from his effort for it to reach past the righteous debates breaking out among the others.

"And you, Henrik, are overstepping your bounds!"

Red-faced guards had nearly gotten Nessix to the doors, but she was bolstered by this sixth voice in support of her. "The Order is meant to defend—"

The rapid pounding of Henrik's gavel punctured the disorder of the hall, his voice piping up between strikes. "Not one more word out of her!"

The doors swung open and Nessix was escorted into a hall now crowded with curious, gossip-seeking eyes. Among those hungry gazes, she caught one set of familiar brown eyes, wide and as horrified as she'd always remember them.

"Talier!" she called above the ruckus of the crowd.

"Silence, General." The command was terse and her title mumbled below the level any of the other soldiers would overhear. "Please."

Nessix appreciated the respectful address, but she could not accept that order. "Find Mathias and tell him—"

She never got to finish her frantic request before another blow to her head sank her into unconsciousness, but Talier hadn't needed to hear the rest of it. Between his sharp ears and the shouting which had erupted in the conference chamber, he'd gathered enough to realize Nessix was in trouble. He'd yet to decipher what that trouble was, but he'd seen Mathias work enough miracles over the past few days. Ducking into the crowd before any suspicious eyes had a chance to identify and detain him as well, Talier slipped away from the commotion and snuck off to the stairwell which led to Mathias's chamber to track down the paladin as Nessix had tried to request.

FOURTEEN

Mathias departed Zeal for Heiligate, trusting neither Henrik to be a decent man nor Nessix to behave as a proper, dignified lady, but with faith enough in her words. She'd let nothing stand in her way of obtaining the help she needed for her army and after the rotten way he'd treated her over the past couple of days, he felt as though he owed her a bit of hard work of his own.

As he'd expected, nothing was amiss in or around Heiligate until he arrived in the middle of the town square. Brave though demons may be and even if each one who called the city home understood Mathias's role in keeping them alive, his sudden appearance in the heart of town was enough to send the passersby scrambling for cover, weapons, or both. He addressed their fears with a tight smile and sheepish raising of his hand.

"Do any of you know where I could find Mehalco this morning?"

His question succeeded in taking the edge off the masses, as business he had with their leader meant business he wouldn't have with them. A one-armed demon of apparent elven descent ventured a few steps Mathias's direction and jerked his head toward the tavern.

"He drank Bronte half dry last night before Vera coaxed him upstairs," he said.

158

Mathias curled his lip. He wasn't in the mood for pulling the most recent plaything away from the town's succubus. "Would one of you mind fetching him, getting him clothed, and sending him out to talk to me? Matters in Zeal require his attention."

Of the dozen demons who had stuck around to hear Mathias's wishes, ten wandered off, grumbling rude excuses at the mention of Zeal. Mathias eyed the remaining two patiently until the skinnier of them spoke.

"I'll do it for a gold."

Mathias blinked and shook his head. Bribery was seldom used against him in Heiligate, and he sorely hoped this didn't hint at an emerging pattern. "A gold?"

"Yeah." The demon looped his thumbs into the waistband of his pants. "Vera's rate's gone up since the attack and the best way to run Mehalco out of her arms is to… well, you know…" He flashed a lewd grin.

Mathias swallowed his grimace and heaved a sigh before slipping his fingers into his coin purse to pull out the requested fee. "You better not be planning on running off with this."

The demon's eyes lit up and he snatched the coin from Mathias's hand. "Running's not the sort of workout I'd had planned."

Contradicting the statement, the demon spun and raced off to the tavern, leaving Mathias to brood over the event he'd just facilitated. At least it had saved him from needing to peel Mehalco from the succubus's arms himself; and any way to avoid the promiscuous demon's advances was certainly worth a gold piece to Mathias.

While respectable cities boasted intricate fountains in their main squares, Heiligate had a stagnant pool of water which grew a lumpy bed of algae on its surface. Something, somehow, lived in the pool's depths to keep the mosquito larvae in check, but whatever it was, it didn't make itself known to Mathias as he walked along the water's edge. Old barrels and crates were stacked around the dismal feature to serve as benches where thoughtful demons could sit and ponder the pool's potential, and after Mathias had made a full pass around the water, looking for the least offensive spot to sit, he surrendered to the notion that one seat was as good as another. He scouted out the least rotted barrel and sat to wait for his messenger to retrieve Mehalco, actively fretting over how Nes fared against the Council. By the time Mehalco was shoved out the tavern's front door and staggered with a bitter snarl in his direction, Mathias was eager to find some other way to occupy his mind.

"Good morning, friend." Mathias fit a pleasant smile on his face and patted the top of the barrel beside him. "I'm pleased to see you doing so well for yourself."

Mehalco glared at Mathias through eyes squinting from the sun's brightness as he walked past to crawl onto the indicated barrel. He maintained that glare in place of giving the paladin a proper, polite answer.

Mathias chuckled and brushed off the demon's ire. Mehalco was still all demon, and Mathias both acknowledged and respected that, but this particular demon's ferocity, at least as it was directed toward Mathias, had always been more bluster than threat. Mathias was confident he'd get what he was after before this conversation was through.

"What do you want?" Mehalco finally spat, pulling his legs atop the barrel with the rest of him to curl into more of a fetal hunch.

"You're… what?" Mathias asked, tilting his head as he scrutinized the demon he'd known for the better part of his existence. "A fourth generation demon? Fifth?"

Mehalco scowled at Mathias from the side of his eyes and spit in the opposite direction. "Third," he snapped. "What of it?"

That was even better than Mathias had hoped for. "I need you to tell me what you know about an ancient named Berann."

A tiny gasp gurgled in Mehalco's throat and he jerked with enough force that he nearly tumbled off the back end of his perch. Glancing around quickly to confirm that nobody was close enough to hear any part of this conversation, the demon left his eyes turned away from Mathias and he cleared his throat. "Never heard of him."

Mathias smiled to himself but had the sense to not display it for Mehalco to catch a glimpse of. "You sure about that? Because it looks to me like you're hiding something."

"I can't hide anything from you, Sagewind," he muttered before caustically adding, "and you know it."

"You're right," Mathias said. "You can't hide a thing from me, which is why you're going to tell me who—"

Mehalco leaned toward Mathias so quickly he almost toppled the entire barrel over and snagged the paladin's arm to jerk him close with such hasty aggression Mathias had to repress his urge to reach for his sword. "You shut your blessed mouth if you value anything you built in this city."

Mathias had watched Mehalco grow from a confused youth in the hells into the leader of the demon haven of Heiligate over the centuries. He'd seen the amusing creature try to establish dominance over him, and he'd gotten used to the reactive demon grabbing him and dragging him around before he was willing to speak, but he'd never seen this depth of a warning in Mehalco's eyes. It spoke of very real threats which would come if Mathias chose to press this matter. It spoke of the danger of pursuing that path. And it assured the paladin in no uncertain terms that the next time he uttered that name, Mehalco would aim to do him harm, despite knowing it would be impossible to do so. Such an aggressive reaction was unusual for the nervous little demon, aligning well with the report Nessix had given him of how Kol had taken to hearing Berann's name. She'd been right. There was more to the dead ancient than the Order had passed on through the ages.

Minding Mehalco's terror, Mathias lowered his voice. "I just have a few questions our records haven't been able to answer."

"And none of our records will have answers, either," Mehalco snapped.

Had Abaeloth not been poised on the verge of imminent chaos, Mathias might have been willing to back down and give Mehalco his right to keep whatever upsetting truths he knew to himself. He might have even been inclined to let the demon stick to his story. Unfortunately, the world needed these answers, Nessix needed these answers, and so Mathias would do whatever he had to in order to get a hold of them.

"And if *you* value what I've built in this city," Mathias said, unbuckling his sword, "you will tell me what you know." Mehalco's jaw dropped at the casual authority Mathias was claiming with his actions and shook his head, but the paladin would not be swayed. "Do you remember the army that marched through here a couple weeks ago?" Considering the patches of fresh construction throughout the town, Mathias could hardly believe otherwise. "I'm not sure how, but Ber—" Mathias allowed Mehalco's sharp hiss to interrupt the name. "The demon I'm asking about is tied to that disaster and you, Mehalco, are the only living being I can count on to help me figure out how that is."

Not ten minutes ago, Mehalco had been lounging, comfortable and warm, in the bed of a succubus, able to ignore his lurking hangover through more appealing sensations. He'd intended to spend the rest of his morning savoring such pleasure, and he'd known from the moment he was told Mathias was here to speak with him that even the most remote notion of peace would be beyond his grasp. But he hadn't expected it to go this far.

The demon gauged Mathias's dedication to what he was after, searching for cracks in the stony resolve on the human's face, in the clench of his jaw and set of his brows. He glanced again at the unbuckled sword, a calm and capable hand resting on the butt end of the hilt, deft fingers ready to draw the blasted weapon at half a moment's notice. Mathias was a pain in Mehalco's ass, but he'd never been unfair and he'd always been willing to find a common ground during negotiations. Even so, this was the sort of thing Mehalco didn't have a ready price to charge.

"I don't know anything." Mehalco slipped off his barrel but before he had the chance to bolt back for the tavern, Mathias grabbed his arm and pulled him over.

"I am in no mood to be lied to, Mehalco."

"Yeah?" The demon's voice ticked with nerves. "Then maybe you should quit asking me your damned questions."

"Answer my damned questions so I can."

Mehalco grit his teeth in the best snarl he could concoct. If the paladin had been less determined and the demon had been even an ounce more confident, that snarl might have resulted in a reaction, if even just a laugh, but Mathias held it firmly, his

162

domineering glower deepening the longer Mehalco tried to stare him down. The demon thought to tug against Mathias's hold but knew it would do him no good, and after another few frantic heartbeats of failing to make Mathias cower, he emitted a shrill whine.

"Fine!" The word burst from him in a near-indecipherable puff. "But not here."

Mathias stood and waved his free hand toward the empty street around them. "Then take me where we can speak in private."

"No," Mehalco hissed. "Not. *Here*." When Mathias raised a brow and shook his head, the demon leaned closer and lowered his voice. "I need you to be able to guarantee my safety if you want me to start talking."

Mathias crossed his arms and cocked his head. "That's what Heiligate was built for."

"Oh, not against the dangers that'd come from this." Mehalco jerked free from Mathias's grasp to cross his arms. "Heiligate was made to protect us from mortals. I'm needing protection from my own kind."

Mathias chuckled and shook his head, casting his gaze toward the distance to keep from glaring at Mehalco. "I cannot take you to Zeal, if that's what you're implying. Even with my escort, you wouldn't make it through the gates and you know it."

Mehalco squared his stance and shrugged his arms tighter, buckling down on his stance with all the might he possessed. "Then I cannot tell you anything more."

Mathias flicked at the buckle of his sword and brought his eyes back to Mehalco, narrowing them keenly. "Cannot and will not do not mean the same thing."

The subtle warnings were not missed by Mehalco, and an annoying shiver raced up his spine. "Look. Mathias. *Friend*. Work with me here."

"I've been trying to."

Mehalco grabbed Mathias by the collar and pulled him to his face. "Demons who go talking about things like this *do not live much longer*." He stared hard into Mathias's serious eyes, this deeper fear of his trumping any reluctance he had of angering the paladin. "Got it?"

Mathias straightened his stance from where Mehalco's sudden move had pulled him forward and swatted the demon's hand off himself. "I'd get it much better if I understood why."

"That's not going to happen. At least not from me."

In all of the centuries Mathias had known Mehalco and learned how to bend him to his will, he had never experienced such difficulties with him. Reluctant to risk coming across as a snitch, yes. Determined to protect his pride or his people, yes. But never so tight-lipped as to not drop any further clues than what Mathias already knew about a situation. The idea of using threats—especially with the knowledge that a better part of him planned to actually follow through on them—was not a pleasant one for Mathias to make, but he was running out of options.

"You've already disclosed enough to pique my curiosity on the matter," Mathias said. "And you know I will get my answers, one way or another." He narrowed his eyes and rubbed his chin in contemplation. "If knowledge of this demon is truly so sensitive, I wonder how long you'd make it if I started asking people to elaborate on what little Mehalco already told me…?" He slid his eyes to the demon before him, both pleased and disheartened to see the color drain from the creature's pasty skin and the shadow of dread rise in his yellow eyes.

"You would stoop to blackmail?" Mehalco squeaked.

Mathias shrugged. "It wouldn't be stooping all that far in these circumstances, now would it?"

Mehalco held Mathias's gaze for moments that felt much longer than they must have been, disbelieving that, after all this time, the paladin would throw away the trust they'd built with each other. "You're treating me like I don't want to help you," Mehalco whispered.

"As far as I can tell, you don't."

Mehalco tried unsuccessfully to speak and half-turned from Mathias to make another sweeping appraisal of the streets, as though surveying the vicinity for an assassin. Sweat glistened on his forehead and his heart beat so strong, Mathias could clearly see his pulse thumping along his throat. Finally, after a few more paranoid searches of the vacant street, Mehalco dragged his gaze back to Mathias, his expression drooping with sickened defeat.

"I don't let any of mine cause trouble for your filthy Order," he said.

"No, you don't," Mathias agreed.

"I've let you know every single time I hear of something amiss as it applies to my kin in the hells."

"Yes, you do."

Encouraged by Mathias's agreement, Mehalco jabbed a finger at the paladin. "I even gave you information about that girlfriend of yours when it came through town, but I *cannot* tell you this."

Mathias had seen Mehalco afraid before; most every visit he made to Heiligate involved some degree of the demon's discomfort, but this was the first time he'd ever been able to consider his fear a genuine paranoia. Mathias suspected he could have resorted to torture and Mehalco would continue to refuse to talk. Just as Nessix had said, no living demon would speak of who Berann was and too many things were beginning to add up. Mathias raised a hand to cup it over Mehalco's and gently encouraged him to lower his arm.

"This really has you bothered, doesn't it?"

Mehalco gulped down the wad of fear which threatened to choke him, but answered without shame. "Yes."

"Because the truth of it will mean retribution far worse than anything a man like me would ever deliver." As Mathias buckled his sword back in its sheath, tears lined the lower lids of Mehalco's eyes as he bit into the insides of his cheeks to keep from frowning. "And you're not just afraid for yourself. That retribution would span beyond you, wouldn't it? To those who count on you for protection?"

Mehalco pinched his lips tighter and swiped a hand across his eyes, shifting anxiously as he cast his gaze away.

"I think I understand enough, friend," Mathias said gently. "Thank you."

Mehalco snapped his gaze back to Mathias, tears squeezing free as he mustered every last ounce of courage out of himself. "If anyone finds out—"

Mathias put a hand on the demon's shoulder. "Nobody will hear you've been covering my tab when I come through." He spoke the excuse loudly enough to divert the suspicions of any who might have been foolish enough to eavesdrop on them. "I'd never dream of causing you more trouble than I already do. Keep your eyes open and your ears sharp."

This still was a less than satisfactory resolution to the problem which Mathias had brought into town, but it beat literally every alternative Mehalco had thought was available to him two minutes ago. "You get back to your books," the demon answered. "The old ones. I don't know what all you've got access to, but…"

Mathias squeezed Mehalco's shoulder. "That's enough."

Mehalco gulped and lowered his head in relief and gratitude that the tension of this encounter had passed in a manner which had hopefully secured both their lives and their friendship before pulling out the wily façade he preferred to bluster toward Mathias when in the public eye. "Then get yourself out of my town!"

Mathias heaved a sigh, guilt creeping up on him for the distress and potential danger he'd brought to Mehalco. "You won't have to tell me twice." Eager to get back to Zeal and see how Nessix was faring, anyway, Mathias flashed his way out of the demon town, leaving Mehalco to sag against the barrel he'd been sitting on, head spinning at how serious matters had just become.

Mathias Sagewind had come asking about Berann, the one demon cleansed from their history. The ache of his hangover embraced him tightly as adrenaline and preoccupation with terror filtered out of his system, and Mehalco pressed the heel of his hand to his temple to stagger back to the tavern.

There wasn't enough mead in Heiligate or all the surrounding towns to wash this from mind.

FIFTEEN

When Nessix woke after being killed, it always happened abruptly, memories of her death—or Kol's—fresh in her mind. She much preferred that alarming sensation to what she crawled through to reach consciousness now. A sharp pain penetrated her shoulders and she shivered on a cold, hard floor, the stench of mildew and waste enhancing the pounding ache in her head. She pinched her closed eyes tight and groaned as her last recollections of the guards hauling her off came to her, but her mind was still too fuzzy to latch onto her concern as to whether or not Talier had escaped notice by the Council or any of those looking to kiss up to them.

She groaned again as the Council tumbled through her thoughts. Mathias had been right to warn her about their behavior, and it seemed as though she had chosen a very poor time to doubt his assessment.

"Mathias told me the two of you had been lovers."

Despite her aching head and the fuzzy thoughts muddling her brain, Nes's eyes flew open as Julianna's blunt question pierced through the ringing in her ears and echoed briefly off naked stone walls. The light was dim, a fact Nes's headache appreciated, the dull glow of a mounted torch the only illumination from the other side of the iron-barred door she was trapped behind.

The High Priestess stood a generous stride's length from the door, arms crossed as she looked down where Nessix lay sprawled on the floor. Nessix shoved herself into a seated position and returned the cold appraisal.

"Not that it's any of your business," Nessix muttered, pressing the heel of her palm to her throbbing temple. "But we had been."

Julianna's lip twitched at the notion, and she narrowed her eyes. *What was Mattie thinking…?*

Do you really want to know? Etha asked. *Because that seems a little inappropriate, given you're his sister and all…*

The scrutiny briefly flashed from Julianna's eyes at the goddess's crude and literal interpretation of her question, and she coughed to fight the flood of blush which raced toward to her cheeks.

Purpose of cooling her daughter's current aggression achieved, Etha gave her a gentler, more serious reply. *Nessix wasn't always this twisted bearer of a broken soul, you know.*

Julianna had spent the past several weeks failing to understand her brother's connection to this demon-perverted woman, and the past few days listening to the panicking Council's ignorant take on the developments surrounding Nessix had done little to help sway her opinions. Etha's reminder was an unwelcome source of rationale which brought Julianna back to her purpose of coming down into the dungeon to speak with Nessix without Henrik's antagonistic manipulations.

"And what were your intentions with him after you'd coaxed him into your bed?"

Nes's headache had matured into a more bearable driving pressure, no longer presenting as the irritating pulse which tried to bar her from functioning, and she lowered her hand. "Please, High Priestess…" she muttered with a halfhearted smirk and shake of her head. "I hadn't coaxed him anywhere. The invitation had been his."

Julianna's bid on authority shrank with the puckering of her lips as she faced yet another unwelcome development in the history Nessix and Mathias shared. "That makes little difference to me." Maybe voicing such an inaccurate statement would help her believe it a bit more. "But you will tell me your intentions."

The question slammed Nessix between the eyes, drawing out the faintest throb in her headache. When she'd gone to Mathias the night before Kol had killed her, she hadn't had any thoughts past that moment. She hadn't even been aware why she'd gone to him until they were already in bed, and from that point on, all that mattered to her was seeing the end of the war, of finding a time of peace for her people so she might have the opportunity to dream again with Mathias by her side. She'd been so close to seeing that fulfilled... so close to being able to be happy... and the demons had taken it all.

She looked away from Julianna, ducking her face toward her shoulder. "My intentions don't matter."

"That wasn't an answer."

Nessix bristled at Julianna's prompt reply, hating her for her arrogance and the ease with which she looked down on the only things Nessix held dear. She sprang to her feet, shaking off the wave of dizziness which accompanied the rapid movement as she strode up to the cell door. Determined to prove to this influential force in Mathias's life that she was strong enough to stand on her own, Nessix refrained from grabbing the bars. Julianna met the unshakeable firmness of her cold glower, held those devastated eyes rimmed with furious and frustrated tears which longed for an escape from this twisted fate which had found her. Nessix had never had the reason to petition to another woman for anything, and the faint wriggle of their common ground of caring for Mathias only served to increase her self-loathing as she spat the answer Julianna had so coldly demanded of her.

"I'd intended to *live*, High Priestess."

Julianna hadn't reacted to Nes's hasty approach, but her expression did twitch with a sympathy she hadn't expected to find as Nessix's words hit her. There *had* been a point when this woman had been a mortal, a time when she'd feared death more than she'd likely admitted. Julianna wasn't a cruel woman, just a skeptical one, and her shoulders slouched from their authoritative firmness as Nessix's words continued to appeal to those aspects which had led her to receive the title of High Priestess.

"I'd intended to see my people through that war and nothing else. But I failed to do that. I died. And now all I can do is try fixing what I'd left broken."

Julianna cleared the sympathy from her throat. "Broken like Mathias?"

There hadn't been the same sharp malice in that question as there had been when this interrogation began, but perhaps that made it that much harder for Nes to swallow. Mathias had done a terrible job hiding his distress from her these past few days. Between her inability to accurately convey what she felt for Kol and the trouble which had followed her to the surface, Nessix was painfully aware that she was a significant part of his frustrations. His loyalty to his Order and his sensibilities as a knight both told him to hate and distrust Nes as much as everyone else in Zeal did, and his speculations of her bond with Kol only gave him an easier time of it.

But he loved her. And because of that, all of his loyalties and sensibilities had amounted to nothing. His judgement was biased toward her, and there was no way to deny that. Maybe Kol and the Order were both right. Maybe there was no salvation for Nessix or her people, and maybe Mathias was simply too blinded by hope and stubborn optimism to see it. Nessix might not have meant for any of this to happen, but that didn't make it any less her fault.

Her knees retracted their assurance of stability, and Nessix grabbed the cell bars with her right hand as she shuffled half a step back into the shadows.

Julianna was a priestess, intimately in tune with the lives around her. Though there was a significant disconnect within Nes's divine threads, she couldn't help but soak in the remorse and helplessness radiating from the woman she'd invested so much energy into finding faults in. It was the first time Julianna had no other choice than to acknowledge the humanity in Nessix. No demon or derivative thereof would have hated themselves this much over mistakes of their past, least of all those which had brought harm to another, and Julianna had trouble continuing to convince herself to hate Nessix, even for the sake and safety of her foolish, lovestruck brother.

"It is best for both you and Mathias to keep in mind how your words and actions reflect on him," Julianna said at last. "I've seen my share of abominations in my time, and while I can't say I've ever seen anything like you before, the Council has made quite a few assumptions about you, as I'm sure you are aware."

Nessix dropped her hand from the bar and drifted back into the shadowed corner of her cell to lean against the stone wall. "Oh, I'm aware. And your damned Council is wrong."

"They often are," Julianna admitted freely, "but they are the ones who make the calls in Zeal."

Nessix gave a dry puff of a laugh, empty eyes cast on the grimy floor. "You and I both know better than that. Mathias does what he wants and I suspect you're prone to doing the same."

Julianna didn't often go up against dignitaries brave—or foolish—enough to call her on her mistakes. One of the highest ranking officials in all of Gelthin, nobody other than Mathias dared to speak to her the way Nessix so casually did, and it was equally infuriating and intriguing to be on this end of such conditioned confidence. Regardless, Julianna's purpose was to establish some degree of Nessix's obedience and respect to try to mitigate the damage done within the conference chamber, and she couldn't let her curiosity as to whether or not this woman was unafraid of her sway her in that mission.

"I honor the Council and its decisions," Julianna said, "for it is the foundation on which Zeal stands."

Nessix crossed her arms and lifted her eyes to challenge the priestess. "I thought your great Etha was the foundation on which Zeal stands? Seems rather blasphemous to put mortals' biased whims ahead of her will."

In the back of Julianna's mind, the goddess giggled. *For a woman who routinely disregards my presence, she does make a good point.*

Etha had stood up in Nessix's defense multiple times now, and Julianna was certain her goddess knew much about the woman's more distant past, but that didn't make the priestess appreciate her mischief right now. "You dare speak on behalf of my most revered Mother Goddess?" she scolded, squinting to try to make out what expression Nessix sent her way through the dark.

"I can only speak for myself," Nessix countered. "But I can tell you that something was watching over me on my journey here. Something kept me ahead of the demons and..." No matter how many times she thought it might be time to hold her breath and confess the sinful manner in which she'd funded her quest, Nessix couldn't quite admit it out loud, least of all to this powerful woman who she still hadn't developed trust in. "And those trying to impede my progress."

Julianna stepped closer to the cell and peered through the darkness to meet eyes which lurked with doubt and fear and a desperate longing to fix the wrongs of the world all on her own. It was an expression Julianna had seen often in her brother, an expression she wished she had the courage to don, herself, and suddenly, her resentment for this victim to the demons' ways seemed less like an abomination and more like a general—strong, but so tired—who would give her life and soul to protect those beneath her, every bit as honorable as Mathias. Seldom one to lose her tongue, Julianna was at a loss for words. Nessix truly did intend to stop the demons or die trying.

"You don't have to trust me," Nessix said to Julianna's silence. "You don't even have to like me. But I am still the only link anyone on the surface has to what the demons are doing in the hells, and you and your precious Council must hear what I have to say. There are thousands of people like me down there, priestess, a reluctant army which the demons plan to use as an undying force against those who oppose them. We are a small force, a green force, trapped within the hells to do the demons' bidding. Not one of us is pleased to be there, and we need help from those who can access divine aid to fix what has happened and to stop the demons from creating more of us."

Even after all of the impossibilities Julianna had faced in her time—the rising of the dead and the ascension of mortals to gods among them—she couldn't fathom the reality of this testament, but Nessix served as tangible evidence to her fears, confirming several of the signs the priestesses had observed and the connections their research had made. *Is she telling the truth, Etha?*

I believe her to be honest, Etha replied. *Though her unnatural qualities*

172

*make it impossible for me to tap into her thoughts under normal circumstances,
her stay in Mathias's chamber did convince me that even if there are flaws in
her report, she truly believes it for herself.*

Julianna frowned. Nessix's honesty—and the magnitude of
what it potentially meant for Abaeloth—complicated her position
in this matter immensely. Law-abiding to a fault, it was Julianna's
duty to support the Council's decisions, but Etha's will and her
intention for the world came before the desires of mortals.

"Please, priestess." Nes's soft words barely squeezed through
the darkness. "My life has never belonged to me. Let your Council
do what they will to me, but find a way to save my people. Find a
way to keep the demons from stealing more souls."

The woman who Julianna had come to hate for the crimes
made against her, the woman who she had convinced herself had
never been and would never be good enough to possess her
brother's heart, the woman who she had consciously allowed the
Council to pass judgement on before so much as speaking to her,
had just thrown the High Priestess against a wall. Nessix had been
goaded into her criminal actions, denied the chance to speak her
truths. If she'd been the vicious beast the Council had painted her
to be, she wouldn't be hiding in the shadows of her cell, softly
petitioning for the sake of those trapped in the demons' clutches.
Julianna had to admit, for the first time, that Mathias's demand that
no evil being would risk their own safety by willfully angering the
demons was true.

"What are your intentions with my brother, General?" Julianna
asked one last time, her voice reaching out with the intent to
understand and the willingness to accept.

Nessix closed her eyes and sank against the wall. "Convince
him to bust me out of here so he and I can save my people. That
seems to be my only option."

"And if you succeed at that?"

That same terrible question had echoed in Nes's mind since
she first woke up in the hells. It had been with her as her fondness
for Kol grew into loyalty and had accompanied her as she led
destruction and brought death across Gelthin. It had been a
pressing thought she'd slammed the door on ever since Mathias's

confession about being bound to Etha; he was a blessed man, and she was a cursed woman. There was still very little about the divine pathways which Nessix understood, but she couldn't imagine there was much of a future waiting for her and Mathias anymore.

"I don't know," she whispered, uncertain if her words even carried to Julianna. She lifted her gaze, grateful for the darkness that it might hide her anguish. "I haven't let myself think that far ahead."

There was a purity to tears, a raw energy which even demons and the undead could express from the frayed bits of divinity which they hadn't lost, and Julianna could no longer doubt Nessix's intentions, neither in Zeal nor with her brother's heart. It was an uncomfortable revelation, but most she had were.

Blessed Mother... she sighed. *How do I keep ending up in these positions...*

Etha said nothing, trusting Julianna already knew the answer.

"General Teradhel, I can do nothing to lighten your current sentence, but I will take to heart what you told me just now," Julianna said.

Relief slammed Nessix hard in the chest and though it didn't chase away her misery of suspecting she'd never find happiness, it did bring back a fistful of hope. She now had the support, or at least the understanding, of the two most powerful voices in all of the Order. She may still be condemned, but there might yet be salvation for her troops. That would have to be enough. "Thank you, High Priestess."

"And take my advice." Julianna stepped the rest of the way up to the bars so she could speak softer. "Keep yourself out of finding more trouble. Though your display of integrity seems to have gained you a handful of allies, you shook the Council quite thoroughly. Speak not unless spoken to, bear all scrutiny as though you are worthy of it and, for Etha's sake, before you or my brother try anything rash, let me attempt to work out a peaceful solution. You survived the demons, Nessix, and you've done an admirable job proving to me that you've maintained the bulk of your decency through their tortures. Do not allow mortals to take any more of it away from you than they already have."

174

It was advice Nessix hated to accept, but words she would be wise to follow. She'd been born into authority and had limited experience taking orders from others, but she'd recognized Julianna's previous malice, saw it for the worry that it was, and couldn't fault the priestess for how she'd behaved. After all, she was no less driven to protect those in her care than Nessix was.

Julianna turned and left the dungeon without looking back, and Nessix closed her eyes in the darkness. Whatever became of her, she'd succeeded in spreading word of her people's plight. It wasn't the heroic charge she'd fantasized about, but it was a start.

SIXTEEN

Thanks to Khin's invitation, Tristan had made himself comfortably at home in the branch of the Citadel's library focused on the history of the undead. Few patrons and even fewer true scholars had ventured near these stacks in the past several days, giving Tristan the freedom and ease to consume the volumes he needed. There were but two complications in his plans to uncover the method the demons had used to bring back the mortals they'd harvested. The first was that Etha's steady presence within the Citadel's blessed marble walls effectively barred Ceredulus from so much as reaching Tristan's thoughts. That was an unfortunate inconvenience, but one Tristan was comfortable working around. The second complication, however, was far more pressing and becoming increasingly distracting.

Tristan was hungry.

Clenching his teeth as the animalistic flaws of his kind screamed at him to remedy this problem, Tristan raised his eyes to the aisle Khin had just disappeared down. The last thing he could afford to do right now was frighten the girl. The fragile little human was his only way into the Citadel and his strongest shield against the Order. As simple as she was, the enchantment he held over her prevented her from connecting that he was anything other than a charming man, and Tristan planned to keep it that way as long as possible.

Which was why his waning strength concerned him so much.

So deep within the confines of those who would consider him an enemy off principle alone, Tristan needed every ounce of strength he could hold onto and for his senses to remain alert even when he was deeply engrossed in the research his god demanded of him. Edmund and his servants had fueled him well, but after his hasty trip from the Swift manor to Zeal and having spent from his defenses to remain functional in the daylight while hunting for Khin, he was weakening by the hour. None of the young priestesses or visiting patrons to the library were safe candidates for a feeding, and Ceredulus still had too many uses for Khin.

Pushed to the limits of his patience and hardly able to concentrate on his work for the demands of his hunger, Tristan shoved his current volume away and blew out a great sigh. Rising slowly to conserve his energy, he quietly stalked down the aisle where Khin strained on the tips of her toes to reach the book in her sights. Approaching her silently, Tristan pulled the book from the shelf for her, receiving an appreciative lowering of her eyes and embarrassed flush in return.

"I'm sorry," she murmured. "I told you I can't read many words. I'm finding your books as fast as I can."

The girl's pace at executing his requests had previously irritated Tristan, but it was now an unexpected boon for his purposes. He gave her a reassuring smile. "That is quite alright. I prefer a job done right than one rushed. Please keep with your work; I've got someone to meet with but will return shortly."

Khin's expression fell and she clutched the two books she'd gathered under her left arm to accept the one Tristan handed to her. "Do you want me to go with you?"

He shouldn't have conditioned her to look after him so well or worked so hard to enamor her. "You will serve me far better locating relevant tomes. I know where I am going and will not be long."

So used to being shoved aside, Khin was slow to release the tight pinch of her lips and allow the concern to drain out of her eyes. Her purpose right now was, after all, finding books that would be of interest to Tristan's studies. Her illiteracy was already making that search take longer than it should, and this distraction he'd found might let her catch up with his requests. Finding a smile that didn't seem quite genuine enough, Khin nodded her acceptance of the orders.

"Very good." Tristan reached forward and brushed his fingers across the girl's cheek, softening her reluctance even further. "Thank you for your dedication." His gentle compliment left Khin's tongue in knots and her heart skipping about, resulting in the silence Tristan had hoped for, and he left the library with nothing else.

He used great care in navigating the halls of the Citadel, avoiding the passage to the temple and carrying himself with the same arrogant authority of every other nobly dressed individual inside. It had been centuries since he'd last been inside the Citadel, back in the days when he'd been a young mortal following his father, but the layout of the great building had remained unchanged, and vampires had superior memories.

Tristan wound his way out of the halls of meeting chambers and the offices of the officials, and headed toward the wing which housed the Order's military. Wary, but hiding it well, he threw his shoulders back another inch, raised his chin, and didn't hesitate to meet the eyes of those knights and apprentices who looked his way, seamlessly conveying to them that he knew where he was going and that he was entitled to be there. The ploy worked, and Tristan soon made it to his last obstacle, the prison's guards.

The upper hall of this part of the Citadel detained prisoners of political esteem—dignitaries who got offended by their peers and offered an untimely slap, their sons who got too drunk at banquet—and Tristan didn't waste his time entertaining what delicious noble he might find there. Instead, he nodded a short acknowledgement to the four guards flanking the entrance of the hallway, and descended the stairs on his left.

The first flight down was as heavily guarded as the first, reserved for those prisoners serving simple sentences and awaiting brisk wrist slaps. The next floor down had but two guards and housed those criminals who were booked for an extended stay in corrective confinement. The third floor down, however, had but one bored guard who leaned against the wall beside a rune-etched door, warded to keep those whose names were posted on it from exiting. This floor imprisoned the worst of Zeal's offenders, those sentenced for execution, and it was where Tristan would find a victim nobody would care to find dead.

It took him reaching the last stair and taking two steps forward for the guard to shake off his boredom and come to attention.

"Halt, sir." The guard held a hand out to reinforce his order. "This is a restricted block and I cannot permit you entry."

Tristan raised his brows in mock outrage, sweeping a quick glance at the door to snag a name before appraising the reluctant shrinking of the guard's posture. "Fool. Do you not know who I am?"

The guard swallowed the insult and his reaction to Tristan's scowl. After all, he was armed and protected by armor. This haughty nobleman was outwardly without weapons and vulnerably dressed in the garb better suited for those of the spoiled life. "I don't much care who you are. This is a restricted block, and I cannot permit you entry."

Tristan sucked his teeth and crossed his arms, narrowing his eyes at the guard as he shook his head. "I am the very lord responsible for throwing Harman Ives in this dreadful pit. Are you telling me I do not have the right to interrogate the one who had wronged me?"

The lie was a gamble, but had been spoken just convincingly enough for the young guard to glance away. "Oh…" he breathed. "L-lord Forlith…?"

Prepared to defend himself if the guard was setting a trap of his own, Tristan uncrossed his arms and held them to his sides. "One and the same."

To Tristan's relief, the guard gave a halfhearted chuckle and backed away a step. "Forgive me, my lord. It's been a busy day down here and we're all a bit on edge."

"Well that is not good at all," Tristan said. "You should try to find some time to relax, get some rest."

The guard heaved a dreamy sigh and squeezed out half a smile. "Yeah," he said. "That'd be nice."

"Yes," Tristan agreed, softening his tone. "It would. Sleep."

Tired and pliable, the guard collapsed in a heap. Tristan caught the dropped polearm before it had the chance to do any harm to its master and gently laid it on the ground, removing the key ring from the guard's belt as he stood once again.

He didn't bother using caution entering the dungeon; he'd made it past everyone who would have tried to stop him, and even if these prisoners were dangerous, they were secured behind sturdy locks and Tristan was confident they'd have their fight cut out for them if they engaged him, even in his depleted state. The hallway was dimly lit by torchlight and broad enough for a prisoner and each of his flanking guards to pass through with enough clearance to avoid the reach of vengeful prisoners. Tristan far favored this drab and dismal environment to the radiance of the main body of the Citadel, and felt more at ease here than he had since he'd first charmed Khin to welcome him inside.

His intention was to go to the last cell on the block to minimize his odds of alarming the prisoners he intended to leave alive. His urge to feed, his thirst for the strength which mortal blood would give him, hastened his stride and twice, a momentary pull of hesitation urged him to stop at the nearest cell simply to satiate himself sooner. He pushed past those primal urges; though he'd be able to protect himself, he couldn't afford to be discovered and chased out of the Citadel. With that in mind, he didn't let himself hesitate again until he passed the most peculiar prisoner.

Tristan had been so focused on ignoring the pull of mortal blood that it took the gentle pulse of an undead's soul, broken though it was, for Tristan to hesitate a third time. The urgency in his gait had almost made him pass the cell completely before the familiarity snagged him, but when it struck, he stopped all forward momentum, turned his attention to his left, and slowly backtracked to face the cell.

It had been Tristan's understanding that all undead had been purged from the reaches of Abaeloth, sealed within the Veil, or in the rare cases such as himself, buried to await Ceredulus's call. But behind the bars of this cell was a young woman of elven descent, pacing away an agitation Tristan related to well, and every bit as unnatural walking the mortal realm as he was. Intrigued by this discovery, having been unaware that the Order would have kept one of his peers imprisoned for so long, Tristan took a step closer to observe the woman more carefully.

She didn't acknowledge him, not even flicking a glance his way, but the enhanced clench of her jaw did convey that she knew he was there. She changed the path of her pacing so she could move closer to the back wall of her cell and deeper into the shadows cast by the torch mounted adjacent to her door. And all the while, Tristan studied her, absorbing all he could so he could ask Ceredulus why he hadn't told him he'd had an ally in the Citadel all along. She moved with the fluid grace of a warrior, but not that of a vampire, and more interesting still was the fact that where vampires' souls had been turned over to the safekeeping of Sergulion, the Abaeloth-bound lord of their kind, this woman still claimed possession of at least a portion of hers.

"Aren't you exquisitely made..." Tristan murmured, taking yet another step closer and hoping to entice her to step into the light.

She flung a scathing glare his way, but stopped both her pacing and her rapidly degrading opinion of Tristan when she saw the curiosity and admiration in his hazel eyes. She looked him over a moment longer, then scoffed and resumed her pacing.

Tristan chuckled at her reaction. "Settle your nerves, sister. I am a friend."

That stopped her again. "Sister?" She spat the word with the venom Tristan had expected to hear from an imprisoned undead, but also with an authority which initially triggered his instinct to obey her.

Ceredulus... Tristan knew there was no point in calling on his god from inside the Citadel, but every honed instinct within the vampire told him he'd stumbled across something vital for Ceredulus to be made aware of. *I believe I've found something of interest...*

"My eyes see truths most others miss," Tristan said, "and right now, they see a woman who has been brought back from the dead.

Thus, you are kin to me."

Her eyes flashed with a sensation Tristan almost considered hope, and she stepped up to the door at last. He stood patiently as she looked him over, watching her with the same intensity she studied him with, trying to solve the puzzle that was her fragmented soul before he was forced to inquire about it. She stuck her arm through the bars and pressed her hand to the center of his chest, an action he allowed as her fingers burrowed against the soft folds of his shirt. Her brows leveled in irritated disappointment, and Tristan reached his hand up to gently encase her fingers.

"Might I—"

She promptly flung his hand off of hers, scoffed, and retreated back into her cell. With an agitated shake of her head, she continued pacing. "You are not kin to me," she muttered.

Tristan cocked his head and pressed his own fingers to where hers had dug at him. "But you do not argue that you are undead?"

She bristled notably at that word and didn't look back at him.

How very curious… "You are in denial of the gift which was given to you?"

Those words stopped her cold in her tracks and she spun on Tristan, stalking briskly up to the door of her cell. Being a vampire, he could have easily evaded her hands as they shot out between the bars and grabbed fistfuls of his coat to pull him closer, but he was more curious to see what she'd do once she had a hold of him.

"The *gift*?" she seethed, eyes fierce enough to suggest to Tristan that perhaps she had powers he hadn't expected. She shoved him back a step and completed another pass through the cell before stalking up to the bars once again. "Who put you up to this?"

"Put me up…?" Tristan raised a hand to his chin as he studied Nessix in all of her self-sustaining strength and splendor. "A… My lord. His name is Ceredulus."

She rolled her eyes and resumed her pacing. "So what rank and title does that prick hold?"

Tristan gasped at her disrespect and fought down the urge to demand she amend her tone. After all, Ceredulus had been all but erased from modern history, and if this undead woman didn't know and respect his name, that meant she was quite possibly a direct link to the exact phenomenon his god had ordered him to look into. Finding her compliant side would be far more beneficial than correcting her tongue.

"Who brought you here?"

"The guards," Nessix spat.

Tristan chuckled and rested his weight on one leg. "Who brought you back to life? That's not a practice that's supposed to be going on anymore."

"Yeah?" she flung a scathing glare at him, shame and hatred contorting what must have otherwise been an attractive face. "Well, there are those who don't give a damn what's supposed to happen."

Tristan cocked his head. "Was it demons?"

The woman jarred to an abrupt stop and stalked up to Tristan again, though this time she stayed out of his reach. "Who are you?"

"My name," he said with a charming smile, "is Lord Tristan Swift." He reached his open hand through the bars. "And even if I am not kin to you, we are very much the same."

Nessix stared at his extended hand and crossed her arms. "Well, Lord Tristan Swift, I am General Nessix Teradhel of Elidae, and I highly doubt we are remotely the same."

General Nessix... of Elidae... A spark of excitement briefly tugged at Tristan, begging him to wrap up his business here so he could report this finding to Ceredulus, but centuries of patience prevented him from acting so hastily.

"Why would an esteemed general such as yourself be in prison?" Tristan asked.

Nessix hissed and rolled her eyes. "Because that damn Council is full of idiots."

Tristan smirked. "I won't argue with that." He watched her a moment longer, enchanted by her movement and comparatively endless source of energy. "I've got a bit of business to tend to down…" he leaned back from the bars to look deeper into the cell block and waved his hand in that general direction. "Down there. But when I'm through, how would you like me to spring you out of there?"

Nessix froze at the offer. She'd have liked it very much, if not for the hunch that it would only buy her more trouble. Besides, she still wasn't convinced this Lord Tristan Swift wasn't affiliated with the Council and thus planning on setting her up.

"I'm here awaiting trial," she answered. "And I intend to represent myself when that time comes."

Tristan winced, his brows tipping toward each other in sympathy. He'd been one of Ceredulus's officers during the Undead War and he'd seen the sorts of punishments this city boasting of justice and goodness delivered to his kind. "You're *sure* you don't want me to get you out of there? Any trial you will receive here in Zeal will not end painlessly for you."

"That's fine." The declaration was much simpler for Nessix to say than it was for her to believe. "I've staked my honor on this trial and will prove it, one way or another."

Tristan looked Nessix over once more, a pitying frown puckering his lips and wrinkling the fair skin between his thin brows. "Suit yourself," he said grimly. "I'll be out by the gallows when it's time for them to think they're executing you. We can talk more then." He gave her an apologetic shrug and resumed walking down the hall as if nothing had happened.

Only after Tristan had faded to nothing more than a shadow did Nessix step the rest of the way to the door to press her face against the bars to look after him.

* * * * *

Tristan had passed all of the barred cells to reach the end of the hallway which housed the prisoners condemned to solitary confinement. Tiny slats were cut into the heavy wooden doors at eye level, and only a few of the prisoners peeked out at him, their expressions ranging from terror to ferocious malice. He ignored them all, unmoved by their motives, until he reached the very last door. He had no idea nor care who occupied the cell he was about to open and went straight to work sorting through the keys to find the one which fit this particular lock.

A pair of empty blue eyes flashed into the tiny portal as the keys jingled on the ring, and though Tristan felt their pressure bearing down on him, he paid their silent threats and promises no heed.

"You alone?" came the inquiry of a deep voice.

Tristan sighed dramatically and tried the next key. "I am."

A chuckle ricocheted off the stone walls of the cell. "They sent a pretty boy like you to fetch me?"

The next key fit the lock perfectly and before Tristan tried it, he looked up to meet the prisoner's cold eyes. "I came to see you to your death." He twisted the key in the lock, and the hollow clunk of the bolt sliding out of place echoed through the relative silence of the cell block.

Before Tristan had moved his hand from the key, the prisoner shoved the door open, slamming the solid wood into Tristan's face. The blow would have dazed a mortal of Tristan's stature, but it only served to enrage a starving vampire. Weakened or not, he was still stronger than an atrophied man, and even as the prisoner leaped forward with hands reached out to grab him, Tristan darted forward with superhuman speed, wrapping one hand around the prisoner's throat, and driving him back to the far wall of the cell.

The prisoner grunted at the impact, but Tristan's grip was tight enough that he couldn't suck in ample breath to gasp. A weaker willed man, one who was less of a psychopath, might have been afraid at this moment, but this prisoner calmly reached his arms around Tristan to wrap him in a great hug to accept the attack, meeting Tristan's hungry eyes with an equal intensity.

His efforts stopped as Tristan's smooth voice spoke a single order. "Freeze."

Having degraded both mentally and physically during his imprisonment, the man had no defenses against the power of Tristan's command. He tried to overcome the impulse to stop the attack, his arms trembling as he fought to will his muscles to obey him and when that failed, he realized he couldn't even let his limbs drop to his sides. Tristan held the man's throat a moment longer, ecstatic at the rate in which his prey's pulse was climbing with fear, and once that heart was beating fast enough to ensure an easy meal, Tristan leaned lower still.

"Silence," he ordered. It would do no good at all to stir up the rest of the cell block with the man's curses or screams.

Only after the order had been delivered did Tristan remove his hand from his prey's neck so he could properly feed.

* * * * *

Mathias's visit to Heiligate hadn't made him any more confident in his limited knowledge of what was going on than before, but at least he'd be able to look Nes in the eye and tell her he believed she was on to something in regards to Berann's influence over the demons. Hoping to avoid causing her any more grief than he was sure she'd already made for herself, he opted to return to his chamber rather than popping back into the conference hall on his return to the Citadel. He still intended to get a full report on what was discussed, but wouldn't give Henrik any other excuses to be more of a belligerent clod than he already was.

Actively sorting through the few details he knew about Berann's relevance as it applied to Zeal's history and adding to them Mehalco's bizarre behavior and Nes's reports, Mathias descended the spire stairs. It was obvious the demon had known something his kin had considered threatening, but what had it been? Something as simple as spoiling battle tactics would have been cause for the demons to celebrate his death and cite him as an example, not instill strict protocol meant to erase him from history. Could the demons have been planning to develop the akhuerai so long ago? To the best of Mathias's knowledge, no mortal had even begun entertaining the idea of such feats, and Ceredulus hadn't even been born at that time.

Mathias had intended for his talk with Mehalco to clarify at least a few of his questions on the matter, but it ended up bringing him more. Before he had the chance to allow himself to dwell over these new ones, Talier's frantic voice greeted him from the landing.

"Mathias, Nessix needs your help."

The door slammed shut on all of those contemplations and curiosities as a far more immediate emergency was thrust into Mathias's hands. "What happened?" he asked, taking the last several stairs two at a time.

"There was a lot of shouting and next thing I knew, a whole army of guards stormed out of that meeting hall, dragging Nessix with them. She told me to find you and then they knocked her out and took her away."

Mathias, still mindful of the unnatural aspects of this nervous man, wanted to insist he'd been mistaken, but with the Council and Nes's temper, he was rather confident it was the whole truth, or at least all of it Talier had been privy to. "Do you know what they did with her?"

Talier gulped. He wasn't certain, at least not yet, but he could track her down. "I know the direction they went, but... um... ducked out before anyone could identify me." He flushed and lowered his gaze, cringing from Mathias as though he expected to be beaten for his sensible actions.

Mathias grasped Talier's shoulder and firmly pushed him into motion. "A direction is good enough to get me started, and you were wise to make yourself scarce. I'd venture a guess that more than one of those guards went back to look for you after Nes called to you for help."

Talier gulped again as he staggered to catch his balance, fear beating out his guilt well enough that he was able to raise his misty eyes to Mathias's. "But I've done nothing wrong." When would he quit being wanted by powers he had no way of fighting?

"Yeah, well, neither has Nessix." Mathias let those words hang in the air between them for a moment, letting them grow stale and frail. "At least I hope she hasn't."

Talier gave a flimsy shrug. "Like I said, I... I don't know what happened to get her in trouble, just that she ended up there."

"Then let's not waste any more breath discussing it." It wasn't often Nessix asked for help, which led Mathias to some rather unpleasant conclusions.

Talier nodded and turned from Mathias to begin tracking the familiarity of Nes's scent. Neither man spoke as they hastened down the halls, Talier too afraid of what he'd let happen and Mathias too preoccupied with what he planned to say to the Council. By the time they reached the eastern wing of the Citadel, Mathias was quite sure he knew what sort of trouble Nes had landed herself in. When Talier balked as he realized they were about to reach the prison, Mathias stopped.

"I can find her from here," he said. "Go put yourself back in your room and act like you don't know what happened."

Talier looked down the hall housing cells and then back at Mathias. He wasn't particularly keen on listening, still stuck trying to work out how he'd explain any of this to Kol when the demon inevitably caught up with him, but eventually relented to Mathias's demands. After all, Mathias was right. There was too high a chance that the guards would be interested in silencing him if he intended to aid a prisoner.

"Will you let me know when she's okay?" he asked, hoping this chain of events would be enough to convince Nessix that she wasn't safe in this holy city so they could leave and he could get them both on the track he needed them to be on.

"As soon as I'm able," Mathias said, wondering when that would be.

Talier stared at him a moment longer, unsure how much he could trust this man who he'd been told to avoid at all costs. Realizing he had no other option, at least in this case, he darted off to the main body of the Citadel. Mathias didn't watch him leave, instead heaving a great sigh before proceeding into the dungeon. One of these days, he'd have to learn how to convince Nessix to try travelling the easy route.

Mathias raged off like a silent storm and it had been fortunate for Talier that he'd been dismissed and thus able to avoid getting caught up in it. Every guard assigned to this wing of the Citadel's prison had been ordered to keep Mathias from gaining access to any part of the cells, but each time one approached him to enforce that order, they shriveled beneath the fury in his eyes and decided they'd much rather receive a formal reprimand worked through the Council than an immediate one delivered by Mathias's interpretation of justice.

When Mathias reached the dungeon floor and found the guard slouched on the ground, snoring, he sneered and saw himself into the dim hall.

"Nes?" he called, unafraid of making a scene, as he'd already done enough of that getting here.

"Sagewind!"

Relief flooded into Mathias's chest as he hurried to the sound of Nes's voice and he found her pressed to the bars of her cell, one arm reached out to him. He took her hand as soon as he was in reach and deftly pressed his lips to her fingers.

"What did you get yourself into this time?"

Nessix heaved a sigh and tilted her head back. "You were right about your Council's sensibilities, I can tell you that much."

Mathias wished he'd have been able to laugh at that. "What happened?"

"The loud guy… Henrik challenged me to a duel, but—"

Mathias's expression drooped instantly, his hope sputtering out like a pathetic campfire in a sudden downpour. "And you *accepted?*"

"Well… yes." She gave a little shrug. "What else was I supposed to do?"

Mathias groaned and shifted his weight from foot to foot. "I left you there unarmed on purpose. Where did you find a sword?"

"I—" Nessix cut herself off and awkwardly glanced away, preemptively shriveling beneath Mathias's coming disapproval. "I drew one off a guard," she mumbled.

Nessix held her shoulders close to her neck and sheepishly worked her jaw as Mathias dropped her hand so he could cover his mouth to stifle a louder groan. After a deep breath to brace himself, Mathias asked the most pressing question. "At any point during your audience did anyone declare it as High Council?"

She bit down on the inside of her cheek and nodded, prompting Mathias to throw his hand down to his side and take a step away to turn around. Apparently, that hadn't been the answer he'd wanted to hear.

"Damn it, Nes…" he whispered as he turned back to her. "Brandishing a weapon at High Council is punishable by death."

Nessix snorted and snuck a glance down the hall to where Tristan had gone before her distraught paladin's fidgeting drew her back to the more immediate issue. "Fine. Let them punish me by death"—she exaggerated the sentence as though mocking its severity—"and toss my corpse out the city walls. Maybe then we can actually accomplish something."

"This isn't a joke, Nes!"

"I can see that." She gripped the cell bars and gave them a stout shake for emphasis. "I'm the one in the cage."

Mathias moaned his frustration and leaned forward to cram his forehead against the cool support of the bars. He'd known better than to agree to let the Council speak to Nes. He'd known better than to leave her alone with them. There might still be a way to get her out of this predicament but, Etha, his mind was already stretched too thin…

Uh oh…

Mathias pinched his eyes shut and held back his frustrated sob at Etha's ominous input. *Could you hold off on the uh ohs…?* he begged. *Just for a little bit. Please?*

Oh, I really, really *wish I could, but it's not an uh oh from* me… the goddess said grudgingly.

"I'm going to be fine, Mathias," Nessix told him gently. "But there's a slightly… bigger concern on my mind than your Council's idiocy."

"A bigger concern than your pending execution?"

Nessix fit him with a scolding glare. "I was promised a trial first."

Continuing to debate the Council's shoddy practices with Nessix would make no difference in her outcome or outlook at this point, and so Mathias settled for a tired sigh. "Alright. What's your concern?"

"How many prisoners… like… me are kept down here?"

That was a strange question. "You're the only akhuerai Zeal has ever seen. It's why everyone's so scared of you."

Nessix shook her head and pulled herself up against the bars so she could lower her voice. "There was a pretty man who introduced himself as Lord Tristan Swift who stopped by my cell and called me his sister on… on account of me having been brought back from the dead."

A sudden chill slid over Mathias and his breath grew quicker. That was a name and blunt description he'd been happy to have left well in his past.

I told you uh oh... Etha whispered.

"He offered to break me out of here," Nessix continued, "after he took care of some other business. Could there be other... undead"—she struggled to use that word in association with herself, the first good sign Mathias had received all day—"down here he might be trying to set free?"

If only it were that simple... "There's no other undead kept down here," he muttered, leaning back to look deeper down the hallway. "Has he come by again?"

"No."

Mathias allowed himself a hushed curse, his pinched lips becoming more of a grimace the longer he thought this over. It did seem about the right time for Ceredulus to throw a complication in what fragile plans he'd scraped together. Mathias glanced back at Nessix and she gave him a smile, the same one which she'd used to rally her troops on Elidae. He doubted she had any way to know the danger lurking deeper in this hall, but neither had she fully realized the extent of the demons' strengths in those early battles. All she knew was that Mathias was rumored to be a hero, and so that was the role he would fill.

"I'll be right back," he grumbled and turned to march stealthily down the hall.

"I'll be waiting right here," she called in reply.

* * * * *

Tristan lounged beside the limp corpse in a euphoric stupor, rolling his lips between his teeth to run his tongue along the residual taste of blood, savoring the way the vital energy he'd taken from the prisoner saturated his muscles as he waited for the full effect of his meal to settle into him. He was so relaxed, so refreshed, and so lost in his satisfaction that he missed the sound of quiet footsteps coming down the hall until the jingle of the key ring separating from the lock alerted him to the presence of a blond man with jaded green eyes who glared down at him with the prejudice of an entire nation. That feeling of peace quickly fled

Tristan, and he shoved himself to his feet.

"What are you doing in here?" Mathias growled, resting his hand on the hilt of his sword.

Tristan glanced at the gesture, then met Mathias's eyes again. He'd only ever seen the White Paladin from afar, but he'd been given enough warnings about what happens when one of his kind attempted to engage this holy man to think twice about attacking him. "I was ridding your fair city of a violent criminal," Tristan said smoothly, gesturing to the dead man at his feet.

Mathias pitied those who made it down to the dungeon, but these prisoners—save Nessix, of course—had earned their punishments. This fact didn't make him any more pleased to hear that the dead man, gray from the lack of blood, had been killed for the benefit of a vampire.

"That's not what I meant." Mathias flicked open the buckle on his scabbard for the second time today. "What are you doing in the Citadel?"

"Research, Sir Sagewind." Tristan, though he knew to be wary around this particular opponent, maintained his calm. As long as he still had answers Mathias was after, he trusted the paladin would not act against him with force. "You must be aware of the goings on affecting the balance of the mortal world." He flashed Mathias a devious grin as he thought of Nessix down the hall. "I've heard rumors that you've got quite a personal interest in these events."

That was far from the most aggressive goading Mathias had tolerated of late, and he brushed it off accordingly. "To whose benefit are you conducting your research?"

Tristan kept that sly smile on his face and lowered his eyes modestly before sending a challenging glance back at Mathias. "Certainly one such as yourself doesn't need to ask such a trivial question."

"And what have you uncovered for your vile lord?"

Tristan chuckled. "I do not have a vile lord, Sir Sagewind."

"Since when did your kind stray from Ceredulus?"

"We've not strayed," Tristan assured, "but it would be wise of you to extend some amount of grace toward my *generous* lord if you want his help."

192

"I don't need his help."

Though Tristan remained cornered in the cell, he shifted his gaze in Nes's direction. "So you've already determined what happened to your pretty little general?"

Mathias bristled, hating how many people had leverage over him due to Nes's misfortune. "Have you?"

Tristan straightened his sleeves and took a slow step closer to Mathias. "If I had, I'd have already gone to report it to—"

"Then you're of no use to me."

Tristan stopped and threw his narrow shoulders back. "*Excuse* me?"

"You are of no use to me," Mathias repeated, "and as such, you have no purpose here."

That euphoric flush faded from Tristan's pale cheeks as Mathias's intentions dawned on him.

Mathias chuckled at the vampire lord's stunned expression, enjoying his advantage over the situation immensely after so long at the mercy of politics. "As long as a Sagewind is present within the Citadel, I hereby declare that you, Tristan Swift, are unwelcome within these walls."

Even rich with power, Tristan could not shrug off the instant pull of Mathias's order. He grit his teeth, clenched fists shaking at his sides as his legs moved of their own accord toward the cell door. Mathias stepped aside to allow the vampire to pass. As Tristan came up next to him, he hissed against the effort but managed to pause.

"Might I at least bid my host farewell?" he seethed through clenched teeth.

Mathias had a special kind of hatred for vampires. Though he'd discovered methods of causing them great harm, he and Etha had yet to find a way for him to permanently dispose of these abominations and, unlike the demons, who'd had their terrible, twisted fates forced upon them by immature gods, vampires had chosen their paths to corruption entirely on their own. Even in this moment, with so much on his mind, Mathias wanted few things more than to deny Tristan his request, if not for the fact that indulging it would lead him directly to who needed to be held

193

responsible for the crime of welcoming a vampire into Etha's sanctuary. Perhaps he'd even be able to negotiate Nes's release by uncovering this culprit.

"Very well," Mathias granted. "But I will accompany you, and you will be quick about it."

The leniency Mathias had just agreed to allowed Tristan's muscles to relax from the forceful tug and he smiled in satisfaction, disregarding Mathias's disgust at the expression. "You are far kinder than my peers had suggested, Sir Sagewind."

"Then get going and don't give me a reason to prove otherwise."

Tristan chuckled quietly and shook his head before continuing down the hallway. Mathias stayed close at his heels, prompting the vampire to keep his ears trained behind himself in anticipation of an attack which never came. They proceeded in silence, Mathias giving Nessix a warning look to demand her silence as they passed, while Tristan allowed his inquisitive gaze to linger on her, giving her a quick wink before Mathias pushed him along. The two men continued in this manner back into the main halls of the Citadel, ignoring the startled and curious glances which followed their procession. And they were silent still as Tristan led the way into the library and predictably turned toward the branch which held the tomes of the undead.

What Mathias hadn't predicted, however, was Khin scuttling out from between the shelves, thin arms stretching to their limits as she pressed a thick stack of books against her chest. Her smile was radiant, her eyes brighter than Mathias had ever seen them and as Tristan hesitated to fling an arrogant smirk in his direction, Mathias's falling heart ignited with rage.

"You son of a bitch!" Mathias spun Tristan around, directing a clenched fist at the beautiful man's smug face.

Khin stifled a scream, her armful of books falling to the floor as she moved both hands to cover her mouth, but Tristan, revitalized from his feeding, caught the paladin's fist with a sharp hiss of disapproval before it had the chance to flatten his nose.

"That is not very polite, Sir Sagewind."

Emboldened by Tristan's presence and comforted by his

apparent control of the situation, Khin glared at Mathias. "What are you doing? He is my guest!"

Mathias jerked his hand free from Tristan's grasp and ran it through his hair as he bit back a bitter chuckle. "*You* are a guest in the Citadel, Khin. You are not authorized to bring in those you find on the street."

"He told me he needed to do research to help with this great cause you've been trying so hard to figure out." Her eyes narrowed and she sneered at the flustered paladin. "Maybe you don't want him here because you're afraid he'll make you look bad by finding the answers you can't."

Tristan smirked and looked away but was wise to keep his laughter hidden. He suspected if Mathias was going to use any amount of aggressive force against him, he'd have done so by now, but that didn't mean it was a good idea to encourage it.

Mathias balled up a fist and shook it at his side, shifting a step away from Khin as he drew a deep breath to force into himself what passed for calm. He raised his heated, suspicious glare at the smirking vampire. "Oh, I very much suspect he has the answers I need."

"Sir Sagewind," Tristan said with feigned humility, "as you can see by the number of books Khin has fetched for me, I have yet to scratch the surface of my hunt. And I must assure you there are many questions regarding these events Khin speaks of still plaguing the minds of those I represent."

The casual reminder of Ceredulus's position in all of this shoved Mathias to his breaking point. He'd tried to spare Khin the cruelty of the truth, but she and her undead companion were making it impossible for him to continue to do so. "Do you know what Tristan is?" he asked the girl.

"He's been more of a friend to me the past couple of days than you have," Khin spat.

Tristan eyed Mathias slyly. His ploy might be up, but he was pleased on all accounts by Khin's firm defense of his character. He sighed dramatically and crossed his arms, turning his attention to the young woman to gauge her response to the coming news.

Mathias stepped closer to Khin so he could lower his voice

from his frustrated shouting in case other ears lurked nearby. "He is a vampire."

A pinch of color drained from the girl's cheeks and her eyes widened with the shock both men had expected, but the expression quickly passed, and she set her jaw in determination. "And?"

Tristan let his arms fall back to his sides, pleased with Khin's response. His careful work in infiltrating and influencing her mind had paid off nicely.

"And there are laws dictating the manner which the undead are to be regarded," Mathias said, exasperated.

Tristan tapped his lips and hummed. "But, Mathias, aren't you and that lovely creature I met in the dungeon, by definition, undead as well?"

Khin raised her brows haughtily as she considered Tristan's educated observation. She crossed her arms and raised her chin high enough to show a single gulp which was the only tell of her concern. "You vowed to keep me safe," she added stubbornly, "so why should I be afraid of those laws?"

Mathias cast a hasty glance at the entryway and clenched his fists tighter to keep from grabbing Khin by the shoulders to shake her. "I cannot protect you from these laws, Khin. Nobody can. Not me, not Julianna, and certainly not him." He nodded in Tristan's direction.

"Then don't tell anyone," Khin reasoned. "Tristan has been here for two days and hasn't caused anyone any trouble yet."

"Hasn't caused any trouble…" Mathias muttered beneath his breath.

"It *would* be such a shame," Tristan added smoothly, "for your name to get tangled up with mine, now wouldn't it, Mathias?" As Mathias continued to glower at the vampire, rapidly forming his next demand to drive Tristan out of the Citadel, Tristan turned back to Khin. "I thank you from the depths of my soul for helping me as much as you have, Khin, but as there *are* laws dictating how Sir Sagewind must treat me, there are laws which I, too, must obey. My welcome has been revoked, and I must honor that."

As much as Mathias wanted to be relieved by Tristan's willingness to leave, Khin's furious glare prevented him from enjoying it.

"But what about your studies?" Khin demanded. "You said they were important."

Tristan smiled in a patient, fatherly manner Mathias saw right through, but Khin ate it up. "My studies will continue, with or without a Sagewind's blessing," Tristan said. "My lord would have it no other way."

Mathias didn't like the way that sounded, but without access to the Citadel's libraries, Tristan would have a difficult time obtaining the sort of information he was likely after. He now had only one other concern on this matter. "And you will leave Khin out of the rest of your intentions, too."

Tristan's brows flattened in a perturbed glower. "Now, Sir Sagewind. She is her own woman, deserving of making her own decisions. Certainly, you can respect that?"

The vampire was laying a brilliantly baited trap, but one Mathias refused to step into. "You were ordered to leave the Citadel, Tristan Swift."

Tristan had been able to brush off the first command after Mathias had granted him the reprieve for this little visit, but he was unable to withstand a reiteration of it. Either way, the seeds of doubt had been planted in Khin, and he considered that victory enough. Legs moving on the compulsion of Mathias's instructions, Tristan barely managed a cordial nod to Khin, and turned to exit the library. Mathias followed to the doorway and carefully studied the vampire's rigid motions as he moved toward the exit of the Citadel. Convinced of the effectiveness of his order and that it would see Tristan out into the streets, Mathias allowed himself that relieved sigh at last.

"He's right, you know."

Khin's voice stabbed at Mathias's back, and though a flutter of irritation woke inside Mathias, he also recognized the chance of gaining insight to what Tristan had learned over the past two days. "About what?"

"I *am* my own woman and I *do* deserve to make my own decisions."

That hadn't been quite the revelation Mathias had wanted to

hear from her, and he swallowed his blunt retort. "I have never said otherwise."

Khin crossed her arms and narrowed her eyes. "He has been kind to me. He's never once told me he had more important things to tend to. He gave me a purpose, not just busywork, and he promised me my family, not just hope."

Anger wrapped around that irritation at the cruel manner which Tristan had manipulated Khin. She'd fallen for his charms, assuring that any direct attack Mathias made on what the vampire had told her would only drive her closer to him, and Mathias didn't have the time to properly sort through this fiasco. "He cannot be trusted."

"And *you* can?"

Mathias clenched his jaw, fifteen ways he could cleanse the evil out of that vile vampire instantly coming to his mind.

"Give me a reason why I shouldn't trust him and I'll forget I ever met him." Khin's words were stubborn, but not entirely closed off to the idea of engaging in a dialogue over the matter.

"I will once I—"

"No," Khin snapped. "Now. If it's so important, you'll make time for it."

With the Council yet to berate and Nessix to get out of prison and Berann's identity to uncover, the last thing Mathias had the patience for was to explain to a naïve civilian why vampires couldn't be trusted. "He kills people for his own benefit."

Khin shrugged. "So do you."

Mathias pinched the bridge of his nose and squeezed his eyes shut. "I kill for justice, Khin. He kills for power."

"Aren't justice and power two parts of the same thing?"

In all of his time serving Abaeloth and upholding Etha's will, Mathias had never thought he'd have to try to convince people that monsters should be feared, not embraced. "I don't have time for this right now," he groaned. "Just… go see if the temple has any more errands for you and I'll sit down with you to answer whatever questions you have after I square away some Council business. Is that fair?"

It *wasn't* fair. Khin hadn't been bluffing or searching for

Mathias's jealousy when she told him how generous and kind Tristan had been to her. She truly felt heard and understood by the man, even if he was a vampire, and that meant a whole lot to a girl who had been shoved aside at every other point in her life. If Tristan was evil or cruel or not to be trusted, he'd have shown some indication of that behavior by now, Khin was sure of it, and all she wanted to do was track him down and reassure him that just because Mathias thought he was a monster, didn't mean she agreed. Which was precisely why she needed an excuse to get out of the Citadel.

"Alright," she murmured, lowering her eyes to shield her developing deceit from Mathias. "I'll go and help how I can."

Mathias was too preoccupied with the other disasters he was managing to even entertain the thought of Khin being up to mischief, and he so desperately wanted to be able to trust anyone right now that he would have been hesitant to call her on it even if he had caught it.

"Thank you, Khin," he said softly. "We'll talk soon."

She lowered her head and gave a brief curtsey as she'd been taught to do in the temple, and slipped past Mathias to find her excuse to go chase after Tristan. Mathias—with much less enthusiasm—left the library to go confront Henrik.

SEVENTEEN

Mathias could recall many times in his endless life when he'd felt his patience wane, but never before had he been so close to his limits with the mortal world he'd been tasked with saving. Had he been less focused on the imminent crisis brewing and what he had to do to resolve the most immediate variable in his reach, he might have felt guilty or selfish for his increasingly cold outlook. As it was, this problem was simply too large to take on all at once. He had no choice but to approach it one step at a time, and that first step was getting Nessix out of prison. He hoped to be able to take a lawful approach in doing so but, acknowledging how aggressively the Council was currently operating, he wouldn't hold his breath.

Etha, remind me again. What is your will?

The goddess recognized Mathias's agitation plainly, but answered his simple request. *My will is to pursue balance on Abaeloth.*

Mathias nodded to himself, his steely glare chasing off the fawning smiles and subtle bows of those he passed as he strode through the marble hall. *And are the demons still the greatest threat to the balance which you seek?*

How Etha wished Mathias was in a less populated part of the Citadel so she could pop up in front of him and give him the proper warnings his intentions were due. *I see where you're going with this.*

Zeal has tried everything to stop the demons, and none of those past attempts have yielded success.

Etha kept her thoughts on the matter to herself as the conference chamber doors came within Mathias's line of sight, regretting that she'd let him keep the entirety of his free will when she'd raised him. Before the great doors, the four guards hastily shifted position, making subtle gestures with their spears as they frantically discussed Mathias's rapid approach.

You would ask me to stop at nothing, Mother, if I could uncover a way to rid Abaeloth of the demons. Am I right?

I will not say what you want me to say, Etha warned. *Though she was driven to them, Nessix chose her actions herself.*

It wasn't often Mathias blatantly defied Etha, but he did so now, unable to stop himself. *She chose none of the fate the demons carved for her, and you know it. Someone has to tend to this crisis. Someone has to solve these problems. I believe Nessix wants to, and I intend to stand beside her to see it done.*

This was a debate Etha could not have with Mathias. Above all, she craved balance, and achieving balance required strict adhesion to the laws she'd laid in place upon Abaeloth's creation. Though Henrik had acted out of line, he'd done nothing to overstep those boundaries, and not even Etha's bias toward her son and his desires could allow her to argue that. Similarly, she knew Mathias's will and soul perhaps even better than he knew them, himself, and he'd carry out his desires whether she wanted him to or not. It didn't help matters that she agreed that he had to do it.

I cannot and will not stop you, she told him carefully, *but you are not to drag me or my will into any part of these negotiations.*

There won't be any negotiations.

Mathias... Etha warned. *Remember that you still need to work with the Council.*

Perhaps they're due a reminder that they *still need to work with* me.

Etha wouldn't fault Mathias for his belligerence, given the unusual amount of stress he'd been under of late and the petty way which the Council had been managing him. *Just... be mindful. Do not risk making matters worse for yourself or for Nessix.*

That gentle reminder did soothe a bit of Mathias's ire, though

201

it wasn't enough to change his mind. He raised his voice to the guards before he was a respectable distance to properly address them. "I demand entry to the conference chamber."

"Sir Sagewind"—the man who spoke was middle-aged and far too soft to have ever seen any true combat—"the Council is busy with—"

Mathias stopped before the group and the two guards closest to the wall nervously crossed their spears before the door. "You mistook my demand for a request. Step aside and allow me entry."

The older man swallowed his doubt and drew upon his training as well as he could, though it did nothing to take the tremor from his voice. "The Council will see you after—"

Etha had forbidden Mathias from using her name in any part of this confrontation, and so he settled for a string of muttered curses and banked on the reluctance these guards had shown him so far as he pushed past the two in front, batted aside the spears with ease, and shoved both doors open to stride inside.

A sudden hush fell over every man and woman in the conference chamber and every wild gaze turned to Mathias's intrusion as though expecting him to be an army of demons. The paladin disregarded their startled responses, sweeping his eyes across Julianna's guilt as she hastily looked away from him before settling his glare on Henrik.

The Head of Court, still flustered from his previous encounters regarding Mathias and the woman he'd attached himself to, coughed and pulled out the confidence he was so skilled at faking. "What is the meaning of this intrusion, Sir Sagewind?"

Mathias smirked and shook his head. From anyone else, he might have accepted the forced outrage, but he was through feigning politeness with Henrik. "I've returned from Heiligate, of course."

Murmurs rippled from both the Council and their modest audience, and color pinched at Henrik's cheeks. "That is fine and well, but what is the meaning of this intrusion?" He repeated the question in a staccato, as though his understanding of syllables would gain him some amount of respect and influence over Mathias.

"You've been so eager for me to report on my actions and findings, I was only trying to act in a manner appropriate for High Council."

The murmurs hushed instantly and Julianna shook her head slowly, mouthing the word "no" to her brother, though he didn't so much as glance at her. After tense moments of silence, Henrik cleared his throat.

"This is not High Council, Sir Sagewind, it is—"

"I am declaring it High Council, by the power granted to my station as the Order's own White Paladin."

"I'll second the motion," Lord Courtenay, Regent of Noble Affairs, Second District, said from the back row.

Julianna groaned and sank her head into her hand as a gentle thunder of fists pounding their agreement on desktops rippled through the chamber. Clearly, Mathias had found Nessix, and clearly, she'd told him what events had transpired to land her in prison. While the foreigner hadn't known the laws which bound High Council, every official present within this chamber could recite them easier than they could recall the names of their own children. Any act of dishonesty made by any member of the Council under these terms would result in instant stripping of title and station, and Mathias had enough ammunition and motive to knock out a fair number of these representatives here and now if he had the mind to do so. When Henrik spoke next, it was with a gruff, trembling voice, and Julianna couldn't blame him for it.

"High Council it is, then, Sir Sagewind. Now, do tell us what grounds you have to interrupt a scheduled audience with these fine gentlemen."

Mathias glanced to the pair of wide-eyed noblemen who had been the Council's previous audience and gave them a curt nod before answering Henrik's request. "The grounds I have for interrupting a scheduled audience are to demand you release General Nessix Teradhel of Elidae from both prison and the charges you had coerced her into."

Henrik gripped the edges of his podium. "That is beyond my power."

"Were you not the one to declare High Council at the

scheduled audience"—he made sure to send another glance at the pair of noblemen—"you had with her?"

Henrik clenched his jaw, his answer stuck in his throat, and the frightened sheen in his eyes was clear even from where Mathias stood.

"High Council demands you answer truthfully, Henrik," Mathias reminded.

"The declaration had been mine," Henrik snapped, "and she had accepted it."

"Had you made the declaration with the suspicion that General Teradhel would have no idea what it meant?"

"I had assumed as a seasoned noblewoman she'd have known how to conduct herself appropriately in official settings."

"Answer what was asked of you, Caldwell," Maxwell Lumley, Director of Public Works, said.

Mathias cocked his head and crossed his arms, bolstered by the support. "Indeed. That wasn't an answer to my question."

Henrik was an argumentative man, but he'd never been a fighter. Born into money and opposed to the notion of sweating, he'd never once entertained the idea of any job outside of politics. He knew how the system worked and how to exploit it, but Mathias had been playing with the Council for generations before Henrik had even been born and, to the Head of Court's knowledge, had never backed down from a fight he'd chosen to engage in. The declaration of High Council meant Henrik could not lie... but it said nothing about him being required to answer an incriminating question. Mouth clamped shut, he turned his gaze to Julianna, who sat with her head bowed, lips rapidly murmuring her side of a private conversation.

Mathias shrugged. "To be open and honest, as this court demands, I'll go ahead and state that I accept your silence as a sign of your guilt. Unless you feel it's necessary to correct me?"

Henrik's eyes darkened and the tips of his ears began to turn red.

Mathias nodded. "Very well." He half-turned and gestured to the doors. "Shall I go spread word of how the Order's esteemed Council has begun treating foreign dignitaries and prisoners of war as felons?"

Henrik slapped a hand on the top of his podium and sprang to his feet. "She drew a sword—stolen one off a guard, even!—during High Council. That *is* a felony, regardless of the status you want to give her."

"I never denied that, but in the name of justice, I simply wanted to be assured that she'd been aware that the action she'd taken was illegal and to hear that she'd been in no way coerced, offered, or otherwise misled into committing this crime."

The chamber remained silent and every eye, save Julianna's—which were still pinched closed beneath rippled brows—locked on the trembling Head of Court, and Mathias smirked.

"You know, as long as we're speaking honestly," the paladin continued, "maybe you'd like to voice your regrets about not finding a way to strip me of my title sooner, eh, Henrik?"

"Enough!" Henrik roared, his voice bouncing off the marble walls of the hushed room. The rapid wheezing of his hyperventilation further punctured the silence. "She is an undead creation of the demons', and as such cannot be permitted access to the Citadel."

The two foreign nobles shrank back into their seats and glanced at the doors, uncertain if the rules of High Council would forbid them from leaving, but beginning to think punishment for doing so may not be their worst decision.

"It's funny you should mention that to your undead champion who just extracted a vampire from the very same Citadel you seem so eager to protect."

Julianna's eyes flew open now and she looked up at Mathias to assess whether or not he'd decided to forfeit his place within the Order for the sake of a poorly timed joke. There was no hint of jest in his eyes, no keen smirk upon his lips. Julianna had known Mathias would be livid after discovering how Nessix had been treated while he was gone, but this was an entirely unrelated anger she saw in him now.

"Sir Sagewind," Willard gasped, "you declared High Council for yourself—"

"And I am not lying, Master Aligoth. This Council has been

busy sending me on pointless missions, demanding paperwork and formal reports, framing the only woman who can guide us to answers, and have neglected the most basic aspects of your responsibility to this installation, to this city, and to the fate of Abaeloth."

Henrik leaned forward. "But you can't prove it."

"Maybe not, but under High Council, you cannot deny it."

Henrik scoffed and flung his glare away from Mathias, keeping the rest of his tirade to himself.

"As for proof of your incompetence," Mathias continued, waving the ring of keys in the air, "the sleeping guard assigned to the dungeon should be able to fill you in on the vampire's visit, and the blood-drained corpse of the man who had been kept in solitary ten should provide you solid evidence."

There wasn't one Council member who *wanted* to speak right now, each of them dreading the negative ramifications which could come with doing so, but Eiluned Fayette, Ambassador of Elven Affairs, had been a child toward the end of the Undead War and remembered the horror of that age well.

"But… the vampires had all been sealed behind the Veil," she murmured, her tiny voice carrying through the stilled chamber.

Enraged or not, the fastest way to appeal to Mathias's compassion was through fear, and he sighed and closed his eyes. "All of them we'd known of, yes." This next bit was more difficult to admit, as it pointed to mistakes the younger version of himself had made and risked further incriminating Nessix. Regardless, he had to make it known. "But something is amiss. Something bigger than the Council and Zeal is at work. Ceredulus has been tethered and muzzled, yet the demons have found a way to bring back the dead. Vampires are showing up once again. This is not the time for talking, but for action. Release Nessix to my custody so she can lead us to what is going on. I can think you're all a bunch of assess and you can all look at me as an uncivilized battering ram, but not one person in this room can doubt my desire to protect Abaeloth."

Willard Aligoth rose first. "I've fielded too many reports regarding the demons of late and I, for one, would like to see them stopped. Etha bless him, I believe Sir Sagewind and motion for the captive general to be released to his custody for the purpose he has proposed."

A handful of agreements popped up through the crowd, but not enough to gain the majority. With time too short to deal with the existing problems, much less new ones that would crop up from what was wasted by the indecisive Council, Mathias sighed. He'd have preferred to not have to go this route.

"I feel it is fair that I also inform you of my intentions to see Nessix out of prison, with or without your permission. This was a courtesy to let you know of the..." He snapped his fingers and looked at Julianna. "What do you call it?"

"Mischief..." Julianna muttered.

Mathias stopped his snapping and pointed at his sister, giving her a charming smile. "That's it. It was a courtesy to let you know of the mischief I'm about to undertake in order to stop the demons from further growing and implementing their army of the undead."

Henrik, more desperate to save face than anything else, stood his ground. "And you, Sir Sagewind, just admitted your intentions to commit a crime at High Council!" He delivered his declaration like it was some great revelation the others hadn't been able to reach on their own.

Mathias quirked his lips to the side, cast a fleeting glance toward the ceiling, and nodded. "Yes," he admitted. "Yes, I am. There is no part of the law preventing me from admitting my intentions. In fact, it'd be more of a crime if I hadn't been honest about it... wouldn't it?" Mathias exaggerated his efforts of thinking over his reasoning, then shrugged. "Anyway, if any of you wish to stop me, you are welcome to try, though I suspect it would require the drawing of weapons..."

Dumbfounded by Mathias's blatant disregard for the law—as well as his seamless and shameless manipulation of it to get what he wanted—not even Henrik was able to object. After all, Mathias always did what he wanted.

Satisfied, Mathias found a small smile at last. "And do remember, High Council remains in effect until the audience is formally dismissed." He turned to the two stunned noblemen and slapped a hand on the nearest one's shoulder. "Take my advice.

Keep your hands off anything pointy."

"This is not through, Sir Sagewind," Henrik said as Mathias began to walk away. His voice had lost half its gusto, but Mathias knew better than to disregard it.

"And once it *is* through, you have my word, by Etha's name and under the constraints of High Council, that I will answer to you for everything I need to."

It was a weighty vow, a serious one, and not even Etha could chime in about how he'd told her he wouldn't use her name in any part of these negotiations. Nobody else tried to stop Mathias after that, and so he departed the silent chamber to go release Nessix from jail.

EIGHTEEN

With time in short supply, Kol and Annin had recruited twenty of their strongest fliers so the burdens of their prisoners could be passed around as each pair tired to avoid slowing their progress to Zeal. The priestesses had begun the flight shrieking, but quieted after the first day in the air, their terror dying out into subtle coos of sobs, and those were hushed by the wind. Auden voiced the occasional squeal, but it was difficult to distinguish if it was of delight or fear. It took the full two days' flight from Elidae to the coast of Gelthin for Kol to shake off his shock that Grell had allowed them to leave the hells yet again, and it wasn't until the peaks of Vesper came into view that Kol finally allowed himself to consider the chance that this plan might work, the faint thrill of hope igniting his spirits for the first time in months.

He didn't get to enjoy the sensation for long before Annin banked over to him from his position on point and rolled to his side to facilitate speaking while in flight.

"We will land in Vesper," Kol shouted past the rip of the wind, "to recover and plan our final approach."

Annin nodded. "I would like to speak with you about that when we land."

Kol frowned and shifted his focus from his path to Annin's bored eyes. Vesper was the most obvious place for them to stop,

209

but the fact that Annin had independently come up with a reason for doing so did not align well with the positive feelings Kol had been trying to enjoy. Desperate to preserve the upswing of his confidence for at least a few more moments, he opted for a nod instead of inquiring about Annin's intentions. His efforts would only buy him another hour with his newfound grasp on sanity.

The party landed on the mountainside, the alar groaning and grumbling in pain and relief, their prisoners collapsing from the same as their legs tried to remember how to negotiate solid ground. Annin separated from the group immediately, spearing Kol with a firm look which demanded he follow. Everyone else was too busy digging through their packs to find their rations, too distracted by their own immediate needs to make much of their leaders' actions, and Kol sighed and obeyed Annin's unspoken instruction.

The oraku didn't acknowledge Kol's compliance, picking his way up the mountainside a couple hundred yards from the rest of the demons. Each step farther from the main group only enhanced Kol's growing dread that Annin was about to propose something he wouldn't want—but would ultimately need—to accept, and his pace slowed accordingly until he reached the spot where Annin had stopped and turned back to face him.

"Alright," Kol said impatiently. "What do you know that can't be discussed around anyone else?"

Annin nodded his curt approval of the authority Kol had found over the past few days, only a little remorseful that he was about to take it away again. "Give me Nessix's soul vessel."

Kol's hand flew to where the pendant rested against his chest, safely tucked beneath his shirt. His eyes flashed with all of the threats and protests Annin had already worked out and his lips curled back in a snarl that would have frightened someone who couldn't manipulate threads. Annin shifted his weight to rest a leg and crossed his arms.

"I told you that you'd never take it from me again," Kol growled, fingers wrinkling the linen of his shirt as he gripped the vessel possessively. "And you told Grell—"

"Is that where we are now?" Annin scoffed. "Basing our actions on what we told *Grell*?"

Kol gnashed his teeth around that snarl. "You said yourself that I need to keep her vessel if we're going to find her."

Annin vented his irritation with a brisk sigh. "We don't need to find her anymore. We know she's in Zeal and we've got a generous payment to exchange for her. You don't *need* to keep her vessel with you, you simply *want* to."

Why should that make any difference? Nessix belonged to Kol! Annin shouldn't have any say in what happened to any part of her. Yet he did. Which meant he'd thought of something Kol's deteriorated concentration hadn't yet come up with. Shoving aside possessiveness and pride enough to open his mind to the idea of listening, Kol narrowed his eyes and let his scowl shrink into a stern frown.

"What do you plan to do with it if I comply?"

Annin squared his stance again and dropped his arms to his sides. "I plan to give it to Lorrin for safe keeping until we secure Nessix and escort her from Zeal."

Kol laughed and shook his head, looking away from Annin to combat the urge to backhand him. "I don't like the idea of parting with her vessel after that trick you pulled on me last time—"

"That trick which put us on her trail, you mean?"

Kol bristled at Annin's provocative logic, but held his ground. "I trust you, Annin, and I don't even want *you* controlling this part of Nessix. The limit of my faith in Lorrin lies in my ability to use him. I will not hand something this important over to the likes of him."

"You won't be," Annin said. "You will be handing it over to me, the demon you just claimed to trust, and I'll be the one handing it over to Lorrin."

Kol sucked his teeth and shook his head again. "That is not a compromise, Annin."

"I'm not looking for one."

Kol's eyes snapped to Annin's and the two stared each other down, both prepared to engage in physical combat over their respective objectives. They were both too spent for either to know which would come out on top, but both were equally committed to their stances. Sensibility demanded they work this out before the first blow was exchanged and, in a great effort to prove he still knew what sensibility was, Kol tried one last time to sway Annin civilly.

"Surrendering Nessix's soul vessel is surrendering the only influence I have over her."

Annin cocked his head. "You don't truly believe that, do you?" A perplexed expression vied to discredit the strictness of Kol's brows and if Annin hadn't known how it would ruin any chance he had at gaining Kol's compliance on the matter, he'd have laughed. "She has fought viciously and violently for you in the past. She has looked to you for aid unprompted. I've witnessed, myself, the same nauseating fondness you feel for her from her toward you. You've already secured your control over her, Kol. Now give me her soul vessel."

Annin's logic didn't quite add up in the thinking parts of Kol's mind—hadn't the oraku accused Kol of stupidity for trusting Nessix wouldn't run off in the first place? But the desperate part of Kol, the fragile side of him which still dreamed about safer, more beautiful things than the Divine Battle, longed to believe Annin's words. Kol knew Nessix relied on him and would obey him once he was physically present in her life once again. Besides, the demonic tendencies which had become increasingly active within Kol of late assured him that even if she did try to fight him once he got his hands on her, he had more than one way to force her obedience. Nessix would trade herself for Auden and the priestesses, Kol had no doubt, but that didn't erase his greater concern.

"Why Lorrin?"

Annin relaxed at the question. Kol was no longer trying to talk his way out of the arrangement and had moved on to gathering information, signaling his willingness to comply. "He's proven reliable and loyal and has already agreed to help us. Vesper is about as far from Zeal and its Sagewind vermin as a haven for demons can get on this continent, and I figured you'd prefer to leave it under some sort of guard than hidden someplace a crow would carry it off from."

Damn Annin and this thoroughness… "I still don't like it."

"I don't care."

Kol drew closer to Annin so he could lower his voice, despite the fact that their troops were too busy poking around at the priestesses to pay attention to this debate. "Lorrin is an oraku," he objected. "He will know there's power in her vessel."

"Lorrin is an idiot," Annin countered. "He'll know it's a pretty treasure, but won't know what else to make of it unless you're dumb enough to tell him. Her vessel will be safer in his ignorant hands than it would be within the reach of anyone on the surface realm who calls themselves a Sagewind."

It was clear that Annin had spent the better part of their flight thinking over how to minimize the risk of this exchange, and Kol finally had to admit to himself that he'd gotten too close to look at all of the variables clearly. As much as he was afraid of parting with Nessix's soul by giving it to Lorrin, the thought of Mathias wrestling it away from him made him want to run back to Grell for the punishment awaiting him. Annin's lack of emotional connection to Nessix would give him the appropriate grounds to appear indifferent about the request, hopefully further deluding Lorrin into thinking the pendant was nothing more than a pretty bauble.

Nothing Annin could say and nothing Kol could do would make this any easier on the alar, and so he held his breath and pulled the chain over his head, thrusting Nessix's soul vessel forward. Annin snatched it instantly, before Kol could process the notion of having second thoughts, and promptly deposited it in his pocket.

"It pleases me to see your sensibilities returning." Annin turned and resumed his trek up the mountain on foot as he called back to Kol. "Gather up the men and our hostages and let's get to the peaks. We've wasted enough time."

Kol watched Annin trudge away for a moment, raising his hand to press against his chest where Nessix's pendant usually caressed him. If this was what it took to get her back, he would manage, though he wouldn't pretend to be happy about it. Grumbling at Annin's parting words, certainly not feeling as sensible as he thought he ought to, Kol hopped into the air to glide back down to his troops and organized them for their approach to Vesper.

* * * * *

Unlike their previous visit to the ancient settlement, there weren't enough demons to offer Kol's unit any trouble, as Lorrin had chosen to keep his troops dispersed instead of recalling them. Even if there had been the inclination for hostility upon their arrival, any desire to stir up trouble for their hell-dwelling brethren simmered away from Lorrin's men in curiosity of the priestesses and mindless man they harbored. Lorrin was particularly eager to catch up with his old friends after the ominous conversation they'd shared earlier in the week and greeted them with a wide smile after taking appraisal of what they'd brought along with them.

"You weren't kidding when you said you had leverage against Zeal. How'd you make such fast work over negotiations with Grell?"

Annin was too focused on his task and Kol too uncomfortable with the current arrangements for either of them to return Lorrin's show of camaraderie, but they did accept it.

"We didn't give him time to think about it," Annin said. "And we've got one more favor to ask of you."

The impulse to scream at Annin that he'd changed his mind struck Kol, and he narrowly hid it behind the clearing of his throat. Accepting that any reactivity on his part would only pique in Lorrin the exact curiosity Kol feared, the alar silently dismissed himself to chase away those surface demons who poked around too closely to the priestesses. Annin noted Kol's departure with care, but outwardly shrugged it off.

Lorrin followed Kol's movement as well, and smirked at the alar's efforts to drive back the boldest of his tribe. "You'll have a soft spot to rest your wings for the night and warm food to fill your bellies if my men get to play with your gifts to Zeal."

Annin frowned, stealing the enthusiasm from Lorrin's grin. "The hospitality had been assumed, and not one of these priestesses will have a finger laid upon her. They are intended to

214

hold value to Zeal and will arrive there in the same condition they are in now."

Lorrin's eye flashed with anger, but it soon fizzled out as he remembered who he was contending against, hiding his grumbling on the matter. "You won't let us go all out on that human you brought, won't let us play with your prisoners, you assume yet another night of our *hospitality*"—he drew that world out tersely — "and claim to have another favor to ask of me."

"That's right."

Lorrin spat and cast an irritated glare toward Kol, wishing the damn alar would step in. He was the only person alive who Lorrin had ever seen successfully control Annin, and it would be nice to borrow some of that security. Frowning, he turned his attention back to the oraku. "So when's any of this going to pay off for me and mine?"

"I thought me and Kol overthrowing the inoga was adequate compensation for a few meals and a bit of that patience you claim to have learned up here on the surface, but if you want to renegotiate—"

Lorrin's eye widened and he shook his head hastily. It had been quite some time since he'd served alongside Annin, but he remembered the oraku's cold practicality. If Lorrin decided to make himself useless in Annin's eyes, Annin wouldn't be opposed to disposing of him.

"No renegotiating necessary," he answered. "Just... ah... looking for ways to keep my troops entertained, you know?"

Annin rolled his eyes, as irritated with his less cultured kin for their lack of dignified self-control as ever. "Does the thought of independent tribes reclaiming their power not entertain them enough?"

Lorrin lowered his head and looked away. "It will be enough," he said, too respectful of Annin's power for any other answer. "So what is this other favor you have to ask of me?"

Annin's expression evened into something which passed as contentment and he shoved his hand in his pocket, ever aware of how carefully Kol monitored his actions. "You have succeeded at each of our requests so far, and I do hope this is the last one I must make of you." He left out the fact that it was more out of his desire to not be indebted to anyone than any notion of inconvenience it might have on Lorrin. "This is an easy task which only requires you to stay alive."

Lorrin's brows wrinkled. "You've never asked me to do something easy before."

"Yes, well, I am now."

"Fine," Lorrin sighed. It wasn't as though he had a choice in the matter. "I'm listening."

Convinced of Lorrin's inclination to obey, Annin pulled Nessix's soul vessel from his pocket, brushing off the flare of agitation Kol telegraphed at the intrigue which sparked to life in Lorrin's eye. "I stole this from Mathias Sagewind some time ago and I'd hate for him to think he could take it back when we inevitably face him outside Zeal."

"Ha!" The residual tension Lorrin had hung onto eased from his shoulders. "Keeping something a Sagewind wants out of his hands? That's not a favor, Annin. That's a privilege."

Lorrin's eagerness pleased Annin, but not so much that he missed the prospect of the simple oraku's likelihood to go parading the valuable pendant around to his subordinates. As much as Annin disliked Nessix, as much as he wished he could have stopped her creation or find some solution to the multitude of problems she'd caused, he did share Kol's fear of what could happen if her soul ended up in someone else's hands. As such, Annin was unable to reciprocate with even a hint of the smile which Lorrin gave him.

"You will keep it hidden and safe." The sharpness of Annin's tone subdued Lorrin's excitement yet again. "The fewer who even know it's here, the better; Mathias does have his ways of getting information out of our kind."

The reminder lurking within Annin's bluff dulled a weighty amount of Lorrin's humor, but didn't impact his willingness to carry out this duty. "If that's what it takes to upset that gnat, I'll see it done."

Annin forbid himself from looking back at Kol, suspecting that would only open the door to more objections, and extended his hand forward. "Remember. I am *quite* fond of this trinket. If anything happens to it…"

"Nothing will." Had Lorrin been making this deal with Kol, he'd have been comfortable simply snatching the pendant away. Since he was dealing with Annin, however, he settled for reaching his open hand forward to wait for Annin to deposit the necklace in his palm. Annin maintained firm eye contact while doing so, confident he'd gained Lorrin's obedience and thus would be able to reassure Kol that they hadn't just made a grave mistake. Showing any further concern over the soul vessel was bound to stoke too much of Lorrin's curiosity, and so Annin allowed his attention to filter away from it as soon as Lorrin crushed it in his grasp.

"I'll keep it on my person until you and Kol return for it," Lorrin said. "No one else will touch it. Now go get yourself something to eat so we can get this inoga-humbling show started."

That was the closest thing to an order Annin ever wanted to receive, but in the interest of satisfying his empty stomach and soothing Kol's building nerves, he gave the surface-bound oraku a nod. "Your service is once again noted."

Lorrin's grin returned at what he interpreted as Annin's praise, and he left for his tent to fetch a pouch to stow the pendant in. Annin turned back to his troops to find the majority of them already eating, the priestesses huddled together in a clump just out of the cookfire's warmth as Auden babbled a nonsensical story to them. Only Kol hadn't taken a seat, his watchfulness sparking into the concern Annin had expected as soon as he registered it was safe to let it do so.

Before the agitated alar had a chance to shout out his worries for the whole camp to hear, Annin raised his hand, putting a prompt hold on Kol's venting. It was a promising sign that Kol obeyed the silent instruction until Annin had reached him.

"Well?" Kol demanded.

Annin gave him a perturbed glare and kept moving toward the fire to serve himself a helping of stew. "Well what? You've got eyes and Lorrin's still alive. All is well, and all will remain well as long as you don't raise any concerns."

Kol froze and clenched his fist at his side. He'd felt so alone after Nessix had chosen to run. Now, without even the faint warmth of her soul vessel, he felt naked and exposed, and Annin's complete lack of regard for that stoked a flare of anger amid his frustration.

"You going to sit down and eat with us?" Annin asked, taking his bowl over to a vacant boulder to sit. "Or do you plan on dropping from fatigue on the flight to Zeal?"

Kol glowered at Annin, hating him for this blatant mockery until he noticed the sly glint in his friend's pale eyes, enhanced by the reflection of the dancing flames. Kol had led Annin through some perilous places of late and he'd grown so accustomed to the oraku's irritation that he'd practically forgotten what his confidence looked like. As it dawned on Kol that Annin—for the first time in months—was beyond positive that they'd successfully achieve their objective, Annin gave him a subtle smirk, shook his head, and invested the remainder of his attention on his food.

All at once, the accumulation of Kol's tension and worry sifted through the soles of his feet, scattering away on the mountain breeze. Zeal was little more than a day's hard flight from here. He couldn't do anything about the damage Nessix might have done with what she knew, but he would be able to ask her to her face why she'd run very soon. Tending to the damage she'd caused could begin once he had her in his grasp.

Feeling the twist of hunger for the first time in weeks, Kol sighed, served himself some food, and enjoyed his sustenance alongside the demons who would soon make history.

NINETEEN

Khin hastened down the steps of the Citadel's grand entry, heart racing as she tried to wrap her head around the task ahead of her. Zeal was one of the largest cities on all of Gelthin, certainly the largest city she'd ever been in. Where was she supposed to start her search for Tristan? What if he'd taken Mathias's rude behavior as a sign to leave Zeal completely? She needed Tristan, no matter what he was. Salvaging the hope Mathias had taught her, Khin raised her eyes to the street and froze in place, gasping, when Tristan uncrossed his legs and leaned forward from where he'd been lounging on a bench right across from the exit.

Khin hadn't been aware that Tristan was a vampire until five minutes ago, nor did she have any way of knowing that he could speak with his god. And it had been that same cunning god who had encouraged Tristan to stay in place and wait for Khin to come find him. Before Khin had the chance to faint from her shock, Tristan smiled and stood, reaching a hand out to beckon her closer than he could comfortably get to the Citadel with the current constraints in place.

Blinking back the tears she hadn't expected to come, it took Khin only a moment to push past her delight and clear the distance between the two of them. "You didn't leave," she breathed.

Tristan smiled gently and turned to face the road leading

toward Zeal's slums. "Sir Sagewind only specified I leave the Citadel." He snuck a glance at Khin as she beamed up at him, pleased to see his enchantment still hard at work. "You didn't think I'd leave you on account of that brute's tantrum, did you?"

Khin blushed furiously and clasped her hands before her, shrugging her shoulders close together. "I've not had much luck with keeping friends," she said quietly. "I didn't know what to think of his... tantrum." Part of Khin felt dirty assigning such a juvenile attribute to the man who had saved her life so many times, but taking that control over her emotions was liberating. She scooted half a step closer to Tristan.

The movement was not missed by the vampire. Being driven from the Citadel hadn't been ideal, but the poor manner which Mathias had handled doing so was of great benefit to Tristan's objectives. Satisfied, he set off down the street. "Mathias would like you to believe I am a monster."

"Mathias would like people to believe a lot of things," Khin muttered, following Tristan like an adoring puppy.

Tristan smirked and shook his head at her feisty retort. "Well, do you? Believe I'm a monster, I mean?"

Khin hadn't yet decided what she believed about Tristan. All she knew about vampires came from the scary stories her brothers used to tell when they'd all stayed up past their bedtime. She could hardly imagine that the charming man who had been nothing but patient with her these past few days could be a monster, but neither had Tristan denied Mathias's claim. Too determined to prove to Mathias that she knew how to live her life better than he did, Khin made up her mind.

"I've known lots of monsters in my time. Nobody as kind as you should be treated as one."

Oh, yes. Tristan's efforts on winning over Khin had paid off, indeed. "Would your opinion of me be the same if I'd told you what I was when we first met?"

Though it had only been a matter of days since Khin had first run into Tristan while on a delivery, she had allowed her initial reservations about him and the intentions he might have with her to fade from mind. Even so, she knew she'd have been frightened if she'd known and believed such a claim then, just as she was uncertain of it now, but she was too determined to stay her course. If Tristan had wanted to hurt her or meant her harm the way Mathias seemed to think he did, he'd had plenty of opportunities to do so by now.

"Would you telling me what you are have changed the way you treated me?" she asked.

Tristan smiled. He'd grown fond of the girl's innocence and fierce loyalty, and he and Ceredulus both looked forward to using those traits in the future. "You can trust me when I say there's not a thing I would have done differently, no matter how any of this played out."

She nodded firmly, resolve solidifying her expression as she forced herself to believe what she was going to say next. "Then my opinion of you would be no different than the one I have now."

"And what opinion do you have of me now?"

Khin stopped suddenly, her sharp gasp startling Tristan, who had been enjoying the confirmations coming from their conversation. He stopped and looked back at her, brows wrinkled in concern.

"You really have to ask?" Tears embellished Khin's words but they hadn't yet made it to her eyes.

Tristan, as far removed from the motives of mortals as he was, hadn't intended to upset the girl and jumped immediately to remedy the results of his clumsiness. "I don't think I do," he answered smoothly. "But I recognize your uncertainty. It might do *you* some good to speak it out loud."

The sense of his words burrowed past Khin's tears and helplessness and her shoulders relaxed. "My opinion is that you've been kinder to me than you had to be and that you deserve to know what's going on as much as anyone else does."

"Oh?" He took a casual step closer to her.

Khin nodded. "And Mathias was wrong to judge you so quickly and forbid you to continue your research."

Tristan smiled, his eyes narrowing with a cunning Khin would have been wary of had she not been so taken by his charm. "My research is still moving forward. Don't worry about that."

"But how? You said you needed what was in the Citadel's libraries."

He reached a hand behind Khin as he turned back down the road, gently pressing against her shoulder to draw her forward again. "I picked up enough knowledge for now and am sure I can count on you to keep me aware of any further developments uncovered by the priestesses." He slid her that sly gaze of his, hooking it deeply into the wide-eyed wonderment of Khin's naïve gaping. "Can't I?"

She tried to pull her eyes away from his, so afraid of disappointing him, but as his focus kept hers locked on him, the routine milling of the city street seemed to blur around her and all that existed was Tristan's gentle request. Unable to look away as shame asked her to, Khin flushed. "I… I can't read."

"You can't read, but you *can* listen. Mathias seemed rather displeased with the idea of upsetting you and though you had to witness a rather… unsavory side of him, he's never been known for cruelty. I'm sure he'll be eager to try to mend those wounds by answering any questions you ask him."

Khin was furious with Mathias and the way which he'd belittled her. She wanted few things more than to prove to him that she was worthwhile and that his assessment of her being nothing but an ignorant, needy child was wrong. The timid ounce of common sense Khin possessed—and had routinely overlooked throughout her lifetime—squeaked out its reservations about trusting Tristan, but her desire to prove she was important shouted over those reasonable concerns. After all, she'd be expected to continue running errands for the temple. Nobody would have to know she was also relaying information to a vampire.

"What kind of information are you looking for?" she asked.

Pleased with her compliance, Tristan released the hold his gaze had on her and turned his attention back to the road so he could navigate Khin away from the main strip and through the crowded residential district. "I need to learn why the demons would want to raise the dead. They're already undying creatures, so they don't need the knowledge for personal use. If you can gain access to the woman named Nessix, I suspect she could tell you much."

Khin harrumphed at the name, her envy of the woman who was so important to Mathias only enhanced by his stony treatment of her. "The priestesses say the demons are building an army out of normal people who the armies here on the surface won't want to fight."

Tristan batted his free hand and rolled his eyes. "The people of the surface *love* to fight. Mortals couldn't survive without something to complain about and go to war over. I won't deny that's a brilliant cover the demons have concocted, but there must be something else tying them to the undead, and my god demands to know what it is."

Up until this point, Khin had been able to justify going along with Tristan's smooth lead, but she physically balked at his use of the word "demands." That gentle hand against her shoulder blade, pressed more firmly and kept her moving. "I… I'm not very smart, Tristan," she tried feebly. "What if I can't find anything?"

Tristan stopped and stepped in front of Khin, gripping both of her shoulders as he stooped over to look her evenly in the eyes. "You will find me all I need and I will see to it you are rewarded for your efforts. Your help so far has been beyond compare. All I ask is for a little bit more. Can you do that for me?"

Khin hadn't lied. She wasn't very smart. Her only education had been what she'd picked up from her working class parents and the cruelty of the world. And perhaps it was this ignorance which had landed her in so many terrible positions, but it was all she knew. She'd been promised a reward she wanted more than anything—more than to regain Mathias's respect, more than her desire to erase her past—and all it would take would be serving as Tristan's friend a little longer. Surely, nobody could fault her for that. Biting her lip, confused as to why her eyes burned with tears, Khin nodded resolutely.

"I can do that for you," she whispered.

Tristan's face softened with a disarming smile. "And will you?"

"I will."

Sliding back to Khin's side, Tristan continued to lead her along. "Very good."

"Where will you stay?"

Tristan's smile sharpened into something more devious as he thought over the irony of the arrangements he'd made for himself. "I've found a place where I can come and go as I please."

A hitch of mischief in his tone gave Khin the distinct impression that his solution was less than legal. "Here in Zeal?"

"Here in Zeal," he answered on a delighted sigh. "And well out of the Citadel's direct gaze. I'll be safe there and you'll have no trouble visiting me."

Khin had never commanded any amount of authority, and her brief attempts at grasping for it in the past had always failed her in a humiliating and dramatic fashion. Whether or not she fully believed it, she'd told Tristan she trusted him and right now, that was the only valid option she had. And so, she followed him through the clean residential streets, past the cramped quarters of the general working class, and into the shady gloom of a slum she hadn't imagined a city like Zeal would host. Past experience warned her of the dangers of the wary eyes which watched her and her handsome companion, and she pressed herself closer to Tristan. She offered no objection as he slid his arm the rest of the way across her shoulders, the firmness of his lean muscles wrapping close around her.

"Nobody will cause you trouble here," he told her quietly. "I'll see to it."

Khin gulped down her fears of what that meant, more aware now than ever of the danger the vampire had the potential to pose. "You won't… you won't hurt anyone, will you?"

"Hurt?" He chuckled, keeping to himself how he'd never understood his peers who preferred to play with their food. "No. But I will make sure they know their place."

Knowing little about vampires and how they worked, knowing even less about the subtle nuances of language, Khin allowed herself to trust Tristan as much now as she had all along. Not far down the filthy dirt road, Tristan drew Khin to a halt outside a sturdy single-room cottage which radiated a clean, secure warmth defiant of its surroundings.

"Welcome to my humble abode."

Khin turned her head to gawk at Tristan, surprised to see a

224

smug smile on his face rather than the sneer she'd expected one as refined as him to show such a simple house. "You… you bought it?" she asked hopefully.

Tristan cocked his head to the side. "It was… abandoned by someone I've got a bit of a past with."

Khin nodded slowly, brain working dutifully at convincing her that Tristan knowing the previous owner somehow made this less questionable. "And it's okay for you to stay here?"

"It's better than me sleeping in the rain and under the noses of knights who judge me by the reputation of my kind."

There were still vital details missing from Tristan's reasoning, but Khin didn't have the experience to put her finger on what they were. Rather, she latched on to the reasonable justifications he'd made and refused to let herself argue any further.

"Please keep trusting me, Khin," Tristan bid at her obvious reluctance. "Please keep helping me. I'm counting on you. Not the Order. Not Mathias. You. I need the help only you can give me."

Given her past, Khin should have been more aware of manipulation when it was presented to her, but after the past few weeks of being made to feel that she was an inconvenience, the girl to be tended to later, always later, the chance to be needed was something she lusted after. "You can count on me."

Tristan grasped her hand and bent low to press his cool lips against her fingertips, looking up at her through his lashes. "Thank you, Khin." She blushed deeply and curled her fingers against his, and he rubbed his thumb across the back of her hand. "Now run back to the Citadel before they start wondering where you've gone. You know what I want, and you know where to find me."

Khin let her fingers rest in Tristan's a moment longer before slowly withdrawing. "I'll try not to keep you waiting long."

Tristan straightened just as slowly, satisfied with his work. "I trust you won't."

Flustered and delighted and reveling in the faint rush of taking part in something that might be just a little wrong, Khin fumbled over a curtsey and bounded back toward the main streets to return to the Citadel. Tristan shook his head in pleased disbelief before turning to let himself into Sazarah's house.

You're doing well, Tristan.

He closed the door behind himself and looked out the window until the girl had slipped out of view. He pulled the curtains closed. "For you, I only aim to please, my lord."

TWENTY

Nessix had run to Zeal knowing she owed the Order answers, but believing she'd be able to secure the help she needed. After Julianna's stony reception, the Council's unprofessional conduct, and Mathias's initial suspicions, her hope for saving her akhuerai army began to slowly roll over to die. She slumped against her cell wall with a weary stream of puffed breaths through puckered lips to break up the dismal grumbles and sobbing of the surrounding prisoners.

There wasn't all that much Nessix fully trusted anymore, but if she trusted anyone, it was Mathias. Whether or not he truly had the clout to force the Council to release her, she believed he'd find a way to break her out. That faith didn't make waiting any easier. Every shift of an adjacent prisoner and echo which bounced down the hall plucked at her nerves, convincing her that one of Henrik's lackeys had come down to torment her, and she couldn't chase Tristan's placid smirk out of her mind.

The undertones of Mathias's voice rudely ordering someone to wake up and do their job cut through the dull commotion of the other prisoners, and Nessix sprang to her feet and returned to the front of the cell to watch for him. As he came into view, she took one glance at the wrinkle between his brows, the tight tuck of his lips and set of his jaw, and her heart fell.

"Am I not getting out?" she asked.

Mathias held out the ring of keys. "No, you're getting out. Just… not quite on the best of terms."

Nessix studied his face as he concentrated all of his attention on locating the key to open her cell, that bit of trust she was willing to invest in anything withering with her hope. "So how long do I have to disappear?"

The lock clunked and Mathias pushed the door open. "No disappearing. If I played my hand right, they're more upset with me than you, which is fine."

Nessix stepped aside to allow the door to swing inward, but otherwise didn't move. "My objective requires you maintaining an influential voice within that Council," she said. "Inwan knows they won't listen to me."

For the first time since he returned to the dungeon, Mathias turned his eyes to Nes's, pressing a brief grimace across his lips. "That objective, Nes. Is it to save yourself or your people?"

Her brows rippled in a proud little fit of indignation. "I have never done a thing to serve myself. You, of all people, should know that."

Mathias pinched his lips tight and nodded, averting his eyes as he stepped back to give Nessix room to exit the cell. "You do understand that you'll have to go back to the hells to see it done."

It was an unpleasant proposition Nessix had done her best to ignore, but a fact which she'd carried in the back of her mind since first slipping free of Kol's grasp. In order to reach her troops again, a feat she had to accomplish to succeed at saving them, she'd have to return to the demons' realm. In her most ideal fantasies, she'd do this with an army of paladins marching with her, but after what had been the disaster of petitioning for the Order's help, she was coming to realize it would be her—and if she was lucky, Mathias—alone. As much as she wanted to think that would be enough, optimism was in rather short supply for Nessix right now.

Ducking her head to avoid looking at Mathias as she passed, Nessix exited her cell and strode down the hall as if she'd never been a prisoner of this city. "I'll do whatever I must."

Mathias remained by the door of the cell as Nes marched so

confidently toward the passageway which would take her back to the main body of the Citadel. "Where are you going?"

She turned her head so her voice would carry, but didn't stop. "To go talk to that idiot Council of yours."

"No, Nes." Mathias's strained objection succeeded in stopping her. "This is not the time for that."

Breathing out her agitation, she turned to face him. "This is the only time for it."

"I had to catch them on technicalities to get you out. If you go back up there and prove yourself to be a problem to them, they'll just throw you back in prison. Possibly execute you."

She puffed a harsh chuckle and lowered her head. "You mean *try* to execute me?"

Mathias sighed out his mental fatigue, feeling no better for doing it. "Yes. I mean try to execute you. And coming back to life won't do anything to help your case in their eyes."

Nessix lifted her gaze to him, the warmth and humor gone from her expression and replaced by the gravity of a jaded general. "Sagewind, I need help. I need the *Order's* help and apparently, I can only get that through convincing the Council to grant it. I gave my word to a couple thousand terrified men and women that I'd rescue them from the demons, and I intend to see it done, with or without your blessing."

Heartbroken, Mathias stared at Nessix as she stood so small and alone and stitched together by nothing but a frayed sense of loyalty and patchworked determination. She had changed so much from the spunky general he'd known on Elidae. Mathias was beginning to accept and understand that it wasn't from any perversions the demons had forced on her, but they had torn her spirit when they'd torn her soul. Mathias had served alongside many grizzled generals in his time and found a certain solidarity in their gruff outlooks of the world, but watching as charismatic Nessix began to fold under the strictness of duty dismayed him. She'd deserved a better life than this.

Her shoulders drooped at Mathias's mournful silence. "Having second thoughts about letting me out?"

If letting her out meant she'd have to go back to the hells, back to Kol, Mathias wanted nothing more than to throw her into the cell and lock the door. He knew she'd march into the demons' realm to save her people, discarding any bit of safety she'd found for herself to fight for their freedom while the Council continued to bicker over whether addressing the threat she foretold was worth more than their pride. Mathias had sworn to Nes's memory, to Brant, to *himself* that he'd save her from the demons, and the only solution to do so meant to send her straight back to them.

"No," he said softly, his voice nearly failing him as he motivated himself to start walking. "No regrets. Just thinking."

Nessix pulled out a convincing smirk and turned to resume walking toward the prison's exit as Mathias caught up to her. "You really ought to quit doing that so much. Improvisation's always suited you better."

Mathias wanted to react to her jest, but that wasn't an option for him. There was simply too much going wrong for him to find humor in the stark realities of the near future. "I've got something more productive than failing to convince the Council to negotiate for you to work on."

Nes's lip curled at her reflection of the Council's inefficiency, but at least she had Mathias's blessing to bypass them. "I'm quite sure anything would be more productive than trying to negotiate with them."

Mathias nodded his agreement and jumped into his explanation before he had a chance to doubt whether or not it was the best idea to encourage Nes to act behind the officials' backs. "I've spoken with one of my contacts and I think you were on to something about Berann."

Finally, a genuine smile, that same brilliant light Mathias had so adored before the world had crammed its injustices into Nes's heart, illuminated her face. "What did you learn?"

"Learn? Nothing. But the response I received for asking about him wasn't much different than the one Kol had given you. You said he'd made you study ancient texts to learn the demons' history?"

Nessix nodded, too excited by Mathias's lead to be disappointed that he hadn't been able to miraculously pull out a complete answer on his own. "I'd venture to say I know more about their history than you do, these days."

Mathias accepted her statement in stride, though he'd be interested in taking her up on that challenge once the immediate crisis was sorted. "And I'm going to guess none of the books he gave you were written in the fleman script?"

"They were the journals he'd kept when he'd been a mortal general marching in the Divine Battle. My people weren't even a thought in your great Etha's mind when they were written."

Nes's reminder of the demons' mortal origins struck Mathias more powerfully than he'd expected it to. Of course, he knew how the demons had come to be, and was aware that many of those ancients still lived, but even he had allowed the bleak reality that they'd once been mortals—fearful, desperate mortals fighting a war they never should have been a part of—to escape his concern. The fact that Kol had let Nessix so deeply into this past which even Mathias had overlooked… Her bond with the demon who'd slain her, who'd bound her to him and raised her from the dead began to make sense to Mathias. What had begun as a relationship based on ownership and manipulation had developed into something far deeper, shared between one defeated general and another. Kol *had* been a mortal. He'd known the struggles of fighting a lost cause. And there was a chance, one Mathias was no longer determined to barricade the door against, that Nessix had found in that ancient demon where those memories lurked. There was a chance she truly had discovered something worth fighting for in that alar.

Uncomfortable with these unwelcome revelations about the demon he was determined to hate, Mathias cleared his throat. "There is a restricted branch of the library, one which holds ancient and classified texts. Several documents had been taken off Berann and his men when they'd been slain, written in a script even the most devout and well-read of our scholars have been unable to translate and that no captured demon has…" Mathias shifted his gaze away "…complied with interpreting for us."

Nessix didn't miss the connotation in that last statement, but was too distracted by what had happened the last time she'd been in the restricted stacks of a library to make anything of it. "With what you say your current standing is with the Council, will you be able to get me in there?"

"I can get us in."

She studied his twisted lips and averted eyes, a bit of that dread which used to crop up in her stomach when Mathias presented her with one of his less-than-brilliant ideas showing itself. "You sure?"

He wasn't completely, but was past the point of civility to get what he needed so he could put this headache behind him. "I'm sure."

Nessix was just as confident in Mathias's answer as he seemed to be, but she shrugged and accepted it for what it was. "Well, then," she sighed, "looks like the Council's going to have to admit I've got a useful contribution to what ought to be their objective, after all."

Mathias echoed her sigh; of all the things he'd missed about Nessix, her condescending tendencies hadn't been among them. "Don't let it get to your head, Nes. Making them listen and getting them to take action on whatever we uncover are two entirely separate feats."

Nessix grumbled her censored opinions and rolled her eyes. Once she figured out what leverage Berann had had over Kol and those he associated with, she wouldn't bother to wait for the Council to tell her what she could and couldn't do. She wasn't a resident of Zeal or even Gelthin, and the only influence they held over her revolved around the services they could provide her. Even if she had to find her way back to Elidae and get Sulik to rally those still loyal to him, she'd stop the demons.

Mathias didn't completely trust Nes's silence, having learned in the past what her mind came up with when it was left to brood over how to tie injustice to her motives, but he wasn't inclined to discourage her now. She'd changed and matured since those days, and though her objective to protect Elidae and fight the demons who threatened it had been a valiant and worthy cause, she'd since accepted the mantle of protecting the whole of Abaeloth, much as Etha had dropped on his own shoulders all those centuries ago. Nessix no longer fought for pride or the causes her ancestors had told her to honor, but for the peace and freedom of those who didn't yet know they were in danger. He snuck a glance at her thoughtful expression. Perhaps a little bit of demon tenacity would serve her well in the days to come, and it did soothe the fears in his heart to see her enthusiasm blossom past frustration once again.

Mathias was careful to lead Nessix through as many of the back halls as possible on their way to the library, making only one brief stop to secure a palatable meal for her. Though he trusted it would take some time for the Council to figure out what to make of his most recent abuse of power, especially while juggling the drudgery of routine meetings for the afternoon, Mathias didn't fancy any further complications.

Conditioned to trust and respect Mathias as the authority figure he was, none of the priestesses objected to his request to access the restricted wing. They kept their suspicious glares on Nessix due to the biased warnings which had trickled from the officials above them, but the determined general wasn't bothered by their responses. It wasn't the first time—and she was sure wouldn't be the last—that she'd been on the receiving end of such hateful looks.

Word that Mathias had arrived at the library reached Khin quickly, and she'd dropped what she was doing to greet him so she could fulfill Tristan's wishes. What she hadn't counted on was for him to be accompanied by a woman who the priestesses recoiled from like she was some kind of hungry viper. The woman was lean and beautiful, with refined cheekbones and softly pointed ears which suggested elven heritage. Though she was short and unarmed, she held herself in a relaxed manner alongside the paladin. Her shoulders were strong and squared, her expression demanding more respect and obedience than even Mathias's did on the day-to-day, and she radiated an aura which blatantly stated that she was unwilling to accept anyone's defiance. Suddenly, Khin felt very small and very unprepared to carry out Tristan's requests. Unfortunately, Mathias had seen her emerge from between the shelves, and before Khin could scamper back into hiding, he smiled at her, and gestured for his company to follow him over in her direction.

"I'm pleased you chose to stay," he told Khin, "and I'm hoping you'll be willing and able to help me."

Khin glanced from Mathias to the woman Khin was certain was this Nessix who had unwittingly caused her so much grief, and back again, a tremble working just beneath her skin. "I'll do what I can."

Mathias gave her that same friendly smile he'd charmed her with when tending to her wounds the night he'd first found her, and she held back the overwhelming urge to tell him to knock it off, shocked that her initial reaction to his warmth was to assume it was an act.

"This is Nessix." Mathias turned a fond gaze toward the woman, missing the brisk clench of Khin's teeth in response to the tenderness in his expression. "She's needed to translate a couple of old documents to help us determine what the demons are up to. Nes"—his smile sank deep into his eyes, the mask of graciousness which he wore about in public softening in a manner Khin hadn't realized she resented until she saw it—"this is Khin. She's been helping the priestesses manage their research, and I suspect she'll be of assistance to us."

Nessix nodded to the young woman, rustling up an entirely new swarm of emotions inside of Khin. This woman who the priestesses were all so wary of had yet to judge her as unworthy, going as far as to give her a gesture of respect greater than anything Mathias had ever delivered to her. He'd been polite in the beginning, but had always viewed her as a dense child to be protected and sheltered, the little girl who didn't have the ability to solve problems. Even now, his assumption that she'd simply obey and help him fetch whatever he was after showed his disregard for her worth. But Nessix hadn't given any indication that she'd judged her.

Conflicted and confused, longing for Tristan's patient voice to tell her what to do, Khin coughed and forced herself to nod. "Of course," she said, her words catching in her throat.

Introductions as complete as they needed to be, Mathias ushered Nessix and Khin through the rest of the library and to an elaborately carved door under guard in the back. The pair of guards straightened to attention as the trio approached and they eyed Mathias cautiously.

"Sir Sagewind, the Council has been issuing complaints about your behavior," the one on the left said.

"Of course they have," Mathias replied. "It's all they can manage to agree on, isn't it?" The guards smirked and offered good-natured chuckles at Mathias's words, but didn't move. Internally grumbling, the paladin modified his approach. "As it is, they demanded I get to work on solving the current crisis, and I've got a friend"—he laid a hand on Nes's shoulder—"who can read the language of the ancients."

The guard on the right narrowed his eyes and leaned forward to look over Nessix carefully. "This isn't the woman who attacked Henrik... is it?"

Nessix scoffed and rolled her eyes, crossing her arms. "I didn't—"

"Henrik and I have sorted that out," Mathias said before Nes had the chance to further incriminate herself. "And she's received her reprimand. I've accepted full custody of her and her actions will directly reflect on me." He spoke that last bit more pointedly, indicating to Nessix his expectations of her good behavior. "She is no danger to any who call themselves a decent person."

It didn't take much for the average solider of the Order to trust Mathias when no other officials were around. Besides, he wouldn't have been able to make it past the dozens of priestesses between the library's main entrance and this dusty corner if he didn't have some sort of authorization to be here. "You accept all responsibility for any damages that happen in there?" the first guard asked for good measure.

"Every last one of them."

The two guards exchanged glances and shrugged before taking wide steps aside to part clearance to the door.

Mathias gave them a hearty smile and stepped forward to open the door. "Thank you both. I'll have a word with your—"

"Please don't," the first said sharply.

Mathias hesitated and sent the young man a quizzical glance.

"If you and the Council are behind this arrangement, there's something you haven't fully disclosed to us." The guard flushed with guilt at his bluntness. "Sir. While we won't demand you elaborate on matters which you wish to hide, we'd both prefer if you kept track of our compliance for yourself."

Mathias tilted his head as he thought over the soundness of their request. "If that's how you'd like it. My gratitude is the same, regardless."

The guards accepted Mathias's thanks and the paladin placed one hand between Nes's shoulder blades and gestured for Khin to come with them as they went through the door. The room within was tidy and comfortably small. Gently illuminated by Etha's grace, a polished wooden table sat centrally in the room, surrounded by six upholstered chairs. A staircase opposite from the entry point delved downwards into the vault of protected knowledge.

"The two of you get settled." Mathias reached forward to pull a chair back for Nessix, driving another nail into Khin's growing fortress of resentment. "I'll get what you need to look at first."

As Nessix sat, Mathias brushed a hand against her shoulder. The warrior woman didn't respond with the glow of warmth Khin would have, her brows strict with focus clearly directed toward the business at hand, but the tender gesture grated on Khin. Mathias disappeared down the stairway, and Khin awkwardly pulled back a chair at the opposite end of the table from Nessix and sat. Nessix was so confident, so beautiful, so important, and Khin squirmed as she settled into her seat. She shouldn't have agreed to gather information on Nessix, no matter how badly she wanted to impress Tristan. This was a task that was simply too big for someone like her.

Gulping down her reservations, Khin rubbed her hands over top of the polished table. "So… how did you meet Mathias?" It seemed like a good place to start. The steady weight of Nessix's eyes shifted to Khin, but the young human didn't have the nerve to look up at them.

"He was sent to help lead my people through a war against the demons," Nessix said.

"Your people?" Khin had a bit of an easier time accepting Mathias's abandonment when she looked at it from the perspective of him dashing off to protect the masses, as opposed to a single woman.

A weary smile softened Nessix's eyes. "I'm a general." She spoke the words with a weight of sorrow Khin had previously thought only she knew. "Between my army and the civilians I was responsible for, I needed all the help I could get. And that's where Mathias stepped in."

Khin caught her breath as she reflected back on how she'd looked to Mathias for the same hope. "Did your people win?"

That smile withered in Nessix's eyes and she briefly worked her jaw back and forth before dropping her eyes to the table. "My people defeated the immediate threat thanks to his leadership. "

Khin hesitated, Nessix's visual cues contradicting the words she'd spoken. "If the demons were defeated, why are they here now?"

Nessix pressed her lips together and gave a temperamental cock of her head as she swallowed a bitter retort. This child, as troubled as she clearly was, didn't need to worry about what all she'd been through. "Abaeloth has underestimated the demons for ages. They can be driven back and pushed around, but they've survived too long to give up on what they want."

"And what do they want?"

The girl's question had been meek but hopeful, frightened of the threat of the demon resurgence but also optimistic that if the mortals could provide the demons with what they wanted, they'd crawl back into their holes. If only it were that easy. Even with the way Nessix had seen Kol change as she returned to him what it meant to live among mortals, despite the persistent fondness she felt for him and the trust she'd developed in him, there were still frightening aspects of him she'd never be able to change. One of these days, she would have to face Kol again. She'd have to make the choice between returning to him or killing him, and if Mathias was with her at the time, she was relatively certain the decision would be made for her. She shivered off the painful twinges of remorse. There was no place for such emotions on the battlefield.

"They seek chaos," she murmured. "They seek destruction and retribution for sins that were never theirs to answer for. Fate

237

wronged them and they chose to fall to that pressure and become the monsters we're fighting now."

Khin shifted in her chair, having never expected to feel so uncomfortable in such a plush seat. "So… what are you looking for here?"

Nessix sighed and jerked her focus away from Kol and back to the task at hand. "We're looking for information on a dead demon named Berann."

Khin wrinkled her nose. "A dead one?"

"Yes. He knew something the rest of his kind would kill to keep from those on the surface. Our hope is that if we can uncover what that is, we can pull ahead of the demons."

All of a sudden, Tristan's request seemed far over Khin's head. She could watch Nessix and try to figure out who she was and where she came from. She could relay what Mathias told her. But this was an actual war, a war against *demons* which had apparently been brewing for some time. Not even a couple of months ago, Khin had been among the ignorant masses which thought demons were nothing but scary stories. This belief had been proven inaccurate in the worst ways possible for the young woman, and the tighter she bound herself between Mathias and Tristan, the more she feared where this revelation was leading her. Scrunching her shoulders closer to her ears, she wrapped her hands around one another and glanced at the exit.

"And what about you?" Nessix's voice gently cut through Khin's fears in the manner of one accustomed to reassuring civilians. "How did you meet—"

"Here it is." Mathias rounded the top of the stairs, carefully holding a discolored and curling piece of leather across his open palms, and saved Khin from the discomfort of answering the question nearly asked of her as Nessix half-rose from her seat to see what he'd brought. "This is the only writing that had been on Berann's person at the time of his death."

Though Kol had taken meticulous care of his old books and scrolls, Nessix had grown accustomed to handling ancient documents and accepted it so casually that Mathias held his breath. The script was written in a less graceful hand than Kol's and the ink had faded with time, but not to the point that it was illegible. Mathias stood behind Nessix to look over her shoulder and a gentle surge of nostalgia eased her back into her seat and into the words before she'd even become conscious she was reading it at all.

"'This feud will be the end of Abaeloth and if you care about her fate as much as you claim, you will listen to me. Violence has become the way of my kind, arrogance the way of yours. Let us speak as peers to overcome our differences.'"

Nessix lowered her hands to the table with a dull thump and raised her eyes to stare at the wall in front of her. Though blunt, that hadn't sounded like the words of a demon out to level cities. She wasn't the only one to reach such a conclusion, and Mathias had to stop himself from demanding Nessix had made it up in some obscure attempt to protect Kol. Her pale cheeks and gaping lips conveyed that she'd been just as shocked to uncover such a straight-forward message.

"He *had* been coming to negotiate…" she murmured.

Stunned by the simplicity of how wrong the Order had been all this time, it took Mathias a moment to organize his thoughts solidly enough for them to reach his tongue. "He ordered whoever this was written for to listen to him," he said, desperate for more proof that the lore he'd been raised on was inaccurate at best. "Listen to him about what?"

Nessix opened her fingers to let the aged document flop down onto the table, her brows stitching together in irritation. "It was three sentences, Sagewind. You heard everything that was written on it."

So much of the history which Mathias had taken as truth contradicted everything about what Nessix had just read, and though he liked to consider himself a far more open minded individual in his advanced years than he'd been in his youth, this was not at all information Mathias had been prepared to accept. "Do you really think he came to seek the Order's aid?"

Nessix lifted one hand from the table in a subtle shrug. "You said he hadn't fought the knights who accosted him at your gates. He was an oraku, an ancient. He'd survived the Divine Battle and thrived after it. There's no way a handful of city guards would have been able to kill him without taking casualties." She loosened the collar of her shirt as the small room became stifling with the approach of revelations she'd been grasping for over the past year, and turned in her seat to face him. "…Sagewind, your Order was wrong. He'd come here for help. He'd had something to tell them that could have stopped his kind from becoming what they are today. Something worth wiping him from their own history to keep hidden."

Mathias pulled back the chair beside Nessix and slumped into it to keep his head from spinning. If Nessix was right—and he was having a hard time denying that—the Order was at least in part responsible for Abaeloth's terrible history with demons. But now, he had a chance to remedy that. "There were other pieces of literature carried by his party." Hating the notion of needing to repent for centuries of misguided actions trickled into him by a fearful and biased organization, Mathias pushed himself to his feet. "A couple journals and some scrolls." He placed a hand on Nes's shoulder, his fingers clammy and trembling. "Khin, come with me. I'll need your help to carry them up here."

Khin frowned at Mathias's blunt order, but obeyed without a fuss, and she and Mathias disappeared into the archives, leaving Nessix to contemplate what was happening.

She'd known—both from Mathias's tales and what she'd uncovered while in the hells—that there had been a faction of the earliest generations of demons who had wanted to forge peace between this realm and theirs, but that was a fact of history still openly mocked in the demons' domain. There was no reason mentioning a demon, even if he'd been a leader of that cause, would merit Kol's response to her question, and even less of a reason why Mathias's connection would have behaved in a similar fashion.

Nessix closed her eyes, reaching out for those foreign sensations of Kol's memories, resenting how part of her she had no way to access knew exactly who this demon was. "What did you know, Berann…?"

Mathias returned before her thoughts could delve much deeper, Khin grudgingly in tow. He deposited a stack of nine worn journals on the table and turned to Khin to relieve her of a linen satchel filled with loose papers and curled scrolls.

"There might be more down there, but this should get you started." Mathias's excitement would have been catching, if not for one factor.

Nessix ran a quick inventory over the selection he'd brought and laughed. "It's a generous start, yes." She lifted her eyes to Mathias's, a faint vein of dread sneaking past her humor. "A *generous* start. You couldn't have pared it down a bit?"

Mathias winced and slid into his chair. "I have no idea what any of it says. How was I supposed to pare it down for you?"

Nessix sighed and slapped her hand atop the first book in the stack to pull it in front of her. "Then I'd better get started…"

Her studies under Kol had been guided and direct, and though she was still enthusiastic to get to the bottom of Berann's secrets, she looked forward to the process with more dread now. Aware of her frustrations, Mathias did his best to keep quiet and avoid asking questions as she thumbed through the pages, and Khin sat in her chair, chewing on the inside of her cheek as she stared up at the ceiling. After fifteen minutes passed, Nessix heaved a labored sigh and looked up at Mathias.

"You want to know what this is?"

His eyes lit up and he inched closer. "Of course I do."

"It's a ledger of the supplies they'd been carrying."

Mathias's expression fell. "*All* of it?"

"So far. They seemed to have a preference for cured meats and were diligent about stopping at damn near every water source they passed." She studied Mathias's disappointment, trying to find humor in it to keep from giving in to her own disappointment. "Do you want me to keep going?"

Mathias ran a finger over the remaining pages in the journal. Nessix had hardly made a dent in it, and for how many other pages there were for vital information to hide, he wanted her to keep going. But he'd also brought another eight volumes with him— hopefully books that would give them more than an ancient's eating habits—and suspected their time for this research was limited before complications would arise. He pulled the scrap of leather written in Berann's own hand over to himself, trying to make sense of the symbols as they applied to Nes's translation.

"Start another one," he said at last.

Nessix nodded once, closed the ledger, and drew the next volume off the top of the stack. This pattern continued for several hours as Nessix identified one volume which logged the geography of the region, another tracking military movement of the knights they'd found on patrol, and the last which chronicled the observed movements of other demons on the surface. It was the last volume which interested Nes and Mathias the most, but Khin covered a great yawn with her hand, reminding them all of how long they'd been sitting there.

Feeling the mental drain from the past day at last, Nessix blinked her exhausted eyes and had trouble opening them again. "I need sleep."

Khin mutely nodded her agreement, and Mathias sighed. They all needed rest after the whirlwind that was the past couple of days, and the room's lack of windows prevented them from knowing how late it had gotten.

"Very well," Mathias granted as he pushed his chair back from the table. "This room is well guarded. We can resume studying in the morning."

For the first time in hours, Khin perked up. "Will I still be needed?"

In truth, Khin had done very little for them today, but it was Mathias's hope that giving her a sense of purpose in a manner which also allowed him to keep an eye on her would move her past her fascination with Tristan. "Both needed and welcome."

The girl pulled out half a smile, but it was unclear if it was so small from insincerity or exhaustion. She wriggled out of the upholstered chair. "Then I'll see you in the morning." She bobbed with an action meant to be a curtsey. "Good night.

After Nessix and Mathias returned the farewell, Khin slipped from the room, leaving the two immortals alone amidst a trove of ancient knowledge neither of them knew what to do with.

"The answer's got to be here." Nessix dragged her weary eyes to Mathias's. "Right?"

He blew out a slow breath and ran a hand through his disheveled hair. "It's here if it's anywhere."

They sat in silence for several moments longer, neither having the heart to vocalize what it would mean if they were hunting for something that didn't exist. Too tired to dwell on it, knowing it wouldn't make any difference, anyway, Nessix sighed and braced her arms against the table to push her chair back. Before she'd expended the force to move the legs, Mathias laid a hand on her forearm to stop her.

"It's probably best if we don't leave this room until we're sure we don't need to get back inside."

Nes's tired eyes pinched in humor and she shook her head. "So you *didn't* have authorization to be in here."

He returned her tired smile. "Of course not. But it's where we needed to be."

Figuring this comfortable chair buried in a guarded room in the Citadel was a better place to sleep than the patches of overgrown grass on the side of roads monitored by assassins and demons, Nessix curled her legs onto the seat and nestled against the back of it as she let her eyes drift closed. "You haven't changed a bit, Mathias."

His heart warmed at her intimate address. She only ever called him by his given name when her guard was down, and it brought him a much-needed bit of peace to know that at least in this moment, she felt safe. Mathias leaned back into his chair and closed his eyes, reaching a hand out to hold hers. Her fingers wrapped around his and he smiled, eased into a content sleep he'd needed for weeks.

TWENTY-ONE

Tristan had been about to head out for some nighttime prowling in the secluded safety of Zeal's slums when Ceredulus gave him the strict order to stay put to greet Khin's imminent arrival. Disappointed but obedient, Tristan settled back into the stiff wooden chair at Sazrah's modest dining table and stared at the door until a timid knock, as though Khin was afraid she'd selected the wrong home in the dark, rapped against it. Donning the smile that worked so well against the girl's sensibilities, Tristan rose to answer her request, opening the door to her wide, bloodshot eyes.

"Do you have information for me?" he asked.

She scooted closer to the door to hide herself from the openness of the moonlit street, and nodded.

Tristan's smile broadened and he stepped aside. "Then come in and share with me what you know."

Khin wasted no time following Tristan's instructions and scuttled into the house. "Mathias brought Nessix to a restricted part of the library."

Tristan quietly closed the door, pleased to hear that the intriguing woman he'd run into in the dungeon had been spared further humiliation and even more interested in where she'd ended up. "Did either of them tell you what they were looking for in a restricted area?"

Khin turned back to Tristan, fidgeting with the skirt of her dress. "They were reading notes and journals from a dead demon named Berann. Mathias said Nessix was the only person able to read them."

The charming façade Tristan wore to enamor Khin slipped in lieu of his interest in her report. "And could she?"

"As far as I could tell. She read things out loud like she knew what they said."

My lord… how would a fleman woman know the ancients' tongue…? "What did you learn of Nessix, herself?"

Khin's shoulders slumped as her arms dropped to her sides. "You, too?"

Tristan's brows knit together and he stepped closer to the dejected girl. He'd worked too hard keeping her compliant to risk offending her now. "What do you mean?"

"Everyone is so interested in that woman." Khin cast her eyes to the floor and picked at the cuticle of a thumb. "The Council's all upset over her, the priestesses whisper about her all day, Mathias is smitten over her like a stag in rut. I'd thought… maybe…" She sneered at herself and turned from Tristan completely as if she'd be able to escape him in this tiny house.

So this woman is *the key*, Ceredulus murmured. *Do not lose your pet's compliance.*

Obeying his god's order, Tristan strode smoothly over to Khin and turned her to face him once again. She didn't fight him, but neither did she look up. "Dear Khin," he murmured. "I've no interest in that creature other than what information she might be able to lend me."

Khin shook her head and snuck a sheepish glance at the handsome man before her. "Creature?"

Tristan cocked his head. "Has nobody told you?" He waited for the girl's brows to furrow and for her to give a subtle shake of her head. "Why, she is far more of an abomination than I have ever been. Just as undead, but where I'd been risen by divine means, it was demons who brought her back to life." Khin's arms tensed in his grasp and he knew he'd snared her yet again. "I have been tasked with understanding *how* this happened. That is my only interest in her. You have my word."

His reassurance worked slowly through Khin's mind and clearly in her troubled eyes. As much as she feared everything tied to the demons now that her grief had had time to settle, Tristan was still counting on her. "I learned very little about her," she said at last, "only that she is a general looking to find out what that Berann demon knew."

Berann… Ceredulus drew the name out slowly. *He was that ancient oraku the blasted Order killed at the onset of the Demon War.*

Spurred by his god's interest, Tristan pressed the topic. "And what did she learn about him?"

Khin lowered her eyes again, ashamed of herself that she'd have to disappoint Tristan. "Not much. At least not that she said out loud. She read a lot of military records and a note Mathias said Berann had carried himself."

"And what did that note say?"

Khin pressed her lips tight as she sifted through her weary memory for the information Tristan sought. "Something about violence being the demons' way and arrogance being Zeal's. Nessix said something about the Order being wrong about him and him wanting to make peace, that his own kind wanted to kill him over what he knew."

Get. That. Note.

Tristan's eyes widened and he drew his shoulders back so sharply that he jerked Khin a step forward. Ceredulus was a powerful god with no end to his frightening potential to those who had the mind to cross him. Tristan had earned his god's trust beyond his peers due to his history of unflinching obedience. As such, Ceredulus had never had a need to make strict demands of this particular servant, but his words now struck Tristan with the first fear he'd experienced in centuries, and the vampire had long ago forgotten how to manage such seizing sensations.

"T-Tristan…?" Khin's timid voice squeezed past the vampire's shock and jolted him back into functioning. "Did I say something wrong…?"

"No, Khin." His voice was raspy and harsh as he tried to press past his fear. "You've done everything right so far."

I order you to obtain that note.

Tristan gulped down the command, feeling Ceredulus's evaporating patience slowly strangling him. "I need you to get a hold of that note of Berann's for me, Khin."

Her eyes widened at the uncharacteristic tension of his strained tone and the request itself. "But that would be stealing from the Order..."

It will not matter for long.

Tristan grit his teeth as his god's pressure caved in on top of him. "You've broken enough laws helping me as it is. One more is nothing."

Khin gulped down the accusation, as she hadn't fully processed the errors of her actions until now. Was this what Mathias had been afraid of? Had he been trying to protect her all along? She glanced at her arm where Tristan's fingers pressed into her flesh and up at his eyes. The warmth had cooled from them, replaced with a desperate urgency Khin almost related to, and she drew a shuddering breath.

"Tristan, it's guarded in the restricted—"

"It's guarded by a buffoon who's too distracted by his girlfriend to notice if one slip of paper goes missing," Tristan insisted.

Khin shrank back at the blunt remark and the sharpness of Tristan's voice, but she didn't put up more of a fuss about it. "I guess I could offer to return it to the archives and slip it up my sleeve." She frowned at the notion of willingly doing something so devious and wrong, but as the strict edge smoothed away from Tristan's features, her concerns lifted with them.

Ceredulus's approval settled over Tristan's shoulders and seeped the relaxation which Khin had grown to assume was the vampire's default through his body. "Thank you, Khin. Was there anything else of merit discussed or uncovered today?"

That tick of apprehension returned to the girl. She had no idea what Tristan was even after; how could she know if something worthwhile had transpired? Either way, as she looked into his eyes, warm and friendly once again, she was reassured that what she was able to provide was enough. "Not that I could tell."

Tristan nodded his acceptance. "You can—"

Invite her to stay the night.

Tristan coughed on Ceredulus's interruption. He'd rather looked forward to a hunt through the slums this evening and Khin's innocence would stand in the way of those plans.

"I can what, Tristan?"

The time is nearing where it will no longer be safe for her to travel the streets on her own and her safety is paramount to my objectives.

That tension which Tristan had just shed crept back to him as he shifted his attention away from the apprehensive girl before him and to his god's ominous implications. "I'd like for you to stay with me tonight."

Khin choked on a sharp gasp, blood rapidly drawing to her fair cheeks as she squeaked Tristan's name, but he didn't immediately respond to her shock.

Is the Order the threat, my lord?

No. Demons are marching on Zeal with valuable cargo. You keep your pet safe and your eyes on the Citadel.

Keep his eyes on the Citadel... A smile toyed at the corners of Tristan's lips but he restrained it in light of Khin's raging uncertainty. *You're sending me inside again?*

If the Sagewinds leave.

Khin tugged against Tristan's hold on her arms and a trill of uncertainty danced in her throat, eyes playing back memories she'd never imagined associating with the charming vampire.

They won't likely stay gone for long. Tristan released his hold on Khin so she could back away from him.

They don't need to. You're to head into the repository to reclaim an artifact of mine. Nothing more.

Tristan lowered his head in submission.

Now, comfort that poor girl before you lose her trust. I need the hands of a compliant mortal to carry my artifact, and she's the only one we've got.

Ceredulus's driving presence left Tristan, and the vampire's concentration on his immediate surroundings snapped into clarity as Khin whimpered a feeble protest.

"But, Tristan, I don't think I—"

"Dear Khin," Tristan sighed. He turned from the girl, giving her the option to try to dart out the door. "The night streets are soon to become dangerous for a young woman to travel on her own." He drew back the covers on the bed and stepped aside. "I've little need of sleep, but you are clearly exhausted. Stay here tonight, where you'll be safe. I'll let no harm find you so long as you're near." It wasn't a lie. She remained the source of his permission to enter the Citadel and his key to getting his hands on the document and artifact his god wanted. He couldn't afford to lose her yet.

Khin didn't move from where she'd backed up against the wall of the tiny house, and Tristan sighed again. Hanging his head, he stepped away from the bed and leaned a shoulder against the wall opposite from the girl.

"I thought you said you trusted me," he said.

Khin's eyes widened and her distraught fingers plucked at the skirt of her dress as she plucked at excuses to appease Tristan. "I *do*…"

"Yet you hold me to the same standards as the filthiest of mortals?"

She lowered her eyes. That was exactly what she'd been doing.

"Hadn't you claimed I was a friend? That I'd been the only one to treat you like your own person?"

The past year of Khin's life hadn't been easy or fair, and Tristan's accusations made it seem all the worse. Her fatigued mind stumbled over what he was saying and what she should do, both in terms of this offer and the dishonest request he'd made of her. But one thing stuck out among all the rest. She *did* trust Tristan.

"I… I'm sorry," she murmured.

He softened his expression. "You've nothing to apologize for. This world has done all it could to lead you to harm. Let me teach you a new way to life. Stay here tonight, Khin. You are safe with me."

Mathias's warnings screamed at her that this was a terrible decision. The stories she'd been told about vampires whimpered over the dangers of letting Tristan any closer than she already had. But he'd promised to help her find her family again. He wanted to lead her to a life she could control. Her mind was fuzzy from emotional overwhelm, muddling her common sense the way exhaustion tingled at her arms and legs.

The night was late. The streets were dark. And Mathias was preoccupied with Nessix. Nobody would have to know where she was, and she'd be safe from anything prowling the streets.

With a great sigh, Khin closed her eyes, her muscles sagging as she finally let go of the tension she'd forced out of herself to function this late. "Sleep would be nice."

Tristan smiled and walked over to her, tenderly taking her arm as he guided her over to the bed. "Yes, it would."

She burrowed beneath the covers and didn't protest as he pulled them up over her shoulders.

"Tomorrow, we will put something beautiful into motion, but for now, you must sleep, dear Khin. Sleep away your stress and your fears."

His words were so smooth and melodic, tempting her mind away from those very concerns he'd mentioned. It wasn't long until the young woman was deep in slumber and, suspecting he'd need more strength tomorrow than he'd expected, Tristan left the girl in the safety of Sazrah's house and slipped out into the streets to accomplish his own objectives.

TWENTY-TWO

Grell hated just about everything about the surface realm. He hated the brightness of the sun. He hated the way the wind made his hair tickle his ears and cheeks. He hated the fresh smell of thriving vegetation and the constant chatter of creatures which hadn't yet been dominated or eradicated by his kind. More than any of that, though, he hated the way Kol seemed to think he'd snatched some semblance of control away from him.

That damn alar's problem now, as it had been since the days they'd all been mortals, was that in his heart, he was a sentimental sap. It was the sole reason, Grell was sure, that he'd remained by the sides of those he'd known the longest, despite the constant deterioration of respect they showed him. It was why he'd been sucked in so close to the mistake that had been Nessix. And it was how Grell knew exactly where Kol would have made his base of operations here on the surface.

His race down the Undersea Pass had worn his massive legs, and as he glared up the mountainside to where the home he'd neither set foot nor thought in for centuries, Grell was grateful his wings would be able to haul him up to Vesper. His memories of the region had faded as he'd grown comfortable in the hells, and an aerial scouting of the peaks would be the fastest way for him to find the village his distant connections allegedly still managed.

He ignored how much harder and faster he had to flap his wings compared to the smaller, more agile alar as he climbed into the purity of the sky, continuing to deny Annin's claim that he wouldn't have been able to keep up with their flight from Elidae. Denial or not, Grell's progress up the mountains of Harborswatch moved at a slower pace than his trip down the passage which connected Elidae to Gelthin, and by the time he could make out the speckles of blue tents nestled on the peak before him, he was ready to land. As the demons who resided in those tents identified who he was and scattered about the encampment upon sighting him, he was even more pleased to do so.

Grell plummeted to a rough landing in the middle of the makeshift village just as Lorrin was stalking toward him. The oraku kept his hands low and his jaw clenched, but his single eye spoke of the keen hatred which triggered memories of this tribe's parting ways in Grell's mind. Unfortunately for Lorrin, Grell had a vague idea of how his powers stacked up against the oraku who still considered the hells their home, and he expressed his lack of respect accordingly.

"This is all you've got left of your pathetic colony?" Grell asked, casting his mocking gaze across the thin number of troops patching together a perimeter around their leader.

Lorrin stopped a good six strides from Grell, close enough to not have to shout, but far enough to give him a second to react on the occasion of Grell attacking. "Our numbers are strong. I've sent several men out on patrol, is all."

Grell crossed his arms and nodded. "And you still haven't found a way to magic yourself a new eye?"

Lorrin bit into his snarl, but not fast enough to stop his tongue. "I'll fix my eye as soon as Annin finds what it takes to fix your face."

Grell worked his jaw back and forth, acutely aware of how the scar which spread from lip to eye pulled against the action, weighing out if he'd be better served to retaliate to the insult or let it go. As it was, the inoga was quite comfortable with his might, and he still had a particular use for Lorrin. He let the jab slide off his back with a deep chuckle.

"Nah…" he sighed. "I don't feel the need to hide from the past like the rest of you. My scars are proof that I survived. What's Annin been up to, anyway?"

"He's—" Grell had thrown that question in so casually that Lorrin nearly missed how out of place it had been, and suddenly the warnings Kol and Annin had given him about Grell's interest in punishing those involved with this missing general seemed much more relevant. "He's been beneath Elidae for the war there, hasn't he?"

When it came to intelligence, Lorrin had Grell beat by just a hair, which still left him pale in comparison to Kol and Annin. Grell knew there was no way his subordinates could have tracked down Nessix with only their petty handful of friends, and the sparse population of Vesper readily pointed toward where the two had found additional help. The question now was why Lorrin found it necessary to try to cover for them. Such generosity wasn't a trait common among demons, and as far as Grell was concerned, Lorrin had no more reason to declare loyalty to Kol—nor should Kol have assumed he'd receive as much from Lorrin—than he did to Grell.

"He *had* been beneath Elidae for the war," Grell replied, "but that's been over for some time now. I'd thought your diligent scouts would have kept you better apprised of Mathias Sagewind's location."

Lorrin shrugged and turned his head to better center Grell in his sight. "That damn paladin comes and goes when he wants. How were we supposed to know—and why should we have *cared*—about the mess you made on Elidae?"

Grell smirked. "So you *did* get reports."

Lorrin didn't bother hiding his grimace. His urge to humble and humiliate Grell had been too strong. Oh well. Nothing he could do about it now, and he was confident in Kol's promise that there would soon be a world without inoga calling the shots. "Why are you here, Grellandier?"

The blunt question and use of the name he'd hated even when he'd been a mortal wiped the smirk from Grell's face, replacing it with a curled lip. "Remind me again what rank and title Kol had given you after rescuing your sorry ass from the dwarves of Hearth."

Not accepting the insult half as gracefully as Grell had swallowed his previous one, Lorrin pressed his toes hard in the soles of his boots, grounding himself for a defensive maneuver.

"Oh, that's right." A haughty snort burst from Grell and brought his smirk out once more. "He hadn't given you one. And do you remember what you had to call me, Lorrin?"

Lorrin's lip twitched, but a brief appraisal of Grell's impatient eyes prompted him to push past his pride and answer the question. "Captain," he muttered.

"Yes, that's right." Grell dropped his arms to his sides and took a slow step forward. "You'd been nothing and I'd been a captain. And now, I am Kol's lord, practically his god, so what do you suppose that makes you?"

Lorrin hadn't needed any more reasons to hate Grell, but the damned inoga was just as skilled at infuriating him as he'd remembered. While he was confident in his skills with magic, inoga were built so dense that reaching the most vital threads was difficult, and though Lorrin commanded greater physical strength than the average oraku, he was still only half Grell's size—and a quarter of his might. Kol and Annin couldn't find this missing lady general of theirs fast enough.

Lorrin looked away, infuriated and shamed by Grell's arrogance but too smart to continue picking this fight. "It makes me nothing."

"*Less* than nothing," Grell corrected. "Which means that if you still answer to Kol, then you answer to me first."

"What makes you think I answer to Kol?" Lorrin asked defensively, retreating a step from Grell's prior advance.

This game was losing its novelty for Grell. He'd wanted—and had expected to gain with little trouble—Lorrin's prompt obedience, through with having those beneath him play him as a fool. He took another step forward, this one larger and with a far more serious purpose.

"I think you answer to Kol because you're going to tell me you do."

Lorrin had two obvious options. He could continue trying to convince Grell that he hadn't seen Kol in years, a feat he'd struggle with more from Grell's suspicions than because it didn't hold an ounce of truth, or he could admit to Kol's passing through Vesper and hope Grell didn't want to know more details than Lorrin was willing to give. One thing was certain, though. Angering the inoga would be a terrible mistake.

"Kol and Annin passed through here for food and rest on their way to Zeal," he admitted at last. "Just because they took my supplies doesn't mean I was answering to them."

The honest answer still wasn't good enough for Grell. "Did they tell you their business in Zeal?"

It had been so long since Lorrin had to stare down an inoga that he had difficulty determining if he saw genuine ignorance or a sly glint in Grell's narrowed eyes. He didn't know nearly enough about his old comrades' plans to determine if Grell would have thought it appropriate for him to know about that Nessix woman or the undead army she was supposed to lead. But he'd also stumbled his way into a corner. Travelling to Zeal was a suicide mission for any demon, and Lorrin had just confirmed knowing of Kol and Annin's intentions to get there. Cursing his foolishness, hating Grell all the more for outsmarting him, Lorrin caved to honesty.

"They said they were going to trade a handful of priestesses for some general they'd brought back from the dead."

Grell's eyes opened a bit wider and he nodded in satisfaction. "About how long ago was that?"

Lorrin's heart raced as he realized he was preparing to betray Annin's trust. Equally as frightened of Annin as he was of Grell, Lorrin had to balance his odds in favor of appeasing the threat which stood before him now. "A couple days ago."

"I see."

Neither demon spoke for long moments, each waiting for the other to make the next move. Finally, Grell, who had gotten bored with the conversation while it had been flowing, cued it up again.

"Why did you try to hide the fact that they'd stopped by? You must have suspected I already knew. What good did you think would come from lying to me about it?"

Lorrin read the unspoken question behind those words so clearly that Grell might as well have stated what had truly been on his mind. He wasn't concerned at all about Kol or Annin being protected, but he cared greatly about what they had been up to. That was an answer Lorrin was simply unable to deliver honestly, but since Grell had taken to hunting out lies, he delivered the closest thing to a confession that he could.

"They said you'd be angry at this general, that you were angry with them over losing track of her."

"I am," Grell replied. "Which begs me to ask again why you thought it was wise to attempt hiding it from me. I am only trying to keep up with their progress and make sure they don't screw this up. Again."

It was of great benefit that Lorrin had known Grell in the past, because he saw straight through the inoga's poor illusion of concern. All of this pointed toward sealing the fact that Lorrin *had* to keep Kol and Annin safe if he hoped to continue entertaining the idea of the inoga's downfall.

"Maybe you demons of the hells have learned to trust each other, but here on the surface, there's too many do-gooders running about trying to foul up our plans. Covering our tracks is an instinct up here, not a choice."

Grell cocked his head. "Why would tracks need to be covered?"

"I…" Lorrin's ability to keep up with Grell's pointed prying faltered as he realized he had no safe answer readily available.

"I'd thought you and your tribe had sworn to be through with the affairs of those of us who stayed in the hells," Grell continued. "What makes Kol the exception to you?"

A flurry of excuses bombarded the oraku, but it was quite possibly the worst one which reached his tongue first. "He wasn't in the hells when he passed through, now was he?"

Had Grell thought there was any chance Lorrin would ever become subservient to him, he'd have found the pathetic attempt humorous. He and Lorrin had only barely gotten along when they were mortals—Grell secretly threatened by Lorrin's competence with battle magic, and Lorrin envying the position Grell's past with Kol had earned him—and the changes which had occurred to them while becoming demons only enhanced their suspicions of one another. There was no doubt in Grell's mind that Lorrin was still hiding information from him, and he was just as certain that there'd be no way to extract it from him. Demons were a tough bunch, and those who chose to live on the surface were among the most resilient of them all. Grell might have been unable to convince Lorrin to confess to him, but he had managed to confirm his theory that Kol and Annin were working one of their schemes and that he'd been right to follow them.

"I'm not in the hells right now, either," Grell said, all humor gone from his voice. "But that's alright. I can cover my own tracks."

The threat registered to Lorrin immediately, but by the time he'd managed to raise his arm to begin frantically tearing at Grell's threads, the inoga's muscular legs had soundly launched him forward to close the distance between them. It wasn't the first time Grell had gone up against an oraku, and Annin had inadvertently taught him a few tricks on simplifying the matter. Before Lorrin had the chance to do more than raise his arm, before any of the demons who remained in Vesper could muster their courage to charge the behemoth attacking their leader, Grell jabbed a finger into Lorrin's remaining eye, burrowing it deep into the socket as the oraku's sweet screams fueled his madness.

No longer able to see the threads he needed to access, unable to even see the familiar surroundings of his home, Lorrin attempted a retreat which was promptly halted by Grell's crushing grip on his bicep. Damn Kol for getting him into this. Damn him straight into Etha's embrace.

Shouts sprang up all around him, the balance of his forces organizing to stand against this monstrous opponent, but Lorrin would never know if their efforts would prevail.

* * * * *

It had taken a brutal attack by a quartet of demons for

Marcoux to lose his carefree nature. It had taken a beating and a dislocated shoulder, watching his younger brother be involved in some bizarre ritual and stabbed through the heart for him to admit that Talier had been right all along. They should have found a respectable job, a safe job, somewhere in the security and stability of a city.

Marcoux hadn't bothered to count the days he'd been a prisoner to these demons, seldom able to keep track of his thoughts past the horrors and tortures they inflicted upon him. He couldn't recall how many prayers he'd said, petitioning for divine intervention to get him out of this situation, but as the hulking, grotesque mass of demon arrived, Marcoux wished he'd specified a bit more clearly on how he'd hoped to be saved.

He couldn't understand a word that passed between the giant demon and the leader of this camp, but when his guard stood, attention focused on the developing confrontation, Marcoux saw his chance sneaking up on him. The two demons continued their discussion, drawing the guard a bit farther away, and the battered human gathered up all that was left of his coherence to scan the soiled straw around him for anything that could assist him with escape or, at the very least, survival. As he spotted a jagged splinter of bone that might be in his reach, a blood-curdling scream broke his concentration. Though he had no fondness for any of the demons he'd encountered, he froze and looked up at the cry of agony, his empty stomach heaving as he witnessed the giant demon scoop the camp leader's eye from its socket, a spray of blood shooting out as veins burst and bundles of nerves snapped.

As much as the resiliency of Marcoux's hope wanted to believe that maybe that monster had come to save him, as the rest of the demons in the camp shouted and prepared to counter the attack, Marcoux knew his place was out of sight and out of mind. His body had long ago forgotten how to tremble, but it took nothing at all to remember how to collapse. Turning his face away from the grunts of combat and wails of death, Marcoux drew upon his ingrained talent for lying, and held his breath.

It could have been thirty seconds or three hours before the final whimper sounded, and still Marcoux laid immobile, his back to the camp which had become a battlefield. A single set of feet clomped across the stony ground, suggesting that it had been the giant who won, and the clattering of metal goods and tearing of fabric as the beast rummaged through nearby tents told Marcoux it wasn't yet safe to move. The monstrous demon completed his looting and Marcoux waited until he heard those heavy steps fade into the distance. He waited until the cackles of carrion birds came to remind him of the death surrounding him. He waited until the sun withdrew its warmth as it passed behind the peaks. And finally, Marcoux allowed himself to open his eyes.

Slowly rolling over, he was grateful for the emptiness of his stomach. Though he'd constantly prayed for his captors to die terrible deaths, he'd never imagined such carnage of broken necks, limbs snapped from their bodies, and so much blood. The crows hopped about the field, barking about their great fortune, and the rapidly dwindling light prompted Marcoux into action before darkness robbed him of the ability to do so.

Locating the shard of bone, he fumbled through picking the locks on his wrists. Legs weak from lack of use and nutrition, the only thing which kept him on his feet was his fear of falling into the gore of the village, and he stumbled to the leader's tent. The giant demon had already ransacked the inside, but Marcoux found a half-eaten plate of cold food and generous piles of furs. Basic needs trumping the flashes of horror behind his eyes and the stench of death which had crept inside with him, Marcoux devoured the meal and buried himself in the furs.

He woke with the sun and to the continued chorus of bickering crows, accepting that the fact that he was still alive meant none of the demons were, and he went to work immediately hunting out clothing and rations. Once his necessities were met, he swallowed the nauseous lump that rose thanks to the previous night's gorged meal, and left the tent. He'd need money—or small valuables to sell—if and when he reached a civilized town.

Creeping through the demon remains as though afraid one of them would grab his ankles, Marcoux picked his way over to where the leader lay crumbled on the ground. At least his head had been spun around so Marcoux didn't have to look into that eyeless face as he pulled rings off cold fingers and the more jingly of the pouches from the demon's belt. The rings alone must have been worth a small fortune, and Marcoux didn't have the nerve to stay in this nightmare any longer.

Unaware that one of these pouches held half the soul of the woman who had brought about all of his misfortune, Marcoux gathered up his supplies and organized his legs the best he could to descend the mountain and leave Vesper behind.

TWENTY-THREE

Nessix woke with a start from her first nightmare in days, more agitated than usual at how her dreams mocked her over the fact that she was so close to uncovering Berann's worth, but still so far away from the same. Mathias stirred as she slipped her hand from his to run it through her hair, and she stretched the night's awkward sleeping position out of her hips and shoulders. Not quite ready to face Mathias's questions and the explanations she'd have to provide him, she tried to be quiet as she straightened her seat to resume reading. Despite her efforts, Mathias, as always, was ready to take action the moment he was awake.

"Did you sleep—"

"No."

Mathias silenced his request at Nes's blunt answer, letting her flip through a few pages of the book she'd ended the previous night's studies in. "Maybe tonight I can get you to an actual bed."

Nessix dumped a brisk sigh from her lungs. "I'm used to sleeping on the ground, Sagewind. The accommodations were just fine."

He frowned at Nes's obvious irritation, having hoped a quiet night would have raised her spirits. Instead, it seemed to have only given her more time to brood over how far they'd yet to go. "We'll find the answers, Nes." He spoke that affirmation as much for

261

himself as he did for her.

She shoved the book away, curling her lips between her teeth as she stared at the page. "But what if we don't?"

"We *will*."

She shook her head. "I should already know what we're looking for, and these damn books don't have anything helpful in them."

Mathias furrowed his brow. "How in Etha's name are you supposed to know? That alar refused to tell you anything."

Nessix winced at the way Mathias spat his reference to Kol but was just frustrated enough with the demon right now to not make anything of it. "There were a lot of things I learned from Kol which he didn't tell me," she muttered. "And of course the one important thing still escapes me…"

Mathias leaned forward to prop his elbow on the table and met Nes's eyes. "What are you saying?"

She held his patient, inquisitive gaze until a distorted sense of shame forced her to look away. "I know about the Divine Battle because I've seen it through Kol's eyes," she muttered. "I told you before, I've *lived* through his memories."

A chill swept across Mathias, pulling his shoulders back as he straightened his position. Nessix had always gravitated toward drama and that was how he'd taken her initial claim, but her hushed tone and the subdued gloss in her eyes assured him she wasn't elaborating a more mundane truth to suit her whims. This entire time, the motive behind Nes's fondness for Kol had escaped Mathias, but if she'd somehow spent the past year experiencing Abaeloth's most devastating day alongside one of its survivors… That was an absolutely valid reason to feel kindred to him.

Mathias cleared his throat, unsure if he wanted to know more. "How?"

"Whatever was done to me, however he'd bound himself to me, I… I relive the moments before he fell in that war in my dreams."

Despite his curiosity about what other details Nessix could provide about the most pivotal period of Abaeloth's history, Mathias lowered his eyes, now feeling like a great ass for asking her

262

how she'd slept. "You're *sure* these are his memories?"

Nessix opened her mouth to answer, but the words didn't come as she felt Kol's trembling arms wrap around her, the warmth of his tears as they pressed against the back of her neck, the rapid pulse of his terrified heart as he tried to let go of past traumas he'd never be able to forget. It was a memory of Nes's which Mathias had no right to, and her fingers curled against the tabletop.

"I'm sure." Her words came out firm but soft. "He never confirmed it to me outright, but he hadn't needed to."

Well, Etha chimed, *this adds some juicy intrigue to her circumstances.*

That wasn't quite how Mathias would have put it. He blew out a slow breath and leaned back in his chair. "And all you managed to learn about Berann was his name?"

Nessix nodded. "A name and a class. That's it. I've met others from Kol's past, alive and demented in the hells, and he told me of the ones who had died. Only Berann was completely unaccounted for, and Kol was adamant I let him stay that way."

Mathias squinted at the ceiling. "Did you ever ask the other demons about him?"

Nessix coughed on her laugh. "After how Kol beat me for it?" Mathias glanced at her, challenging her devotion to the alar. "Kol *liked* me and he made me regret mentioning Berann's name. I'm impulsive, Sagewind, not stupid."

Before Mathias had the opportunity to press back on where Nes's loyalties lie, the door creaked open. Both of them jerked to attention, fearing they'd been found out, but all that peeked through was the current shift's guard who looked right past Nessix to Mathias.

"Sir, Khin has returned to assist your studies."

Nessix relaxed instantly, relieved that the disruption had distracted Mathias from the uncomfortable topic they'd been approaching, and she pulled her book close again.

"Thank you," Mathias said. "Send her in."

The girl squeezed through the door quickly, as though acutely aware that she was doing something wrong, and went immediately to her seat from yesterday. The door was an inch from closing when the sharp gasps and stammered excuses from the guards preceded the door flinging open once again to reveal a stern Julianna. Khin yelped in surprise, Nessix snapped to attention, prepared for the inevitable conflict the High Priestess had brought with her, but Mathias was the one to scramble to his feet to rush around the table and intercept whatever intentions his sister had. After all, he was the one who had manipulated his way to access the restricted area.

"Guests aren't supposed to enter this part of the library." Julianna's words snapped with authority as Mathias neared.

"I know." There was no use lying over this, so Mathias buckled down on the honest approach. "But Nessix can read the language of the ancients, and she's got valid reason to suspect Berann had been hiding something his kin didn't want us to know."

Julianna shook her head and braced her delicate fingers against her forehead. "Oh, for Etha's... *You* of all people should know the history—"

"I, of all people, know the history which the Order painted for the world." Mathias sent a pleading glance Nes's direction, giving her worried expression a tight frown. "The evidence in here already points to a mortal bias against what he'd actually been up to."

Julianna stared at her brother hard, delving for hints that he doubted what he'd just said, but the desperate light in his eyes and the pained optimism in the angle of his brows stated clearly that the evidence he spoke of was tangible. Realizing she had no ground to stand on with the limited information she had, Julianna sighed.

"Well, any research either of you are hoping to accomplish will have to wait."

Nessix straightened in her chair at Julianna's snipped tone, but she remained silent, content to let Mathias negotiate whatever was happening.

"The Council," Julianna continued, "would like another meeting. With both of you."

Now, Nessix pushed herself to her feet, heated remarks fresh on her tongue. Mathias hadn't even needed to turn his attention to the sound of her movement before he held a hand back to her and claimed the duty of navigating these conditions himself.

"We've got more important, pressing matters to tend to," he

countered. "We'll meet with the Council once we've found what we need."

Julianna turned a skeptical eye at the withered old tomes on the table and the combative glint in Nessix's eyes. "It would benefit the both of you to come with me willingly. The Council has sworn—to me and Etha both—that you will be given a fair audience."

"Fair on whose terms?" Mathias asked.

Julianna shifted her authoritative gaze to her brother. "Mine. Or are you and I at odds with one another now, too?"

The question hung in the air like a side of beef at the butcher's. Nessix had only a slim reason to trust Julianna after how she'd been treated over the past few days, but Mathias knew his sister's heart and mind well. She was afraid, though she wouldn't admit it. She was afraid just as she had been when her desperate prayers had prompted Etha to first raise Mathias from the dead. Julianna often sat in on Council business, but had learned to allow the mortal-appointed officials to handle what transpired in the courtroom. If she'd managed to arrange for them to surrender the bulk of their authority to her calm sensibilities, Mathias and Nessix might be alright.

"Will you give me your word that both Nessix and I will be released as free individuals to return to our research as soon as the Council's immediate concerns have been addressed?" Mathias asked.

Julianna crossed her arms, her head tilting in an argumentative fashion. "That all depends on— "

"It depends on nothing," Mathias said, gaining the shocked attention of both women he'd invited into the room. "If you want me to agree to your terms, you will agree to mine."

Julianna's gaze slid to Nessix then pointed back to Mathias. "I cannot protect either of you from the ramifications of another physical assault."

Mathias crossed his arms and backed up to lean his weight against the table. "Tell the officials to not give us a reason to and you won't have to worry about it."

Nessix felt the beginning of a smirk toy at her lips. It would be nice to see those dolts humbled and unable to provoke her. Maybe then something productive could be accomplished.

"Deal," Julianna said after a long moment of consideration. "But we leave now."

Mathias dropped his arms to his sides and stood up. "*Now?* We haven't even had breakfast."

"It's fine, Sagewind." Nessix stepped around the table, calm and relaxed, and gave him a smile. "Let's give them what they want so we can get back to work without needing to dwell over their nonsense. We can eat later."

Julianna raised her eyebrows in pleasant surprise and approval. "You were right, Mattie. She does have sensibility in her."

Nes's eyes narrowed at the backhanded compliment, but she recognized the advantage her opponent was seeking and refused to offer such an opening. She grasped Mathias's elbow and stepped forward.

"I suspect I'm the most sensible one in this entire city," she said. "Let's go."

Once again, Nessix was far calmer and infinitely more sure of herself than Mathias was. She'd already seen the worst of the Council's behavior, yet she was ready and willing to face them again. This couldn't end well…

Trapped between Julianna's expectations and Nessix's composure, Mathias groaned and allowed Nessix to lead him out the door behind his sister.

Khin sat, forgotten as usual, by herself in one of the most restricted rooms in the Citadel. And before her on the table sat that little note Tristan had asked for. Biting her lip, she glanced down the staircase and back at the closed door, hardly believing nobody was here to watch her.

Let Mathias leave her alone. Let Nessix be the one who demanded everyone's attention. Khin had only one person to please, and she would do so.

* * * * *

To say Nessix had grown fed up with the Council would have

been to say she thought Inwan had been a decent god. They'd separated her from Mathias, keeping him standing centered before their panel and ordering her to sit off to the side under a modest guard, and after nearly an hour of listening to these alleged dignitaries debate whether or not she could be trusted—a debate everyone in the room, except Nessix herself, had been allowed to weigh in on—Nessix had gotten to the point where she could anticipate each member's argument before it was even formed. How Mathias had ever managed to get anything done in this city was well beyond her. It was no wonder he'd leapt at the chance to go fight demons on Elidae.

The first bit of excitement to catch Nes's interest arrived in the form of a pimply young man, wrinkled uniform stained with sweat as he squeezed through the cracked doors and scooted across the floor as though none of the eyes facing him would be able to see him.

"This is a closed meeting!" Henrik roared, and Nessix enjoyed a brief moment of reprieve as the pompous man's frustration was directed at someone other than her and Mathias.

The young man bowed his head and nodded profusely, continuing forward, though his feet dragged with reluctance. "Yes, sir. I know, sir. Forgive me, sir, but—"

"Then you will see yourself out!"

The young man cringed lower still, his nodding growing increasingly frantic as his gait slowed even further. "Yes, sir. But the southern gates are requesting Sir Sagewind and his charge."

Henrik cast his accusing glare at Mathias, eyes narrowing as he went to work contemplating what sort of diversion the paladin had arranged. Mathias answered the critical appraisal with a shrug that was everything but apologetic, and smirked as he turned to face the young man. Nessix sat up straight now that the room's activities were taking an alternate path and looked over the heads of her guards, trying to eavesdrop from across the room. Her efforts of hearing what the flustered youth was reporting didn't work, but she did catch Mathias's prolonged look her way, the color draining from her cheeks as his expression filtered from amusement at the Council's expense into a deeper concern which Nessix and her life spent commanding an army had taught her to know well.

Mathias pulled a coin from the pouch on his belt and passed it to the messenger, speaking soft words of encouragement and giving him a hearty pat on the shoulder before sending him back out the door. After the young man had disappeared from the chamber, Mathias strode to Nessix's platform.

"Move," he ordered the pair of guards before her.

In their position by official orders, the guards shifted uncomfortably at the notion of ignoring their superior's instruction as he delivered it a foot from their faces.

"Sir Sagewind, we are not done here, and you will take your hands off our—"

Mathias spun, the ferocity in his glare enough to silence Henrik's complaint. "If you call her your prisoner, Henrik, I will come back for you as soon as I'm through with whatever business I have at the gates."

Henrik growled and gnashed his teeth. "This is nonsense!"

"And I am inclined to disagree, but in order for me to see what it *is*, I need access to Nessix. I've asked you nicely once. And now I'll ask you rudely." Mathias turned back to the guards in front of Nessix. "Get out of my way. You do not want me to make the request a third time."

"Oh, for Etha's…" Julianna huffed and rolled her eyes from her seat on the opposite side of the room. "Stand down and let my brother do as he needs to."

"And trust that this isn't some setup of his to make sure he and his girlfriend can escape prosecution?"

Mathias wheeled to face the podium. "*Prosecution?*" He enunciated the word clearly. "I was assured this was meant to be a civil meeting. What is it, Henrik, that you seek to prosecute either of us for?"

"That has yet to be determined—"

Julianna spun on the officials now, eyes flashing in an entitled rage. "Prosecute either or both of them all you'd like on your own time. If you simply must pry, there is a suspicious man asking to see Nessix at the gates. The guards have sent for Mathias's expertise, and I trust Mathias is requesting Nessix's." She turned to the pair.

"Am I right?"

Mathias, more shocked by his sister's sudden backing than by the thought that the Council was trying to come up with some sort of manner to act against him, nodded. "That is right."

Julianna curtly returned the gesture. "And there you have it. He and Nessix will proceed to the gates and now you"— she strode over beside her brother and physically swatted the polearms aside from the two guards in the front—"will allow him to carry out this mission. As we don't yet know the nature of this event, I encourage all of you to remain in your seats until matters have been tended to, as this chamber is the most secure location in the realm."

Mathias often envied how Julianna got away with such subtle assaults as that one. If he'd have tried it, he'd have been in for a tedious debate he had neither the time nor patience for right now. Either way, he wouldn't overlook the unexpected boon Julianna had given him, and thanked her with a quick smile as he offered a hand to help Nessix hop off her little platform.

"Do not make me regret this," Julianna muttered from between clenched teeth.

Mathias gave her a wink. "I'd love to make that promise, but don't know what I'll find yet."

Julianna threw her gaze aside as Mathias hastened Nessix out the chamber and, looking back at the frustrated faces of the Council members, shrugged, and followed them. Whatever was causing trouble at the gates would be much better for her sanity than being locked up in the conference chamber, listening to entitled dignitaries yell at one another about how they were all too right to be wrong.

The trio exited the Citadel with haste and headed toward the southern gate as instructed, where plentiful shouts encouraged their speed even more. Firm orders for someone to calm down soon became clear and incoherent hollers responded to them, as though the man in question thought he was under attack. Zeal's guards were among the most professional Mathias had ever seen and he doubted they'd mistreat anyone they'd detained for an audience with him, even if doing so came at the price of their own safety or sanity.

As much as Mathias hurried toward the commotion, however, the instant Nessix heard the shouts, they struck her with a fervent desperation and sorrow she'd known from her time in the hells. She matched Mathias's gait until she was able to spot the pair of guards standing over a man who rolled around in the dirt like a child throwing a tantrum. She'd seen her fair share of beggars driven mad by their circumstances, but didn't quite know what to make of this scene until the man on the ground flopped to his belly and looked at her His face split into a wide grin and he scrambled his limbs to gracelessly push himself to his feet.

"Nessix!"

Nessix and her two escorts slammed to a halt, and she let Mathias's question of, "Do you know this man?" slide past her as she squinted forward to identify who he was. The sandy colored hair. The genial smile. The square jaw and eyes which spoke fondly of a past he wasn't afraid to revisit in his dreams. Outwardly, Auden maintained all of his warmth, but all sense of coherence was missing from the dear man. A dark, damp spot the size of Nes's fist stained through the thick canvas of his shirt over his heart.

"No…" Nessix murmured, shaking her head once to see if that might change who she saw. When Auden continued to grin at her, waving a splayed hand as he told the guards beside him, "See? Nessix! See? General!" she released a heartfelt sob and ran forward.

"Auden, what have they done to you?"

The man jabbered blissfully at Nessix's arrival, making various arrangements of her name and title to convey to the guards how well he knew her. Nessix grasped him by the shoulders to try to get a better look at him and he laughed heartily at her actions as he attempted to mimic her movements, ducking his head every time she ducked hers and thinking it was a grand game. The only thing he didn't mirror from Nessix was the uncontrolled cascade of tears.

Moments later, Mathias and Julianna arrived behind Nessix.

"Do you know this man, Nes?" Mathias tried again.

Nessix turned to wipe her nose on her shoulder and nodded, pinching her eyes shut. "This is Auden Clement. He is… I guess… was… my second in command."

Mathias winced at the fact that Nessix was needing to deal

with a very obvious change in personality in one she'd considered a brother in arms. She'd lost Brant through horrific means she'd yet to find the nerve to ask him about. She'd had to walk away from Sulik on her quest to reach Mathias. And now her surviving commander of the akhuerai army had been rendered a babbling fool and released to come find her. Mathias blinked and turned his gaze out the gates before addressing the guards.

"Did this man come here alone?"

"Yes, sir," the guard replied immediately. "He was caught picking the lilies. When he was approached and ordered to stop, he just sort of stumbled his way down here, asking for General Nessix."

Mathias squinted out over those white fields, searching through every reach of his logic to come up with a better answer than the one he was rapidly approaching. "Nes, when was the last time you saw Auden?"

"A couple weeks before I was set free on Elidae."

"And I assume he was... of more sound mind at that time?"

Nessix hung her head briefly to hide a fresh surge of tears, then looked up to stroke the hair out of Auden's wholesome brown eyes. "He was sharp and sensible. I'd accepted him as my second in command for a reason. You know I'd never intentionally leave an army set up for failure..."

Mathias laid a hand on Nes's shoulder and briefly studied Auden, searching for ways to connect the pieces he knew of Nes's horrific past with the demons to this man's arrival and noticed immediately that Auden's soul was missing. Not fractured and mourning, like Nes's was, but completely gone. Pulling his hand from Nessix, as it wasn't doing her any good, he reached forward and tore Auden's shirt open to expose an open wound the size of a thumbnail which spurted a bubble of blood each time his heart beat. It bled slowly enough to not kill the man, but the size of the stain centered on Auden's shirt suggested it had been seeping like this for some time. Auden didn't seem to notice that there was a wound there, chattering contentedly about his general, and Nes's knees weakened to the point that she had to slump to the ground to prevent an uncontrolled collapse.

She breathed heavily and Auden plopped down beside her, asking her repeatedly what was wrong. She couldn't form the words to tell him that she was sorry she'd failed him. She couldn't look up at his clueless face to witness how her actions had led to his destruction. It was her relationship with Auden which had resulted in his current state, and the fact that he was now this pathetic madman was her fault.

"At least we know what that ring's for," Julianna murmured.

Mathias silenced her with a firm glare as Nessix wept on the ground, mimicked as if it was some great joke by the man who had once been her loyal commander.

Numb to the world around her, Nessix didn't react to the sound of the horns rising from the southwest wall, but Mathias and Julianna did, the bitter jest leaving the High Priestess in the same instant. Their sound was haunting, and their second blare cut through Nes's disbelief enough to raise the hairs on the back of her neck. Auden pursed his lips and voiced a cheerful, "do-DOO!" back at them. Feeling Mathias's agitation where he stood beside her, Nessix looked up to his face and saw his clenched jaw as he stared out to the distance.

"What's happening?"

"Exactly what I was afraid was happening." His lips twitched toward a snarl, eyes darkening with a deep loathing Nessix had never seen before. "The demons have come for you."

TWENTY-FOUR

Outside a secluded side entrance on the eastern side of the Citadel, Tristan sat perched on the edge of a bench, thin fingers holding the scrap of curled leather Khin had brought him with the utmost care. He'd given up trying to decipher the words stained on it, and not even Ceredulus had been able to understand what it said, yet he couldn't take his eyes off of it. To think that such an insignificant piece of animal hide could be so important... Beside him, Khin plucked at the fraying hem of her satchel as it sat on her lap, gnawing her anxiety into the inside of her cheek as she waited to hear what purpose she'd serve next.

The Sagewinds have left the Citadel. Be quick.

Ceredulus's solemn instruction beat with an eagerness unbecoming of gods, but not entirely unexpected, given how long he'd spent patiently waiting for this very moment. Tristan looked up and stood by his god's compulsion, carefully sliding Berann's note into his right pocket.

"Come, Khin," he commanded. "It is time for us to find the answers the entire Citadel has overlooked."

Khin rose with far more reluctance than Tristan had, but with no less obedience. She'd already fallen too deeply into whatever scheme the vampire had concocted and was determined to receive the payout he continued to promise her by following through to its

273

end. She'd dedicated the first part of her morning to sniffing out where the repository of divine artifacts was located, and though she worried about how Tristan planned to actually get into the guarded chamber, the delicate brush of his fingers against her back as she led him through the halls of the Citadel chased her doubts away and gave her a delicious shiver of anticipation. For once, she was going to do something important.

The pair made quick progress toward their goal, having tactically positioned themselves at a rear entrance nearest the vault, and though Khin's feet tried to drag as the guards and their spears came into view, Tristan's confidence continued to wash over her and press her onward.

"I will cover the negotiations," he murmured to her tension. "You are simply serving as my chaperone."

His voice was so smooth and calm, reminding Khin all over again why she'd invested so much of her limited trust in him. The guards, in diligent guard fashion, straightened their stances as it became apparent that the pair was heading toward their post, and Tristan dropped his hand from Khin's back to stick it into his left pocket.

"Good sirs," Tristan hailed with a brightness Khin didn't quite recognize. "Thank all that is just and good I've reached here at last!"

Unlike Mathias's instant effect on the Citadel's guards, these two remained at attention, brows firm and lips tight. Khin's stomach coiled around itself and she tightened her grip on the strap of her satchel to keep from further expressing her worry.

"What is the nature of your business?" asked the guard on the right.

Tristan stopped, a feigned confusion rippling across his elegant brow. "I am Ripley Wudekind, Baron of Fallsmouth. Certainly, Zeal has received word of the fall of Edmund Swift?"

The two guards exchanged brief glances, the one on the right shrugging, the one of the left shaking his head.

Tristan scoffed. "*Edmund Swift*," he repeated. "Of the Ceredulus-serving line of Swifts?"

Dropping the evil god's name did stir a reaction from the

guards and this time, their expressions were much more concerned. "His fall?" the first asked as the second lifted the butt end of his spear from the ground to dash off to relay the report. "Does that mean he's risen—"

"Oh, no." Tristan chuckled and batted his free hand at the guards' nervous reactions. "He's quite dead and bound to stay that way, I'm sure. But when running inventory of his estate—as is my duty and right as Baron of Fallsmouth—I uncovered this."

With a grand flourish, Tristan revealed a golden ring he'd had hidden in his pocket. The band was too thick to suit the elegance he preferred for his own embellishments, and it was set with a ruby big enough to choke on. Beveled onto the underside of the massive gem was the image of a chalice wreathed with roses. As Khin and the two guards gawked at the ring, fixated on its splendor, Tristan took the opportunity to smirk at how smoothly this plan was playing out.

"This is the crest of Ceredulus, is it not?"

The second guard scratched the back of his head, unable to draw his eyes from the artifact's pull, and the first nodded slowly. "It appears so." With effort, he looked up to Tristan. "You said this came from *the* Swift family manor?"

Tristan closed his fingers over the ring to break the spell it had put over his modest mortal audience. "Indeed. And I am fulfilling my civic duty of bearing what might be a dangerous divine artifact to the security of the Citadel's repository."

The first guard held out his hand. "Zeal thanks you for your service, Ripley Wudekind, Baron of Fallsmouth."

Tristan quickly withdrew his hand and took a step back from the guard. Though he wouldn't mind a couple quick meals, Ceredulus had specifically ordered him to be as brisk and clean as possible, and he hoped to ensure as much by avoiding unnecessary complications. "Begging your pardon, sirs, but it is my region's duty to ensure this artifact is properly stowed away, and I will see it done with my own eyes."

Khin held her breath as the guards sized up Tristan once more, but let it out as the first lowered his head and reached back for the door's handle.

275

"The girl is your escort from the temple?"

Tristan turned his warm gaze to Khin and gave her a friendly smile which let her swallow the lump in her throat. All three men waited expectantly until Khin gasped, her nervous flush mistaken for embarrassment as she fished the writ of access Tristan had forged from her satchel. She cleared her throat and held it toward the guards.

"From the temple, sir," she said.

The guard reviewed the document and scrutinized her timid face before giving her a nod. As Khin hastily crammed the note back in her satchel, the guard on the left opened the door, standing aside to let her and Tristan pass into a narrow hallway lined with doors. Arcane characters Tristan had no doubt were meant to ward away anything more powerful than him covered those in immediate sight. The guard kept the door propped open with one foot as he lit a torch, letting it fall shut as they stepped into the hall.

"It's awful dark in here…" Khin's observation trembled and bounced off the bare walls.

"No need to waste resources keeping it lit," the soldier answered. "It's less of a trove of resources and more a prison for powers better kept from the hands of mortals."

Tristan frowned at the reference. "There is nothing to be learned from the artifacts contained here?"

The guard shrugged. "That's not for me to say. All I know is that the bits and baubles kept in here are considered dangerous, and that's all I *need* to know."

Khin snuck a concerned glance at Tristan, silently asking him if he knew of these dangerous aspects which their guard implied, but he brushed off her concern as the guard stopped before a door labeled with his god's name. It had been centuries since the artifacts within had been in the hands of those worthy of them, and Tristan's fingers curled in anticipation. The guard pulled a ring of keys from his belt and unlocked the door, the wards before it dissipating like dust.

"Here we are." He pushed the door open and held his torch high. "Ceredulus's vault."

The light only illuminated the first ten feet of the room, but that was all Tristan needed to see to choke on a shocked gasp. His god's raw power radiated from within the room, calling to him, welcoming him, but it wasn't this overwhelming might which had stolen his voice. The sacred artifacts of his god, tools the devout and dedicated of his priests had used to craft the most flawless army Abacloth had ever seen, had been haphazardly tossed into the room as though refuse to be swept away after a county fair. Most of the items had made it onto a mound in the middle of the room, but several had fallen from the pile and sat sad and disrespected on the dusty floor.

"Well, toss the ring in and let's go."

Tristan spun his heated glare toward the guard, unable to help himself. "This is a disgrace."

"I—" The guard shook his head. "What?"

"Is this truly how this holy city treats divine relics?"

The guard shrugged again. "Relics of this beast? Sure."

Tristan grit his teeth, his shoulders drawing back slowly as he fought to suck back his outrage. He clearly felt no fewer than a dozen specific artifacts which would let him wipe this guard's indifference from his face and earn himself a servant even more loyal than Khin, but then the girl shuffled beside him, bringing him back to Ceredulus's specific orders and the reminder of the tight time frame they were operating on. He hissed out a slow breath and unclenched his fingers from around the ring.

"So, this"—he raised the bauble up before them again—"just gets tossed on the pile and that's all there is to it?"

The guard's eyes lingered on the ruby once more, its facets twinkling in the torch's light. "That's all there is to it."

Tristan nodded and closed his fingers over the ring once more. "I've got one more request for you."

The guard blinked and looked up into Tristan's eyes.

"Sleep."

Khin stifled a startled yelp as the guard's eyes rolled back into his head, and she scuttled back against the wall as his knees caved out from beneath him. Without blinking, Tristan's free hand snapped forward and caught the torch before it fell from the guard's limp hand, and he turned to enter the storehouse of his god's most precious possessions.

"Wh- Is he…?"

"He will wake when I'm ready for him to," Tristan assured nonchalantly, hungry eyes scanning the room for the item he was after.

Ambition was a trait which ran strong in all of Ceredulus's followers, and though Tristan could have raised hordes of servants by utilizing just a handful of these relics, he remained as true as ever to his god's wishes. There would be time for conquest after Ceredulus had gained a proper foothold.

"We are looking for a wooden box," he told Khin as he scanned the outermost layer of the central pile. "Long and narrow, about half the length of your forearm."

Khin repeated his description on a murmur, edging her way through the room which buzzed with a presence which left her trembling in awe. Tristan voiced an irritated huff and crouched down to sort through the central pile as Khin settled herself at the cluttered corner in the back. Just as with every other task she'd attempted to take on in her life, she had little idea what she was doing, but even as Tristan grumbled and cursed, a sense of achievement settled over Khin as she sorted through the pile of knives and chalices, bowls and idols. She dislodged a statue of a golden crow, causing a brief and noisy cascade of surrounding items which revealed a dark spot in the pile of artifacts.

Surrounded by riches cast in all manners of precious metals and inlaid with gems of every color, this was the first item which didn't glisten in the torchlight. Holding her breath, Khin reached forward and pressed her fingers against the worn smoothness of wood. She gasped Tristan's name and he turned to her as she tugged it free from the pile.

"A wooden box like this?"

She held it out for him to see, and his eyes lit up in delight. It was a nondescript wooden box with a simple compass mounted on the lid and a metal locking plate. The cost of crafting a replica would have been nominal compared to any other relic in this room, but since it was the one item Ceredulus had requested, it was the third most beautiful thing in this room, next to Tristan himself and his loyal little mortal.

"Exactly like that!" Tristan lodged his torch in the pile of his god's treasures and sprang to his feet to accept the box with one hand and help Khin to her feet with the other. "You have done *well*, Khin. Thank you."

Unaccustomed to praise, Khin blushed and glanced at Tristan's hand as it gently supported her elbow. She'd done well! She had located the item she'd been told would lead to the answers neither the priestesses nor Mathias nor Nessix had been able to find. And she'd done it for the first man she'd ever truly been able to consider a friend. Her heart fluttered and her hands returned to the strap of her satchel.

"Now what?" she asked.

"Now," Tristan said, carefully slipping his treasure into Khin's satchel and nestling it between scrolls to mask its rigid shape, "we wake the guard and leave. No one gets hurt. No one gets in trouble."

She grinned, elated by every aspect of this outcome, and Tristan returned the expression, eternally grateful that Mathias had practically driven this girl into his hands.

"Come. We must be out of the Citadel before Mathias returns."

Mention of the paladin dulled Khin's smile but didn't steal it completely, and she followed Tristan as he retrieved the torch and returned to the doorway. Khin positioned herself back in the hallway and held her breath as Tristan knelt down to shake the guard's shoulder.

"Wake! Sir! Are you well?"

The guard groaned and pinched his eyes tighter.

"You really shouldn't lock your knees on duty." Tristan slipped his arm around the man's shoulders to help him sit up. "You fainted hard."

"I…" the guard peered his eyes open to make an appraisal of Khin's shocked face and Tristan's worried one. "How long was I out?"

"But a few moments," Tristan said. "It's a good thing I caught you, or else you could have taken quite a nasty blow."

The guard shook his head, brows furrowing as he pawed about to locate his spear. Grounding it into the floor, he used it to push himself back to his feet. "Right, then. The ring?"

Tristan stood and supplied the item once again from his pocket. "Ready to be rid of it."

The guard swept his hand toward the room in a welcoming manner, and Tristan flicked it onto the pile of his god's most precious and powerful possessions as though it was a coin in a wishing well. Nodding in satisfaction, the groggy guard pulled the door shut, secured the lock once again, and led his charges back out of the hallway. Exchanging brief pleasantries with the second guard, Tristan and Khin hastened out of the Citadel where the vampire guided his young friend to a quiet little grove of trees.

"Ceredulus is pleased with you," he told the girl.

The brightness dimmed from her smile. "Are you?"

"Of course I am," he assured, "but he is truly the one you should aim to impress. And you have. He rewards loyalty and service generously."

Khin, still so naïve and ignorant to the workings of the divine realm, didn't know what to do with Tristan's statement, but she did like the sound of it. "What do we do with the box now that we have it?"

"I'll hide it in my shelter for now." He reached his hand into Khin's satchel and dug out the artifact, admiring its deceptive simplicity here in the dappled sunlight. "Come to me again tomorrow night, and I will teach you how it works."

Khin's grin split across her face. Not even Mathias had volunteered to teach her something special without her begging for it. "Tomorrow night?"

"Tomorrow night."

She scrunched her shoulders close to her ears and, before she knew what she was doing, leaned forward and kissed Tristan's cool cheek. "I'll be there!"

A flood of blush colored her cheeks, enticing a side of Tristan she couldn't have possibly meant to wake, but he let his hunger settle in lieu of the more unique benefits he'd discovered he could get from the girl. Flustered by her actions, Khin gave one more giddy shrug and skipped back into the Citadel. Tristan watched her leave, caressing the artifact his god had wanted so badly.

Tomorrow, the real hunt would begin.

TWENTY-FIVE

Julianna stood at Mathias's shoulder opposite from Nessix and scanned her narrowed eyes up the hill before them. "There are twenty-two demons and four mortals." She glanced at Mathias then leaned forward to bare her gaze on Nessix. She could dislike this warrior woman all she wanted, but she had experienced enough interactions with the demons to know what they were after now… and they'd brought leverage to ensure they'd get it. Mathias's stony expression suggested he'd reached the same conclusion, but his clenched jaw also conveyed that he would die trying to save every last life involved in the demons' plans. "What's our move, Mathias?"

"We wait." He crossed his arms and stepped forward to position himself between Nessix and the city gate. "Patience isn't a strength of demons. We'll wait for them to get anxious and snag the advantage then."

From her position behind Mathias, Nessix shook her head. "Not these demons." Her voice was timid and small. "They've got enough patience to wait you out for eternity."

Both Sagewinds diverted their attention to look at Nessix, the guards standing nearby shifting their weight in uncertainty as they awaited orders on how to proceed.

"You know the demons who came here?" Mathias asked.

Nessix stared up that hill of lilies, past every silhouette except for one. Amid the anticipatory shuffling, one alar paced the width of the road before his allies. Nessix couldn't explain how she knew it was Kol, but neither could she explain why she had his dreams, why she knew these terrible whispers of his past. She could only assume Annin had accompanied him, but she knew for a fact that Kol had come for her at last, just as he'd promised he would. On the verge of facing a showdown between the human she loved and the demon who possessed her, Nessix didn't want to see how any of this would play out. Gulping down the threat of tears, she nodded.

"I know at least one of them, and because I know him as well as I do, I suspect he's got an oraku with him. An ancient."

Julianna pulled her inquisitive gaze from Nessix to stare at the group of demons again. An ancient oraku would be well in range to attack those gathered near the gate from where he stood, and she shivered at the notion that he was intentionally letting them think they had the upper hand. The High Priestess might have had untold power, but using her gifts in such close proximity to the city promised devastating results for those caught in the crossfire of any action she made in their defense. Quietly, Julianna braced herself to make decisions she wasn't pleased to contemplate.

"Is the one you know Kol?" Mathias asked quietly, his question deep and menacing.

Swallowing the lump of tears and terror crawling up from her stomach, Nessix nodded again.

The paladin grit his teeth, his fist clenching tight as it twitched over toward his left hip, and Nessix gently grasped his forearm. She couldn't tell him that she wanted Kol's life spared, but neither could she deny that she wanted Mathias to keep her from needing to go back to the hells under these circumstances. She'd carved out a comfortable life for herself down there at one point; not a great one, but tolerable. But after her rebellion, after how many demons she'd left dead in her wake, after having begged and pleaded about the plight of her people to whoever would listen to her here in Zeal…

Nessix had seen what tortures demons delighted in, and she

felt Kol's eagerness and disapproval beat down on her from on top of this hill. Despite what duty and logic firmly told her, there was no way she could go back. But she didn't want Kol dead to ensure it.

Mathias, on the other hand, as gentle and kind as he always tried to be, had lost himself countless nights over the past several months fantasizing about the ways he'd kill the alar who had taken Nessix from him. His one reservation, as Julianna's, was Nes's quiet warning that Kol was likely accompanied by an ancient oraku, the Spirit Binder named Annin, by Mathias's guess. The paladin could not be killed in the traditional sense of the word, but that wouldn't stop an oraku from using his magic to drop him before he had the chance to defend anybody, Nessix included. This should have been a fight he'd have been able to handle, and it was one that was long overdue. A growl of frustration rumbled in his throat.

"That alar's a coward."

Nes's heart ached as she thought back on the times Kol had protected her from Grell, risking his own life to make sure the inoga didn't end hers. She thought of how he'd saved her from the assault by Inek's officers, how he'd lost his mind in defense of her to the point of barbaric madness, bloodying himself like a deranged butcher as he cut down those who meant to do her harm. She thought of how even after he'd beat her into submission, he'd expressed regret for the actions he'd taken, tenderly assuring her that he never wanted to see her hurt. And now, she thought about how Mathias would do whatever he could to see Kol dead, how she was certain Kol would reciprocate the notion if given the option, and her heart tore in two, cleaved clean in half between devotion and loyalty.

Before Nessix was able to form a reply to Mathias's insult, a single demon separated from the pack, dragging with him a person wearing filthy, tattered robes with their hands tethered together. He held his wings folded close to his back, displaying that he had neither the intention of fleeing nor trying to use them in defense while simultaneously protecting them from ranged attacks, and raised both his free hand and the one pulling his prisoner along to his sides.

Julianna frowned and addressed her brother, still staring ahead. "Mind going to see what he has to say?"

Mathias reached the arm Nessix had her hand on across to his hip and unbuckled his sword. "Not at all. Nes, stay here with Julianna."

Nessix didn't know if Mathias had sensed her reluctance for him to finally face Kol, and part of her resented his order, but unarmed and without the protection of her armor, she wasn't able to do anything about it. Unlike the guards in the conference hall, these soldiers dutifully surrounded Nessix at Mathias's word to protect her, and Julianna kept an attentive eye trained on the surrounding threats as Mathias departed.

He approached the alar, a gangly, awkward demon who Mathias suspected was still well in the mortal age range. Youth and inexperience aside, this demon still had the same resigned eyes as his ancient brothers and sisters, still sneered at the purity of the field of lilies surrounding them. He stopped as Mathias neared, staying closer to his allies than he'd let the paladin stay to his own, and the priestess behind him gave her gender away with a warbled and weak cry.

"Sir Sagewind, find me mercy! Please!"

The young alar displayed his predictable cruelty as he gave a sharp jerk of his arm to pull the priestess out from behind him and fling her to the ground. She tumbled down the hill until the tether caught her, her arms extending painfully at her shoulders as the momentum of her slight bodyweight flung against the demon's hold. Mathias hastened his gait up the hill to assist the filthy young woman, but as he bent down to receive her, the alar heaved the rope and pulled her just out of his reach. Mathias scowled and glared up at the demon.

"You are too young to be wise, so let me give you some advice," Mathias said. "Release this woman if you value your life."

The alar spat on the bedraggled woman at his feet. Head tucked beneath her arms, she didn't respond past a continuation of the same sobs she'd heaved for days now. "How many demons do you think truly value their lives?"

"Not many who cross me, that's for sure."

The demon smirked. "Yet you haven't killed me."

Mathias spared one more look at the priestess and her torn and filthy robes. He had no idea who she was or how long she'd been in the demons' hands, but she'd remained in the sacred vestments assigned to her by the temple, an unusual comfort for demons to grant their prisoners. After assessing that the priestess was as physically sound as a survivor of the demons' torments could be, Mathias raised his gaze to the beast before him.

"I haven't killed you yet because I need information and you have control over someone I consider dear. Do not think I haven't cut you down out of some concept of leniency."

"I wouldn't dream of it." The alar hauled on the rope again, shortening it like a sailor pulling his boat up to the dock as he dragged the priestess to her feet, her knees trembling so hard he had to grab her by the arm to keep her standing. "You and your sister are supposed to be smart. You're supposed to be able to see and feel things others can't. If you're as smart as you think you are, you know that this isn't the only whiny bitch we've brought with us."

Mathias tasted the bile rising in his throat. There was no way he'd be able to negotiate with the Council in the terms he knew were coming, and that made him want to kill demons even more than ever... except for the fact that they'd retained enough leverage to guarantee his good behavior. Holding his rage behind sweltering breaths and fingers which ached to draw his sword, Mathias met the demon's grinning eyes once more.

"And it seems you understand what we're after," the demon said. "We're giving you this one in good faith. Do what you like with her. Then you bring us Nessix, and we'll hand over the other three priestesses. Can we be gentlemen about this? Or will there be bloodshed?"

Mathias ached for there to be bloodshed, for him to forget about what it meant to be a gentleman, but there were lives on the line, lives the entire city had thought were lost, and ones he'd been given the chance to reclaim. He wouldn't show weakness to this demon but, Etha, it tore at him. Despite disruptions from both the Council and the temple, Nessix had given them valuable information in the few days she'd been here, enough to give them leads. Enough to give Mathias motivation to do something he hated even more than cooperating with demons. Nessix was strong. She was a fighter. And Mathias knew deep in his heart that she would always spare the lives of the innocent, even if it meant sacrificing her own. He'd find an answer, as he always did, but for now, he had to save the priestesses.

"Do we have ourselves a deal?" the demon asked, pulling the priestess back against his chest and holding her close to keep her out of Mathias's reach.

Why did there have to be four of them…? "We have a deal," Mathias said.

"And if you don't come back with Nessix in tow—"

"I know. I'll have her here shortly."

"No dawdling?"

"None at all."

The demon sneered as he appraised Mathias's waiting stance more carefully. As young as he was, he'd only ever heard stories of how Mathias fought, having not had the chance to see him up close or in action. The human didn't look like someone who had earned such ferocious legends to be penned about him, but then again… Annin didn't appear the least bit imposing, either, and no demon alive liked the idea of the oraku being out of his line of sight. Not that being *in* his sight would make any difference if Annin wanted to attack.

Satisfied with Mathias's compliance, the demon shoved the priestess forward. Mathias caught her in his left arm, preparing his right to draw a weapon in case this demon planned to use her as a distraction to attack, but when the alar grunted and spun to trudge back up the hill, Mathias carefully turned the battered woman around and supported her back toward the city gates.

Her eyes were wide and filled with tears, and she looked around herself frantically as if she didn't recognize where she was. The fields were still lovely, the Citadel's watchful eyes as soothing as she'd remembered them, but it was all such a stark, clean difference from the dark hole of torture and despair she'd suffered in for the past three years, and she felt as though she was unworthy of entering the splendor graciously awaiting her now.

"You're going to be alright," Mathias said, speaking those words now since he doubted he'd be able to make this same claim to the woman he loved. "I've got you and once you're back in the city walls, you will be safe. You know that."

She hummed a vague affirmative and leaned against Mathias's side.

He wrapped his arm around her and when she didn't object to the restraint of his touch, held her closer still. "Warm food and a hot bath are just ahead." Keeping the comfort of optimism in his voice was a battle Mathias feared he'd lose. "The Citadel still stands safe, warm, and waiting for you."

The priestess's entire body trembled against his and she made a tiny, garbled choke in response to his offers.

There would never be a time when Mathias didn't revere Etha, but it gutted him knowing this young woman had suffered through years of the demons' torment and torture simply because of her devotion to the Mother Goddess. *Etha—*

You don't have to bother. I'm already watching them.

And Nessix?

Etha remained quiet for a quarter of Mathias's trip down the hill and then had to break her son's heart all over again. *There is no way to get her out of this, at least not right now. I'm working on a solution, but you must turn her over to the demons if you want to spare the other priestesses. Which, I must tell you—*

I know, Mathias snapped before he had to hear it from his goddess. *It must be done.*

It was a terrible request to make of her dear paladin who had already given so much in her name, but Etha accepted his words as his vow to honor the agreement he'd made.

When Mathias had made it halfway down the hill, Julianna broke from the crowd to rush to the pair, tears in her eyes as she cupped the young woman's face in her hands. "Oh, Sybil!" She kissed each of the filthy girl's cheeks and smudged at the dirt and grime which flawed her skin. "You are home now. Blessed Mother, you've made it home!"

Sybil promptly left Mathias's sturdy arms to curl into those of the woman who had practically raised her since she was a child, sobbing into the cleanliness of Julianna's gown. Mathias cast one more glance over his shoulder to ensure the demon mass behind them was behaving, and stepped up in line beside the two women. He went to work untying the binds on Sybil's wrists.

"The other three?" Julianna asked her brother as she continued to stroke the feeble young woman's hair.

"They're more priestesses," Mathias confirmed, refusing to look up from his task.

Julianna's eyes hardened and she lifted her gaze from her student to her brother, knowing how her next statement would hurt him. "And they want a trade."

"They do."

Mathias lacked the courage to elaborate any further. He knew why the demons were there, they all did, but it was as if refusing to speak of it could prolong Nes's fate a little bit longer. He'd only just found her again... he wasn't ready to let her go.

"You know we have to—"

"Yes."

The snappiness of Mathias's interruption and the abrupt manner in which he flung the rope to the ground once Sybil's hands were free silenced Julianna into a gloomy silence. She didn't doubt her brother's intentions to make the correct decision, but it was clear that he was far from at peace with it. Angry enough, perhaps, to go disappearing once again as he tried to chase down his lover after the demons took her away. Julianna had spent so long trying to safeguard Mathias from his own actions that she'd given up trying to do so, and she vowed to let him do whatever he deemed necessary as long as he could reclaim the last three priestesses the demons had in their possession.

Playing favorites, as she was so fond of doing, Etha spared Julianna the gentle warning of being more mindful about what she wished for, because she knew exactly the sorts of plans Mathias was playing around with right now. And, balance-hungry or otherwise, Etha couldn't say she completely disagreed with the actions he was contemplating.

The siblings moved back toward the city gates in silence,

Mathias closed off from the notion of talking and Julianna afraid of pushing either her brother or the frightened priestess in her arms over the edge.

As soon as they reached the modest group of Zeal's curious and horrified residents gathered by the gates, Julianna gestured for some of the braver young women who had trickled out of the Citadel to come forward to support their lost sister then moved to prepare to back up her brother, should Nessix put up a fight to the inevitable.

Mathias parted through the growing crowd, focus grounded solely on Nessix and holding her eyes so firmly that even if she'd had a desire to look anywhere else, she wouldn't have been able to. He approached her silently, not with the kind expression she'd hoped to see, but with a resigned coldness which made her heart slow down to nothing. He stayed silent as he walked up to her, silent as he reached both of his hands to her face and brushed the hair away from her cheeks, silent as he bent forward and gave her the lingering kiss she'd been waiting for since he'd come dashing to her aid in Fairmont.

The warmth of Mathias's tears spattered on Nes's cheeks for just a moment before he pulled away, and by the time he'd straightened fully, they were gone, hidden behind duty and discipline. Nessix knew where this was going, knew what her own duty demanded of her, but she hated to believe it. Mathias briefly gripped a fistful of Nes's hair then slid his hand down her shoulder to press against her back as he gruffly delivered his order.

"We're moving out."

Having thought she'd have had more time to prepare herself, and some sort of control over the timing of her return to the hells, Nessix resisted Mathias's gentle order and he gave her a firm shove to get her going.

"Nes," he said softly, "you knew you'd have to go back to save your people. We need to go."

"Not yet," she murmured, her voice a subdued murmur meant just for him. Her tear-rimmed eyes remained focused up the hill, watching Kol as he paced before his group of soldiers, arms crossed and gaze locked on her position as he moved. "We're getting so close... I can't go back yet."

"What choice do we have?" he asked. "The demons have hostages. Innocent girls. And they have unrestricted access to your army. Do not give them a reason to make this any worse."

Duty forbid Nessix to debate Mathias's logic, but that didn't make her any more eager to swallow it. "We haven't figured out how to make any of it better to begin with."

Mathias shifted his gaze away from hers. "You put me on the right track. I'll find the answers we need."

"How?"

He flinched at the ridicule in her tone, registering from it exactly what she'd intended for him to. He couldn't understand the texts they needed to read, but such hurdles hadn't stopped him from miracles in the past. "I *will*."

Nessix had trusted Mathias through some of the greatest impossibilities she'd ever faced but this one, uncovering the knowledge of a long-dead demon erased from history... Determination and confidence weren't quite the same thing, and Nes's fear of what waited for her back in the hells prevented her from crossing her arms at Mathias's stubborn excuse, though it did nothing to cover her skeptical glare.

It would have been delightful to have Etha's input and encouragement at the moment, but that kiss Mathias had taken for himself, the one he should have taken the moment Nessix first came back to life in his chamber, dulled the goddess's voice to a tinny chatter in the back of his mind. He knew he couldn't be with Nessix, not the way he longed to be, and still keep true to his vows to Etha, but if he could find a way to have them both...

"This must be done," he said, coughing out his regret before it threatened to overtake him. "You are brave. You are strong. Your people need you, Nes. Please. Trust me. I know what's going on now. I'll find a way to you."

Nessix found the motivation to continue forward in the image of the bedraggled priestess Mathias had just supported down the hill, in the clueless void of Auden's eyes, and the undying terror which lurked in her buried army. The tug of morality's influence and Mathias's persistent guidance kept her moving, despite the resounding screams to flee which chaos rang through her entire being. Kol quit his pacing as Nessix and Mathias made progress his direction, his arms dropping to his sides and posture drawing up taller.

"Come with me," Nessix murmured, a hot sweat beading on the back of her neck as her anticipation of the joy that would come from being near Kol once again melded with the fear of what he'd do to her for her disobedience. "You told me I wouldn't have to do this alone."

Mathias grit his teeth against Nes's gentle plea and gave up on answering her. Trying to rationalize anything she objected to had always been a trial and in this terrible moment as she trembled beneath his steady touch, Mathias didn't have it in him to keep up with her debates.

"Every advantage I had is gone," she said. "I don't even have my sword. And my armor's still being repaired…"

Mathias's fingers rubbed at the tension beneath them, urging Nessix bravely on. "You have everything you need, Nes. *Nothing* has ever managed to stop you. Not demons. Not death."

"At least one of us has faith," she muttered.

"That has always been your weak point. So forget faith if it won't serve you. Draw on your strengths."

Had Nessix not been half-nauseous with dread, she'd have laughed at Mathias's suggestion. Her strengths were luck and charisma, both traits she was relatively certain would no longer be of service to her in the hells. "I'll do what I can."

"That's all I ask of you and more than I want to."

They neared the halfway point up the hill, the location which Mathias assumed they would make this horrible trade, and so he pulled Nessix to a stop to force the demons to come to them. From the top of the hill, Kol watched Nes's wavering resolve, a frown sullying his handsome face as his eyes smoldered with all of the disappointment she deserved.

"Is this going to become a spectacle?" Mathias called to the demons before Nessix had another chance to voice her doubts about the outcome of this exchange.

Kol shifted in anticipation but was held back by a subtle

292

gesture and brief statement from the demon Mathias recognized from the scene of Nes's death as the Spirit Binder. After Kol huffed his irritation, eyes fixated on Nessix as if nothing else in the world existed, Annin gestured for a detail of seven demons to lead the last three priestesses from the back of the crowd.

The proof of life satisfied Mathias, and each of the terrified young women was at least as functional as the first had been. The demons shoved their prisoners forward, stopping halfway to Mathias and Nessix as they waited for their next set of instructions to be delivered.

"I have an amendment to our terms," Annin called down to Mathias.

Mathias bristled. He should have known better than to think he could trust demons. "The deal has been made, oraku. I've brought who you wanted."

"Send with her the Afflicted we'd assigned to find her."

Mathias blinked his shock but did well to hide it, having never in his wildest dreams believed a man as timid and clueless as Talier would have survived three seconds under the demons' control. Someone as soft as him would have perished from fear alone within moments of entering the hells, not to mention been physically unable to withstand their typical methods of handling mortals. This was a most unexpected development, and one Mathias was bitterly determined to investigate further, provided he could keep track of Talier.

"Afflicted?" Mathias called out his bluff with perfectly constructed confusion. "I'm afraid I'm the only Afflicted I know of who was searching for her. And you couldn't possibly want to have me any closer than I am now."

Habitually, Nessix cringed as Annin flashed a vicious scowl and she watched him closely for the subtle tells of an attack. One of the least excitable demons Nessix had encountered, the oraku steadied his resolve with a slow breath, but before he was able to speak, Kol gripped his arm and engaged him in a fierce, hushed debate.

"He didn't mean...?" Nessix couldn't quite finish her whispered question.

"Oh, he did. It seems Talier was sent to find you on their behalf," Mathias muttered, monitoring the exchange on the hilltop as Kol's increasing signs of aggression toward his comrade suggested there might soon be trouble.

Mathias maintained his schooled focus on the spectacle above, but Nessix nearly vomited with the sudden realization of Talier's betrayal, hot waves of shock threatening to take her trembling knees out from under her.

She'd trusted Talier to lead her to Zeal. How far off course had he led her before fortune had driven her to Fairmont? How much time had she lost? How close had he led her—ignorant and willing—to Kol? That man had convinced her that he was half useless—and truly, she believed he was—and she'd bought into the ploy.

Nessix had always hated Annin off principle. Today, she learned to hate him more.

The debate between Kol and Annin came to an abrupt end, with Annin throwing a shoulder from the alar and Kol gesturing to his subordinates to continue forward. They clomped down the hill, coming to a stop ten yards from where Mathias stood stoic guard over Nessix. The one demon not personally escorting a priestess separated from the group and continued forward, removing a pair of shackles from his belt.

Nessix recoiled from this demon's approach, even before he was within striking distance, but Mathias's firm hand remained pressed to her back, reinforcing her status and station, assuring her that he would be with her until the end.

The demon marched closer and closer, stopping before the pair when he was but a few feet away. He carried himself with the authority of an older demon, one who had seen Mathias in combat once or twice in his life, and he disregarded the valuable prize which Nessix was to keep a watchful eye on the paladin's stony glower.

"I'm here for what's ours," the demon said.

Nessix clenched her jaw and glared at this demon, longing for the days when she'd been able to influence the lesser ranked of these fiends due to her connection to Kol. The last card of that game had been played, leaving Nessix with far more dismal—and painful—prospects ahead of her. The chaos Kol had imparted in her thrashed at her discipline until Mathias's fingers gently gripped the back of her shirt, his touch caressing her trembling back.

"Give me your hands, bitch."

Nessix snarled at the cocky underling and drew her arms back. With so many disadvantages stacked against her, this demon would have to kill her here, before Mathias and Kol both, for her to surrender the use of her hands. "What's wrong?" she asked. "Afraid you can't handle me?"

The demon spat to the side, unimpressed by her bluster. "I can handle you just fine. It's your master who wants to make sure you learn your place."

Against all of her battle instincts, Nes's focus flew past the demon before her to where Kol watched her, his possessive eyes laughing at her last stand of defiance and failed attempts to outwit him. Mathias was supposed to be her champion, the one to rescue her from this madness, and he was helpless to do anything but hand her over, shackled like a prisoner, to the demon who had turned her into this abomination.

"Your paladin there said he didn't want a spectacle," the demon said. "Are you planning on making it one?"

Nessix was too focused on Kol to acknowledge this demon until he grumbled and reached out to grab her wrist. As his hand brushed hers, she redirected her glare to him and swatted his hand away. He growled and drew his arm back to strike her, but Nessix was quick to drop back enough to draw a knife from Mathias's belt. Seeing no positive outcome if Nes's belligerence remained unchecked, Mathias caught her arm and jerked her away from the offending demon. She spun on Mathias, face contorted in outrage but a shadow swept up to them before she could open her mouth to order him to let her go. The demon who had come to collect Nessix yelped his surprise and staggered back three steps as Kol landed before the struggling pair.

Nessix froze, transfixed by the disapproval in Kol's stern eyes and Mathias was struck by the insatiable urge to release her so he could tear into this Etha-forsaken beast he'd concocted so many terrible ways to destroy. But the priestesses stood in a tidy line just behind this loathsome creature, his oraku lurking someplace at the top of the hill. No matter how badly Mathias wanted to skin Kol alive, he had to restrain himself. At least for now.

Kol smirked as he acknowledged Mathias's poorly executed restraint and he swiped the shackles from his subordinate's hands. "Go back to the others," he said. "I've got this handled."

As the lower ranked alar accepted his instructions, Kol flung one last amused glance at Mathias then stalked up to Nessix, caressing her paled cheek.

"I told you I'd find you, little one. It wasn't worth the fight before, and it isn't worth one now." He glanced at Mathias. "I suppose some amount of gratitude is owed to you for finding her for me, Mathias Sagewind. I'll make sure word of your deeds reaches every ear in my realm."

Nessix couldn't breathe as Kol stood before her, too trapped by her bizarre obedience to him and terrified of the promises lying dormant in his eyes. Kol dropped his hand from her face to grab her free arm and she swatted at him, earning a brisk slap in response. Mathias's hand wrapped tighter around her wrist to restrain them both from retaliation which would only complicate the delicate situation, and Kol's second attempt at seizing Nessix's arm was successful. He wrenched the cuff around her wrist, then grabbed her other arm, his hand brushing Mathias's as he met the paladin's eyes again.

"I've got her now, if you don't mind."

Mathias pulled Nessix closer to him, drawing Kol's attention with the movement, and when he met the demon's orange eyes, he growled the promise he'd carried in his heart for nearly two years. "First chance I get, I *will* kill you."

"Oh?" Kol asked. "You've got a chance now. What's stopping you?"

The muffled sobs of the priestesses squeezed through the enraged ringing in Mathias's ears, and the pressure of Annin's presence continued to hang over the growing crowd of spectators gathering at the gates. Kol knew damn well what was stopping Mathias, and the paladin seared his threats at the demon, scathing

296

him with his hatred and the promises of what he'd do when they met on fair terms. Wishing Nessix would have skipped the fit she'd thrown so he could have had one more quiet moment to reassure her that she was the only one capable of fulfilling this role, to remind her that he would find her and that none of her suffering would be in vain, Mathias gave her arm one last squeeze and commanded his hand to release its grip on her.

Kol wasted no time clamping the other shackle around her wrist. "Drop the knife, little one." When Nessix only replied with a curled lip and narrowed eyes, he spat out a sigh and torqued her wrist against its binds until she was forced to drop the weapon. Satisfied, Kol gave Mathias one last, defiant smirk and tugged sharply on his end of Nes's bindings. "Come now. It's best we don't keep Grell waiting."

The reminder that there were demons more powerful than Kol who she'd have to answer to, ones he might not be able to protect her from and which her army may have to face due to her misbehavior, stole the feisty rebellion from Nessix, leaving an opening for regret to sneak past her determination. She didn't know the last time she'd had access to dream stop, and she'd never faced a crisis this crippling in any previous phase of her life. Not during her first death, not through any of the trials when she'd been pretending to be an obedient little akhuerai to please Kol, not when chased by the threats of corrective measures by the assassins' guild. Trapped like a feral animal between her fears, her pride, and her duty, Nessix tried a fierce tug against Kol's hold. Not even glancing back at her, he gave the tether a stout yank and Nessix staggered to keep from falling, certain Kol would have no qualms dragging her behind him. She looked up to where a cluster of demons stood guard over a trio of traumatized priestesses, and she bowed her head, wondering how long she'd be able to withstand Kol's new opinion of her before she became so empty.

As Kol led Nessix past the demons holding the priestesses, he gave them the nod to let their prisoners go. All three women stumbled, falling to the ground and scrambling on bound hands and knees toward Mathias and the safety he represented. Their demon keepers filed in behind Kol to guard his progress back toward the rest of the group, ensuring that even if Nessix escaped his iron grip, she'd have nowhere to flee. With their backs to him, Mathias allowed himself to cave to his remorse, his anguished weeping disguised as empathy for the three women awaiting his protection.

Pulling his eyes from Nes's squared shoulders and loose hair, Mathias reached his numb hands down to help the priestesses to their feet. Having handicapped himself by kissing Nessix farewell, all he could do at the moment was guide them down the hill, and he kept himself steady and focused on that task until an eruption of Nes's anger and cackles of laughter amid a flurry of wings vied for his attention. Kol barked a correction at his subordinates which brought them back in line, but Nes's voice persisted, cursing her captors, reminding Mathias that he'd done nothing to shield her from this fate.

Gritting his teeth, Mathias prayed for Nessix to keep her strength, that she wouldn't be broken by the punishment awaiting her. Etha would hear his prayers, whether or not he'd be able to hear her response right now, but standing by as Nes's scathing taunts faded in the distance, answered by the amused chuckles of her guards left Mathias defeated and doubting everything he stood for.

If he couldn't save the most important woman in his world, how did he think he could save anyone?

Halfway down the hill, Mathias stopped, and looked back up to see the remainder of the group of demons close in around Nessix, only the oraku turned away from her to monitor Zeal's response to this exchange. Nes had stepped up her fight, kicking at shins and flinging her shackled hands at her captors' heads and for the first time, Mathias pitied her for her tenacity and the pain it would cause her. He prayed the oraku would take her out quickly, before she had a chance to compound her sentence. He prayed she'd wake up rested and of clear mind and believe her memories of when he said he'd never stop trying to save her. He prayed, yet again, that she still could be saved.

"Mattie, we need to get the girls home."

Julianna's gentle voice cut through the ringing in Mathias's ears, and he wanted to turn to her and sob against her breast just the same as the priestesses who she'd come to comfort. He knew Julianna disapproved of Nessix. He knew she mistrusted her. And he accepted that. But she could not deny that Nessix had been the best thing to happen to Mathias after he'd been resurrected, and he'd just let her go.

TWENTY-SIX

Word had spread quickly throughout the Citadel that demons had approached the gates, and the halls were alive with frightened nobles scurrying to their rooms and soldiers rushing to their stations. Mathias strode through the buzzing crowd as if it wasn't there, not even registering the requests for guidance which came his way. Temporarily deaf to Etha, there was no calm voice to ground him out of his brewing madness, and the greater part of him was just fine with that.

From down the hall, Talier staggered toward him like a lost puppy that had gone a week without food, and Mathias, eager to point the blame on someone other than himself, growled and lengthened his stride. Julianna had been preoccupied making arrangements for the rescued priestesses but was quick to pass off the immediate responsibility to one of her senior aides as she saw her brother charge the scrawny man. Though she wasn't fast enough to stop him from grabbing Talier by the shoulders to fling him to the ground, she did manage to pull Mathias back as the terrified man scooted away before he moved in for a more substantial blow.

"How much sooner could she have been here?" Mathias spat, trembling as he leaned against the restraint of Julianna's hold.

Talier raised a guarding arm and ducked his head beneath it, only able to shoot quick glances up at the furious paladin. "W-what…?"

Mathias attempted to lunge forward, but Julianna still commanded the entirety of her divine connections while Mathias had traded the majority of his away. "How far did you lead her off course, you pathetic waste of your father's—"

"*Mathias!*"

Julianna's scolding successfully cut through her brother's tirade and though Talier was far too frightened to form words to thank her for restraining the terrifying man, it allowed him to gather his thoughts enough to make a second request. "What… what happened?"

Mathias gave another stout jerk against Julianna's hold, but her grip did not falter. "I figured you'd be able to explain that."

"I don't…" Talier sent Julianna a hasty glance, begging her to help him, though her eyes spoke of a curt demand for his compliance. "I don't know what you mean."

Mathias, dizzy from the rush of blood coursing through his head, roared his frustration and drew his leg back to kick the floored man. As his balance shifted, Julianna flung him backwards and placed herself between her brother and the subject of his anger. Talier scrambled to his feet as Mathias regained his balance, and when Julianna cast a fuming glare back at her brother, he knew he wouldn't get past her again.

Pacing like a caged jungle cat, Mathias's glare bore into Talier. "The demons have taken Nessix," he seethed. "What can you tell me about that?"

Having barely found his feet past his fear of the just man's bout of violence, those words pummeled Talier every bit as hard as he imagined that kick would have struck him. Face growing cold, hands growing numb, Talier staggered backwards a step. This wasn't how any of this was supposed to happen. "What do you mean they *took* Nessix?"

Mathias balled his fists at his sides and had to turn from Talier to stalk a few paces away. After Julianna assessed that he truly was trying to calm himself from his initial outburst, she dug out the diplomacy she wished she didn't have to use and answered Talier herself.

"The demons arrived with hostages, proposing an exchange." She held a preparatory hand back at her brother and slid half her attention his direction. "Accepting their terms was the only bloodless solution we had; we could not allow the priestesses to remain in the demons' custody."

Talier's stomach twisted and he whimpered against the urge to vomit. "But… but Nessix was all I had to… to…" Feeling left his knees and though he was mostly certain he still stood, it certainly felt like he was falling.

In a flash, Mathias was at Julianna's back, his agitation beating against her so strong she defensively straightened her stance. "Nessix was all you had to *what*?" he demanded.

Julianna held up her hand to Mathias and though he swatted it away, he respected her unspoken command. "We intend to send forces to aid her, Mister Dalton—"

"But that will be too late!" Talier shook his empty hands in front of himself, helpless, hopeless, and pleading to the last two people on Abaeloth who could possibly do anything to help him.

"Too late for what, Talier?"

The hushed, calm manner which Mathias asked his question was enough to raise shivers on the back of Julianna's neck, and Talier retreated another step.

"What my brother means—"

Talier's tears spilled over and he took the final step back he needed to sag against the wall. "No…" he moaned. "It doesn't matter. It's all… it's all over now…"

Mathias stepped past his sister with such an air of authority that, even with him handicapped as he currently was, she didn't favor the idea of trying to stop him. "What do you know, Talier?"

"Not much," he blubbered. "Not enough. The demons… they have my brother…"

Mathias bristled at the confession, the slightest bit of compassion singing its virtue amidst all of his turmoil and suffering, twisting his tongue in manners which prompted him to say things his anger forbid him to. Julianna spoke the words Mathias couldn't.

"And you were hoping to use Nessix as leverage to save him?"

The High Priestess's eyes showed no more warmth than they had before, still cool and logical, but at least she'd been trying to protect him from Mathias. "She was the only thing they wanted, the only thing keeping Marcoux alive…"

"So that oraku had been honest?" Mathias asked. "You'd made a deal with them?"

Talier lowered his head and nodded, looking away from both of the Sagewinds in an attempt to avoid the influx of fear which would come when either of them approached to deliver the final blow. "They told me to find her… to direct her away from Zeal…" He tried to gulp down the nerves which accompanied his incriminating words, but they got stuck in his throat and his last statement croaked in a pathetic squeak as he peered at Mathias. "And from you, specifically."

Fury engulfed Mathias—fury at Talier for having been stupid and selfish enough to help demons, fury at the demons for having destroyed the beauty that had been Nessix, fury at himself for being unable to stop any of it—and he snapped under its pressure. How much sooner might he have found Nessix if not for this man? How many fewer innocents might Nessix have killed on her road to get here? Disregarding his limitations, Mathias shoved Julianna aside and dashed forward, grabbing Talier's collar as the wimpy man screamed at the clenched and cocked fist aimed at his face.

Talier's scream persisted even as Mathias flew backwards as if being unseated from a horse by a lance to the gut, persisted as the paladin's unyielding grip on his collar tore the front of his shirt as he was launched across the hall. Mathias hit the opposite wall with a heavy thud and a surprised rush of breath and Julianna stood between the two men, stance broad and sturdy, with her right arm reached behind her as though she had physically tossed Mathias aside. Humbled by the intervention, but no less enraged from it, Mathias grit his teeth against the pain of the sudden impact and curled his legs to prepare to stand before Julianna spun her commanding glare on him. She hadn't wanted to humiliate her brother so publicly, but neither could she risk him harming a key witness—or his own fragile reputation—while he wasn't thinking soundly. He scathed her with a hateful glower, but lowered his eyes after a few heavy heartbeats, conceding to the fact that Julianna was better equipped in every regard to handle the situation.

Accepting her brother's submission, though not convinced it would stick for long, Julianna turned back to where Talier had flattened himself against the wall. "Where do they have your brother?"

His fingers itched to reach for his pocket, but with as little influence as he clearly had right now, he refused to clue this pair in on the valuable trinket hidden inside of it. "I don't know…"

"Think hard, child," Julianna said curtly, "because I won't be able to subdue my brother indefinitely, and he both deserves and needs these answers."

Talier cringed. "I don't know! If I did, I'd have tried to take Nessix there to have her free him."

The filthy glare Mathias had fit Talier with grew downright menacing and he pushed himself to his feet, adrenaline strengthening his movement. Of course, this piece of trash would have used Nessix for his own purposes. Of course, he'd never intended to help her.

Julianna's calm voice broke through and silenced Mathias's rampaging thoughts. "Then their plans with her, Mister Dalton. Why did the demons want Nessix?"

Talier, now convinced there would be no escape from explaining what little he knew, caved at last. Perhaps this would be how death would find him. Marcoux was already dead, by his estimation. "Kol… he said she was the general of his army, that she'd tried to escape him and he needed her back. I…" he shook his hands out in front of himself. "You have to believe me. I didn't have a choice."

Mathias struck a single step forward, but stopped as he caught the slightest tilt of Julianna's head in his direction. "There is *always* a choice!"

Talier hung his head. There'd been a time when he'd believed that, but there'd also been a time when he'd thought the Order had done its job and made demons nothing but beasts of scary stories passed over campfires. "You have no idea what they could have done to me or Marcoux…"

The haunting song of Mathias's bitter laughter silenced Talier's blabbering and Julianna caught her breath as she felt the final bindings of her brother's sympathy slip free from him. "You ignorant *fool*," Mathias hissed, a malicious edge lacing his words. "There is nobody alive who better understands what demons are capable than I am. And now they have the woman I—" Finishing that statement proved too much for Mathias, and he gagged on his words before anger demanded he finish chastising this traitor. "The woman who could uncover their plans and spare the rest of Abaeloth their tortures. Demons punish those who disobey them, Talier." Part of Mathias savored the way the man crumbled at that warning. "And Nessix disobeyed them greatly. *You* played a part in this."

"I'm... I'm sorry."

"Sorry."

Talier nodded and ducked his head to his shoulder, praying for the death blow to come quicker from Mathias than it would from Kol or Annin.

"*Sorry.*"

Julianna squared her shoulders and turned to face her brother, prepared to intervene in whatever means necessary as Mathias clearly telegraphed his intent to punish Talier for the hand he'd played in Nes's ultimate demise. That anticipated attack never came, but something far more wicked from the man she'd looked up to since she was a mortal toddler did.

"I will say my prayers for a quick and merciful end for your brother," Mathias said quietly, each word enunciated with deliberate care. "But I will also pray you are forced to answer for your sins. Etha shines her favor on me—"

"Mathias..."

He ignored his sister's attempt to remind him that he was a gracious and benevolent man. "And all you've got working for you is an oraku's curiosity. Think over those odds carefully, Talier Dalton."

Through speaking his mind, strangely fulfilled by the open threat he'd just laid before the sniveling Afflicted creature who could have played a significant role in Nes's salvation had he not been so pathetic, Mathias spun on his heel and stalked down the hall before he had a chance to either fall apart or snap again.

Julianna kept herself in position, watching her brother's fist rhythmically clench and relax as he struggled to hold himself together enough to maintain what was left of his heroic front until he disappeared around the turn which led him toward the temple. *Etha, watch over him, for he cannot watch over himself…*

"I… What do I do now…?"

Talier's whimpered question snagged Julianna's attention, and she allowed herself to drink in a bit of her own irritation and outrage over the part this man had played in recent events. "You, Mister Dalton, will stay here, within the Citadel."

The last pinches of color drained from Talier's cheeks as his eyes darted to where Mathias had disappeared, but he'd lost the strength to even shake his head. "Stay here. In the Citadel. Where he can find me?"

"You give yourself too much credit, Mister Dalton. Mathias has addressed you and presently, he has allowed you to live. He has far more pressing matters to tend to right now than any desire for vengeance, and as afraid as you are of the demons who indentured you, you must believe me, on my word as High Priestess, that inside this Citadel is safer than anywhere else on Abaeloth."

"But… what about… my…" He couldn't finish voicing his fear, deciding too late that he didn't actually want to know the answer.

"In all likelihood, your brother is dead. Return to your chamber and I will send a priestess to pray with you as soon as I am able."

Talier made no indication of moving, not out of a lack of desire, but out of a lack of ability to do so. Just as Mathias had too much to deal with to be bogged down by the inconvenience of Talier, Julianna had just as much. Summoning more grace than Mathias would have been able to command on his best days, Julianna turned to face Talier.

"I do believe you've mistaken my words as advice rather than the order they were, Mister Dalton. I can call upon armed guards to escort you to a cell, or you can take yourself back to the quarters you've been graciously granted. I leave the decision to you."

Mathias's physical assault had frightened the wits out of Talier, returning to him the horrific memories of the fight against the giant demons in Fairmont, but the calm which Julianna continued to command frightened him even more, and he understood well that he was a prisoner to the Order until this matter was resolved. As if it ever would be…

"I'll go," he choked out on a hoarse voice.

"That is wise," Julianna said. "Do not let me receive word that you changed your mind."

Julianna dismissed herself promptly to tend to the rescued priestesses, leaving Talier trembling in the hallway, and though he'd promised to return to his room, he sank to the floor, there in the hallway, and sobbed.

* * * * *

Mehalco was a demon of simple desires, and the biggest one he had was to be left alone. He understood that a certain degree of disorder came with running a demon haven on the surface realm, especially one tucked so close to Zeal, but it wasn't since the attack arranged by his darker, hell-dwelling brethren two months prior that he'd heard such a commotion in his streets. Just as he'd begun to debate whether to creep outside his ramshackle house to see what the fuss was about or to crawl into his hidden shelter and wait for this next disaster to pass, his door flew open to reveal Bronte and the burly Rax. So startled by their intrusion, Mehalco fumbled with the correction that was due to them.

"Mehalco, it's Mathias! He's out for blood!"

The mayor of Heiligate sat up straighter and snuck a quick glance at the trap door in his floor. The idea of hiding looked increasingly appealing. "Whose blood?"

"Everyone's!"

Mehalco had known Mathias for centuries. He was accustomed to the paladin's interrogations and persuasive nature, and he knew the human was not above threats of force to gain the compliance of those who called Heiligate home. Above all, though,

Mathias had been fair and was the one ally these surface-bound demons had to call on to protect them from persecution and death by the Order of the White Circle. There was only one thing Mehalco could imagine Mathias would violently be after so soon following his most recent visit, and Mehalco eased himself to his feet, eyeing his cubby hole once more.

"Go ask him what he wants."

"He wants *you*," Bronte insisted.

"Then go and extend my invi—"

Rax, as bound by etiquette as any demon alive, grabbed Mehalco by the arm and hauled him toward the door. "You're not running and leaving us to solve this problem. Not this time."

Mehalco squirmed in the larger demon's crushing grasp, sweat pouring down the back of his neck as Bronte joined the procession by prodding him in the back.

"Now, listen, fools. *I* am in charge—"

Rax flung the door open and dragged Mehalco down the uneven steps of his home and onto the main thoroughfare. The streets were clearing rapidly, the demons who called Heiligate home scattering and ducking for cover as Mathias stormed, sword drawn, toward Mehalco's humble house. As the first eyes sighted the unwilling arrival of their leader, desperate cries for Mehalco to come do something about the paladin were raised, and Mathias turned his righteous eyes to his intended target, his pace hastening to a charge.

It took a certain degree of courage and finesse to run a tavern in a city full of demons, but Bronte and Rax hadn't stayed alive in their occupation as long as they had by being stupid, and Mathias was doing a far poorer job than usual hiding his intentions. Without so much as a mutter of good luck to their fearful leader, they shoved Mehalco forward and bolted in opposite directions to hide with the rest of their kin.

Mathias ignored the fears expressed by every other demon in town, focusing solely on Mehalco's attempt to catch himself. The demon's efforts were briskly interrupted as Mathias's left hand wrapped around his throat. The paladin's charge launched the flimsy demon backwards, and all Mehalco could register was the

308

rage in Mathias's eyes until the breath was launched out of him when his back slammed against a wall. Mathias drove himself up on the demon until the brunt of his weight pressed against Mehalco's heaving chest. Aligning his lips with the demon's ear, Mathias growled his demand in a harsh tone Mehalco had never witnessed from the reasonable paladin before.

"Friendship only goes so far. You will tell me who Berann is."

Mehalco wasn't a particularly courageous demon, and though he had experienced no end of fear in his time, often as a direct result of Mathias's demands, he'd have soiled himself from terror had he not recently relieved himself properly. He was very much so afraid of Mathias's rage, fully believing that the paladin had every intention of getting an answer to his question one way or another. However, Mehalco was even more afraid of what would happen to him if he chose to provide that answer. Tears welled up in his eyes at the simple fact that Mathias had openly spoken that name.

"I can't—" Mehalco choked against the crush of Mathias's hold, struggling to speak against it. When the paladin's grip maintained its intensity and he didn't so much as flinch at the demon's struggles, Mehalco realized he had no choice but to continue. "Tell you."

"Oh, you *will* tell me, friend. I am past the point of politeness on the matter."

"Death comes to those who speak of—"

Mathias leaned in closer still. "And death will seem like a great reward if you don't. Etha's not holding me back right now, the Council has been anxious for me to level this town for decades, and I've got every intention to uncover what I'm after, no matter what measures I must take to do that. Am I clear?"

The tears spilled free from Mehalco's eyes as he faced these terrible ultimatums. Death by his peers, or an eternity of suffering in whatever way Mathias's deranged mind had come up with. He gave a push against Mathias's hold, receiving a firm shove back against the wall in response, and had to accept the most immediate threat.

"Promise you'll keep me safe…"

"Your safety will be my next objective."

Mehalco's frown deepened. "That's not good enough."

"That's the best I can do," Mathias answered. "It's more than I should do. Your unwillingness to speak to me about this earlier led to the current circumstances and that is my sole priority."

The demon's eyes widened. "This... it's not about your girl, is it?"

Mathias shoved his weight against Mehalco again. "You will talk."

Mehalco exaggerated a gag as he tried to draw the breath to reply and feebly lifted his hands to point at Mathias's hold around his neck. Slowly, Mathias loosened his grip, keeping a watchful eye on Mehalco as he took a step back and allowed the demon to settle on his feet.

"Just to be clear, I want no part of whatever you're getting ready to start." Mehalco still trembled as he brushed himself off from Mathias's manhandling.

"We're past the wants of individuals."

"But isn't this all about your want of—"

Mathias lunged toward Mehalco again, resulting in a prompt cringe from the demon, and he restrained himself from a second attack. It wouldn't do him any good. "This is about the fate of Abaeloth. I have been an advocate for you and your crew for long enough, and it's time for me to collect on that. You will give me what I'm after."

Mehalco tried unsuccessfully to stare Mathias down, knowing, as he always did, that he didn't stand a chance at doing so. Through the generations in which the two had known each other, stretching clear back to when Mehalco had been an ignorant demon child playing bones in the hells, he'd never seen Mathias this sort of mad before, and the survivor inside of him assured him that the absolute best option was to play to the powerful human's desires. Mehalco bowed his head.

"This is to be discussed in private."

"Lead the way."

It was a small relief that Mathias was still rational enough to accept Mehalco's request for privacy, and the demon managed to suppress his urge to attempt darting off and away from the paladin as he turned to go back to his home.

Mathias followed closely as Mehalco led the way past the thorny bushes along his walkway. He remained silent as they walked, honoring Mehalco's reluctance to speak of the sensitive subject, despite the nagging urge to demand answers now. The worn wooden steps creaked as the two climbed onto the porch and after Mehalco ushered his unwelcome guest inside, he closed the door, bolted it, and dragged a heavy chair in front of it.

"Is this private enough?" Mathias asked, failing to keep the impatience from his voice.

Mehalco glanced about the entry of his house, his attention snagging on the window beside the door. It was as private as they were going to get. "We speak quietly," he said, lowering his voice accordingly.

As eager as he was, as angry as he was, a thrill of excitement swept across Mathias as it became evident that he had the demon's compliance at last. He sheathed his sword and took a step closer to Mehalco, crossing his arms to show that he was willing to leave his intentions to hurt him outside. "We can speak quietly."

Mehalco grimaced as though he was about to be ill and looked out the window again. The other residents of Heiligate hadn't come out of hiding quite yet, and so he still had some time before suspicions would arise. Or so he hoped. "The demon you speak of… what is it your records told of him?"

"That he was who initiated the Demon War when he and his handful of alar stormed Zeal."

Mehalco opened his mouth to comment on Mathias's answer, then his brows wrinkled and that nauseated frown returned. "Wouldn't it just be easier for you to keep believing that?"

Mathias heaved a brusque sigh and lowered his right arm, freeing it to potentially grasp a weapon. "We're past the point of ease, Mehalco. I already know that this demon is important. I just need to know why."

Mehalco stared at Mathias, not trying to intimidate him, but trying to decide how badly he valued his life. He'd trusted this human for centuries and Mathias had proven worthy of that trust and had given his word—at least in a round about way—that he would do what he could to continue protecting him, even if those he needed protection from were hordes of demons.

"You know he was an ancient," Mehalco whispered at last, a fresh wave of tears falling freely as he faced the truth which had been wiped from all written and spoken history the demons had collected. "So he was around since the beginning." He stopped, waiting hopefully for Mathias to change his mind. He wouldn't be so lucky.

"Right. I've been led to believe he was an oraku who worked closely with an alar named Kol and an oraku named Annin. I need to know why he's not to be spoken of."

Mehalco winced. "Of course you do..." He huffed and harrumphed as nerves petitioned for him to just accept whatever punishment Mathias had in mind, and he scooted even closer to the paladin. "He was an ancient," Mehalco repeated. "Well before my own time. But the stories said... I mean... the whispers that made it through the halls..." Mehalco clenched his teeth and scrunched his face up as he viciously battled his fears of speaking the lore which had been beaten out of him as a child. "Not all of the ancients wanted war, you know."

"That is how it is told." Indeed, the Order's own records clearly stated that the demons had spent a great deal of effort attempting to incorporate back into the natural world but had been routinely driven off by the mortals who had survived the Divine Battle unscathed. "Where are you going with this?"

"Ber— He— That demon..." Mehalco lowered his voice so much that the words barely came out as sounds at all. "He found a way to *undo our curse*."

"Undo..." Mathias gaped at the revelation, wishing beyond anything other than having Nessix standing beside him that he was able to discuss what this meant with Etha. All of these years... how had they not known such a vital element about the demons? "So the rumor that he'd come to Zeal petitioning for help..."

Mehalco shrugged and couldn't meet Mathias's eyes.

The news soaked into Mathias, triggering all of his demon hunting instincts and elevating his heart rate with hope and excitement and an insatiable urge to take action. There was an alternative beyond simply killing these abominations and leaving their souls to suffer in nothingness. It was such a simple answer, one the Order had systematically convinced all of their knights was an impossibility, and one that had the potential to free Abaeloth from the darkness which lurked in her core.

"I will ensure you are safe within the Citadel itself if you tell me how to achieve this undoing," Mathias said, his voice raising in excitement.

Mehalco cringed lower and peeked a nervous glance up at Mathias. "None of us know how," he squeaked. "We just know that he knew."

The light died in Mathias's eyes, replaced by the same chill which had carried him into town. "This is not the time to be toying with me, Mehalco."

"I'm not!" the demon sputtered. "It's said only a couple of those ancients had any idea what that method was, and he was the only one of the group who wanted peace. He fled the hells, seeking the Order's help when they killed him, and that's all I know." He rolled his lips between his teeth and sent a pleading gaze at Mathias. "Please believe me. That is *all* I know."

Frustration begged Mathias to demand more of an explanation, but even as he opened his mouth to insist on it, humility struck him at last. Mehalco had never been a willing informant, but he'd always been a reliable and honest one. He knew his place and had served Mathias faithfully for decades. The poor fool had been brought to tears over Mathias's question, genuine fear not only for himself but for the entirety of his race coursing from him freely. Demons weren't meant to show such emotions, and Mehalco had always been a terrible liar. Mathias took a deep breath and let it out in a slower sigh, closing his eyes against the beginning of a headache.

"That's all you know," he murmured back. "He was the only demon to make it to the surface who knew this method, and the Order killed him."

Even more uncertain now that Mathias had backed down, Mehalco slunk a step back. "If any others know, they haven't whispered a word of it. Everyone who did was culled generations ago."

Mathias nodded slowly. Nes's time in the hells hadn't uncovered anything to help shed light on this. Her limited reading of the ancient texts within the Order's vaults had done nothing more than confirm Berann's connection to the demons she'd served. The demons, as they were so skilled at doing, had successfully hidden their greatest weakness from the rest of the world, coldly and cruelly erasing all evidence of the one demon who could have saved Abaeloth from so much suffering.

And there was only one surefire way to tap into that knowledge.

"Thank you for your courage and honesty, friend," Mathias said, his tone having lost its fervor for a more resigned hush. He clapped a hand on Mehalco's shoulder, gaining a flinch from the demon who was convinced he'd be struck down any second now. "I owe you more than I will ever be able to repay."

Mehalco gulped on his reservations of the increasingly unsettling developments with this conversation. "Yeah, well, word gets out that I even told you that much…"

Mathias blinked the clarity back into his eyes, accepting the guilt for having asked Mehalco to pay such a price. He pulled the chair away from the door. "I'll ensure you are protected before that connection can ever be made. You have my word."

Heiligate had been founded on Mathias's vow to protect the demons who called it home, and in the decades it had stood as the crippled, ugly stepsister to Zeal's splendor, he had only had to cull three demons from its population. Mathias had always managed to keep the Order's eyes turned far enough away to not cause the demons any undue problems and had always ensured the humble city had access to the resources it needed. It was an unspoken oath of his, a responsibility he'd shouldered on his own which the demons of Heiligate all remembered but often took for granted. But this was the first time in all of Mehalco's shrewd recollection that Mathias had vowed to protect Mehalco himself. It was an honor the demon would have preferred to die a hundred deaths before ever needing to accept.

"Just… If you want to keep anyone safe, don't keep poking

around about this. Least of all around here."

Mathias pressed his lips together in a dissatisfied frown, his eyes growing distant in introspection as he unbolted the lock. "I've got no more questions about this that anyone in Heiligate can help me with. Thank you, Mehalco. I'll be in touch."

The demon opened his mouth to reply, but Mathias had already seen himself out the door, walking down the street as if in a daze. The frightened residents of Heiligate crept out of their hiding spots one by one to watch the paladin's departure, and Mehalco couldn't help but think that his foolish friend had finally gotten in over his head. As activity resumed outside, Mehalco pulled the door of his ramshackle house closed, picked up a dusty bottle of wine, and ripped the cork from it with his teeth.

TWENTY-SEVEN

The demons had departed Zeal by flying into the sun to blind their opponents to their location, but their worn wings weren't strong enough to carry them all the way to safety. As soon as they were clear of Zeal's eyes, they landed to continue their journey on foot. After all, with Nessix in their custody, they could comfortably slow their pace.

Nessix had denied Kol the conversations he'd tried to make with her, too busy erecting the walls she'd need to withstand the punishment awaiting her and desperately searching for a new plan to help her people. They'd been counting on her. She'd left them in peril with nothing but the promise that she'd bring the Order to free them, and she'd been unable to secure the reinforcements they so badly needed. She hadn't even been able to sway one man to come along with her. The shackles on her wrists and the manner which Kol refused to pass her off to any of his comrades assured her he wouldn't allow her to escape a second time, and Nessix was still stuck with the inconvenient truth that though she hated what Kol stood for, she couldn't quite wish him dead. Running low on hope and even lower on resilience, Nessix had to entertain the thought that there may no longer be a way to accomplish her goal.

Annin savored every moment of Nessix's struggles, even the shrillest of her screams, after the headache she'd put him through.

He loved the way her voice had grown hoarse from her objections. He loved the way her thrashing at the end of her tether made her lose balance so she fell to the ground, dragged through the dirt and rocks until Kol stopped to jerk her back to her feet. He loved the way her wrists bled and bruised from the intensity with which she fought her restraints. And he absolutely adored the way Kol didn't feel as though he had to coddle her through any of it.

It was wonderful to see Kol finally remember what it meant to be a demon. He'd likely crumble back to his sappy devotion once his immediate anger wore off but for now, he was a demon again. He had a hold of a prisoner, one he'd long ago claimed for himself, and he willingly stood by as she struggled against him solely to prove his superiority to her. It was a refreshing change in Kol which Annin had been waiting to see for over a year now. Kol was coming back to himself and because of that, they may still be able to overthrow the inoga.

The troop of demons stopped to camp once the sun set, and when Nessix didn't pick at the meal Kol presented her, he settled for letting her choose to go hungry. Driving the ring of her shackles into the ground with a stake, he slept holding her through the night.

Nessix didn't dream that night, as she had the other time when Kol had been so near, and she was fine with that. She didn't trust her dreams any more than she trusted reality, and though her stomach demanded she accept his offer of food and the sedative effects of dream stop, she wouldn't give Kol the pleasure of seeing her take care of herself. She'd now witnessed what the demons would do to akhuerai who misbehaved, and though she suspected she'd have had her ring torn out by now if that was Kol's plan for her, she didn't put it past any of the inoga or even the underlings to rip her soul out when he wasn't looking.

There had been part of her which had fancied the notion that Kol might be so relieved to see her again that he'd decide to be gentle with her, to revisit that tenderness which he'd shown her even in her more violent stints of disobedience; the first time she'd laid eyes on him after being brought back to life, she'd nearly sawed through his neck, and that conversation had ended with him gifting her clothes and a fatherly kiss on the forehead. But now, Nessix faced a demon who treated her like a scrap of meat, contemplating whether or not Mathias truly would be able to uncover what they needed for her to save her army and guide Abaeloth to a hopeful future.

She spent the night listening for the sounds of knights charging to back her up, but as the hours passed, her memories of the Council's petty bickering and senseless accusations outweighed that hope. The Order, the great, Etha-fearing pillar of justice Mathias had spoken so highly of back on Elidae would not help her rescue the akhuerai. Or her. At least she'd managed to be part of protecting those priestesses. At least Auden, as broken as he was, had managed to escape. Kol's arm slid further around her as he shifted in his sleep, and Nessix bit down on the insides of her cheeks to keep from screaming.

She'd been so close, but not fast enough.

Morning broke and Nessix, as exhausted as she was and continuing to refuse food, staggered behind Kol as they resumed their journey southwest. As the day wore on, her thoughts shifted away from her grand failure and to the tortures exclusive to her kind. Auden had been sent into Zeal both as a summons and a warning. By the way Kol continued to flaunt his doting possession of her as he dragged her down the road, she suspected she was considered too valuable to meet her end in a similar fashion, but she'd been routinely reminded that what made her the ideal leader for an army of frightened once-mortals was her instinct to watch over and guard those beneath her. The fastest way to break Nessix would be to break those she cared about, those she'd vowed to protect, and she had an entire army the demons could force her to witness the ends of.

They continued through the day, marching at a pace just brisk enough to stick a cramp in Nessix's side. Annin halted their journey upon arriving at an outcropping of open hills as evening set in, allowing the entire procession to sigh with relief. The oraku assigned troops to watch the perimeter of their little camp, taking the most vulnerable northeastern corner for himself, and leaving Kol—far more sane now that he'd reclaimed his toy—in charge of the balance of the troops.

The alar ignored his duties of leadership to focus his attention on Nessix, but she stubbornly remained hunched within the circle of demons, avoiding eye contact with him. She hadn't spoken all day, and the raking soreness left in her throat from her furious screams promised she'd have a difficult time at it even if she had something she wanted to say.

"You will eat tonight," Kol told her as he pulled a handful of rations from his pouch. He'd learned from his previous attempts that she'd feign being unable to coordinate her bound hands to feed herself and held a bite forward for her. She didn't so much as glance at the sustenance presented to her, and the alar glowered. Starvation would not kill Nessix the way it would kill a mortal, but she needed a minimum amount of strength to make the rest of the trip back to the hells without complicating the logistics of their travel plans.

"Just dominate her and be through with it, Kol," one of the demons behind him snickered.

Kol cocked his head at the suggestion, drinking in the way Nessix's suffering eyes shriveled even closer to defeat. "Is that what you'd like, little one?" he asked her quietly. "Do I need to treat you the way demons treat their toys for you to respect me as a demon?"

Nessix lowered her chin, resigned to her misery and whatever threats Kol wanted to send her way. What good would fighting do for her, anyway?

Kol grabbed her chin with his free hand to turn her face toward his. She allowed the movement, but kept her eyes lowered, and Kol crouched down to her level. His fiery eyes bore into what was left of her resolve, stripping her confidence naked and quietly wrapping its shreds in restraints which he bound to his whims. There had been a time when Nessix had thought it would be fun to play games with a demon who was receptive to them, but that novelty had worn off, replaced by so much regret.

"All of you are on leave for the next half hour." Kol had raised his voice to address the demons behind him, but kept his eyes locked on Nessix. She snuck the briefest, disbelieving glance at him but quickly looked away from the possessive calm which he held her with. "Tell Annin to leave us alone."

The group of demons laughed and complained that Kol was taking all of the fun out of their night, but they did as they were told, venturing up the hills to reinforce the perimeter and give Kol his privacy. Nessix lowered her eyes even further under the pressure of Kol's leering, a faint tremble working through her body as she accepted the fact that she was about to lose any influence she'd ever had over him.

He dropped the food he'd tried to offer her and grabbed her bound wrists to haul her to her feet as he stood. Nessix didn't have the chance to fight him as he pushed her backwards, driving her off the cleared site of their camp and into a field of grass which stood nearly up to her waist. She struggled to coordinate her steps, and after just a few domineering strides, Kol hooked his foot behind her ankle and tripped her. Nessix fell backwards, unable to use her arms to catch herself, and Kol let the rope of her bindings slide through his slacked hands. She struck the ground hard enough to pummel the breath from her, and before she'd recovered, Kol kicked her knees apart and knelt between them.

Nessix had known Kol for months now, had convinced herself she'd known him well, and she hadn't felt this sort of threat from him since the day she'd first been brought back to life. He'd treated her so respectfully that part of her had dismissed the notion that he was a demon and capable of horrendous acts, but as he spread his wings to counterbalance his movement, legs sliding her knees apart wider as he pinned her left shoulder to the ground with the heel of his right hand, she realized that Kol, the alar who had been patient with her in instances which would have tried the most lenient of mortals, the demon she had begun to think was an exception to what these terrible creatures were, had done this before. He lowered his torso over hers, left arm sliding in the dirt by her head until his elbow supported him and his fingers slid into her hair. Swallowing her sob, Nessix looked away.

"Why did you leave me, little one?" he asked, hot breath tickling her ear and sending a disgusted trail of shudders through her entire frame.

Nessix tried to organize her thoughts, tried to rally herself to

320

fight him or attempt negotiating her way out of what was coming, but she couldn't even begin to fathom what she could say or do to amend the situation. She'd gotten away with too much as it was.

"I do *not* want to hurt you," Kol said quietly when it became apparent that Nessix hadn't the means or courage to answer him. "And I *will* not hurt you unless you force my hand, but you have put me in a very dangerous place, and that's a dangerous place for anyone affiliated with me, yourself included."

The words, far from the lewd taunts Nessix had expected, seeped through her dread and she shifted her gaze to Kol, drawing upon the memories of how she'd hated him when he'd first killed her. Unlike the well-nourished and spirited version of her past self, she was too dehydrated to spit at him. "I don't care about me." Her voice was low and raspy from the day she'd spent screaming.

Kol's eyes softened. "I know you don't." His fingers idly squeezed her hair. "That's why you ran off. You were trying to rescue your army, weren't you?"

She looked away from him again, wishing he'd just hurry up and get this over with.

"Were you ever obedient to me, little one? Did you ever care for me the way I cared for you?"

Nessix's eyes snapped back to his, soaking in the depth of his longing for her. He'd devoted so many years learning how to create akhuerai. He'd hand-picked her, bound himself to her, invested all of his waking hours into forging her into the most brilliant weapon Abaeloth had ever known, and he *adored* her for that. Had Nessix ever felt such adoration for him? Had she not tried to give her life to protect him when Grell attacked? Had she not found solace in his embrace the night they'd dreamed together of the horrors of his past? She longed to return to that time, to remember what it was like to know that she had someone protecting her the way she protect him, but she couldn't let herself admit that she cared about him. Doing so would mean she'd quit caring about everyone whose life he'd destroyed, the people who weren't strong enough to stand and fight on their own. The people she'd abandoned.

The truth was, Nessix didn't know what she wanted anymore. She didn't even know if her thoughts were her own or some construct fed into her by the forces vying to influence her. What she did know, based on the fact that Kol had been so cruel to her in front of his peers, yet had adopted a more sensible nature now that he had her alone, was that she *was* safe with him. His promise that he didn't want to hurt her was as genuine as a demon could ever be, and if she was going to find any sort of safety or redemption ever again, she had to trust him now.

"Not the way you cared for me, I'm sure," she answered at last.

Kol breathed a sigh at her willingness to engage him in this conversation. "Then in what way?"

Nessix would have preferred him to go ahead and assault her over prying into these thoughts. Physical abuse, she'd learned to tolerate, from the battlefield and Veed and the demons themselves. But mental abuse, she'd routinely fallen victim to, from her father's sugared lies to inflate her confidence, to Mathias's lies meant to embolden her into foolishness, to the very lies she now believed had been the basis of her relationship with Kol.

"Does it matter what I think?" she asked. "Just do what you have planned for me, and take me back to my troops."

Kol cocked his head and frowned. "I told you I don't want to hurt you, but you are hurting now, aren't you?"

If she'd had even an ounce more confidence, Nessix would have laughed. "You don't care."

"What makes you say that?"

"Because you don't." Nessix flashed her stony glare at him, holding his inquisitive gaze without flinching. "You killed me, stole my soul, and raised me from the dead. You forced me to recruit an undead army to carry out your horrendous plots against the mortal realm, then chased me halfway across the world, and broke my—" She bit off the cascade of her thoughts and shook her head until she'd pressed her cheek into the ground to look away from Kol. "If you cared, if you didn't want me hurt, you'd have never done this to me." That laugh made it out of her now, but she didn't feel any better for it. "How stupid am I for trying to explain this to a demon…"

Kol leaned lower over her and stroked the hair from her face with his right hand, promptly stealing from her the hint of confidence her bitterness had loaned her. "You beautiful, beautiful fool..." he murmured. "Did you learn nothing at all from our studies together?"

Nessix gulped down the wave of nauseous fear which swept over her as Kol pressed closer against her, every instinct inside her screaming conflicting assessments over what was happening. Even if he chose decency, he was asking her to trust him. She'd thought she'd been the one playing him all this time, but he'd always been a fierce opponent. Had he been the one conditioning—and gaining—blind trust from her, and not the other way around? And now that she was helpless, at his mercy in every sense, he was asking her to open that door again. Tears burned at the backs of her eyes, but they were of sheer frustration, not fear. Kol, clever, conniving Kol, had never stopped being a demon, but Nessix had somehow let herself forget that. A tremble worked through her body and he brushed his thumb across her cheek to still her.

"You were, indeed, intended to carry out my horrendous plots," he told her, his voice low and deep, smoothly confirming that same cunning Nessix had just identified. "But it was never mortals you were designed to strike."

Nessix struggled to tear her mind from the immediate concern of the physical advantage Kol held over her, but her eyes widened at the hateful snap at the end of his statement. He *had* been intending to strike against his own people. Nessix had few reasons to trust him, but as she thought back to all she knew about demon hierarchy, about Kol's casual explanation of all of the ways he planned to use the akhuerai, about how carefully he made sure she never forgot how to fight—and hate—his kind, she realized that he had even fewer reasons to lie to her.

"Why are you telling me this?" she whispered.

Kol lowered his forehead to hers, closing his eyes as his relief of finally being in a position to explain to Nessix his true intentions met a sudden flood of anxiety about what he was about to launch into action. "Because your rebellion has landed me solidly in Grell's sights. I would *die* for you, little one, and my sentence very well may be in place, but if any of us—your troops, yourself, or even I—are going to make it out of this alive, I need your compliance. I need your obedience. I need to know I can trust you."

Whether by Kol's physical nearness, his spiritual connection to her, or simply their shared motivation in ridding the hells of Grell and those who stood in his defense, Nessix couldn't form the words to respond.

Kol's fingers curled tighter in her hair, and his lips brushed her cheek as he whispered, "Were you *ever* loyal to me, Nessix?"

She'd always hated hearing him call her by her given name, having made an association with it and some claim of station or authority over her, but this time was different. This was him addressing her as an officer, as a valued member of his army, and Nessix was struck by his intention of speaking to her so privately. He was afraid, and he believed he was alone.

The part of her which had been torn away from Mathias, forced to abandon her mission to save her people screamed a resounding no, but the answer wasn't that simple, not anymore. "I don't know," she admitted quietly.

Kol opened his eyes and drew his face back from Nessix's, fine wrinkles between his brows betraying a fragile emotion he'd never allowed her to look upon before. "I need you, little one." He pinched his eyes shut, lips working between a frown and a snarl, before he opened them again, and he briefly flicked his attention back toward where Annin had stationed himself on guard. "My intentions are not as secret as I'd like them to be and I've quickly lost allies and influence due to your actions. I need someone I can trust. Will you be that person for me?"

Nessix looked up at Kol as he loomed over her, finding her fear of him had been battered about by the faint, but steady drumming of loyalty. This could still be a plot of his, but he'd stayed true to his claim of not wanting to hurt her when there was nothing at all holding him back from doing that and so much more. All her life, Nessix had told herself she was destined to protect innocents, that the only way to determine her worth was by how well she could obtain and maintain peace and safety. That responsibility had stretched well past Elidae and to the rest of Abaeloth after Kol had forced his way into her life, and she suddenly had to wonder if what she'd viewed as a devastating interception of fate had actually been what put her on a straighter path to achieve that very goal.

Resolve returned to her eyes and she shifted her weight beneath Kol to twist her arms around and prop herself up with an elbow so she could meet his eyes. "I am a general for and of the people," she said firmly. "And I will not quit fighting until the last person who wants freedom from their oppressors has found it."

Kol's expression lost its strictness and he closed his eyes once more, releasing his grip on Nessix's hair. "Play your part for me, little one," he ordered softly. "Show me obedience. Show me loyalty. And we will change the hells."

Nessix wasn't quite sure she was confident enough to verbally agree with him, but neither did she object. After all, even if this was a ploy of Kol's, even if there was only a slim chance matters would work out in her favor, it was the only option she currently had.

Kol sat back on his knees and tugged Nessix's shirt out from where she'd had it tucked in her pants then tore the neckline at her shoulder. After unfastening his belt, he stood and jerked Nessix to her feet. No more comfortable with this arrangement than she'd been two minutes ago, Nessix bowed her head to avoid the believability of Kol's malicious smirk and allowed him to lead her back to the campsite. If he needed her to play her part, that was what she'd do.

* * * * *

Annin didn't accept failure well and he'd hoped he'd put it behind himself now that they had Nessix back in their possession. As he stared into his scrying bowl as his blood cooled after his third attempt to reach Lorrin, his frustration crept back to him. When the procession of alar climbed his hill, irritation wrapped its arm around him in a smothering embrace. And when he realized both Kol and Nessix were missing from the group, he flung the blood from his bowl and spun to face his underlings.

"Where is Kol?"

The demons snickered and passed about crude jokes until one

of them piped up. "He's getting to know his pet a bit better."

Annin frowned, his eyes flashing at the danger those words implied. The last thing any of them needed, Kol chief among them, was for Nessix to hook her claws even deeper into him. As unstable as Kol had been of late, any act of domination he might make against Nessix could easily be used against him by the crafty woman. Growling, Annin turned to begin heading back down the hill.

"I... wouldn't do that if I were you, sir," another of the demons said. "Kol asked for half an hour."

More laughter bubbled up from the group and Annin grit his teeth.

"Son of a bitch..." he muttered.

Annin had known Kol longer than he'd known anyone else living or dead, and he knew the alar's mannerisms well. Kol seldom participated in the more carnal displays of dominance used by their peers, much preferring the cruelties of psychological manipulation, but once he did reach the point to shift from playing with the mind to the flesh, it was never an event he rushed through. Half an hour wouldn't have come close to satisfying his objectives of dominating anyone, least of all his rebellious toy. And Nessix, Annin knew, had enforced her own psychological advantages over Kol long ago. No, whatever Kol had planned, it was not the fun these demons chortled about now. Annin clenched his fists and resumed heading toward the camp.

The laughter stopped immediately. "Um, Annin. Kol specifically told us—"

Annin stopped abruptly and swung around to the group. "Which one of you put him up to this?"

A brutish alar with small eyes smirked. "I did, s—"

Annin flicked his hand through the air as though batting away a fly, and the demon's words were cut off by a shrill scream as his kneecap rolled to the side of his leg. Shaking his head in disgust at the incompetence of the men he had to depend on, Annin continued down the hill, not meeting another gasp of debate from his subordinates.

"He's not doing what you think he's doing," the oraku

muttered, though he doubted the group could hear him. *He's doing something much worse…*

Annin trudged down the hill and watched as Kol stood from the tall grass opposite the campsite, dragging Nessix to her feet. The alar proceeded to pull his prisoner, her hands still bound, back to the clearing of their camp and held his friend's commanding gaze firmly as they neared each other. Not one part of Annin believed Kol had assaulted Nessix, despite the roguish glint in his eyes and the cockeyed smile he wore. Annin may have known Kol and the nature of his desires and ambitions too well to believe that any form of intimacy, consensual or otherwise, had been shared between the two of them, but he didn't know Nessix well enough to gauge why she only allowed herself a timid peek at him before hunching her shoulders and staring pointedly at the ground as Kol jerked her forward and into his grasp.

"I thought I'd sent orders that I wasn't to be disturbed," Kol said.

Annin studied his friend hard. "You did, but clearly you overestimated your stamina."

Nessix, already uncomfortable with her role in this charade, attempted to turn away from Annin at the blatant insult, but Kol held her fast, his fingers digging into her waist with a possessiveness even she believed for a moment.

"Exposed in the open, there are chances I'm unwilling to take," Kol answered sharply. "I ensured everything necessary was conveyed."

"I'll bet it was," Annin scoffed.

Kol met that judgement without flinching. "When we reach a more secure location, I'll take care of matters properly. Don't worry."

Annin stared at Kol for a long while, acutely aware of when Nessix raised her eyes to appraise him. Kol had conveyed something to Nessix, there was no doubt, and it was unusual for the alar to attempt such measures to try keeping a secret from him. "Very well," Annin granted. "I will go tell the troops that they've got clearance to return to their meals."

Night progressed, and the weary band began to bed down to

rest their wings and nerves. The watch rotation was assigned and as Kol gathered up the slack of Nessix's guide rope to drag her up the hill for his shift, Annin stepped up beside him and grasped a hold of her shackle chain. Kol froze and met Annin's eyes.

The oraku held them firmly. "It's my turn with her now," he said loudly enough for the rest of the camp to hear.

Kol's eyes flared as he prepared to argue, but he knew Annin had pieced together the lie he'd attempted to pass on him. While the transparency should have shamed him on some level, and the words Annin had just used to express his intentions stoked a bitter fire inside of him, Kol couldn't fight the request, not with so many troops witnessing their exchange. Besides, Annin had made it blatantly clear to Kol that he'd rather castrate himself than take Nessix to bed, and had claimed multiple times that he truly did want Nessix functioning enough to carry out her objective.

There were so many requests Kol wanted to make of Annin right now, for him to be fair to her, to not hold his stupidity against her, to not frighten her to the point that she would disregard the headway he'd just made. But there was no way he could word any of those requests to reflect positively on him or his intentions of appearing like the domineering beast he'd spent the earlier part of the evening establishing himself as. Instead, Kol swallowed the debates spurred by his affection for Nessix and nodded once to Annin. He gave Nessix a kiss on top of her head, passed her rope to the oraku, and turned to walk off to his post.

Though Kol hadn't had any more time to explain to Nessix what his plans were, and though part of her still believed she was a fool to cave to his request so readily, Nessix swallowed her pride and dug out her courage as Annin dragged her away from the campsite. No matter what intentions Annin had with her, fighting him was an even stupider notion than trying to fight Kol. As resigned as before, Nessix followed without a fuss and retreated as far as her tether allowed when he stopped and crossed behind her to shove her farther from camp.

"Sit," Annin ordered, and Nessix obeyed before he had the chance or excuse to throw her to the ground.

He sat across from her, extending his wings to block the

troops' view of what he was up to.

"You have put us in a very precarious position, Nessix," Annin said at last.

Generous cloud cover washed out most of the moonlight, casting Annin as an ominous silhouette against the darkness. Nessix didn't need to see him clearly to know she hated him.

"And you continue to do so the longer you keep Kol enthralled with you."

Nessix shook her head, losing her fear of what Annin had planned. She'd never trusted the oraku but she was comfortable engaging him over this. "You think I *want* a demon doting over me like some hyperactive mother hen?"

Had this been a situation worth laughing over, Annin would have chuckled at the analogy. "We are taking you back to the hells, and we are going to ensure you lead your army to our whims. We've got movements that are too important for you to screw up again, and the manner in which you keep Kol under your thumb risks endangering all of them. Has he already told you what Grell's been thinking?"

Nessix was grateful for the way the darkness hid her contemplative expression. Kol had implied he didn't know how much he could trust Annin, and that did very little to improve her own opinion of the oraku. The fact that Annin had chosen to speak to her in a civil manner made her appreciate the circumstances even less. "He told me Grell's angry at him for losing me."

"Angry?" Annin asked, his voice as calm and even as ever. "He's livid. He allowed us to come to the surface to look for you twice before, and we had to return empty handed both times. But even now that we have you in tow, do not think that will be enough to satisfy him. He'll need to make an example of someone, and he may very well consider you too valuable to fill that role. Is this a chance you're willing to take?"

So fresh from her private encounter with Kol, Nessix knew exactly who Annin implied would accept punishment in her stead, and the truth was, she didn't know if that was a risk she wanted to flirt with at all. "I've already tried to die for Kol in the past. That should be answer enough for both of you."

"But you've also tried to get him killed."

"I've done no such thing!" The excuse flew from Nessix's lips before she had a chance to catch it, and she flushed and looked away, realizing her hasty defense of Kol had confirmed Annin's suspicions that less intimacy had passed between her and the alar than either of them had tried to convey.

Annin allowed her to wallow in her fumble, hiding his own reaction as he often did. "Perhaps not on purpose, but if you're as smart as he always rattles on about, you knew the moment you committed yourself to plunging a knife into that first guard that your actions could lead to his death." Annin cocked his head as Nessix's threads beat with a rapid uncertainty. "I suspect he used his time with you to ask for your obedience?"

Nessix choked on her reservations of disclosing more than she already had. Annin had always been wary of her and operated on a faster level than she did. She knew she wouldn't be able to lie to him, and thus decided it was better to aim for honesty. "He did."

"And did you give it to him?"

Nessix was trapped by this interrogation, just as she had been when Mathias had demanded similar answers from her. It was nobody's business but her own who she'd forged alliances with, but she wasn't in a hurry to find out what Annin would do if she tested his patience. "I did."

Annin heaved a weary sigh, startling Nessix as his wings slouched an inch lower. Though he'd known better for months now, he'd hoped it wouldn't have come to this. "Kol has not been of sound mind lately, and I'm sure you've pieced together your value within the hells. I am not Kol. I do not believe you can easily be controlled. But I do suspect you can be manipulated."

Nessix shook her head, having expected this turn of events even less than the ones Kol had led her down earlier. "What's that supposed to mean?"

"Distance yourself from Kol if you have any vested interest in his future. That is all I will say."

"But what—"

Nessix's question cut off abruptly as Annin quietly snapped her thread of consciousness. She slumped down to the ground like a rag doll, twisting awkwardly over her bound hands. Annin eyed the dark blob she formed in the moonlight, speculating on how easy it would be to do whatever he wanted with her, how easy it would be to drag her back to camp and pass her around to the underlings who had been anxiously voicing their desires to have some fun, but even Annin had standards. Even Annin understood what obedience was.

He tucked his wings close at his sides and crawled over to Nessix, pushing her over to her side to prevent her muscles from cramping, and laid down on his belly beside her, resting his chin on his folded hands as he stared into the darkness. They might have had Nessix back in their hands and she might have sworn her loyalty to Kol, but it wasn't the first time they'd reached either of these achievements. It wasn't often that Annin doubted his plans, especially those as thought out and long studied as the akhuerai, and he didn't welcome the feeling now. Hissing at his own foolishness, Annin closed his eyes.

TWENTY-EIGHT

Mathias missed Etha's gentle words—even her strict scolding—but he didn't regret his bittersweet farewell to Nessix. The recovered priestesses preoccupied the goddess too much for her to manifest to him right now, leaving Mathias to figure out his next plan of action on his own, which led him nowhere he wanted to go.

There was no way to deny that Berann had been important to the demons obtaining the might they now commanded. Whether Nes's hunch was correct and he'd been looking for help, or the Order's lore was true and he'd been the catalyst to the Demon War, he'd been key to Abaeloth's greatest and most persistent heartache. And Mathias needed to know the truth of it all.

Speaking to the souls of the departed was something Mathias was capable of when he dipped into the divine realm, but the residue of Nes's curse which he carried barred him from entering that sacred plane. Even if it didn't, no departed demon had ever crossed those borders. Nobody knew where the twisted remains of demon souls went when they died, at least not anybody Mathias considered trustworthy. Logic told him exactly who would have the best theories on the matter, and though he hated entertaining that avenue, he hated the thought of what would happen from his inaction even more.

Mathias didn't find Khin in the libraries, nor when he inquired at the temple, but he tracked her down to the room she'd been granted in the general living quarters. She answered his knock promptly, likely assuming he was someone from the temple looking to send her on an errand, and when she saw it was him, her lips twisted in a scowl as she turned her eyes to the side.

"Do you need something?" The girl's sour tone struck Mathias right where she'd intended, but she'd expected a guilty flush from him, not the fierce narrowing of his eyes.

"Where has Tristan gone into hiding?"

Her eyes widened at Mathias's question, as she'd contently let herself believe Mathias had thought him gone. Desperate to protect the vampire, to continue making him proud, Khin crossed her arms and leaned against the door frame. "You kicked him out. *Remember*?" When Mathias's frown and stony glower persisted, she shrank back an inch into her room. "What makes you think he's still here?"

Mathias ran a hand through his hair and blew out a slow breath to buy time for patience to find him. "Because, Khin, you've been happy the past couple of days, and you've been sneaking out of the Citadel every chance you get." Her arms slowly melted back down to her sides, lips parting in a silent gasp that she'd been so easily found out by the man she'd convinced herself hadn't been paying any attention to her. "Circumstances have... changed," Mathias added. "And I need to know where Tristan has been staying."

Khin didn't appreciate the firmness of Mathias's tone nor her assumption that his desire to speak with Tristan would result in more inconveniences for her friend. Tristan had told her he was proud of her. He counted on her. And she still had to meet with him—here in Zeal—tonight. Maybe, if she played her cards right with Mathias, she could do even more to help the vampire. She crossed her arms again, keeping them in place by tightening her hunched shoulders.

"Circumstances have changed, like he can come back home?" she asked.

The patience Mathias had been searching for hadn't quite

taken root, and he tapped his fingers on his thighs to vent some of his anxious energy. "The Citadel is not his home, Khin."

She raised her chin and gulped down her courage before it fled out her throat. "But can he come back?"

Mathias drew a sweltering breath. "No."

Cheeks pale, Khin shrugged and backed into the room, grabbing the door to push it shut. "Then I don't know where he—"

Mathias slammed his hand against the door so hard it flung out of the girl's grip, prompting her to wring her hands and retreat a couple steps away from him. She'd given up on Mathias caring about her the way she wanted him to, and she had no way of understanding how fragile his self-control was, but though she'd convinced herself that Mathias was not the grand gentleman he pretended to be, she'd never imagined he'd express such aggression toward her. Her wide eyes petitioned to the paladin's sensibilities, mocking his virtue and emphasizing a greater flaw in his character than he'd been prepared to accept.

He'd frightened this girl when a vampire hadn't.

Flexing his fingers, struggling to release the accumulation of his tension, Mathias tried to soften his approach in a manner Khin might be receptive to. "I need to have a talk with him."

She studied Mathias for a long, quiet moment before she was able to believe that he wouldn't hurt her. "Sure," she sneered, parking herself firmly within the safety of her room. "A talk."

Mathias held his empty hands before himself. "A talk and nothing else. If you help me and he behaves himself, that's all it will amount to."

Khin's distrustful eyes raked him over, reminding him of all the times he'd brushed her off and let her down. *Tristan,* those eyes told him, *has never told me to wait on him.* "You won't hear where he's at," she snapped. "Not from me."

After receiving the girl's harsh opinion of the priorities Abaeloth's pending crisis had forced him to make, Mathias truly was at a disadvantage. Unfortunately for his desire to work out his differences with Khin, he had no choice but to obtain what he was after. If that left her hating him for the rest of her life, it wouldn't be the first time he'd let a desperate woman down.

334

"Khin…" he drew her name out along the last remaining thread of patience he had. "If you force me to go searching for him, that will involve others, others who won't be as inclined to overlook the fact that you've befriended a vampire as I am. Do you understand what I'm saying?"

Khin tucked her lips in a tight frown, her gaze tumbling to the floor. Though she resented Mathias for the cruelty he'd shown her and his unjust treatment of Tristan, he could have easily pursued much more aggressive measures in driving the vampire away. He was obligated by his station to uphold the law and, as far as Khin could tell, he'd chosen to avoid incriminating her or leading a hunt to track down Tristan. Mathias may not *want* the vampire in his holy city, but he'd had enough time to make things much worse. Perhaps working with him would entice him to continue with such leniency.

"What do you need to talk to him about?"

Mathias hesitated as protocol dictated he not disclose such sensitive information to the general public. Word of the demons' interaction with Zeal had already entered the Citadel, though, and it wouldn't be long before the details worked through the temple. It was better for Khin to hear the truth now than after a few dozen interpretations had a chance to skew the details.

"I am about to go to war against the demons—"

A brief yelp of a startled laugh left Khin. "*You* are?" Her voice rattled in a haunting mixture of disbelief and fear. "Alone?"

Mathias pinched his eyes shut. It wasn't the most ideal arrangement by far, but with the Council routinely shutting him down and Etha unable to accompany him, what other option did he have? "Right now, yes." He sighed from the soles of his feet, mental and physical exhaustion pulling at him. "And I need to know more about demon souls than anyone affiliated with the Order can tell me if I hope to make it out of the hells again."

As angry as Khin had been with Mathias, there wasn't one part of her which wanted to see him hurt. "Tristan can speak to souls…" she murmured.

"I know he can." Mathias's voice had lost its terse edge, more a tired plea now than anything else.

"If I help you," Khin said slowly, "can he be granted safety here in Zeal?"

Mathias could hardly imagine the vampire wanted to stay in the blessed city longer than necessary, but wouldn't fault Khin for her hope. "That is not my decision to make and right now, my word holds very little weight to those who get to make that call."

Khin blew a quick laugh out her nose, not entirely believing Mathias's excuse but unwilling to fight him on it. If she could get him to see that there was something good and useful in Tristan... Mathias might not be able to grant the vampire citizenship or safety, but he could continue to turn a blind eye to his presence. "All you want to do is talk to him?"

"Believe me. That is all I hope it will be."

Khin stared at him hard as she balanced out the different aches in her heart and head. Finally, she stepped forward and grabbed the edge of the door, clinging to it like it might offer her moral support. "He's staying in the slum." Afraid of her confession and the trouble it might cause Tristan, she pushed the door halfway closed, hiding her body behind it so only her head and shoulders peeked out. "In an abandoned house he said belonged to an old friend of his."

Mathias bit down on his reaction to frown. He was quite sure Sazrah was one of only three acquaintances any vampire would have in Zeal, and he was even more certain that Tristan's selection of accommodations after being driven out of the Citadel had been an intentional slap at him. Khin had no reason to be drawn into such petty drama.

"I know the place," Mathias said.

Khin nodded shortly. "Do you need anything else from me?"

"No, Khin," Mathias replied. "You've been of great help. Thank you."

For having waited weeks now to hear such kind words from Mathias, Khin shrugged off his gratitude and looked down once more as she closed the door.

"Etha, what did I do to deserve this..." Mathias muttered.

He didn't expect an answer and suspected he wouldn't have been all that thrilled with any the goddess might have given him, anyway. So troubled, so exhausted, Mathias turned and marched out of the Citadel to go confront a vampire. His fierce aura prevented anyone from thinking it was a good idea to follow him, and familiarity more than thought carried him to the dirty street where Sazrah's little house was tucked away. The curtains were drawn, the front step swept clean, confirming Mathias's suspicion that Tristan had carefully selected this residence specifically to irritate him.

"Behave yourself…" he muttered to himself—and Tristan—as he ascended the step. He leaned his forearm against the doorframe, using the tiny cottage's sturdiness for support. "I know you're in there, Tristan." He didn't bother to hush his voice, through caring whether or not the vampire was aiming for secrecy. "Neither of us want to cause a scene."

There was no sound from inside the cottage and the paladin scowled before drawing the breath to make his next demand. The door opened as his mouth did the same, and Mathias quickly looked up at the elegant young man who had taken up residence in the vacant home.

"Ah, Sir Sagewind." Tristan's hazel eyes seeped the same deceptive warmth he used to charm those far more naïve to the darker sides of Abaeloth, his voice smooth and calm as it toyed at gaining influence over Mathias's sensibilities. "My lord informed me that you would be stopping by." He flicked his gaze up and down Mathias, smirking at the paladin's disheveled appearance and bloodshot glower. "I do hope you didn't threaten my dear little Khin the way you threatened that half-witted Afflicted in order to locate me."

Patience spent, Mathias scowled at how much information the vampire had milked out of the young woman. "It may be difficult for one such as yourself to believe, but I make it a point to avoid harming those who haven't earned it."

One corner of Tristan's lips raised in an antagonistic smirk. "Are you still telling yourself that lie? Have you not come to terms with the fact that you hurt every single person you bring into your life?"

On most any other day, Mathias would have been able to

chuckle at this goading and tuck the guilt which came along with it into the compartments where he hid inconvenient truths. But today had already presented him with a lengthy list of people who he had failed, whose involvement with him had brought immeasurable suffering to, and the sting of Tristan's observation struck Mathias as much more of a pointed attack. He'd intentionally left his sword back at the Citadel, well aware of the current limits of his self-control, and his scowl etched deeper across his face as he gripped a fist until his knuckles creaked.

Tristan's smirk remained in place and though he would have delighted in pushing Mathias further, the reaction doing so would gain was not in his agenda. "Well," he said with a lofty sigh and arrogant arch of his thin brows. "I cannot imagine you hunted me out simply to receive revelations you have always carried with you, so please." Tristan took a step back and swept his arm into the modest interior of the single-room home. "Enter."

Mathias's link to the divine realm granted him immunity from most of a vampire's abilities, even in his current handicap, but the suggestion laced within the command word melded with his past day's emotional toils. He caught himself as a subtle tug in his knees attempted to force him to step forward, and briefly caught Tristan's laughing eyes before regaining control of his actions and striding inside the dwelling fully on his own accord. Not wasting a moment, he pulled the door from the vampire's grip and slammed it shut.

"Tell me everything you know about what happens to demons' souls after they die."

Tristan's smirk broadened into a smile and he shook his head. "Truly, you flatter me, Sir Sagewind. I am but a humble servant of my lord. What would possibly make you think I have knowledge to mysteries even your great Order has been unable to uncover?"

"Do you and your god need to hear it?" When Tristan's eyes narrowed, Mathias continued. "Ceredulus is no fool. He knows what dangers the world is facing. He woke you and risked sending you into the Citadel for a reason, and if you have any interest in remaining here in Zeal, unharmed, you will tell me what you learned in the library."

"You mean before you kicked me out?" A chuckle enhanced

Tristan's smile and he turned his back to Mathias as he casually moved toward the room's table. He drummed his fingers against the worn wood then sat, neglecting to offer—or command—Mathias to join him. "All I was able to discover was that their souls do, in fact, remain among this realm when they pass."

"Where?"

An agitated frown wiped the elegance from the vampire's lips. "Did you not comprehend my words, or are you simply being difficult? I do not know where they lie, only that they remain. If you would invite me back into the library—"

"You know your kind are forbidden to enter the Citadel."

Tristan shrugged and lowered his eyes as he set to scratching out the rough edge of a thumb nail. "That didn't stop me from finding an invitation before." He glanced up, and delivered his challenge on a crooked smile.

The tell-tale tremors of rage crept into Mathias's arms and legs and he instinctively jerked his hand toward a sword which wasn't there. "I am not playing games, Tristan."

Tristan sprang to his feet, slapping the top of the table and digging his nails into its surface as he restrained himself from leaping forward to engage Mathias. "And neither is Ceredulus!" His words hissed with the first hints of aggression he'd displayed since first arriving in Zeal. "He knows what you long for, and he suspects he knows how to obtain it. The question is, are you willing to pay for it?"

"And what is it your god thinks I long for?" Mathias asked.

Tristan chuckled and eased himself back into the chair, casually crossing his legs. "Rumors spread awful fast within the divine realm. You know that." His laughing eyes swept over Mathias's rigid expression. "The demons have a hold of that intriguing girlfriend of yours again. Bets are already being placed on what you'll do to try to get her back and how long the demons will keep you locked up when they catch you sneaking about their realm."

Mathias had always known the new children gods shared a special sort of disrespect for him, but he could have done without the reminders of how he'd failed to protect Nessix and his past

339

imprisonment in the hells. Unarmed and unbacked by Etha as he faced a rather vibrant vampire who was clearly in communication with his own god, Mathias wasn't so foolish or too proud to realize that he needed favors right now. He crossed his arms, too flustered and afraid of offending the last lead he had to form an appropriate response.

The smile didn't leave Tristan's eyes as he leaned forward. "Did I strike a nerve, Sir Sagewind?" Mathias didn't answer, and Tristan shook his head. "What good will knowing the fate of demon souls do for you, anyway?"

Mathias had hoped this race had ended once he'd found Nessix, but the eager glint in Tristan's eyes assured him that he was far from finished. "That is no concern of yours."

"Is this about Berann?" Tristan asked without hesitation.

"Who told—?" Tristan's smile grew slier, shedding a most unwanted light on the motives behind Khin's interest in aiding Nes's studies. "Damn it, child…"

"Ceredulus would help you," Tristan said. "You must believe that."

Still hung up on his own stupidity, Mathias glared at the vampire, longing to blame him for this turn of events. "That beastly god has no intention of helping me, only himself."

Tristan gave an irritated sigh and waved a dismissive hand in the air as he leaned back into his chair. "Suit yourself. All I'm saying is that it would be a shame if a feud that was settled—and in your favor!—centuries ago was the reason your beloved became even more of a plaything to that handsome alar than she already is."

Mathias could tolerate stabs at his pride. He could take the constant reminders that Ceredulus had access to tactics nobody else on Abaeloth could provide him. But the matter-of-fact way which Tristan played into the nagging fear which had been chasing him all this time was one thing Mathias, worn to his emotional limits as it was, could not overlook. He might have been unarmed, but he was far from helpless. Dashing forward, he caught a laughing Tristan by the neck, continuing his charge to topple the chair backwards and lifting his arm to pin the vampire against the back wall of the tiny home.

"What. Do. You. Know?"

Tristan, well-fed and unthreatened by Mathias's brutish display, met the paladin's feral glare with glittering eyes and pointed to the hand wrapped around his throat. It took Mathias a few heavy breaths to settle his fury enough to loosen his grip and a few more still to release his hold completely. Tristan nodded in approval and straightened the wrinkles from his collar.

"I told you all I know," he said evenly. "I do suspect my lord has reached his fair share of his own conclusions, but he hasn't yet shared them with me."

"Could Berann's soul be located?"

"Could it be?" Tristan made one final adjustment to his collar and lifted his eyes to Mathias's. "I'm sure. But the real question is, what would *you*, White Paladin, do with it if you found it?"

"Get answers."

Tristan took a step closer to Mathias, meeting his glare without flinching. When he spoke, it was with a low, hushed voice. "And how would you do that without the aid of my lord?"

Mathias held Tristan's challenging gaze as long as he could. Ceredulus truly was the most patient and intelligent of the new children gods and was not to be underestimated. Tristan was loyal to his god—he had no choice but to be—and Mathias, even with Etha in his corner, would not be able to force or pry answers from him. Hope rapidly dying, Mathias staggered backwards.

"I could have helped you, Tristan."

The vampire smirked at the strain in Mathias's voice. "I have no need for your help. I've already got everything I need. It is Ceredulus who you need to help. Set him free from the Veil, Sir Sagewind, and he will lead you straight to the answers you seek. You do know my lord keeps his promises."

Mathias shook his head, a dry laugh accentuating his bitterness. "Even if I wanted to grant him freedom, I have no influence over the management of the Veil."

Tristan rolled his eyes and backed up to lean against the wall. "I'm sure you could pull a few favors on the matter." Mathias's glower never changed, and Tristan smiled. "Take your time and think it over. Ceredulus is a patient god and he is far more generous than you boorish barbarians of the Order like to think."

Mathias clenched his teeth. He'd lost his chance at a peaceful eternity because of Ceredulus. He'd watched the fall and perversion of so many innocent people because of him. There wasn't much of Mathias's heart that had room for hatred, but Ceredulus had been crammed into that corner, keeping it warm centuries before Veed or Kol had even been known to Mathias. "I will *not* play any part in unleashing your god's plague on Abaeloth."

Tristan exaggerated a gasp and pressed his hand to his chest. "*Plague*? That's a bit harsh, don't you think?" His hand fluttered down as he crossed his arms and his feigned disgust immediately melded with a far crueler tone. "Ceredulus can wait on you. But are you sure Nessix can?"

Nes's reluctant resignation to return to the hells came back to Mathias, her hushed attempts to negotiate with him not to send her back to Kol alone, her enraged retaliation to the demons' wandering hands. Nessix was strong, but Etha, she was tired. She was frightened. And she needed whatever help could be sent her way.

But freeing Ceredulus…?

Mathias had been a hopeful fool to come here expecting Tristan to simply provide him the answers he was after. There wasn't a vampire ever raised who wasn't blindly loyal and fiercely devoted to Ceredulus, and there was only one goal the god of the undead had since being caged behind the Veil. There were other means for Mathias to find what he was after… there had to be. Unleashing Ceredulus on Abaeloth, allowing his influence to leak out into the mortal world, was an unacceptable solution, even if it was the fastest one.

"You let me worry about Nessix," Mathias spat, and Tristan raised his brows in amusement. "Your god can continue to rot in his prison." Not trusting himself to stay in this house any longer, Mathias spun and tore open the door.

"Best of luck," Tristan called to his back. The door slammed shut, shaking the walls of the tiny house. "I'm sure I'll be seeing you soon…"

The conversation could have gone better, but neither

Ceredulus nor Tristan had been surprised by the outcome. All of the appropriate seeds had been planted, and that was enough for this evening. Pushing himself away from the wall, Tristan crossed the room to the bed and flipped the mattress to retrieve the box holding Berann's precious note. Night would be here soon, and he and Khin had such a grand adventure awaiting them.

TWENTY-NINE

A sharp pain braced across Nes's shoulder blades, branching into her neck as her cold arms stretched above her. Though her brain struggled to connect the dots between where she was and how she got there, the agony drove hard enough to spur her awake, allowing her to identify that she was bound by her arms and legs to a horizontal pole, suspended above the ground. Memories of where she was headed leaked back through her fuzzy mind, and panic barreled straight past the limitations of her compromised position. A startled yelp announced to her captors that the magical restraint which had been placed over her had worn off.

Her limbs secured and of little use to escape attempts, Nessix squirmed violently to search of leverage, digging her binds more firmly into her aching joints. She cried out again, this time in pain rather than fright, the sound driven out of her in an abrupt gasp at the end of a brisk fall as the demon in front of her dropped his end of the pole she'd been hung up on.

Instantly confirming that she was on solid ground, Nessix rolled to her side and twisted about to try stretching the driving cramps from her arms and shoulders among the cackles of her demon guards.

That's right… she thought bitterly. *Annin's the last person I spoke to.*

She groaned and raised her head to look for the blasted oraku, finding him at the head of the procession, his biting grip restraining Kol from rushing to her aid. Both of them had trained their focus on Nessix and her alone, Annin's cold eyes reminding her of the ultimatum he'd given her and Kol's subtly pleading gaze silently repeating his request for her obedience. In her current position, limited in every regard, Nessix had no choice but to submit to them both and, with one last, silent promise sent Kol's way, she lowered her eyes.

"Free her ankles and drag her if she won't get to her feet," Annin barked. "We need to keep moving."

The underlings Kol and Annin had brought along with them had made no great secret of their desires to watch Nessix suffer, and after one cut the rope binding her feet, she organized her tingling legs beneath herself to scramble upright before they had a chance to implement the dragging option. Annin only briefly acknowledged her effort before turning to resume walking, but Kol hung back a moment longer, casting a warning glare across his subordinates as he bit back his demand that Nessix be treated with care. Before those warnings developed any further, Annin pulled the alar around. Nessix's tether was snatched up and she was jerked forward, stumbling over the discarded pole, as the rest of the troops followed their leaders.

Nessix ignored the lewd comments slid her way by the demons prodding her along and grit her teeth through the occasional poke and fondle, all the while keeping her eyes on Kol's back. He threw quick glares over his shoulder each time his men got too rowdy, reinforcing for Nessix the fact that he still commanded some amount of fear and respect among his ranks, and she let herself find comfort in that since there were few other places left for her to look for it.

Kol had conveyed much to Nessix in that field, possibly more than he'd meant to, and she was reasonably confident he'd honor his intentions to protect her and her army as long as she fulfilled her role. With so many secrets shared between them, both spoken and not, she was safe with him. But safety hadn't been her mission; if it had been, she'd have continued to trudge along in the predictability of her studies and training of her troops. She'd made a promise to a frightened and desperate army that she'd bring them help and when she'd failed to do that, she'd turned around and promised the same to the very demon responsible for putting them in that position.

What was she supposed to tell the akhuerai now?

She wanted to believe that Mathias was coming to rescue her people as he had in the past, but she could hardly imagine he'd be able to sway the Council or organize any number of knights to the cause after the disastrous past week. And what about their hunt for the secret which Berann had carried? As if overhearing her thoughts, Kol sent a quick glance back at her, and she hastily looked away. Mathias, as intelligent as he could be when he stopped long enough to think straight, wouldn't be able to make it through those books in a timely manner, and attempting to ask Kol for more information about this forbidden demon would do everything but prove her obedience to him.

Nessix had always thrived off challenges. Her entire life had been wrapped up in serving those who needed her, hunting for the approval and respect of the few people who outranked her. But as she marched along, an undead prisoner of the demons, recruited to serve as the general of an army meant to overthrow inoga, she finally had to consider the idea that she may have found a challenge bigger than she knew how to take on.

A shadow zipped over the pathway, interrupting Nessix's dismal contemplations, followed promptly by one of Annin's breathless sentinels crashing to the ground in his haste to land. The entire procession jerked to a halt and grabbed for their weapons. With Annin distracted, Kol fell back amid the troops and snatched Nessix's tether from her current keeper to pull her close. Whatever threat had chased the sentinel back in such a humiliating display of urgency, there wasn't a demon alive who would protect Nessix more fiercely than Kol would. The rapid deterioration of the unit's confidence was not lost on Nessix, and though she inched closer to Kol and the safety he represented, she held her breath, torn between her hope that reinforcements had come her way and the fear of what that would mean for the fate of the demon she'd just aligned herself with.

The sentinel cried out his brief report and stole all inclination of hope from Nessix. "Sirs! It's Grell!"

While Nessix coughed on a startled gasp and took a much more noticeable step toward Kol, the rest of the demons, Annin included closed in tighter around her. The underlings eyed their leaders speculatively, afraid of what the inoga's unexpected arrival pointed toward. They'd all been assured that this movement had been cleared and approved by that grotesque beast, but it was a well-circulated fact in the hells that he'd been yearning to act out over Nessix's escape for weeks now.

The slack of Nessix's tether trembled in Kol's grasp. Just as she opened her mouth to beg him to release her from her binds and arm her, Grell plummeted out of the sky like a cannon ball. He caught the momentum of his slide with his massive hands, leaving ruts to mark the trail of his landing, and straightened abruptly, clapping the dirt and gravel from his fingers as he grinned at the gaping group.

"I see you were finally successful in capturing your little wench," he said, his voice too pleasant to be trusted as genuine.

Among the shocked and startled alar, Annin was the first to find his tongue, but only after he'd swallowed the hitch of his reluctance. "You didn't need to come all the way to the surface to find that out. I'd planned to scry you with the good news once we reached the safety of Vesper."

Grell crammed his meaty hand into his pocket. "I'll bet you were. Ran into your friend on my way passing through that old camp." A look of contentment settled over his disfigured face as his fingers wrapped around the band of Lorrin's eye patch. He pulled it out, briefly dangled it in front of Annin, then tossed it to land at Kol's feet. "He told me how to find you."

Annin used the flight of the item as an excuse to turn to face Kol. *Do. Not,* his tense glare warned. *We will still make this right.*

But Kol hadn't been looking at Annin and his logic. He'd been staring at the eye patch of the demon—now long dead by Grell's hands, he was certain—who he'd entrusted his half of Nessix's soul to. If Grell had known Lorrin was hiding such a valuable item, he'd have taken it before the eye patch, and if he'd taken it, he wouldn't have hesitated to flaunt it before Kol. Now the only problem was how to get to Vesper and figure out where Lorrin had hidden the vessel before anyone other than Annin learned it was missing.

Kol had only just rediscovered his confidence and Grell's untimely arrival actively shoved him back toward the pathetic instability Annin had worked so hard to remedy. "You hate the surface," the oraku continued before Grell's domineering presence overtook Kol completely. "What inspired you to come here?"

"I'd sent you to catch such a slippery little worm." Though Grell called his answer back to Annin, he remained facing Kol, cocking his head at the way Nessix shifted behind him. "I thought I'd lend a hand to make sure she doesn't escape you." He flicked his gaze from Nessix to Kol. "Again."

"I assure you, we have her under control."

Grell snapped his attention to Annin, granting Kol a momentary reprieve from his mounting tension. "Just as you had her under control while she was teaching her army how to kill us?"

Annin had developed a healthy dose of wary respect for Grell ever since they'd discovered what the Divine Battle had done for him, but this was the first time the oraku recalled feeling a tiny flutter of reservation spurred by the madness in his eyes. The oraku kept both of his hands low and still, aware of Grell's watchful eyes, but mentally prepared himself for a rapid defense. "Certainly the akhuerai don't intimidate you, of all people, my lord?"

Grell snarled at the hint of sarcasm he imagined in Annin's voice then threw his sneer at Kol and Nessix once more. "Of course the akhuerai don't intimidate me," he said, scattering the handful of underlings as he meandered closer to the frozen pair. "Because she will not disobey our rule again." He stopped two feet from Kol and looked own at him with a pitying scowl. "*Will* she?"

Kol held his breath, summoning every last ounce of courage he had as Nessix attempted another step back. Just as she needed to play her part in this grand ruse, however, Kol's survival required him to play his, and he held fast to Nessix's tether, keeping her in place. Her fear was palpable, serving Kol's motives of claiming dominance over her well. Unfortunately, his own fear raced past what Nessix expressed as Grell shot his hand forward and ripped the tether from his grasp. Neither Nessix nor Kol had the time to react to the inoga's sudden movement, and he threw his arm back to jerk the startled woman forward.

Nessix stumbled from the force, but was saved by a rough upward jerk before she crashed to the ground. Moments later, Grell's free hand gripped her chin, holding her face immobile as he leaned down to scrutinize her weary, frightened expression. A smile slowly spread across the inoga's face. "No sharp tongue from you this time?"

To Nessix's credit, she hid her fear and loathing well, if not for a glisten of unfallen tears. She met Grell's eyes for a heartbeat at a time until his wickedness cowed her too much for her to believe her memories of how she'd slain two inoga a few short days ago.

Objective complete and still gripping Nessix's chin, Grell grunted his satisfaction and dropped the end of the tether to stick his thick fingers into the pack tied at his hip. "Here, *little one*." Kol bristled at Grell's use of his term of endearment, only sweetening this moment for the inoga. "I brought you something."

He produced a withered chunk of dream stop which Nessix eyed cautiously. She'd successfully turned down all of Kol's attempts to force her to eat the sedative, but Grell's pinching grasp prevented her from so much as flinching away from him. She'd gained a decent grasp on her withdrawal symptoms during her stay in the Citadel and had hoped to avoid having her thoughts dulled and to keep close to her ability to draw on her chaotic impulses if needed. But, as they so often did, Grell's motives did not align with hers. Her throat pressed against the heel of the inoga's palm as she gulped down her hesitance.

"You will eat this willingly or by force," Grell said, his voice soft and menacing. "It makes no difference to me which method you choose, but you will eat it."

Nessix didn't move to obey Grell, nor did she try the improbable feat of escaping him. With his hold on her, he could snap her neck with little more than a flick of his wrist and if she thought being drugged was a disadvantage, her death would prove worse yet. Torn between duty and fear, determination and resentment, it took Kol's firm shove against her back to make her move at all.

"Eat it," he barked.

Unable to turn to assess the alar's demeanor or to see around Grell's massive frame to try to get a read on Annin, Nessix held her breath as long as her racing heart allowed. Kol's push had been rough and impersonal, colder than he'd ever touched her in the past, his command firm and lacking the concern Nessix hoped still protected her.

She'd given her word that she'd show Kol obedience, and despite his outward cruelty, she did believe doing so was the smartest option, but she'd made that promise before thinking Grell would show up. This great beast was who she was destined to defy on Kol's behalf, the creature her alar needed her to destroy before his objectives could be obtained. Nessix had tried to kill Grell in the past, and though she'd since defeated two of his peers, she was two days into exhaustion and malnourishment, arms tied and weaponless, and honor-bound to the one demon who wanted to keep her safe.

You have everything you need, Nes. Nothing *has ever managed to stop you. Not demons. Not death.*

Nessix pinched her eyes shut, forced another swallow past the restricting pressure of Grell's hand, and parted her lips.

Grell grunted an amused laugh and shoved the chunk of dream stop in her mouth. With a shift of his wrist, he lifted her chin to close her jaws around it and when she began chewing, grimacing at the bitter taste she'd been content to leave behind with the other drudgeries of the hells, Grell raised his free hand to pat her on the head.

"You did a good job on her, Kol."

Kol's glower openly advertised his hatred for the liberties Grell was taking, but he managed the slightest decline of his head. "Thank you, my lord."

Grell kept his wicked eyes on Nessix as she finished chewing and choking down the dream stop, but he tilted his chin in Kol's direction. "And I can assume she's been properly punished for her insubordination?"

All of the demons around them, save Annin, chuckled and muttered their takes on the misadventure that hadn't actually happened, and Kol tightened his jaw and drew his shoulders back. "She has."

Grell glanced about the hungry and humored leers of the troops and leaned his ear to his shoulder, eyes narrowing. He'd known Kol all his life and the implications passed along by these underlings didn't sound much like the man he knew. He'd been suspicious of Kol's methods of handling this particular akhuerai for some time, and was determined to bear witness to her submission now or humble Kol by forcing the subject on them both. Shoving Nessix back to Kol, Grell took careful note of the hastiness used to catch her and her lack of objecting to Kol's touch.

"Prove it."

More cackles and hoots sprang up from the troops who had been forbidden to spectate on the previous display of Kol's domination over Nessix. Kol's fingers bit into her arms as she trembled in his grasp, both of them sharing a brief, unspoken acceptance that, one way or another, Grell was going to get his way, no matter what they tried to do to avoid it. After so long without its influence, the dream stop had already begun to soothe Nessix, but it didn't stop her from shuddering as Kol slid a hand to her hip.

"My lord."

Kol froze and Nessix held her breath as Annin's terse interruption drew Grell's attention from them. There wasn't one part of the bitter oraku that cared what nature of torment befell Nessix, but there was a substantial part of him that refused to stand by and let Kol come up with any more excuses to claim fondness for the blasted woman.

"The Order is on our trail," Annin continued. "There is no time to waste on proving something which has no need to be verified."

Grell's narrowed eyes scoured Annin's even expression, digging for signs of a hidden motive, but he'd never been able to reliably read a damn thing about the eerie man, not when they'd been mortals and certainly not now. The inoga swung his skeptical agitation back toward Kol's dark glower—a hateful look which

Grell couldn't decide if it was directed toward him for making the demand or Annin for opposing it—and made note of Nessix's hunched shoulders and ducked head. As much as he resented Annin's public disregard for his power, as much as he hated the fact that Kol had been given an excuse to disregard his order, Grell could not debate the threat which lurked around them. Nessix had reached Zeal, and Mathias Sagewind could not have been pleased to have her taken from him. If only to alleviate the risk of complications, Grell accepted Annin's words.

"Then I'll orchestrate the punishment I see fit for her during our flight back to Elidae."

Kol's wince at what the promises in Grell's declaration entailed was masked by a greater shock. "Elidae?" He needed to get to Vesper to locate Nessix's missing soul vessel.

Grell might have had one victory taken from him, but the discomfort in Kol's question was an adequate consolation. "You heard Annin. The Order's after us. Flying back home will be much faster than trekking all the way down the Undersea Pass where mortals can easily follow us. Besides"—Grell smirked in satisfaction. He had no idea why Kol seemed so keen on getting back to Vesper, but preventing him from doing so was pleasure enough. "It's not like there's anything left for you on that mountain."

It was that last jab that struck Kol past his fear of the tortures Grell had fantasized about inflicting on him, and his hand clamped down harder on Nessix's arm as he fought to restrain himself from reacting. He *had* to get back to Vesper. He *had* to get a hold of the other half of Nessix's soul. Gritting his teeth as Grell shifted his mass to address the rest of the troops, trembling with the urge to scream, Kol speared Annin with his furious glare. *This is all your fault...*

After the trouble the alar had caused him, Annin met Kol's anger without flinching, but not without his own, seldom-displayed hint of trepidation which sprouted from the same place as Kol's building agitation. Nothing could be done to resolve this problem anytime soon, and Annin subtly shook his head, advising Kol to let it go for now.

Kol had always trusted Annin, quite possibly the only living being to ever do so, and though everything about their current circumstances criticized him for it, Kol choked down his terror and uncertainty and trusted Annin yet again. After all, the oraku was second only to Kol in demanding that Nessix was too valuable to risk losing, and he knew better than anyone else the importance of commanding the external portion of her soul. Kol couldn't fathom what solution Annin had for this problem but, after all of the disasters the oraku had already managed, he trusted it would be solved.

Grell motivated the underlings into the air with little problem and, after Kol scooped Nessix into his arms, he joined them and set off for Elidae.

THIRTY

Mathias had allowed his frustration to push him to carelessness, convinced the greatest of his personal problems had been solved now that he knew where Nessix was. That carelessness had rapidly burned up all the leniency he could milk from the Council, and he knew there would be no easy way to gain their support in mobilizing the demon hunters to go chasing after her. Those men and women were tough and carried few fears in their hearts, but even so, Mathias would have a difficult time swaying them to march out with him after where he'd recently positioned himself in Henrik's sights.

Nessix had told him more than once that she expected them to have to fix this problem themselves, and Mathias was finally ready to accept that.

There were few languages Mathias hadn't managed to master after immortality had given him the time to do so, and though Nessix had only given him the three sentences on that little slip of leather which had been taken off Berann, he'd make that be enough to pick up the tongue of the ancients. He *would* find out what Berann knew, and he would carry that knowledge back into the hells to personally remind the demons who they'd decided to go to war with. The set of his brows and clench of his jaw were the only clearance he needed to gain prompt access back into the restricted room of the library. He found the books Nessix had strewn across the desk exactly where she'd left them, the scrolls yet untouched, and he shuffled the volumes around to look for Berann's note.

"I don't have time for this..." he muttered, flipping the open covers closed to search beneath them.

He pressed the covers flat to see if it might have slipped between the pages and lifted and restacked each scroll to see if it had been tucked between them. Heart beating faster, he dropped to his hands and knees and looked beneath the table. Nothing. He rocked back to his haunches and covered his mouth with his hand as a cruel reality tried to settle over him. The note was *gone?*

"No, no, NO!"

Frantically, he shoved his fingers between the seat cushions of the chairs, pulling at the seams of the upholstery in his search. He patted down his own clothing to see if it had somehow fallen on his person. Just as he was about to dart down the stairs in case he'd simply forgotten that he'd returned it, the door burst open and he spun around.

"Mathias!"

Julianna had always been more calm and collected than her brother, even in the most trying of times, but terror shook her voice and her big green eyes were rimmed with tears. Only knowing that her expression must have matched his own, Mathias organized his numbing legs to carry him around the table.

"The repository," she breathed, reaching out her hands to grasp his so they could support each other. "Ce-Ceredulus's vault... It's been broken into."

Mathias choked on the coincidence of what Julianna's broken report and the mystery of the disappearing document rapidly pointed toward.

"That vampire you claimed was in the Citadel... who was he?" she asked.

"Swift," Mathias spat.

Julianna pulled her hands from Mathias's and turned back to the door as if to run from the room. "And how had he gained access to the Citadel?"

Mathias choked down his rage and barely managed to whisper

Khin's name. *Child, what have you done…?* He slid past his fretting sister, past the bewildered guards outside the door, and strode through the library. That damn vampire and his foul god wanted his attention? Well, they had it now.

"Etha!" Mathias roared in the serenity of the library. "I need your help!" He stalked past the startled gawks and disapproving frowns of those who were quietly studying, not caring what sort of impression he made as he departed the library and turned toward the Citadel's exit.

The tiny padding of Julianna's feet rushed up behind him and she grasped his hand with both of hers. "Mattie, what are you planning?"

Julianna's timid question snuck past his rage and he swallowed the hateful remark on his tongue and stopped his march. Looking over at his sister's wide eyes, still begging him for guidance despite her own immense power, tempered his emotions and reminded him that getting Etha's attention was only the first hurdle he had to conquer. He tightened his hold Julianna's hand and turned to face her.

"I'm going to have Etha help me figure out where they've run off to," he said. It was only partly a lie. "You should go back to the temple and tend to the rescued priestesses before the Council has their turn tormenting them."

There were few forces on Abaeloth Julianna was unable to contest, but she'd always fallen back on Mathias when times got tough. She nodded. "And when you find them?"

Mathias sighed and feigned interest in the activity down the hall to avoid Julianna's pleading eyes when he delivered what was much closer to a lie than the first. "I'll do what I can to recover the missing artifacts and, if I'm able, fling Tristan Swift into the Veil to properly reunite him with his god."

Julianna gulped down her reservations. "And Khin?"

And Khin…

Both Mathias and Julianna had failed that child and both of them carried that guilt with them now. The law demanded she be arrested and tried for conspiring with a vampire, breaking and entry, and theft of restricted artifacts, but Mathias couldn't quite separate himself from those crimes. "I'll... I'll see how things look once I find her."

It was a shady answer, but Julianna nodded and squeezed Mathias's hand. "Be careful, Mattie. You're still at a disadvantage to fight such formidable foes."

"I'll be fine." He went ahead and left out the part of him having a divine barrier between himself and the audience he truly intended to find. "Worry about those who need you now."

Julianna scoured Mathias's eyes a moment longer, but he'd already closed himself off to further concerns. He had made up his mind, he had his mission, and he would see it done. Giving his hand one more squeeze, not bothering to ask him again to stay safe, Julianna slipped away to go tend to the priestesses.

Mathias watched her disappear and waited longer still until he was confident she wouldn't come rushing back around the corner, and turned to exit the Citadel to go battle the god of the undead.

* * * * *

"Do you have *any* idea how dangerous it was for you to kiss Nessix like that with the demons standing right behind you?"

While Mathias was relieved to hear the chime of Etha's voice, her goading didn't lift his spirits in the way it often did, and he opted instead to focus on the coarseness of Ceraphlaks's mane in his hands and the way his goddess didn't even bother to hold onto him for support as she perched behind him.

"Because it was *quite* dangerous. You had no idea if they were going to try anything that would require my grace. And what about those little priestesses? They could have used your healing touch."

Enough was enough, even from his goddess. "Mother, can I just wallow in the reflections of my failure in silence?"

Etha's hands wrapped around the back of his neck and rubbed at his tense muscles. "It's not a failure until you give up. And the fact that you're riding Ceraphlaks to the west, under the cover of night... without telling Julianna what you're actually up to..."

Mathias hefted a sigh. "Yeah. I'm counting this as a failure of mine, too."

"But you haven't even asked Ceredulus how he plans to help you yet."

Mathias turned to cast a perturbed look at his goddess, the shift of his weight dragging Ceraphlaks's flight to the right. "Why are you so excited over the idea of me going to talk to Ceredulus? I thought we hated him."

"We do."

"Then why are we entertaining the idea of trusting him?"

"Because I've been listening to Khin's prayers about some pretty vampire lord solving our problems. We've hit so many dead ends… maybe it's time to seek some undead options?"

Mathias didn't find half the humor in that remark as Etha did. "Yeah. Well. If you'd bothered to tell me when that pretty vampire entered the Citadel, I could have done something about him before this mess erupted."

"Ah, but he's the reason you're heading to the Veil, isn't he? The information he found about demon souls? You really should have a talk with the priestesses about cross referencing between the branches of the library. I'll bet they'd have had this solved months ago if they'd have thought to look in the *other* dusty tomes."

"Reminding me that this should have been over and done with months ago is doing nothing at all to raise my spirits."

Etha stilled herself and wrapped her arms around Mathias, unsuccessfully trying to draw out his pain and heartache. "You told Nessix you'd find her again, and you don't lie."

"And not one of us believes that damned alar will leave us another opening as long as he lives." His voice shrank into the wind, but carried well to Etha's divine ears. "Mother, what have I done…?"

She rested her forehead against his back. "You did exactly what you should have done, and you'll make it right, just wait and see."

Mathias shook his head, reluctant to call Etha wrong but neither able to see how what she was telling him could possibly be true. "And you're sure Ceredulus is who I need to make it right?"

"Well, he's most likely how you'll make *this* right. How you'll make the stuff you screw up by working with him right…? Now, that's another basket of worms."

Just once, Mathias wished he could have a normal relationship with his mother, that she'd let him sulk and be miserable all on his own. It wouldn't change the way he served her or looked after Abaeloth, but he deserved to dwell in his misery without Etha's interference, at least for a little while.

Ceraphlaks blew a sharp breath through his nostrils, signaling that he'd sighted the hazy border of the Veil, and Etha released her hold on Mathias to clap her dainty hands. "And here we are! Will the two of you play nice this time, or do you need me to come act as a moderator again?"

Mathias was too afraid of what he'd say and do when facing Ceredulus to want Etha around when they met. She wouldn't have spent so much effort encouraging him to go talk to the god if she suspected he'd disappoint her, but the dark path which Mathias eyed now was one he was so frightened to step down. Etha would always be with him, but there were still very mortal fears this immortal longed to hide from his goddess.

"This is something I need to sort out by myself," Mathias murmured at last. "Please, preserve your goodness. Let me make this sin all on my own."

After several moments of Ceraphlaks's wide circles as he spiraled toward the ground, Etha's arms tightened around Mathias, her lips brushed the back of his neck, and then she was gone. The chill of the night air blew against Mathias's back, chilling the sacred steel of his armor, and he wondered, not for the first time, how he'd let himself get to this point.

Ceraphlaks landed soon after and carried his rider to the divine barrier, tiny ears flicking about, alert for lurking dangers. Moments later, the form of a tall man materialized on the path which welcomed the most unfortunate into the Veil, and Mathias stopped Ceraphlaks and dismounted.

"Stay where I can find you for now, friend," he bid the pegasus. "I'm not yet sure how this is going to end up."

Ceraphlaks blew out a brisk acceptance of Mathias's request and cautiously retreated to give his rider his space. The pair had first been introduced to each other due to the vile workings of the same god Mathias was preparing to speak to, and Ceraphlaks had no desire to be involved in any part of this conversation.

Ceredulus swept up to the edge of his side of the Veil, his timely arrival and smug expression confirming to Mathias that this had all been a carefully coordinated plan all along. The god paced the width of the road like a caged tiger, cunning eyes bright with the knowledge of how much destruction he could cause if only he weren't contained. Grumbling to himself and commanding his heart to quit racing quite so fast, Mathias stalked closer to the barrier.

"It is good to see you've come to your senses, Mathias."

The paladin clenched his jaw and stopped two paces from the invisible wall.

Ceredulus mirrored his guest and crossed his arms, looking over Mathias as though he was a slab of spoiled meat. "Or perhaps you haven't. Have you come simply to cry to me some more?"

"I've come because I was assured you had the answers I need." Patience depleted hours ago, Mathias snapped his statement without regard to the offense it may cause his audience.

Ceredulus was not fazed by Mathias's sharp tongue and nodded slowly, sly eyes keeping a steady watch on the paladin's face. "I know what you must do to solve this problem. All it would take is for you to let me out so I can go secure those means for you."

"Like I would free you from the Veil after the sacrifices made to put you in there."

Ceredulus shrugged. "I suppose that is your call to make." He swept his gaze across Mathias's tense shoulders and the strained tendons in his neck, studying the way he nervously tapped one thumb against the side of his index finger. This was exactly where Ceredulus wanted him. "Your girlfriend is not in a very safe place, you know. And you were the one who sent her there." He held up a hand as Mathias blustered up a debate. "I know it couldn't be helped, but I'd have thought you'd want to do *something* to get her out of the trouble she's in."

Mathias choked back his anger. Though he hated admitting it, Ceredulus was one of the few children gods who had always been more than eager to negotiate without the use of threats and right now, Mathias much preferred the easy route. "Nessix knew she'd be going back to the hells."

"Yes, but she'd been assured it would be on her own accord, after the two of you had sorted out how she could make those caverns crumble from the inside. She'd never imagined it would be because you threw her into her demon master's arms after a mere week of petty arguments which kept anyone in Zeal from moving past the fact that she was still alive."

The cunning glint in Ceredulus's eyes raked Mathias's remaining nerves raw. He should have banished Tristan from Zeal the moment he found him. To the hells with Khin's infatuation with the vampire. If Tristan had been gone, Ceredulus wouldn't have been fed so many facts to be used against Mathias. None of the artifacts held locked up in the Citadel would have gone missing. Khin would have still had a chance at a bright future.

"Why did you come here, Mathias?"

Mathias bristled at Ceredulus's casual tone. "Because you know souls better than anyone else in all the realms."

The god straightened his posture with a little shake of his shoulders, a self-satisfied smirk touching his lips. "I do."

Mathias took a step closer to the Veil. "And you are going to tell me how to free Nes's soul before the demons drag her out of divine reach and into the hells."

Ceredulus jerked back an inch and his arms fell to his sides. "I'm *what?*"

"I will not repeat myself."

A bitter chuckle left the god and he briefly turned his face from Mathias so he could dispose of his scowl in a neutral fashion. "Idiot," he sneered, sliding his glare back to Mathias. "There is no way to free her soul, not as it currently exists. It has been fractured, made unwhole. Both parts would have to be obtained and not even I know what means would have to be taken before they could be rejoined. Rending souls is my expertise, Mathias. Mending them is not."

It was unusual for any god to admit their shortcomings, and while Mathias would have loved to bask into Ceredulus's bout of honesty, all sense of humor had left him. "You said you know how to obtain what I want."

"No," Ceredulus drew the word out to ensure Mathias's rattled brain understood it. "I said I knew how to solve your problem. Ripping what's left of your girlfriend's soul from her, hoping we can get our hands on the other half of it, is not how to do that."

Mathias should have known this was all a grand waste of time… "Then what is?"

Ceredulus puffed out a brisk sigh and crossed his arms again. "Free me from the Veil and I will tell you."

The god was too calm, too sure of himself, to have been bluffing about the knowledge he had, and though lawful to a fault, he was far too selfish to accept any terms Mathias might try to negotiate in Abaeloth's favor. No, Ceredulus knew something Mathias needed to hear, and he wouldn't give it up for anything less than what he wanted. But was that a price Mathias could pay? Did he even have a right to do so?

"Time is wasting, Mathias." Ceredulus sighed the observation as though bored with the paladin's inner struggle. "The demons have her in flight to Elidae while you stand there giving me filthy looks."

Mathias cocked his head at the free nugget of information. "Elidae?" That didn't make the least bit of sense, not when there were closer holes for the demons to crawl down. "Why Elidae?"

Ceredulus's brows dipped in a sharp V of irritation. "How would *I* know?" He waved a hand at the shimmering barrier which stood between them. "It's not like I can go ask them myself, now is it?"

So this had been a ploy, too… Mathias shook his head. "I will not allow you to set foot outside the Veil."

Ceredulus lowered his chin, spearing Mathias with a menacing eye. "Then condemn your Nessix to her fate and move on with your life."

The blow struck precisely where Ceredulus had aimed it, and Mathias had to clench his jaw and fling his gaze aside to keep from crying out for some other option. He grappled with his emotions, with logic and tactics, and the only answer he could come up with

362

was the one he'd spent the majority of his existence denying.

"You're asking me to *trust* you," Mathias whispered harshly.

"I am."

Excuses and justifications assaulted Mathias faster than he was able to grab any of them, overwhelming him with an indecisiveness Ceredulus was only too pleased to take advantage of.

"Need I remind you that my influence has already begun to spread, unchecked without my oversight? My most loyal servant freely walks the realm"—Ceredulus's eyes narrowed as one corner of his lips raised—"and he's got with him the most darling priestess in training—"

Mathias's eyes flashed and had he not been without Etha's grace—a fact the cunning god he faced had to have noted by now—he'd have charged inside the Veil to properly reprimand Ceredulus. "You leave that child alone," he growled.

"Like you did?" Ceredulus closed his eyes and gave a soft laugh. "Oh, no. She's thriving under my gentle influence. She needs me in her life. She *wants* me there."

Mathias held the god's gaze with admirable intensity, but Ceredulus didn't miss the way his confidence was slowly chipped away by the same desires that struck all of those still preoccupied with the mortal world. Mathias would cave, just as Ceredulus expected. The poor man had no other choice. His beloved was in peril, the demons stood poised to storm Abaeloth, and the child he'd vowed to protect was wandering down a path the paladin was morally opposed to. And Ceredulus was the only one able to offer assistance in remedying any of this.

"It takes a mortal's hands to manipulate a soul not meant to become wholly mine," Ceredulus said, drawing Mathias's heroic tendencies closer to his striking distance. "So Tristan had to recruit help to find Berann. And Khin... well... she's still quite weak in her command of my will. It would be an absolute shame if our old rivalry is what caused harm to befall her. Would it not?"

"Call them off their search." Mathias's demand left no room for debate.

Unfortunately for the paladin, Ceredulus was operating on facts. "Oh, it's too late for that. Khin has already bound herself to the demon's trail. Do you truly think she's got the strength to withstand the power of an ancient oraku?" Ceredulus soaked in Mathias's rage as it boiled over the limits of his self-control; he'd found the right angle to strike at. "I advise you, yet again, to free me so I might aid her."

Mathias shook his head until his jaw loosened enough to reply. "There will be no freeing you and no raising of anything else in this conflict."

Ceredulus leaned his weight onto one leg and rubbed his chin. "Then how do you propose gleaning what Berann knew? You *need* that knowledge to save Nessix, Mathias, to save her people! And you know the only path you have to gain it."

Mathias held Ceredulus's gaze through the god's careful goading until the glaze of dampness covered his eyes, forcing him to blink. When they opened again, the dampness was gone, replaced with a rigid loathing, and Mathias spun on a heel to stride away from the border of the Veil.

Furrowing his brow, having been certain he'd played the human to his favor, Ceredulus shifted uncomfortably as he held himself back from trying the impossible task of following Mathias. Desperate to salvage the advantage he'd so tediously choreographed, Ceredulus called out, "Need I remind you—"

"Silence yourself, child!"

Ceredulus put up with more than his peers did, but the sharpness of Mathias's growled response peeled on his nerves; it was never easy for those of such boundless might as the gods to accept the fact that the Sagewind siblings held seniority over them. Influence over the situation in peril, Ceredulus prepared to pitch another demand for Mathias's respect, when the paladin's fingers loosened a velvet pouch at his hip to withdraw a small silver bowl. The ire bubbled away into amusement.

"Blood magic, Mathias?"

"I told you to shut up."

Ceredulus would give Mathias that one, and smiled smugly to himself. He hadn't lost his leverage, after all. Twirling a finger toward the ground, the god conjured up a plush armchair and settled himself in its seat to wait for what would happen next. Oh, how the just Sir Sagewind had fallen.

Ever aware of Ceredulus's amused eyes watching him, Mathias prepared his scry and awaited Sazrah's answer. It didn't take her long and Mathias, too distraught over what he was preparing to do, forewent a proper greeting to jump into what he had to discuss.

"What is the current state of affairs on Elidae?"

Sazrah replied promptly, assuming Mathias was being responsible and checking in as he always promised he would. "Tense but stable. Those of us—"

"Have the demons been active?"

Sazrah furrowed her brow and allowed herself a brief, perturbed frown at Mathias's interruption, but continued obediently. "Nothing worth noting. Why?"

Mathias flexed his jaw and glanced away from the woman's image. "You know how you always suspect I'm about to do something stupid?"

A grumble which sounded an awful lot like, "Damn it, Mathias," filtered through the dish of blood before Sazrah huffed out a clearer reply. "Yes."

"Well." Mathias cleared his throat and failed to shed the pressure of Ceredulus's knowing gaze from his back. "I'm getting ready to do something… extremely stupid. Even for me." He coughed. "*Especially* for me."

Sazrah allowed a fully developed groan to come out this time, and her image briefly flickered as she repositioned her scrying bowl so she could rub her temple. "What are you about to do?"

"Matters have gotten… complicated. I'll elaborate once I know how it will turn out."

That wasn't good enough for Sazrah. "Mathias, if you bring one more—"

"I need you on your guard, Saz." This interruption slipped out of him much faster than the first, unplanned and raw, and it halted the warrior woman's firm debate instantly. "All you need to know right now is that a highly motivated troop of alar is bringing Nessix back to Elidae."

"Wait." Sazrah's hand dropped from the side of her head. "You *lost* her?"

"I don't really want to talk about it," Mathias muttered.

"Of course you don't."

Neither party spoke for a long moment, their frustrations stewing with one another from across the world. Sazrah's image, her jaw clenched and lips tucked in a tight, disapproving frown, began to dim as the viable heat drained from Mathias's blood, and he sighed.

"Just... be ready for them," he murmured. "Save Nes for me if you can."

Sazrah shifted her glower to him, but didn't offer a comment.

"I'll... be in touch in a couple of days. I promise."

She rolled her eyes and cast her gaze away from him once more.

"Thank you, Sazrah," he said, voice subdued. Though she hadn't verbally accepted his request, she hadn't denied it, either, and Mathias trusted her experience and loyalty to not let him down.

The blood cooled and Sazrah's face faded from view. After flinging the blood to the ground, Mathias replaced his bowl in its pouch and strode back up to a grinning Ceredulus as the god rocked up to his feet, chair disappearing in a puff of fog.

"I'll give you one day," the paladin said.

That grin promptly dashed from Ceredulus's face and he coughed. "*One* day?"

"That's more than you deserve."

"And not nearly enough time if you want my freedom to prove worthwhile to you. A week. You will give me a full week."

"This is not open for debate."

Resolve had settled across Mathias now that he'd made his decision, his eyes no longer burning at the thought of offending Ceredulus, and the god felt his chance at freedom rapidly escaping his grasp. "Then save your own damsel."

The god snapped around and purposefully strode away from Mathias. But not without holding his breath. He'd waited so long for this opportunity to arrive and was certain another wouldn't rise for quite some time.

Mathias watched as his one guaranteed way to tap into the information Nessix had convinced him the world needed to know faded deeper into the Veil. Even Etha had encouraged him to make this decision, and he was letting it turn its back and walk away all because of his deeply ingrained hatred. Ceredulus was evil, yes, but he was also the most lawful denizen of the divine realm. He would honor whatever agreement they settled on, and that agreement could save Nessix, save her people, save *Abaeloth*. Mathias couldn't deny it any longer.

"Wait."

The demand was pathetic and small, but more than adequate to reach the attention of a highly attentive deity. Ceredulus allowed himself a victorious smile, but was careful to tuck it away before turning around and sauntering back toward Mathias. "For what?"

"If I let you out," Mathias spoke deliberately, "if I give you a week of freedom, your sole objective will be to aid in Nessix's safe recovery."

Ceredulus frowned at Mathias's terms and gave a temperamental twist of his head. "My sole objective will be to punish the demons for the liberties they've taken with my art. Aiding your Nessix is part of that plan."

"And the rest of your plan?"

Ceredulus chuckled at the harsh implications in Mathias's question. "I am not after some wild spree to defile Abaeloth. I'm no fool; I've learned the lesson you and your sister forced me through."

"After the underhanded tactics you've already employed to get me here, I can't be so sure."

"Oh, Mathias, that wasn't underhanded, simply my efforts to survive, just like you. Just like Nessix. And part of my survival, part of your lover's survival, is me addressing the demons' blasphemy. Quit with your whining. Quit with your fear. And let me *help* you."

Mathias clenched his teeth repeatedly. Every ounce of his sensibility and honor screamed at him to walk away from the god's silver tongue, but he'd been so beaten down by despair, worn so thin by Etha's persistence on this matter, that sensibility no longer seemed like the most logical option. And the longer he put this off, the harder it would be for him to go through with it. Drawing his sword with a clammy, trembling hand, Mathias stalked up to the

Veil.

"One week," he growled. "And you stay by my side throughout."

Ceredulus's displeasure in that final stipulation was limited to a subtle wrinkle between his brows. He'd make it work. "If I can't have it any other way, very well."

Before the promises Mathias had made to Abaeloth centuries ago had the chance to talk him out of it, he blew out a deep breath and jabbed his sword through the wall of the Veil. The barrier screeched in tortured delight as the blessed steel sliced through it and lazy sparks of divinity popped and danced as Mathias used his blade to pry open a seam for Ceredulus to crawl through.

The god of the undead ducked low and held his arms close around his torso to avoid catching the throbbing laceration in his prison's wall as he stepped into the dawn, and he straightened to a height he'd forgotten once he'd cleared the barrier. The air out here was fresh and moving, carrying with it a warmth his realm of death and misery had been without. His senses flew wildly from the immediate vicinity, reaching for the endless scope of the world with all the restraint of a toddler set loose in a sweets shop. Mathias jerked his sword free from the Veil, slamming it back into its sheath, and as the barrier groaned and stitched itself back together, Ceredulus turned his wicked grin back toward the paladin.

"Let us go hunt the soul of a demon."

Not waiting for Mathias's reply, not caring for whatever one would be given, Ceredulus clasped the paladin's forearm and forcibly dragged him into the divine pathways in pursuit of Tristan and Khin.

THIRTY-ONE

The mountainside was cold and windy this time of year, sapping away most of the soldiers' patience and a great deal of their discipline. They'd set camp near the demons' portal, on a rocky landing devoid of any sort of decent shelter, and hadn't seen so much as a ruffle of an alar's wings in the cloudless sky.

"Nothing's coming," groused Captain Karst Boulderchoke, a blond-bearded dwarf who had served as one of Sazrah's more seasoned officers for the past few decades. He vigorously rubbed his hands before the campfire to work warmth into them.

Sazrah hefted a weary sigh. How she wished she could have brought Sulik with her for this mission! The middle-aged fleman commander was far better equipped to handle these constant, nagging complaints than she was. And it wasn't like Sazrah didn't have gripes of her own to add to them...

"Just wait a bit longer." Her glum tone did little to convince her captain and the surrounding troops that she was any less displeased with the situation.

"You've been saying that since last night." Karst didn't flinch at the sharp look his general gave him; he'd served Sazrah long enough to have a fair grasp on her temperament. "And nothing's shown yet. Maybe it's finally happened that Sir Sagewind's lost his mind."

Sazrah bit back her inclination to agree and brought her tired green eyes back to the sky above the mountaintops. "He took the time to warn me that he was planning something stupid."

Karst glanced at Sazrah's distant focus then shook his head and plopped down beside the fire. "I guess I'm not seeing how that stands out from his normal behavior."

"Because," Sazrah sighed, "he does stupid things all the time. The fact that he bothered to tell me instead of just doing it?" She shook her head, still trying to figure out where this nagging dread she'd picked up after her last conversation with Mathias fit in her mind. "The demons will be here. And we need to intercept them."

Karst refrained from rolling his eyes until he was certain Sazrah's focus was centered on the horizon and he'd turned his face from hers. After the past year of civil unrest as Elidae's nobles squabbled for power without the unifying force of the Teradhel line, the troops they'd brought up here to watch the demons' portal—fifty men and women in all—wouldn't tolerate this much longer. Sazrah had been a bold, unifying force for those who claimed loyalty to Mathias before he'd left on his quest of tracking down the demons who had stolen Nessix's soul, but even her influence was wearing thin. Grumbling to himself, Karst leaned his weight back to rock himself to his feet but froze mid-movement as a solitary horn to the east delivered its lonely warning cry.

Sazrah was on her feet in an instant, the rest of the unit pulling themselves to attention as though roused from slumber. As Sazrah had promised, as Mathias had foretold, the demons were returning to Elidae.

* * * * *

"We're almost there, little one."

Kol's voice, strained with fatigue, burrowed into Nessix's addled mind. She couldn't recall much of the flight from Gelthin after the third root of dream stop Grell had forced her to eat in the first half day's travels, but she was grateful the ignorant brute had allowed Kol to be her escort for this journey. Her added weight wore on Kol over the brisk, extended flight, and he was ever-aware

370

of Annin's careful eyes, but he didn't object to his burden.

His observation of Elidae's shores was echoed by the alar who had made it this far—one had been left behind on the second island they'd stopped on for a break, another dropped into the ocean by Annin after his complaining became more than the oraku would tolerate, successfully putting a halt on anyone else expressing their grievances—but their remarks were soon cut short by the bleating of a horn.

Demons were Abaeloth's original survivors, and every ear in the procession instantly registered the hazard that solitary call pointed to. Nessix raised her head from Kol's shoulder in response to the sound, but couldn't sort out if she was comforted or dismayed by its song. While the entire unit slowed to reassess their approach, Grell, as stubborn and spoiled with confidence as always, made it another dozen yards before awkwardly rebalancing his momentum to bank back to his troops.

"You cowards!" he spat above the wind. "Are you truly afraid of a few mortals we've bested in the past?"

Not one demon, not even Annin, had the nerve to mutter the truth that the flemans had been the ones to soundly best them.

"Our portal's just on the other side of these peaks," Grell continued. "And then you can rest. Then you can be scared." He flashed his eyes—dark with rancor of the self-imposed exhaustion he wouldn't openly admit to—to Kol's, delving deep into the alar's composure. "Then we can ensure all debts are properly paid."

Annin flicked an observant glance at the twitch in Kol's arms as he instinctively tightened his grip around the drugged woman before addressing the rest of the troops. "You have your orders. Let's move out."

It wouldn't be the first time Grell resented the way his subordinates acted more on their fear of Annin than their fear of him, but he was tired and eager to put the trials tied to Nessix behind him. Once they got her back in the hells, he'd personally see to it that she never thought of defying them again. Reluctantly, the troop of alar mustered their courage and resumed their approach.

"Move… up…"

Kol missed Nessix's murmured instruction over the whip of

371

the wind and pounding of his heart and it took her squirm to try to get closer to his ear for him to divert his attention from his flight pattern to her.

"Fly… higher."

He looked across his unit as they flew in a close formation toward the mountains. He'd always credited Nessix for her tactical mind and had taken great care in enhancing her expertise through studies of his people's take on warfare, but she had no reason or way to understand aerial tactics. The overdose of dream stop had been impacting the clarity of her thinking, and Kol wouldn't fault her for this oversight.

"This is a defensible formation," he assured her.

"Fly. Higher." When Kol ignored her demand, she drew in a heavy, sleepy breath to try explaining herself. "Archer's horn. Fly higher, out of range."

Kol's racing heart nearly ceased beating. Nessix had vowed her loyalty to him and had shown it well so far, but he hadn't been able to discern if she'd implemented it as means to protect herself and her army or out of genuine observation of the virtue. Nessix knew fleman tactics better than anyone, and even sedated half out of her mind, she had identified the greatest danger an alar could face, and she'd pushed herself past the dream stop's debilitating effects to deliver the warning to him. His safety had surpassed any lingering desires she had to escape the hells. Kol didn't need Nessix's soul vessel to feel the warmth of his connection to her now, and he inwardly embraced the forgotten comfort of unconditional compassion for the first time in centuries.

Silently, Kol caught an updraft and shot himself and Nessix higher in the air. His abrupt movement caught the attention of the demons behind him, causing them to stall in their flight and further weaken their formation. Moments later, the first arrow zipped into the group of demons, piercing an underling's wing. As he rapidly dropped toward the hungry ocean, a second arrow flew toward the demons, this one sinking into Grell's right breast.

The inoga bellowed in fury and left the rest of the unit behind as he plummeted toward the offending attacker and just as Kol was beginning to contemplate the idea of sneaking himself and Nessix away, Annin swept up in front of him.

"Grell's got the mortals distracted," he said. "Now's our time. Move!"

All potential cover blown, Kol spared a glance at where Grell had just crashed into an unfortunate trio of flemans perched among the mountain's peaks, and followed Annin's hasty approach toward land. He'd quit thinking luck was a viable force in life, but if any of it still existed, perhaps Grell would succumb to the mortals he so often underestimated. It was a long shot, but one Kol would be delighted to accept. The remaining alar clustered in close to their officers on this descent, following through with their orders to ensure Nessix made it back into the hells. Just as they were about to pass the point where Grell had landed, the inoga launched back into the sky, spattered with blood and grinning like a maniac.

"Flushed 'em out, huh, Kol?"

The mass of wings around him kept Kol's scowl obscured from Grell, but he'd caught the inoga's suspicions clearly as they crested the mountaintop. They rapidly coasted down its side until their portal to the hells—guarded by a force of four dozen knights, demon hunters, and furious flemans—came into view. And, positioned at the head of this opposition stood Sazrah the Shade.

"Annin!" Grell roared. "Collapse the ridge!"

Kol snuck an appraising look at his friend. Annin commanded untold power with his magic, but Kol's limited understanding of thread manipulation suggested crippling men and crippling the world itself were two different challenges. Annin's wide eyes and sharp grimace confirmed he hadn't been too far off on his assessment.

"Sir, I—"

"Collapse the ridge before I launch you down there to deal with them!"

Annin hated many things and chief among them was displaying weakness. A feat of this magnitude would come close to killing him, but pride forbid him to openly admit that. Instead, all he allowed himself was a brief glance back at Kol, the idiot who had bought him his life when they'd been mortal youths, the idiot who had led him down this path of destruction. And he let that weakness be seen before beating his wings to shift himself upright to focus on the task demanded of him.

Kol hadn't missed the ripple of uncertainty Annin had tossed his way and though he wouldn't entrust Nessix in the hands of anyone else, he wasn't helpless. Annin had saved his life too many times. Darting in front of the pair of alar to his right, Kol rose up before them.

"Move to support Annin. If you let him fall, I'll kill you myself."

Of the eighteen remaining alar assigned to this mission, not one of them knew what to make of it anymore, but these two obeyed Kol's order and separated from the main body of the group to flank the oraku. Annin's brief dance with fear had ended, his intense gaze glazed over with that sociopathic sheen expected of him. He raised his arms in the air, fingers splayed wide as his eyes darted across the landscape, seizing the most relevant threads to carry out his order. Drawing in a deep breath, he closed his fingers to bind Abaeloth's threads to his own and, keeping his eyes open to witness what might be his final—and most impressive—display of might, Annin threw his arms to his sides.

The mountainside screamed in agony, just as the trembling battlefield which had turned him into a demon had, and as the ground crumbled away to swallow up the opposing soldiers, Annin's wings quit beating.

* * * * *

Based on Mathias's unusual behavior, Sazrah hadn't expected this mission to be easy, and she'd carefully selected her most experienced soldiers to support her with that in mind. She'd anticipated the ancient oraku and his obsessive alar. She'd even been willing to entertain the idea of facing an inoga. What she hadn't expected, what she'd had no reason to expect, was for the ground which her elite troops stood on to give way beneath their feet.

There had been no warning, only a scattering of alar as the archers opened fire and a heart-stopping shriek from the mountain itself as it fell away. Startled yelps punctuated the crash of rocks and groans of the mountainside and Sazrah, cursed with the uncanny reflexes of her heritage and positioned farthest from the epicenter of the collapse, sprang from rock slide to rock slide, leaping and diving between the debris which devoured her troops. Mathias had asked her to intercept these demons to rescue Nessix, but these fools had just made matters personal.

She scrambled up to firm ground just in time to see the oraku drop into the arms of two of his alar companions. At least that pest was out of commission. The remainder of the alar, including a dark haired one carrying the drooping body of a woman Sazrah suspected was Nessix, banked toward the opening in the mountainside, and Sazrah growled and raced toward the cavern.

If Mathias said getting Nessix away from the demons would anger them, that was precisely what she would do.

The oraku and his escorts disappeared into the hole first, followed by two unburdened alar. She was close enough now to acknowledge the strict hatred in the orange eyes of the one carrying Nessix, but as Sazrah pulled a throwing knife from her hip, the force of half a dozen chargers collided with her back. The impact itself left her gasping with lungs too stunned to function and threw her off her feat, her forehead smacking hard against the ground. The attack would have taken a normal warrior out of the fight, but Sazrah wasn't quite normal. Unfortunately, her opponent knew that, a fact which became apparent as she was hoisted upside down and into the air by her right leg. She'd lost her grip on her sword and knife due to the shock of that first blow and her vision quit spinning just in time to witness the orange-eyed alar disappear into the cavern.

Furious on so many levels, she scissored her free leg upward, connecting solidly with a firm mass, the crunch of a jaw snapping shut commending her for a job well done. That moment of victory was short lived, however, as she sailed through the air, still connected to the beast behind her, and met an abrupt stop with the ground. This time, there was more than a sudden jarring and her tendons ignited in pain as her leg hyperextended and, ultimately, rolled free from her hip joint.

Sazrah had spent most of her life in some sort of combat. She'd survived torture trapped deep within the hells. But even she wasn't immune to the agony of a dislocated limb. She didn't scream, emitting instead a trembling hum as her non-functioning limb flopped down to the ground. This was too pathetic of a way to go, and Sazrah still had three working limbs to humble this inoga who loomed into her field of vision. She grabbed her short sword, but before she managed to straighten her arm to draw it, the demon stomped down on her elbow. This time, Sazrah did scream as the metal of her armor bent and bit through the padding of her gambeson.

"You could have spared all of your men their lives if you'd only left us alone." The inoga spoke down to her, as though she was a dull child.

Swallowing her gasps of pain, Sazrah found a strained smile upon seeing the blood dripping from the demon's mouth. "Go fuck yourself."

He crossed his arms and studied Sazrah like she was a pig being measured for slaughter. "It's quite the coincidence that you and your men were out here, waiting for us while we brought your surrogate's girlfriend back home."

"Nothing coincidental about wanting you dead." Sazrah tried to shift her weight to see if she might be able to use her right arm for one last attack, but even the subtlest movements pulled against her injuries and a hot wave of panic swept over her. She grimaced as she fought to slow her climbing respiration rate.

"Was it worth it?" the inoga asked, ignoring Sazrah's efforts, even the frustrations tied to her failed attempts to organize an attack. "You must have known you didn't stand a chance against us, yet you came anyway and lost all of your men."

Sazrah quit her attempts to move to focus all of her energy into a fierce glare. "I thought I told you to go fuck yourself."

The demon dropped his arms to his sides and crouched to give Sazrah a better look at his scarred face to make sure she'd remember him in the future. "It's not going to work, you know."

"What's not going to work?"

"Goading me into killing you."

Sazrah's glare was made all the fiercer by the underlying pain screaming through her eyes.

"No, little Sagewind." The inoga chuckled as Sazrah flung her glare aside, trying to hide from the truth the same as she always had. "We've got so many more ways to play with you; it's not my place to ruin that fun." He stood, bloody smile pulled lopsided by the massive scar across his face. "Think over how you'll tell Mathias how you failed today, and come after me again once you're able to offer a challenge. You'll get there. Some day."

The inoga didn't give her another glance as he walked off toward the cavern his subordinates had disappeared into, leaving Sazrah broken on the demolished mountainside. She sank into the pain radiating from her arm and leg, tapping into that agony to keep coherent enough to listen for signs that any of her troops had survived the cave-in.

Based on Mathias's unusual behavior, Sazrah hadn't expected this mission to be easy. And based on that inoga's parting words to her, she was prepared to take every hard road she had to in order to see him dead. She didn't know what sort of complications Mathias had run into, but one thing was clear. Whatever it was he was planning, whatever stupid decision he was in the process of making, he owed her an explanation. These demons would die. And she would be part of orchestrating it.

The Afflicted Saga

Deliverance

Tale of the Fallen: Book VI

DEMONS WILL ONCE AGAIN BECOME LEGENDS...

Chilled from blood loss and numb from pain, Sazrah succeeded in locating her scrying bowl just to have it slip out of her shaking grasp and tumble five yards away from where she lay on the ground. Still in her sights, it was well out of reach, and the beating she'd suffered at the hands of that inoga barred her from making any sort of rapid progress toward it. Yes, the filthy power of her own demon blood would see her through this ordeal, but it wouldn't pop her leg back into place or properly set her broken arm. And it wouldn't do a damn thing for her troops who had perished when the side of the mountain had given out.

Gritting her teeth against the pain of dragging her broken body across the ground, Sazrah clawed her functional hand forward and gave a feeble push with her working leg. A jolt of agony raced up her spine, forcibly seizing her strength and will to move toward her misplaced scrying bowl, and she cried out in pain and frustration. Curling her fingers into the coarse dirt, she bowed her head toward the cursed mountainside. She'd survived countless dismal situations in the past, but all of them had posed to impact her alone. Now Mathias, her troops, potentially all of Abaeloth, relied on her being able to force her body through these simple motions it refused to execute.

A heavy clomping of footsteps crunched her way across the dirt and stones, and before dread or desperation had a chance to settle amid her swell of guilt and shame, Sazrah heard something beautiful.

"You still with the living, Shade?"

Sazrah closed her eyes and lowered her forehead to the ground, allowing a brief round of tears to be soaked up by the dirt. "I am, Karst."

The steps pounded at a faster rate and within moments, the dwarf, battered and bruised but far from defeated, crouched down before her. His rough hands cupped her chin and raised her weary face to his. "Bless the Mother. Tell me what you need."

"I need to hunt down the son of a bitch who buried my men and—"

Karst's weathered brows sagged in exhaustion. "What would you be needing *now*? Something that I can be doing for you?"

Sazrah bit back the defensive impulse to correct Karst for interrupting her and counted her blessings that he'd survived the attack at all. Her anger was not with him, and she did need his help. "I need to speak with Mathias, but I dropped my scrying bowl."

Karst stood before she had to voice a formal request for it, and located the device from nothing more than following her gaze.

"I thought I'd lost everyone," Sazrah admitted as the dwarf returned and knelt down to steady the bowl for her use.

"You should know a dwarf can handle a couple tumbling rocks." He assisted her in righting herself onto her sound elbow and plucked a knife from his belt. "Dragged thirteen more soldiers out of the rubble who were still breathing. It wasn't a complete loss."

Sazrah grimaced and nodded at the hand of her broken arm for Karst to do the honors of slicing her thumb open. "That still leaves thirty-five"—she barely felt the blade bite through her flesh from the pain of her greater injuries—"unaccounted for. And we failed our objective."

Karst dropped his knife to the ground and dutifully squeezed Sazrah's blood into the little silver bowl. "Yeah. Well. We had no way of knowing the demons planned to bury us. Mathias will have some ridiculous work around like he always does. Just you wait."

Often times, Mathias did have a ridiculous work around for

when plans turned south, but this time, Sazrah wasn't so sure he would. This time, as it had been when the demons had captured her from a long-ago battlefield, matters were personal to him. She'd already witnessed the paladin preparing to make some terrible decisions in regards to relocating Nessix, and he'd told her himself he intended to make even more if he had to. He'd been counting on her and she'd been honor-bound to deliver on his faith, but she had failed in a tremendous fashion. The blood in the bowl rippled to reveal Mathias's face, and just a glance at him made the battle-hardened woman wish she would have found some other method to contact him.

His brows were knit together in a strict line, a fierce scowl curling his lips and carving wrinkles in the bridge of his nose. His eyes were cold with the sort of darkness he reserved for facing only the cruelest of opponents. He didn't even glance at Sazrah's reflection, focused instead on some point she couldn't view, when he addressed her.

"Tell me something good, Saz."

She gulped at Mathias's curt tone, ashamed of herself all over again, though she knew he had no way to fault her for what had happened. "I can't."

He flicked a glance her direction at her unusually timid tone and his expression faltered toward softness for just a moment before he returned his focus to his prior point of interest. "Then deliver the report you have."

Sazrah swallowed her disgust in her failure, salvaging the ability to persevere from her staunch adhesion to duty. "I led fifty soldiers to wait for Nessix and her captors. The demons were fronted by a winged inoga and an oraku who collapsed the ridge we stood on. Current count suggests we've taken thirty-five casualties from this single attack. I am wounded beyond my own repair, and the demons still have Nessix."

Mathias's lips pressed together briefly, nostrils flaring with a labored sigh, but Sazrah didn't detect the disappointment she'd felt due. That had to have meant that whatever stupid plan he'd been brewing had been a success, that Karst's suggestion of the paladin having a solution was accurate. While that should have comforted

Sazrah, it didn't.

"Had Sulik been among the men you'd brought with you?" Mathias asked.

Sazrah closed her eyes against a brisk rush of tears. "No. He'd offered to come, but I convinced him one of us should man the temple and he agreed I was better qualified to fight demons." A rush of self-loathing flooded Sazrah's resolve. For all that faith Sulik had put in her, she'd fared no better than he would have, and may have even lost one of his sons in this tragedy. "Mathias—" Sazrah's voice cracked and Karst respectfully looked away from her surrender to unchecked emotions. "I need your help."

That frown pulled even lower on Mathias's face. "What injuries did you sustain?"

"Broken sword arm and dislocated leg, as far as I can tell. I won't be able to make it back to the temple as I am now."

"Of those alive and accounted for, are any of you mobile?"

Sazrah looked up at Karst and the dwarf shook his head. "Only Karst Boulderchoke, and he's already spent himself dragging our survivors from the rubble. Please, Mathias. I don't know what you're preoccupied with, but we're defenseless targets if the demons come out to see what's left of us."

Mathias closed his eyes, lips trembling as he drew in a ragged breath. "I can be there within a day."

"Within a—" Sazrah initially clamped her mouth shut around her argument, but as pain squeezed past her barriers and the muffled sobs and groans of her wounded petitioned for her advocacy, she couldn't hold it back. "I need you *now*."

Mathias ducked his head away from the firmness of Sazrah's plea. "Believe me, Saz, I would much rather be by your side, patching you up so you can go charging into the hells for vengeance, than where I am now. I'll be there as soon as I'm able. Has Karst set a bone before?"

Sazrah and the dwarf dodged each other's doubtful looks. "He has, but—"

"Then have him do it. I'm guessing he's even rolled one of his own legs back into place at some point, tough dwarf as he is. See if he can help you with that, too."

"No, Mathias." Sazrah, dizzy from pain and the adrenaline needed to talk back to her trusted mentor, balanced on the precarious cusp between panic and anger. "You owe me answers. You owe me the truth. What is going on?"

The image of Mathias's face rippled, as though he was preparing to fling the blood out of his bowl, but stabilized after he'd opened his eyes. "Nothing good," he said softly. "And I will give you more answers than you could possibly want after I'm sure nothing else goes wrong."

If nothing else goes wrong... Part of Mathias's frustrating charm came from his propensity to play games, but from his defeated tone, his refusal to look at her as she begged for his aid, Sazrah knew games were the farthest thing from his mind, just as she knew that now was not the time to ask what had gone wrong to land them in this current disaster. Sazrah had seen many battles over the past few decades, but this was the first time since she and Mathias had united to quell the undead that she had to accept the fact that they were facing the dawn of a war in which Mathias played a central role.

"I need more than that if you want me prepared to help you," Sazrah said.

Mathias's cheeks inflated and his eyes shifted from hers as he blew out little puffs of breath. The last bit was released in one, tired sigh, and he tilted his face back toward his bowl, though his eyes remained averted. "There may be a way to negate the demons' curse, a way to cure them of the corruption they'd sustained."

Sazrah stared at Mathias, eyes wide as she internally cursed him for his stubborn avoidance. A way to negate the demons' curse? To strip from them of the essence which made them the disgusting abominations they were? How had nobody discovered this sooner? She narrowed her eyes at Mathias's shiftiness, clearly reading his discomfort in what should have been a heartening discovery. "Is there a reason you chose not to implement this cure against those who took Nessix and killed my men?"

The grimace Mathias responded with was not the one of guilt which Sazrah had expected, but one of regret. "I don't know what it is."

"Then why even bother mentioning it?"

"Because I—" Mathias cut off his hasty response, lips turning down as though he was suffering a bad taste. "I've got a strong lead on it. But that is all I can tell you for now. Just… trust me. Please."

Karst grunted his rude opinion of Mathias's request. "Trusting him's what got us out here in the first place."

Sazrah chastised her captain with a firm glare, but didn't correct him otherwise. The dwarf spoke a sound truth. "Mathias. My troops were decimated. I have no way to aid the few survivors and no idea when the demons will return to finish what they started. I want nothing more than to trust you, but I need answers. I need help."

The corners of Mathias's eyes pinched lower with a deep sorrow he wouldn't let himself express any further. Sazrah seldomly asked for help. "I have given you all of the answers I currently have and will deliver the rest as soon as I can. I swear this to you, Sazrah."

Oh, how she wanted to continue arguing with Mathias, to demand he drop what he was doing and help her figure out what she was supposed to do to keep Elidae safe in the days to come, but duty and discipline stifled those words. Mathias wanted to be trapped in his circumstances no more than she did.

"Yes, sir," she answered at last. "Please hurry."

"I will. You and Karst stay well. I'll do my best to not keep you waiting longer than you must."

Sazrah nodded to Karst to dump her blood from the bowl and she lowered her head to the ground once more. Whatever Mathias had planned, she would help him as much as she could, but the longer she thought over what it was he'd started, the less she believed she'd be able to.

"I know you look to that man as your father," Karst grumbled, "but your dad's a reckless idiot, thinking I'm some sort of field surgeon."

Sazrah grit her teeth, hearing more in Karst's criticism than his words conveyed. "Maybe so, but he wasn't wrong. My body's going to try to heal around these wounds and if he can't get here…" The concept still didn't add up to her, but she was out of influence on the matter. "I'd rather have my captain's best effort than a useless sword arm."

The dwarf pushed himself to his feet to trundle around in search of something long and sturdy enough to use as a splint. "Just don't demote me when it hurts or doesn't turn out right. This is a job for Etha-blessed paladins, not some battle-weary dwarf."

Sazrah couldn't have agreed more, but was too distracted to argue. Of all the frustrations Mathias had caused her in the past, he'd never left her in peril if he'd had any other option. *Whatever you're doing, Mathias… let it work…*

Keep up to date at www.katikaschneider.com

Thank you for reading. If you enjoy The Afflicted Saga, please consider telling your friends and leaving reviews. That's the best way to keep an author fed and show them you appreciate what they do.

ABOUT THE AUTHOR

A lover of literary adventure and notorious breaker of writing rules, Katika Schneider's been an obsessive writer for most of her life. She started out writing for herself before surrendering to her characters' demands, and began pursuing publication in 2014. She's a firm believer that everyone has a story to tell.

Holding her degree in Animal Science, Kat planned on attending veterinary school until incisions started making her faint. She lives with her husband and their abundant family of critters.